P9-CMF-380

The forest, so mysterious and inviting

THE
BLAZED TRAIL

By
Stewart Edward White

GROSSET & DUNLAP

NEW YORK   PUBLISHERS

PRINTED AT THE *Country Life Press*, GARDEN CITY, N. Y., U. S. A.

CONTENTS

PART I

THE FOREST

CONTENTS

PART I
THE FOREST

THE BLAZED TRAIL

CHAPTER ONE

WHEN history has granted him the justice of perspective, we shall know the American Pioneer as one of the most picturesque of her many figures. Resourceful, self-reliant, bold; adapting himself with fluidity to diverse circumstances and conditions; meeting with equal cheerfulness of confidence and completeness of capability both unknown dangers and the perils by which he has been educated; seizing the useful in the lives of the beasts and men nearest him, and assimilating it with marvellous rapidity; he presents to the world a picture of complete adequacy which it would be difficult to match in any other walk of life. He is a strong man, with a strong man's virtues and a strong man's vices. In him the passions are elemental, the dramas epic, for he lives in the age when men are close to nature, and draw from her their forces. He satisfies his needs direct from the earth. Stripped of all the towns can give him, he merely resorts to a facile substitution. It becomes an affair of rawhide for leather, buckskin for cloth, venison for canned tomatoes. We feel that his steps are planted on solid earth, for civilizations may crumble without disturbing his magnificent self-poise. In him we perceive dimly his environment. He has something about him which other men do not possess—a frank clearness of the eye, a swing of the shoulder, a carriage of the hips, a tilt of the hat, an air of muscular well-being—which marks him as belonging to the advance guard, whether he wears buckskin, mackinaw, sombrero, or broadcloth. The woods are there, the plains, the rivers. Snow is there, and the line of the prairie. Mountain peaks and still pine forests have impressed themselves subtly; so that when we turn to admire his unconsciously graceful swing, we seem to hear the ax biting the pine, or the prospector's pick tapping the rock. And in his eye is the capability of quiet humor, which is just the quality that the surmounting of many difficulties will give a man.

Like the nature he has fought until he understands, his disposition is at once kindly and terrible. Outside the subtleties of his calling, he sees only red. Relieved of the strenuousness of his occupation, he turns all the force of the wonderful energies that have carried him far where other men would have halted, to channels in which a gentle current makes flood enough. It is the mountain torrent and the canal. Instead of pleasure he seeks

orgies. He runs to wild excesses of drinking, fighting, and carousing—which would frighten most
men to sobriety—with a happy, reckless spirit that
carries him beyond the limits of even his extraordinary forces.

This is not the moment to judge him. And yet
one cannot help admiring the magnificently picturesque spectacle of such energies running riot. The
power is still in evidence, though beyond its proper
application.

CHAPTER TWO

IN the network of streams draining the eastern portion of Michigan and known as the Saginaw waters, the great firm of Morrison & Daly had for many years carried on extensive logging operations in the wilderness. The number of their camps was legion, of their employees a multitude. Each spring they had gathered in their capacious booms from thirty to fifty million feet of pine logs.

Now at last, in the early eighties, they reached the end of their holdings. Another winter would finish the cut. Two summers would see the great mills at Beeson Lake dismantled or sold, while Mr. Daly, the " woods partner " of the combination, would flit away to the scenes of new and perhaps more extensive operations. At this juncture Mr. Daly called to him John Radway, a man whom he knew to possess extensive experience, a little capital, and a desire for more of both.

" Radway," said he, when the two found themselves alone in the mill office, " we expect to cut this year some fifty millions, which will finish our pine holdings in the Saginaw waters. Most of this timber lies over in the Crooked Lake district, and

6

that we expect to put in ourselves. We own, however, five million on the Cass Branch which we
would like to log on contract. Would you care to
take the job?"

"How much a thousand do you give?" asked
Radway.

"Four dollars," replied the lumberman.

"I'll look at it," replied the jobber.

So Radway got the "descriptions" and a little
map divided into townships, sections, and quarter
sections; and went out to look at it. He searched
until he found a "blaze" on a tree, the marking
on which indicated it as the corner of a section.
From this corner the boundary lines were blazed at
right angles in either direction. Radway followed
the blazed lines. Thus he was able accurately to
locate isolated "forties" (forty acres), "eighties,"
quarter sections, and sections in a primeval wilderness. The feat, however, required considerable
woodcraft, an exact sense of direction, and a pocket
compass.

These resources were still further drawn upon for
the next task. Radway tramped the woods, hills,
and valleys to determine the most practical route
over which to build a logging road from the standing timber to the shores of Cass Branch. He found
it to be an affair of some puzzlement. The pines
stood on a country rolling with hills, deep with potholes. It became necessary to dodge in and out,

here and there, between the knolls, around or through the swamps, still keeping, however, the same general direction, and preserving always the requisite level or down grade. Radway had no vantage point from which to survey the country. A city man would promptly have lost himself in the tangle; but the woodsman emerged at last on the banks of the stream, leaving behind him a meandering trail of clipped trees that wound, twisted, doubled, and turned, but kept ever to a country without steep hills. From the main road he purposed arteries to tap the most distant parts.

"I'll take it," said he to Daly.

Now Radway happened to be in his way a peculiar character. He was acutely sensitive to the human side of those with whom he had dealings. In fact, he was more inclined to take their point of view than to hold his own. For that reason, the subtler disputes were likely to go against him. His desire to avoid coming into direct collision of opinion with the other man, veiled whatever of justice might reside in his own contention. Consequently it was difficult for him to combat sophistry or a plausible appearance of right. Daly was perfectly aware of Radway's peculiarities, and so proceeded to drive a sharp bargain with him.

Customarily a jobber is paid a certain proportion of the agreed price as each stage of the work is completed—so much when the timber is cut; so much when it is skidded, or piled; so much when it is stacked at the river, or banked; so much when the "drive" down the waters of the river is finished. Daly objected to this method of procedure.

"You see, Radway," he explained, "it is our last season in the country. When this lot is in, we want to pull up stakes, so we can't take any chances on not getting that timber in. If you don't finish your job, it keeps us here another season. There can be no doubt, therefore, that you finish your job. In other words, we can't take any chances. If you start the thing, you've got to carry it 'way through."

"I think I can, Mr. Daly," the jobber assured him.

"For that reason," went on Daly, "we object to paying you as the work progresses. We've got to have a guarantee that you don't quit on us, and that those logs will be driven down the branch as far as the river in time to catch our drive. Therefore I'm going to make you a good price per thousand, but payable only when the logs are delivered to our rivermen."

Radway, with his usual mental attitude of one anxious to justify the other man, ended by seeing only his employer's argument. He did not perceive that the latter's proposition introduced into the transaction a gambling element. It became possible for Morrison & Daly to get a certain amount of work, short of absolute completion, done for nothing.

How much does the timber estimate?" he inquired finally.

"About five millions."

"I'd need a camp of forty or fifty men then. I don't see how I can run such a camp without borrowing."

"You have some money, haven't you?"

"Yes; a little. But I have a family, too."

"That's all right. Now look here." Daly drew toward him a sheet of paper and began to set down figures showing how the financing could be done. Finally it was agreed. Radway was permitted to draw on the Company's warehouse for what provisions he would need. Daly let him feel it as a concession.

All this was in August. Radway, who was a good practical woodsman, set about the job immediately. He gathered a crew, established his camp, and began at once to cut roads through the country he had already blazed on his former trip.

Those of us who have ever paused to watch a group of farmers working out their road taxes, must have gathered a formidable impression of roadclearing. And the few of us who, besides, have experienced the adventure of a drive over the same highway after the tax has been pronounced liquidated, must have indulged in varied reflections as to the inadequacy of the result.

Radway's task was not merely to level out and

ballast the six feet of a road-bed already constructed, but to cut a way for five miles through the unbroken wilderness. The way had moreover to be not less than twenty-five feet wide, needed to be absolutely level and free from any kind of obstructions, and required in the swamps liberal ballasting with poles, called corduroys. To one who will take the trouble to recall the variety of woods, thickets, and jungles that go to make up a wooded country—especially in the creek bottoms where a logging road finds often its levelest way—and the piles of windfalls, vines, bushes, and scrubs that choke the thickets with a discouraging and inextricable tangle, the clearing of five miles to street width will look like an almost hopeless undertaking. Not only must the growth be removed, but the roots must be cut out, and the inequalities of the ground levelled or filled up. Reflect further that Radway had but a brief time at his disposal—but a few months at most—and you will then be in a position to gauge the first difficulties of those the American pioneer expects to encounter as a matter of course. The cutting of the road was a mere incident in the battle with the wilderness.

The jobber, of course, pushed his roads as rapidly as possible, but was greatly handicapped by lack of men. Winter set in early and surprised him with several of the smaller branches yet to finish. The main line, however, was done.

At intervals squares were cut out alongside. In them two long timbers, or skids, were laid andironwise for the reception of the piles of logs which would be dragged from the fallen trees. They were called skidways. Then finally the season's cut began.

The men who were to fell the trees, Radway distributed along one boundary of a "forty." They were instructed to move forward across the forty in a straight line, felling every pine tree over eight inches in diameter. While the "saw-gangs," three in number, prepared to fell the first trees, other men, called "swampers," were busy cutting and clearing of roots narrow little trails down through the forest from the pine to the skidway at the edge of the logging road. The trails were perhaps three feet wide, and marvels of smoothness, although no attempt was made to level mere inequalities of the ground. They were called travoy roads (French *travois*). Down them the logs would be dragged and hauled, either by means of heavy steel tongs or a short sledge on which one end of the timber would be chained.

Meantime the sawyers were busy. Each pair of men selected a tree, the first they encountered over the blazed line of their "forty." After determining in which direction it was to fall, they set to work to chop a deep gash in that side of the trunk.

Tom Broadhead and Henry Paul picked out a

tremendous pine which they determined to throw across a little open space in proximity to the travoy road. One stood to right, the other to left, and alternately their axes bit deep. It was a beautiful sight this, of experts wielding their tools. The craft of the woodsman means incidentally such a free swing of the shoulders and hips, such a directness of stroke as the blade of one sinks accurately in the gash made by the other, that one never tires of watching the grace of it. Tom glanced up as a sailor looks aloft.

" She'll do, Hank," he said.

The two then with a dozen half clips of the ax, removed the inequalities of the bark from the saw's path. The long, flexible ribbon of steel began to sing, bending so adaptably to the hands and motions of the men manipulating, that it did not seem possible so mobile an instrument could cut the rough pine. In a moment the song changed timbre. Without a word the men straightened their backs. Tom flirted along the blade a thin stream of kerosene oil from a bottle in his hip pocket, and the sawyers again bent to their work, swaying back and forth rhythmically, their muscles rippling under the texture of their woolens like those of a panther under its skin. The outer edge of the saw-blade disappeared.

" Better wedge her, Tom," advised Hank.

They paused while, with a heavy sledge, Tom

drove a triangle of steel into the crack made by the sawing. This prevented the weight of the tree from pinching the saw, which is a ruin at once to the instrument and the temper of the filer. Then the rhythmical *z-z-z! z-z-z!* again took up its song.

When the trunk was nearly severed, Tom drove another and thicker wedge.

" Tim*ber*! " hallooed Hank in a long-drawn melodious call that melted through the woods into the distance. The swampers ceased work and withdrew to safety.

But the tree stood obstinately upright. So the saw leaped back and forth a few strokes more.

" *Crack!* " called the tree.

Hank coolly unhooked his saw handle, and Tom drew the blade through and out the other side.

The tree shivered, then leaned ever so slightly from the perpendicular, then fell, at first gently, afterwards with a crescendo rush, tearing through the branches of other trees, bending the small timber, breaking the smallest, and at last hitting with a tremendous crash and bang which filled the air with a fog of small twigs, needles, and the powder of snow, that settled but slowly. There is nothing more impressive than this rush of a pine top, excepting it be a charge of cavalry or the fall of Niagara. Old woodsmen sometimes shout aloud with the mere excitement into which it lifts them.

Then the swampers, who had by now finished the travoy road, trimmed the prostrate trunk clear of all protuberances. It required fairly skillful ax work. The branches had to be shaved close and clear, and at the same time the trunk must not be gashed. And often a man was forced to wield his instrument from a constrained position.

The chopped branches and limbs had now to be dragged clear and piled. While this was being finished, Tom and Hank marked off and sawed the log lengths, paying due attention to the necessity of avoiding knots, forks, and rotten places. Thus some of the logs were eighteen, some sixteen, or fourteen, and some only twelve feet in length.

Next appeared the teamsters with their little wooden sledges, their steel chains, and their tongs. They had been helping the skidders to place the parallel and level beams, or skids, on which the logs were to be piled by the side of the road. The tree which Tom and Hank had just felled, lay up a gentle slope from the new travoy road, so little Fabian Laveque, the teamster, clamped the bite of his tongs to the end of the largest, or butt, log.

" Allez, Molly! " he cried.

The horse, huge, elephantine, her head down, nose close to her chest, intelligently spying her steps, moved. The log half rolled over, slid three feet, and menaced a stump.

" Gee! " cried Laveque.

Molly stepped twice directly sideways, planted her fore foot on a root she had seen, and pulled sharply. The end of the log slid around the stump. " Allez! " commanded Laveque.

And Molly started gingerly down the hill. She pulled the timber, heavy as an iron safe, here and there through the brush, missing no steps, making no false moves, backing, and finally getting out of the way of an unexpected roll with the ease and intelligence of Laveque himself. In five minutes the burden lay by the travoy road. In two minutes more one end of it had been rolled on the little flat wooden sledge and, the other end dragging, it was winding majestically down through the ancient forest. The little Frenchman stood high on the forward end. Molly stepped ahead carefully, with the strange intelligence of the logger's horse. Through the tall, straight, decorative trunks of trees the little convoy moved with the massive pomp of a dead warrior's cortège. And little Fabian Laveque, singing, a midget in the vastness, typified the indomitable spirit of these conquerors of a wilderness.

When Molly and Fabian had travoyed the log to the skidway, they drew it with a bump across the two parallel skids, and left it there to be rolled to the top of the pile.

Then Mike McGovern and Bob Stratton and Jim Gladys took charge of it. Mike and Bob were run-

ning the cant-hooks, while Jim stood on top of the
great pile of logs already decked. A slender, pliable
steel chain, like a gray snake, ran over the top of the
pile and disappeared through a pulley to an invisible horse—Jenny, the mate of Molly. Jim
threw the end of this chain down. Bob passed it
over and under the log and returned it to Jim, who
reached down after it with the hook of his imple-
ment. Thus the stick of timber rested in a long
loop, one end of which led to the invisible horse,
and the other Jim made fast to the top of the pile.
He did so by jamming into another log the steel
swamp-hook with which the chain was armed.
When all was made fast, the horse started.

" She's a bumper! " said Bob. " Look out,
Mike! "

The log slid to the foot of the two parallel poles
laid slanting up the face of the pile. Then it trembled on the ascent. But one end stuck for an instant, and at once the log took on a dangerous slant.
Quick as light Bob and Mike sprang forward,
gripped the hooks of the cant-hooks, like great
thumbs and forefingers, and, while one held with all
his power, the other gave a sharp twist upward.
The log straightened. It was a master feat of
power, and the knack of applying strength justly.

At the top of the little incline, the timber hovered
for a second.

" One more! " sang out Jim to the driver. He

poised, stepped lightly up and over, and avoided by the safe hair's breadth being crushed when the log rolled. But it did not lie quite straight and even. So Mike cut a short thick block, and all three stirred the heavy timber sufficiently to admit of the billet's insertion.

Then the chain was thrown down for another.

Jenny, harnessed only to a straight short bar with a hook in it, leaned to her collar and dug in her hoofs at the word of command. The driver, close to her tail, held fast the slender steel chain by an ingenious hitch about the ever-useful swamp-hook. When Jim shouted "whoa!" from the top of the skidway, the driver did not trouble to stop the horse —he merely let go the hook. So the power was shut off suddenly, as is meet and proper in such ticklish business. He turned and walked back, and Jenny, like a dog, without the necessity of command, followed him in slow patience.

Now came Dyer, the scaler, rapidly down the logging road, a small slender man with a little, turned-up mustache. The men disliked him because of his affectation of a city smartness, and because he never ate with them, even when there was plenty of room. Radway had confidence in him because he lived in the same shanty with him. This one fact a good deal explains Radway's character. The scaler's duty at present was to measure the diameter of the logs in each skidway, and so compute the number of board feet. At the office he tended van, kept the books, and looked after supplies.

He approached the skidway swiftly, laid his flexible rule across the face of each log, made a mark on his pine tablets in the column to which the log belonged, thrust the tablet in the pocket of his coat, seized a blue crayon, in a long holder, with which he made an 8 as indication that the log had been scaled, and finally tapped several times strongly with a sledge hammer. On the face of the hammer in relief was an M inside of a delta. This was the Company's brand, and so the log was branded as belonging to them. He swarmed all over the skidway, rapid and absorbed, in strange contrast of activity to the slower power of the actual skidding. In a moment he moved on to the next scene of operations without having said a word to any of the men.

"A fine t'ing!" said Mike, spitting.

So day after day the work went on. Radway spent his time tramping through the woods, figuring on new work, showing the men how to do things better or differently, discussing minute expedients with the blacksmith, the carpenter, the cook.

He was not without his troubles. First he had not enough men; the snow lacked, and then came too abundantly; horses fell sick of colic or caulked themselves; supplies ran low unexpectedly; trees turned out "punk"; a certain bit of ground proved soft for travoying, and so on. At election-time, of course, a number of the men went out.

And one evening, two days after election-time, another and important character entered the North woods and our story.

CHAPTER THREE

ON the evening in question, some thirty or forty miles southeast of Radway's camp, a train was crawling over a badly laid track which led toward the Saginaw Valley. The whole affair was very crude. To the edge of the right-of-way pushed the dense swamp, like a black curtain shutting the virgin country from the view of civilization. Even by daylight the sight could have penetrated but a few feet. The right-of-way itself was rough with upturned stumps, blackened by fire, and gouged by many and varied furrows. Across the snow were tracks of animals.

The train consisted of a string of freight cars, one coach divided half and half between baggage and smoker, and a day car occupied by two silent, awkward women and a child. In the smoker lounged a dozen men. They were of various sizes and descriptions, but they all wore heavy blanket mackinaw coats, rubber shoes, and thick German socks tied at the knee. This constituted, as it were, a sort of uniform. The air was so thick with smoke that the men had difficulty in distinguishing objects across the length of the car.

The passengers sprawled in various attitudes. Some hung their legs over the arms of the seats; others perched their feet on the backs of the seats in front; still others slouched in corners, half reclining. Their occupations were as diverse. Three nearest the baggage-room door attempted to sing, but without much success. A man in the corner breathed softly through a mouth organ, to the music of which his seat mate, leaning his head sideways, gave close attention. One big fellow with a square beard swaggered back and forth down the aisle offering to everyone refreshment from a quart bottle. It was rarely refused. Of the dozen, probably three quarters were more or less drunk.

After a time the smoke became too dense. A short, thick-set fellow with an evil dark face coolly thrust his heel through a window. The conductor, who, with the brakeman and baggage master, was seated in the baggage van, heard the jingle of glass. He arose.

" Guess I'll take up tickets," he remarked. " Perhaps it will quiet the boys down a little."

The conductor was a big man, raw-boned and broad, with a hawk face. His every motion showed lean, quick, panther-like power.

" Let her went," replied the brakeman, rising as a matter of course to follow his chief.

The brakeman was stocky, short, and long armed. In the old fighting days Michigan railroads chose their train officials with an eye to their superior deltoids. A conductor who could not throw an undesirable fare through a car window lived a short official life. The two men loomed on the noisy smoking compartment.

"Tickets, please!" clicked the conductor sharply.

Most of the men began to fumble about in their pockets, but the three singers and the one who had been offering the quart bottle did not stir.

"Ticket, Jack!" repeated the conductor, "come on, now."

The big bearded man leaned uncertainly against the seat.

"Now look here, Bud," he urged in wheedling tones, "I ain't got no ticket. You know how it is, Bud. I blows my stake." He fished uncertainly in his pocket and produced the quart bottle, nearly empty, "Have a drink?"

"No," said the conductor sharply.

"A' right," replied Jack, amiably, "take one myself." He tipped the bottle, emptied it, and hurled it through a window. The conductor paid no apparent attention to the breaking of the glass.

"If you haven't any ticket, you'll have to get off," said he.

The big man straightened up.

"You go to hell!" he snorted, and with the sole of his spiked boot delivered a mighty kick at the conductor's thigh.

The official, agile as a wild cat, leaped back, then forward, and knocked the man half the length of the car. You see, he was used to it. Before Jack could regain his feet the official stood over him.

The three men in the corner had also risen, and were staggering down the aisle intent on battle. The conductor took in the chances with professional rapidity.

"Get at 'em, Jimmy," said he.

And as the big man finally swayed to his feet, he was seized by the collar and trousers in the grip known to "bouncers" everywhere, hustled to the door, which some one obligingly opened, and hurled from the moving train into the snow. The conductor did not care a straw whether the obstreperous Jack lit on his head or his feet, hit a snowbank or a pile of ties. Those were rough days, and the preservation of authority demanded harsh measures.

Jimmy had got at 'em in a method of his own. He gathered himself into a ball of potential trouble, and hurled himself bodily at the legs of his opponents which he gathered in a mighty bear hug. It would have been poor fighting had Jimmy to carry the affair to a finish by himself, but considered as an expedient to gain time for the ejectment proceedings, it was admirable. The conductor returned to find a kicking, rolling, gouging mass of kinetic energy knocking the varnish off all one end of the car. A head appearing, he coolly batted it three times against a corner of the seat arm, after which he pulled the contestant out by the hair and threw him into a seat where he lay limp. Then it could be seen that Jimmy had clasped tight in his embrace a leg each of the other two. He hugged them close to his breast, and jammed his face down against them to protect his features. They could pound the top of his head and welcome. The only thing he really feared was a kick in the side, and for that there was hardly room.

The conductor stood over the heap, at a manifest advantage.

" You lumber-jacks had enough, or do you want to catch it plenty? "

The men, drunk though they were, realized their helplessness. They signified they had had enough. Jimmy thereupon released them and stood up, brushing down his tousled hair with his stubby fingers.

" Now is it ticket or bounce? " inquired the conductor.

After some difficulty and grumbling, the two paid their fare and that of the third, who was still dazed. In return the conductor gave them slips. Then he picked his lantern from the overhead rack whither he had tossed it, slung it on his left arm, and sauntered on down the aisle punching tickets. Behind him followed Jimmy. When he came to the door he swung across the platform with the easy lurch of the trainman, and entered the other car, where he took the tickets of the two women and the boy. One sitting in the second car would have been unable to guess from the bearing or manner of the two officials that anything had gone wrong.

The interested spectators of the little drama included two men near the water-cooler who were perfectly sober. One of them was perhaps a little past the best of life, but still straight and vigorous. His lean face was leather-brown in contrast to a long mustache and heavy eyebrows bleached nearly white, his eyes were a clear steady blue, and his frame was slender but wiry. He wore the regulation mackinaw blanket coat, a peaked cap with an extraordinarily high crown, and buckskin moccasins over long stockings.

The other was younger, not more than twenty-six perhaps, with the clean-cut, regular features we have come to consider typically American. Eyebrows that curved far down along the temples, and eye-lashes of a darkness in contrast to the prevailing note of his complexion combined to lend him a rather brooding, soft, and melancholy air which a very cursory second examination showed to be fictitious. His eyes, like the woodsman's, were steady, but inquiring. His jaw was square and settled, his mouth straight. One would be likely to sum him up as a man whose actions would be little influenced by glamour or even by the sentiments. And yet, equally, it was difficult to rid the mind of the impression produced by his eyes. Unlike the other inmates of the car, he wore an ordinary business suit, somewhat worn, but of good cut, and a style that showed even over the soft flannel shirt. The trousers were, however, bound inside the usual socks and rubbers.

The two seat-mates had occupied their time each in his own fashion. To the elder the journey was an evil to be endured with the patience learned in watching deer runways, so he stared straight before him, and spat with a certain periodicity into the centre of the aisle. The younger stretched back lazily in an attitude of ease which spoke of the habit of travelling. Sometimes he smoked a pipe. Thrice he read over a letter. It was from his sister, and announced her arrival at the little rural village in which he had made arrangements for her to stay. "It is interesting—now," she wrote, "though the resources do not look as though they would wear well. I am learning under Mrs. Renwick to sweep and dust and bake and stew and do a multitude of other things which I always vaguely supposed came ready-made. I like it; but after I have learned it all, I do not believe the practice will appeal to me much. However, I can stand it well enough for a year or two or three, for I am young; and then you will have made your everlasting fortune, of course."

Harry Thorpe experienced a glow of pride each

27

time he read this part of the letter. He liked the frankness of the lack of pretence; he admired the penetration and self-analysis which had taught her the truth that, although learning a new thing is always interesting, the practising of an old one is monotonous. And her pluck appealed to him. It is not easy for a girl to step from the position of mistress of servants to that of helping about the housework of a small family in a small town for the sake of the home to be found in it.

"She's a trump!" said Thorpe to himself, "and she shall have her everlasting fortune, if there's such a thing in the country."

He jingled the three dollars and sixty cents in his pocket, and smiled. That was the extent of his everlasting fortune at present.

The letter had been answered from Detroit.

"I am glad you are settled," he wrote. "At least I know you have enough to eat and a roof over you. I hope sincerely that you will do your best to fit yourself to your new conditions. I know it is hard, but with my lack of experience and my ignorance as to where to take hold, it may be a good many years before we can do any better."

When Helen Thorpe read this, she cried. Things had gone wrong that morning, and an encouraging word would have helped her. The sombre tone of her brother's communication threw her into a fit of the blues from which, for the first time, she saw her surroundings in a depressing and distasteful light. And yet he had written as he did with the kindest possible motives.

Thorpe had the misfortune to be one of those individuals who, though careless of what people in general may think of them, are in a corresponding degree sensitive to the opinion of the few they love. This feeling was further exaggerated by a constitutional shrinking from any outward manifestation of the emotions. As a natural result, he was often thought indifferent or discouraging when in reality his natural affections were at their liveliest. A failure to procure for a friend certain favors or pleasures dejected him, not only because of that friend's disappointment, but because, also, he imagined the failure earned him a certain blame. Blame from his heart's intimates he shrank from. His life outside the inner circles of his affections was apt to be so militant and so divorced from considerations of amity, that as a matter of natural reaction he became inclined to exaggerate the importance of small objections, little reproaches, slight criticisms from his real friends. Such criticisms seemed to bring into a sphere he would have liked to keep solely for the mutual reliance of loving kindness, something of the hard utilitarianism of the world at large. In consequence he gradually came to choose the line of least resistance, to avoid instinctively even the slightly disagreeable. Perhaps for this reason he was never entirely sincere with those he loved. He never gave assent to, manifested approval of, or showed enthusiasm over any plan suggested by them, for the reason that he never dared offer a merely problematical anticipation. The affair had to be absolutely certain in his own mind before he ventured to admit any one to the pleasure of looking forward to it—and simply because he so feared the disappointment in case anything should go wrong. He did not realize that not only is the pleasure of anticipation often the best, but that even disappointment, provided it happen through excusable causes, strengthens the bonds of affection through sympathy. We do not want merely results from a friend— merely finished products. We like to be in at the making, even though the product spoil.

This unfortunate tendency, together with his reserve, lent him the false attitude of a rather cold, self-centred man, discouraging suggestions at first only to adopt them later in the most inexplicable fashion, and conferring favors in a ready-made impersonal manner which destroyed utterly their quality as favors. In reality his heart hungered for the affection which this false attitude generally repelled. He threw the wet blanket of doubt over warm young enthusiasms because his mind worked with a certain deliberateness which did not at once permit him to see the practicability of the scheme. Later he would approve. But by that time, probably, the wet blanket had effectually extinguished the glow. You cannot always savor your pleasures cold.

So after the disgrace of his father, Harry Thorpe did a great deal of thinking and planning which he kept carefully to himself. He considered in turn the different occupations to which he could turn his hand, and negatived them one by one. Few business firms would care to employ the son of as shrewd an embezzler as Henry Thorpe. Finally he came to a decision. He communicated this decision to his sister. It would have commended itself more logically to her had she been able to follow step by step the considerations that had led her brother to it. As the event turned, she was forced to accept it blindly. She knew that her brother intended going West, but as to his hopes and plans she was in ignorance. A little sympathy, a little mutual understanding would have meant a great deal to her, for a girl whose mother she but dimly remembers, turns naturally to her next of kin. Helen Thorpe had always admired her brother, but had never before needed him. She had looked upon him as strong, self-contained, a little moody. Now the tone of his letter caused her to wonder whether he were not also a trifle hard and cold. So she wept on receiving it, and the tears watered the ground for discontent.

At the beginning of the row in the smoking car, Thorpe laid aside his letter and watched with keen appreciation the direct practicality of the trainmen's method. When the bearded man fell before the conductor's blow, he turned to the individual at his side.

"He knows how to hit, doesn't he!" he observed. "That fellow was knocked well off his feet."

"He does," agreed the other dryly.

They fell into a desultory conversation of fits and starts. Woodsmen of the genuine sort are never talkative; and Thorpe, as has been explained, was constitutionally reticent. In the course of their disjointed remarks Thorpe explained that he was looking for work in the woods, and intended, first of all, to try the Morrison & Daly camps at Beeson Lake.

"Know anything about logging?" inquired the stranger.

"Nothing," Thorpe confessed.

"Ain't much show for anything but lumber-jacks. What did you think of doing?"

"I don't know," said Thorpe, doubtfully. "I have driven horses a good deal; I thought I might drive team."

The woodsman turned slowly and looked Thorpe over with a quizzical eye. Then he faced to the front again and spat.

"Quite like," he replied still more dryly.

The boy's remark had amused him, and he had showed it, as much as he ever showed anything. Excepting always the riverman, the driver of a team

commands the highest wages among out-of-door
workers. He has to be able to guide his horses by
little steps over, through, and around slippery and
bristling difficulties. He must acquire the knack of
facing them square about in their tracks. He must
hold them under a control that will throw into their
collars, at command, from five pounds to their full
power of pull, lasting from five seconds to five minutes. And above all, he must be able to keep them
out of the way of tremendous loads of logs on a
road which constant sprinkling has rendered smooth
and glassy, at the same time preventing the long
tongue from sweeping them bodily against leg-
breaking *débris* when a curve in the road is reached.
It is easier to drive a fire-engine than a logging team.

But in spite of the *naïveté* of the remark, the
woodsman had seen something in Thorpe he liked.
Such men become rather expert in the reading of
character, and often in a log shanty you will hear
opinions of a shrewdness to surprise you. He re-
vised his first intention to let the conversation drop.

"I think M. & D. is rather full up just now," he
remarked. "I'm walkin'-boss there. The roads is
about all made, and road-making is what a greenhorn tackles first. They's more chance earlier in the
year. But if the *Old* Fellow" (he strongly ac-
cented the first word) "h'aint nothin' for you, just
ask for Tim Shearer, an' I'll try to put you on the
trail for some jobber's camp."

The whistle of the locomotive blew, and the conductor appeared in the doorway.

"Where's that fellow's turkey?" he inquired.

Several men looked toward Thorpe, who, not understanding this *argot* of the camps, was a little bewildered. Shearer reached over his head and took from the rack a heavy canvas bag, which he handed to the conductor.

"That's the 'turkey'"—he explained, "his war bag. Bud'll throw it off at Scott's, and Jack'll get it there."

"How far back is he?" asked Thorpe.

"About ten mile. He'll hoof it in all right."

A number of men descended at Scott's. The three who had come into collision with Jimmy and Bud were getting noisier. They had produced a stone jug, and had collected the remainder of the passengers—with the exception of Shearer and Thorpe—and now were passing the jug rapidly from hand to hand. Soon they became musical, striking up one of the weird long-drawn-out chants so popular with the shanty boy. Thorpe shrewdly guessed his companion to be a man of weight, and did not hesitate to ascribe his immunity from annoyance to the other's presence.

"It's a bad thing," said the walking-boss, "I used to be at it myself, and I know. When I wanted whiskey, I needed it worse than a scalded pup does a snowbank. The first year I had a hundred and fifty dollars, and I blew her all in six days. Next year I had a little more, but she lasted me three weeks. That was better. Next year, I says to myself, I'll just save fifty of that stake, and blow the rest. So I did. After that I got to be scaler, and sort've quit. I just made a deal with the *Old* Fellow to leave my stake with headquarters no matter whether I call for it or not. I got quite a lot coming, now."

"Bees'n Lake!" cried Jimmy fiercely through an aperture of the door.

"You'll find th' boardin'-house just across over the track," said the woodsman, holding out his hand, "so long. See you again if you don't find a job with the *Old* Fellow. My name's Shearer."

"Mine is Thorpe," replied the other. "Thank you."

The woodsman stepped forward past the carousers to the baggage compartment, where he disappeared. The revelers stumbled out the other door.

Thorpe followed and found himself on the frozen platform of a little dark railway station. As he walked, the boards shrieked under his feet and the sharp air nipped at his face and caught his lungs. Beyond the fence-rail protection to the side of the platform he thought he saw the suggestion of a broad reach of snow, a distant lurking forest, a few shadowy buildings looming mysterious in the night.

The air was twinkling with frost and the brilliant stars of the north country.

Directly across the track from the railway station, a single building was pricked from the dark by a solitary lamp in a lower-story room. The four who had descended before Thorpe made over toward this light, stumbling and laughing uncertainly, so he knew it was probably in the boarding-house, and prepared to follow them. Shearer and the station agent—an individual much muffled—turned to the disposition of some light freight that had been dropped from the baggage car.

The five were met at the steps by the proprietor of the boarding-house. This man was short and stout, with a harelip and cleft palate, which at once gave him the well-known slurring speech of persons so afflicted, and imparted also to the timbre of his voice a peculiarly hollow, resonant, trumpet-like note. He stumped about energetically on a wooden leg of home manufacture. It was a cumbersome instrument, heavy, with deep pine socket for the stump, and a projecting brace which passed under a leather belt around the man's waist. This instrument he used with the dexterity of a third hand. As Thorpe watched him, he drove in a projecting nail, kicked two " turkeys " dexterously inside the open door, and stuck the armed end of his peg-leg through the top and bottom of the whiskey jug that one of the new arrivals had set down near the door.

THE FOREST

The whiskey promptly ran out. At this the cripple flirted the impaled jug from the wooden leg far out over the rail of the veranda into the snow.

A growl went up.

" What'n hell's that for! " snarled one of the owners of the whiskey threateningly.

" Don't allow no whiskey here," snuffed the hare-lip.

The men were very angry. They advanced toward the cripple, who retreated with astonishing agility to the lighted room. There he bent the wooden leg behind him, slipped the end of the brace from beneath the leather belt, seized the other, peg end in his right hand, and so became possessed of a murderous bludgeon. This he brandished, hopping at the same time back and forth in such perfect poise and yet with so ludicrous an effect of popping corn, that the men were surprised into laughing.

" Bully for you, peg-leg! " they cried.

" Rules 'n regerlations, boys," replied the latter, without, however, a shade of compromising in his tones. " Had supper? "

On receiving a reply in the affirmative, he caught up the lamp, and, having resumed his artificial leg in one deft motion, led the way to narrow little rooms.

CHAPTER FOUR

THORPE was awakened a long time before daylight by the ringing of a noisy bell. He dressed, shivering, and stumbled down-stairs to a round stove, big as a boiler, into which the cripple dumped huge logs of wood from time to time. After breakfast Thorpe returned to this stove and sat half dozing for what seemed to him untold ages. The cold of the north country was initiating him.

Men came in, smoked a brief pipe, and went out. Shearer was one of them. The woodsman nodded curtly to the young man, his cordiality quite gone. Thorpe vaguely wondered why. After a time he himself put on his overcoat and ventured out into the town. It seemed to Thorpe a meagre affair, built of lumber, mostly unpainted, with always the dark, menacing fringe of the forest behind. The great saw-mill, with its tall stacks and its row of water-barrels—protection against fire—on top, was the dominant note. Near the mill crouched a little red-painted structure from whose stovepipe a column of white smoke rose, attesting the cold, a clear hundred feet straight upward, and to whose door a number of men were directing their steps through the snow. Over the door Thorpe could distinguish the word " Office." He followed and entered.

In a narrow aisle railed off from the main part of the room waited Thorpe's companions of the night before. The remainder of the office gave accommodation to three clerks. One of these glanced up inquiringly as Thorpe came in.

" I am looking for work," said Thorpe.

" Wait there," briefly commanded the clerk.

In a few moments the door of the inner room opened, and Shearer came out. A man's head peered from within.

" Come on, boys," said he.

The five applicants shuffled through. Thorpe found himself in the presence of a man whom he felt to be the natural leader of these wild, independent spirits. He was already a little past middle life, and his form had lost the elastic vigor of youth. But his eye was keen, clear, and wrinkled to a certain dry facetiousness; and his figure was of that bulk which gives an impression of a subtler weight and power than the merely physical. This peculiarity impresses us in the portraits of such men as Daniel Webster and others of the old jurists. The manner of the man was easy, good-natured, perhaps a little facetious, but these qualities were worn rather as garments than exhibited as characteristics. He could afford them, not because he had fewer difficulties to overcome or battles to fight than another, but because his strength was so sufficient to them that mere battles or difficulties could not affect the deliberateness of his humor. You felt his superiority even when he was most comradely with you. This man Thorpe was to meet under other conditions, wherein the steel hand would more plainly clink the metal.

He was now seated in a worn office chair before a littered desk. In the close air hung the smell of stale cigars and the clear fragrance of pine.

"What is it, Dennis?" he asked the first of the men.

"I've been out," replied the lumberman. "Have you got anything for me, Mr. Daly?"

The mill owner laughed.

"I guess so. Report to Shearer. Did you vote for the right man, Denny?"

The lumberman grinned sheepishly. "I don't know, sir. I didn't get that far."

"Better let it alone. I suppose you and Bill want to come back, too?" he added, turning to the next two in the line. "All right, report to Tim. Do you want work?" he inquired of the last of the quartette, a big bashful man with the shoulders of a Hercules.

"Yes, sir," answered the latter uncomfortably.

"What do you do?"

"I'm a cant-hook man, sir."

"Where have you worked?"

"I had a job with Morgan & Stebbins on the Clear River last winter."

"All right, we need cant-hook men. Report at 'seven,' and if they don't want you there, go to 'thirteen.'"

Daly looked directly at the man with an air of finality. The lumberman still lingered uneasily, twisting his cap in his hands.

"Anything you want?" asked Daly at last.

"Yes, sir," blurted the big man. "If I come down here and tell you I want three days off and fifty dollars to bury my mother, I wish you'd tell me to go to hell! I buried her three times last winter!"

Daly chuckled a little.

"All right, Bub," said he, "to hell it is."

The man went out. Daly turned to Thorpe with the last flickers of amusement in his eyes.

"What can I do for you?" he inquired in a little crisper tones. Thorpe felt that he was not treated with the same careless familiarity, because, potentially, he might be more of a force to deal with. He underwent, too, the man's keen scrutiny, and knew that every detail of his appearance had found its comment in the other's experienced brain.

"I am looking for work," Thorpe replied.

"What kind of work?"

"Any kind, so I can learn something about the lumber business."

The older man studied him keenly for a few moments.

" Have you had any other business experience? "

" None."

" What have you been doing? "

" Nothing."

The lumberman's eyes hardened.

" We are a very busy firm here," he said with a certain deliberation; " we do not carry a big force of men in any one department, and each of those men has to fill his place and slop some over the sides. We do not pretend or attempt to teach here. If you want to be a lumberman, you must learn the lumber business more directly than through the windows of a bookkeeper's office. Go into the woods. Learn a few first principles. Find out the difference between Norway and white pine, anyway."

Daly, being what is termed a self-made man, entertained a prejudice against youths of the leisure class. He did not believe in their earnestness of purpose, their capacity for knowledge, nor their perseverance in anything. That a man of twenty-six should be looking for his first situation was incomprehensible to him. He made no effort to conceal his prejudice. because the class to which the young man had belonged enjoyed his hearty contempt.

The truth is. he had taken Thorpe's ignorance a little too much for granted. Before leaving his home, and while the project of emigration was still

in the air, the young fellow had, with the quiet enthusiasm of men of his habit of mind, applied himself to the mastering of whatever the books could
teach. That is not much. The literature on lumbering seems to be singularly limited. Still he knew
the trees, and had sketched an outline into which to
paint experience. He said nothing of this to the
man before him, because of that strange streak in
his nature which prompted him to conceal what he
felt most strongly; to leave to others the task of
guessing out his attitude; to stand on appearances
without attempting to justify them, no matter how
simple the justification might be. A moment's
frank, straightforward talk might have caught
Daly's attention, for the lumberman was, after all,
a shrewd reader of character where his prejudices
were not concerned. Then events would have turned
out very differently.

After his speech the business man had whirled
back to his desk.

"Have you anything for me to do in the woods,
then?" the other asked quietly.

"No," said Daly over his shoulder.

Thorpe went out.

Before leaving Detroit he had, on the advice of
friends, visited the city office of Morrison & Daly.
There he had been told positively that the firm were
hiring men. Now, without five dollars in his pocket,
he made the elementary discovery that even in chop-

ping wood skilled labor counts. He did not know where to turn next, and he would not have had the money to go far in any case. So, although Shearer's brusque greeting that morning had argued a lack of cordiality, he resolved to remind the riverman of his promised assistance.

That noon he carried out his resolve. To his surprise Shearer was cordial—in his way. He came afterward to appreciate the subtle *nuances* of manner and treatment by which a boss retains his moral supremacy in a lumber country — repels that too great familiarity which breeds contempt, without imperiling the trust and comradeship which breeds willingness. In the morning Thorpe had been a prospective employee of the firm, and so a possible subordinate of Shearer himself. Now he was Shearer's equal.

"Go up and tackle Radway. He's jobbing for us on the Cass Branch. He needs men for roadin', I know, because he's behind. You'll get a job there."

"Where is it?" asked Thorpe.

"Ten miles from here. She's blazed, but you better wait for th' supply team, Friday. If you try to make her yourself, you'll get lost on some of th' old loggin' roads."

Thorpe considered.

"I'm busted," he said at last frankly.

"Oh, that's all right," replied the walking-boss. "Marshall, come here!"

The peg-legged boarding-house keeper stumped in.
" What is it? " he trumpeted snuffingly.

" This boy wants a job till Friday. Then he's
going up to Radway's with the supply team. Now
quit your hollerin' for a chore-boy for a few days."

" All right," snorted Marshall, " take that ax and
split some dry wood that you'll find behind th'
house."

" I'm very much obliged to you," began Thorpe
to the walking-boss, " and——"

" That's all right," interrupted the latter, " some
day you can give me a job."

CHAPTER FIVE

FOR five days Thorpe cut wood, made fires, drew water, swept floors, and ran errands. Sometimes he would look across the broad stump-dotted plain to the distant forest. He had imagination. No business man succeeds without it. With him the great struggle to wrest from an impassive and aloof nature what she has so long held securely as her own, took on the proportions of a battle. The distant forest was the front. To it went the new bands of fighters. From it came the caissons for food, that ammunition of the frontier; messengers bringing tidings of defeat or victory; sometimes men groaning on their litters from the twisting and crushing and breaking inflicted on them by the calm, ruthless enemy; once a dead man bearing still on his chest the mark of the tree that had killed him. Here at headquarters sat the general, map in hand, issuing his orders, directing his forces.

And out of the forest came mystery. Hunters brought deer on sledges. Indians, observant and grave, swung silently across the reaches on their snowshoes, and silently back again carrying their meagre purchases. In the daytime ravens wheeled and croaked about the outskirts of the town, bearing the shadow of the woods on their plumes and of the north-wind in the sombre quality of their voices; rare eagles wheeled gracefully to and fro; snow squalls coquetted with the landscape. At night the many creatures of the forest ventured out across the plains in search of food—weasels; big white hares; deer, planting daintily their little sharp hoofs where the frozen turnips were most plentiful; porcupines in quest of anything they could get their keen teeth into;—and often the big timber wolves would send shivering across the waste a long whining howl. And in the morning their tracks would embroider the snow with many stories.

The talk about the great stove in the boarding-house office also possessed the charm of balsam fragrance. One told the other occult facts about the "Southeast of the southwest of eight." The second in turn vouchsafed information about another point of the compass. Thorpe heard of many curious practical expedients. He learned that one can pre-vent awkward air-holes in lakes by "tapping" the ice with an ax—for the air must get out, naturally or artificially; that the top log on a load should not be large because of the probability, when one side has dumped with a rush, of its falling straight down from its original height, so breaking the sleigh; that a thin slice of salt pork well peppered is good when tied about a sore throat; that choking a horse will cause him to swell up and float on the top of the wate., thus rendering it easy to slide him out on the ice from a hole he may have broken into; that a tree lodged against another may be brought to the ground by felling a third against it; that snowshoes made of caribou hide do not become baggy, because caribou shrinks when wet, whereas other rawhide stretches. These, and many other things too complicated to elaborate here, he heard discussed by expert opinion. Gradually he acquired an enthusiasm for the woods, just as a boy conceives a longing for the out-of-door life of which he hears in the conversation of his elders about the winter fire. He became eager to get away to the front, to stand among the pines, to grapple with the difficulties of thicket, hill, snow, and cold that nature silently interposes between the man and his task.

At the end of the week he received four dollars from his employer; dumped his valise into a low bobsleigh driven by a man muffled in a fur coat; assisted in loading the sleigh with a variety of things, from Spearhead plug to raisins; and turned his face at last toward the land of his hopes and desires.

The long drive to camp was at once a delight and a misery to him. Its miles stretched longer and longer as time went on; and the miles of a route new to a man are always one and a half at least. The forest, so mysterious and inviting from afar, drew within itself coldly when Thorpe entered it. He was as yet a stranger. The snow became the

48

prevailing note. The white was everywhere, concealing jealously beneath rounded uniformity the secrets of the woods. And it was cold. First Thorpe's feet became numb, then his hands, then his nose was nipped, and finally his warm clothes were lifted from him by invisible hands, and he was left naked to shivers and tremblings. He found it torture to sit still on the top of the bale of hay; and yet he could not bear to contemplate the cold shock of jumping from the sleigh to the ground— of touching foot to the chilling snow. The driver pulled up to breathe his horses at the top of a hill, and to fasten under one runner a heavy chain, which, grinding into the snow, would act as a brake on the descent.

"You're dressed pretty light," he advised; "better hoof it a ways and get warm."

The words tipped the balance of Thorpe's decision. He descended stiffly, conscious of a disagreeable shock from a six-inch jump.

In ten minutes, the wallowing, slipping, and leaping after the tail of the sled had sent his blood tingling to the last of his protesting members. Cold withdrew. He saw now that the pines were beautiful and solemn and still; and that in the temple of their columns dwelt winter enthroned. Across the carpet of the snow wandered the trails of her creatures—the stately regular prints of the partridge; the series of pairs made by the squirrel; those of the

49

weasel and mink, just like the squirrels' except that the prints were not quite side by side, and that between every other pair stretched the mark of the animal's long, slender body; the delicate tracery of the deer mouse; the fan of the rabbit; the print of a baby's hand that the raccoon left; the broad pad of a lynx; the dog-like trail of wolves;—these, and a dozen others, all equally unknown, gave Thorpe the impression of a great mysterious multitude of living things which moved about him invisible. In a thicket of cedar and scrub willow near the bed of a stream, he encountered one of those strangely assorted bands of woods-creatures which are always cruising it through the country. He heard the cheerful little chickadee; he saw the grave nuthatch with its appearance of a total lack of humor; he glimpsed a black-and-white woodpecker or so, and was reviled by a ribald blue jay. Already the wilderness was taking its character to him.

After a little while, they arrived by way of a hill, over which they plunged into the middle of the camp. Thorpe saw three large buildings, backed end to end, and two smaller ones, all built of heavy logs, roofed with plank, and lighted sparsely through one or two windows apiece. The driver pulled up opposite the space between two of the larger buildings, and began to unload his provisions. Thorpe set about aiding him, and so found himself for the first time in a " cook camp."

It was a commodious building—Thorpe had no idea a log structure ever contained so much room. One end furnished space for two cooking ranges and two bunks placed one over the other. Along one side ran a broad table-shelf, with other shelves over it and numerous barrels underneath, all filled with cans, loaves of bread, cookies, and pies. The centre was occupied by four long bench-flanked tables, down whose middle straggled utensils containing sugar, apple-butter, condiments, and sauces, and whose edges were set with tin dishes for about forty men. The cook, a rather thin-faced man with a mustache, directed where the provisions were to be stowed; and the " cookee," a hulking youth, assisted Thorpe and the driver to carry them in. During the course of the work Thorpe made a mistake.

" That stuff doesn't come here," objected the cookee, indicating a box of tobacco the newcomer was carrying. " She goes to the ' van.' "

Thorpe did not know what the " van " might be, but he replaced the tobacco on the sleigh. In a few moments the task was finished, with the exception of a half dozen other cases, which the driver designated as also for the " van." The horses were unhitched, and stabled in the third of the big log buildings. The driver indicated the second.

" Better go into the men's camp and sit down till th' boss gets in," he advised.

Thorpe entered a dim, over-heated structure, lined

on two sides by a double tier of large bunks parti-
tioned from one another like cabins of boats, and
centred by a huge stove over which hung slender
poles. The latter were to dry clothes on. Just outside the bunks ran a straight hard bench. Thorpe
stood at the entrance trying to accustom his eyes to
the dimness.

"Set down," said a voice, "on th' floor if you
want to; but I'd prefer th' deacon seat."

Thorpe obediently took position on the bench, or
"deacon seat." His eyes, more used to the light,
could make out a thin, tall, bent old man, with bare
cranium, two visible teeth, and a three days' stubble
of white beard over his meagre, twisted face.

He caught, perhaps, Thorpe's surprised expression.

"You think th' old man's no good, do you?" he
cackled, without the slightest malice, "looks is de-
ceivin'!" He sprang up swiftly, seized the toe of
his right foot in his left hand, and jumped his left
foot through the loop thus formed. Then he sat
down again, and laughed at Thorpe's astonishment.

"Old Jackson's still purty smart," said he. "I'm
barn-boss. They ain't a man in th' country knows
as much about hosses as I do. We ain't had but two
sick this fall, an' between you an' me, they's a skate
lot. You're a greenhorn, ain't you?"

"Yes," confessed Thorpe.

"Well," said Jackson, reflectively but rapidly, "Le Fabian, he's quiet but bad; and O'Grady, he talks loud but you can bluff him; and Perry, he's only bad when he gets full of red likker; and Norton he's bad when he gets mad-like, and will use axes."

Thorpe did not know he was getting valuable points on the camp bullies. The old man hitched nearer and peered in his face.

"They don't bluff you a bit," he said, "unless you likes them, and then they can back you way off the skidway."

Thorpe smiled at the old fellow's volubility. He did not know how near to the truth the woodsman's shrewdness had hit; for to himself, as to most strong characters, his peculiarities were the normal, and therefore the unnoticed. His habit of thought in respect to other people was rather objective than subjective. He inquired so impersonally the significance of whatever was before him, that it lost the human quality both as to itself and himself. To him men were things. This attitude relieved him of self-consciousness. He never bothered his head as to what the other man thought of him, his ignorance, or his awkwardness, simply because to him the other man was nothing but an element in his problem. So in such circumstances he learned fast. Once introduce the human element, however, and his absurdly sensitive self-consciousness asserted itself. He was, as Jackson expressed it, backed off the skidway.

At dark the old man lit two lamps, which served dimly to gloze the shadows, and thrust logs of wood into the cast-iron stove. Soon after, the men came in. They were a queer, mixed lot. Some carried the indisputable stamp of the frontiersman in their bearing and glance; others looked to be mere day-laborers, capable of performing whatever task they were set to, and of finding the trail home again. There were active, clean-built, precise Frenchmen, with small hands and feet, and a peculiarly trim way of wearing their rough garments; typical native-born American lumber-jacks powerful in frame, rakish in air, reckless in manner; big blonde Scandinavians and Swedes, strong men at the sawing; an Indian or so, strangely in contrast to the rest; and a variety of Irishmen, Englishmen, and Canadians. These men tramped in without a word, and set busily to work at various tasks. Some sat on the " deacon seat " and began to take off their socks and rubbers; others washed at a little wooden sink; still others selected and lit lanterns from a pendant row near the window, and followed old Jackson out of doors. They were the teamsters.

" You'll find the old man in the office," said Jackson.

Thorpe made his way across to the small log cabin indicated as the office, and pushed open the door. He found himself in a little room containing two bunks, a stove, a counter and desk, and a number of shelves full of supplies. About the walls hung fire-arms, snowshoes, and a variety of clothes.

A man sat at the desk placing figures on a sheet of paper. He obtained the figures from statistics penciled on three thin leaves of beech-wood riveted together. In a chair by the stove lounged a bulkier figure, which Thorpe concluded to be that of the " old man."

" I was sent here by Shearer," said Thorpe directly; " he said you might give me some work."

So long a silence fell that the applicant began to wonder if his question had been heard.

" I might," replied the man dryly at last.

" Well, will you? " Thorpe inquired, the humor of the situation overcoming him.

" Have you ever worked in the woods? "

" No."

The man smoked silently.

" I'll put you on the road in the morning," he concluded, as though this were the deciding qualification.

One of the men entered abruptly and approached the counter. The writer at the desk laid aside his tablets.

" What is it, Albert? " he added.

" Jot of chewin'," was the reply.

The scaler took from the shelf a long plug of tobacco and cut off two inches.

" Ain't hitting the van much, are you, Albert? "

he commented, putting the man's name and the amount in a little book. Thorpe went out, after leaving his name for the time book, enlightened as to the method of obtaining supplies. He promised himself some warm clothing from the van, when he should have worked out the necessary credit.

At supper he learned something else—that he must not talk at table. A moment's reflection taught him the common sense of the rule. For one thing, supper was a much briefer affair than it would have been had every man felt privileged to take his will in conversation; not to speak of the absence of noise and the presence of peace. Each man asked for what he wanted.

"Please pass the beans," he said with the deliberate intonation of a man who does not expect that his request will be granted.

Besides the beans were fried salt pork, boiled potatoes, canned corn, mince pie, a variety of cookies and doughnuts, and strong green tea. Thorpe found himself eating ravenously of the crude fare.

That evening he underwent a catechism, a few practical jokes, which he took good-naturedly, and a vast deal of chaffing. At nine the lights were all out. By daylight he and a dozen other men were at work, hewing a road that had to be as smooth and level as a New York boulevard.

CHAPTER SIX

THORPE and four others were set to work on this road, which was to be cut through a creek bottom leading, he was told, to " seventeen." The figures meant nothing to him. Later, each number came to possess an individuality of its own. He learned to use a double-bitted axe.

Thorpe's intelligence was of the practical sort that wonderfully helps experience. He watched closely one of the older men, and analyzed the relation borne by each one of his movements to the object in view. In a short time he perceived that one hand and arm are mere continuations of the helve, attaching the blade of the axe to the shoulder of the wielder; and that the other hand directs the stroke. He acquired the knack thus of throwing the bit of steel into the gash as though it were a baseball on the end of a string; and so accomplished power. By experiment he learned just when to slide the guiding hand down the helve; and so gained accuracy. He suffered none of those accidents so common to new choppers. His axe did not twist itself from his hands, nor glance to cut his foot. He attained the method of the double bit, and how to knock roots by alternate employment of the edge and flat. In a few days his hands became hard and used to the cold.

From shortly after daylight he worked. Four other men bore him company, and twice Radway himself came by, watched their operations for a moment, and moved on without comment. After Thorpe had caught his second wind, he enjoyed his task, proving a certain pleasure in the ease with which he handled his tool.

At the end of an interminable period, a faint, musical halloo swelled, echoed, and died through the forest, beautiful as a spirit. It was taken up by another voice and repeated. Then by another. Now near at hand, now far away it rang as hollow as a bell. The sawyers, the swampers, the skidders, and the team men turned and put on their heavy blanket coats.

Down on the road Thorpe heard it too, and wondered what it might be.

"Come on, Bub! she means chew!" explained old man Heath kindly. Old man Heath was a veteran woodsman who had come to swamping in his old age. He knew the game thoroughly, but could never save his "stake" when Pat McGinnis, the saloon man, enticed him in. Throughout the morning he had kept an eye on the newcomer, and was secretly pleased in his heart of the professional at the readiness with which the young fellow learned.

Thorpe resumed his coat, and fell in behind the
little procession. After a short time he came upon a
horse and sledge. Beyond it the cookee had built a
little camp fire, around and over which he had
grouped big fifty-pound lard-tins, half full of hot
things to eat. Each man, as he approached, picked
up a tin plate and cup from a pile near at hand.

The cookee was plainly master of the situation.
He issued peremptory orders. When Erickson, the
blonde Swede, attempted surreptitiously to appropriate a doughnut, the youth turned on him savagely.

"Get out of that, you big tow-head!" he cried
with an oath.

A dozen Canada jays, fluffy, impatient, perched
near by or made little short circles over and back.
They awaited the remains of the dinner. Bob Stratton and a devil-may-care giant by the name of Nolan
constructed a joke wherewith to amuse the interim.
They cut a long pole, and placed it across a log and
through a bush, so that one extremity projected beyond the bush. Then diplomacy won a piece of
meat from the cookee. This they nailed to the end
of the pole by means of a pine sliver. The Canada
jays gazed on the morsel with covetous eyes. When
the men had retired, they swooped. One big fellow
arrived first, and lit in defiance of the rest.

"Give it to 'im!" whispered Nolan, who had
been watching.

Bob hit the other end of the pole a mighty whack

with his ax. The astonished jay, projected straight upward by the shock, gave a startled squawk and cut a hole through the air for the tall timber. Stratton and Nolan went into convulsions of laughter.

" Get at it! " cried the cookee, as though setting a pack of dogs on their prey.

The men ate, perched in various attitudes and places. Thorpe found it difficult to keep warm. The violent exercise had heated him through, and now the north country cold penetrated to his bones. He huddled close to the fire, and drank hot tea, but t did not do him very much good. In his secret mind he resolved to buy one of the blanket mackinaws that very evening. He began to see that the costumes of each country have their origin in practicality.

That evening he picked out one of the best. As he was about to inquire the price, Radway drew the van book toward him, inquiring:

" Let's see; what's the name? "

In an instant Thorpe was charged on the book with three dollars and a half, although his work that day had earned him less than a dollar. On his way back to the men's shanty he could not help thinking how easy it would be for him to leave the next morning two dollars and a half ahead. He wondered if this method of procedure obtained in all the camps.

The newcomer's first day of hard work had tired

him completely. He was ready for nothing so much
as his bunk. But he had forgotten that it was Saturday night. His status was still to assure.

They began with a few mild tricks. Shuffle the
Brogan followed Hot Back. Thorpe took all of it
good-naturedly. Finally a tall individual with a
thin white face, a reptilian forehead, reddish hair,
and long baboon arms, suggested tossing in a blanket. Thorpe looked at the low ceiling, and declined.

"I'm with the game as long as you say, boys,"
said he, "and I'll have as much fun as anybody, but
that's going too far for a tired man."

The reptilian gentleman let out a string of oaths
whose meaning might be translated, "We'll see
about that!"

Thorpe was a good boxer, but he knew by now
the lumber-jack's method of fighting—anything to
hurt the other fellow. And in a genuine old-fashioned knock-down-and-drag-out rough-and-tumble
your woodsman is about the toughest customer to
handle you will be likely to meet. He is brought
up on fighting. Nothing pleases him better than to
get drunk and, with a few companions, to embark
on an earnest effort to "clean out" a rival town.
And he will accept cheerfully punishment enough
to kill three ordinary men. It takes one of his kind
really to hurt him.

Thorpe, at the first hostile movement, sprang back
to the door, seized one of the three-foot billets of

hardwood intended for the stove, and faced his opponents.

" I don't know which of you boys is coming first," said he quietly, " but he's going to get it good and plenty."

If the affair had been serious, these men would never have recoiled before the mere danger of a stick of hardwood. The American woodsman is afraid of nothing human. But this was a good-natured bit of foolery, a test of nerve, and there was no object in getting a broken head for that. The reptilian gentleman alone grumbled at the abandonment of the attack, mumbling something profane.

" If you hanker for trouble so much," drawled the unexpected voice of old Jackson from the corner, " mebbe you could put on th' gloves."

The idea was acclaimed. Somebody tossed out a dirty torn old set of buckskin boxing gloves.

The rest was farce. Thorpe was built on the true athletic lines, broad, straight shoulders, narrow flanks, long, clean, smooth muscles. He possessed, besides, that hereditary toughness and bulk which no gymnasium training will ever quite supply. The other man, while powerful and ugly in his rushes, was clumsy and did not use his head. Thorpe planted his hard straight blows at will. In this game he was as manifestly superior as his opponent would probably have been had the rules permitted kicking, gouging, and wrestling. Finally he saw his opening and let out with a swinging pivot blow. The other picked himself out of a corner, and drew off the gloves. Thorpe's status was assured.

A Frenchman took down his fiddle and began to squeak. In the course of the dance old Jackson and old Heath found themselves together, smoking their pipes of Peerless.

"The young feller's all right," observed Heath; "he cuffed Ben up to a peak all right."

"Went down like a peck of wet fish-nets," replied Jackson tranquilly.

CHAPTER SEVEN

IN the office shanty one evening about a week
later, Radway and his scaler happened to be
talking over the situation. The scaler, whose name
was Dyer, slouched back in the shadow, watching
his great honest superior as a crafty, dainty cat
might watch the blunderings of a St. Bernard.
When he spoke, it was with a mockery so subtle as
quite to escape the perceptions of the lumberman.
Dyer had a precise little black mustache whose ends
he was constantly twisting into points, black eyebrows, and long effeminate black lashes. You would
have expected his dress in the city to be just a trifle
flashy, not enough so to be loud, but sinning as to
the trifles of good taste. The two men conversed
in short elliptical sentences, using many technical
terms.

"That 'seventeen' white pine is going to under-
run," said Dyer. "It won't skid over three hundred thousand."

"It's small stuff," agreed Radway, "and so much
the worse for us; but the Company'll stand in on it
because small stuff like that always over-runs on the
mill-cut."

64

The scaler nodded comprehension.

"When you going to dray-haul that Norway across Pike Lake?"

"To-morrow. She's springy, but the books say five inches of ice will hold a team, and there's more than that. How much are we putting in a day, now?"

"About forty thousand."

Radway fell silent.

"That's mighty little for such a crew," he observed at last, doubtfully.

"I always said you were too easy with them. You got to drive them more."

"Well, it's a rough country," apologized Radway, trying, as was his custom, to find excuses for the other party as soon as he was agreed with in his blame, "there's any amount of potholes; and, then, we've had so much snow the ground ain't really froze underneath. It gets pretty soft in some of them swamps. Can't figure on putting up as much in this country as we used to down on the Muskegon."

The scaler smiled a thin smile all to himself behind the stove. Big John Radway depended so much on the moral effect of approval or disapproval by those with whom he lived. It amused Dyer to withhold the timely word, so leaving the jobber to flounder between his easy nature and his sense of what should be done.

Dyer knew perfectly well that the work was be-hind, and he knew the reason. For some time the men had been relaxing their efforts. They had worked honestly enough, but a certain snap and vim had lacked. This was because Radway had been too easy on them.

Your true lumber-jack adores of all things in creation a man whom he feels to be stronger than himself. If his employer is big enough to drive him, then he is willing to be driven to the last ounce of his strength. But once he gets the notion that his " boss " is afraid of, or for, him or his feelings or his health, he loses interest in working for that man. So a little effort to lighten or expedite his work, a little leniency in excusing the dilatory finishing of a job, a little easing-up under stress of weather, are taken as so many indications of a desire to conciliate. And conciliation means weakness every time. Your lumber-jack likes to be met front to front, one strong man to another. As you value your authority, the love of your men, and the completion of your work, keep a bluff brow and an unbending singleness of purpose.

Radway's peculiar temperament rendered him liable to just this mistake. It was so much easier for him to do the thing himself than to be harsh to the point of forcing another to it, that he was inclined to take the line of least resistance when it came to a question of even ordinary diligence. He sought often in his own mind excuses for dereliction in favor of a man who would not have dreamed of seeking them for himself. A good many people would call this kindness of heart. Perhaps it was; the question is a little puzzling. But the facts were as stated.

Thorpe had already commented on the feeling among the men, though, owing to his inexperience, he was not able to estimate its full value. The men were inclined to a semi-apologetic air when they spoke of their connection with the camp. Instead of being honored as one of a series of jobs, this seemed to be considered as merely a temporary halting-place in which they took no pride, and from which they looked forward in anticipation or back in memory to better things.

"Old Shearer, he's the bully boy," said Bob Stratton. "I remember when he was foreman for M. & D. at Camp O. Say, we did hustle them saw-logs in! I should rise to remark! Out in th' woods by first streak o' day. I recall one mornin' she was pretty cold, an' the boys grumbled some about turnin' out. 'Cold,' says Tim, 'you sons of guns! You got your ch'ice. It may be too cold for you in the woods, but i.'s a damm sight too hot fer you in hell, an' you're going to one or the other!' And he meant it too. Them was great days! Forty million a year, and not a hitch."

One man said nothing in the general discussion.

It was his first winter in the woods, and plainly in the eyes of the veterans this experience did not count. It was a *faute de mieux*, in which one would give an honest day's work, and no more.

As has been hinted, even the inexperienced newcomer noticed the lack of enthusiasm, of unity. Had he known the loyalty, devotion, and adoration that a thoroughly competent man wins from his "hands," the state of affairs would have seemed even more surprising. The lumber-jack will work sixteen, eighteen hours a day, sometimes up to the waist in water full of floating ice; sleep wet on the ground by a little fire; and then next morning will spring to work at daylight with an "Oh, no, not tired; just a little stiff, sir!" in cheerful reply to his master's inquiry—for the right man! Only it must be a strong man—with the strength of the wilderness in his eye.

The next morning Radway transferred Molly and Jenny, with little Fabian Laveque and two of the younger men, to Pike Lake. There, earlier in the season, a number of pines had been felled out on the ice, cut in logs, and left in expectation of ice thick enough to bear the travoy "dray." Owing to the fact that the shores of Pike Lake were extremely precipitous, it had been impossible to travoy the logs up over the hill.

Radway had sounded carefully the thickness of the ice with an ax. Although the weather had of late been sufficiently cold for the time of year, the snow, as often happens, had fallen before the temperature. Under the warm white blanket, the actual freezing had been slight. However, there seemed to be at least eight inches of clear ice, which would suffice.

Some of the logs in question were found to be half imbedded in the ice. It became necessary first of all to free them. Young Henrys cut a strong bar six or eight feet long, while Pat McGuire chopped a hole alongside the log. Then one end of the bar was thrust into the hole, the logging chain fastened to the other; and, behold, a monster lever, whose fulcrum was the ice and whose power was applied by Molly, hitched to the end of the chain. In this simple manner a task was accomplished in five minutes which would have taken a dozen men an hour. When the log had been cat-a-cornered from its bed, the chain was fastened around one end by means of the ever-useful steel swamp-hook, and it was yanked across the dray. Then the travoy took its careful way across the ice to where a dip in the shore gave access to a skidway.

Four logs had thus been safely hauled. The fifth was on its journey across the lake. Suddenly without warning, and with scarcely a sound, both horses sank through the ice, which bubbled up around them and over their backs in irregular rotted pieces. Little Fabian Laveque shouted, and jumped down from his log. Pat McGuire and young Henrys came running.

The horses had broken through an air-hole, about which the ice was strong. Fabian had already seized Molly by the bit, and was holding her head easily above water.

" Kitch Jenny by dat he't! " he cried to Pat.

Thus the two men, without exertion, sustained the noses of the team above the surface. The position demanded absolutely no haste, for it could have been maintained for a good half hour. Molly and Jenny, their soft eyes full of the intelligence of the situation, rested easily in full confidence. But Pat and Henrys, new to this sort of emergency, were badly frightened and excited. To them the affair had come to a deadlock.

" Oh, Lord! " cried Pat, clinging desperately to Jenny's headpiece. " What will we'z be doin'? We can't niver haul them two horses on the ice."

" Tak' de log chain," said Fabian to Henrys, " an' tie him around de nec' of Jenny."

Henrys, after much difficulty and nervous fumbling, managed to loosen the swamp-hook; and after much more difficulty and nervous fumbling succeeded in making it fast about the gray mare's neck. Fabian intended with this to choke the animal to that peculiar state when she would float like a balloon on the water, and two men could with ease

draw her over the edge of the ice. Then the unexpected happened.

The instant Henrys had passed the end of the
chain through the knot, Pat, possessed by some
Hibernian notion that now all was fast, let go of
the bit. Jenny's head at once went under, and the
end of the logging chain glided over the ice and fell
plump in the hole.

Immediately all was confusion. Jenny kicked
and struggled, churning the water, throwing it
about, kicking out in every direction. Once a horse's
head dips strongly, the game is over. No animal
drowns more quickly. The two young boys scrambled away, and French oaths could not induce them
to approach. Molly, still upheld by Fabian, looked
at him piteously with her strange intelligent eyes,
holding herself motionless and rigid with complete
confidence in this master who had never failed her
before. Fabian dug his heels into the ice, but could
not hang on. The drowning horse was more than a
dead weight. Presently it became a question of letting go or being dragged into the lake on top of the
animals. With a sob the little Frenchman relin-
quished his hold. The water seemed slowly to rise
and over-film the troubled look of pleading in
Molly's eyes.

"Assassins!" hissed Laveque at the two unfortunate youths. That was all.

When the surface of the waters had again mirrored the clouds, they hauled the carcasses out on the ice and stripped the harness. Then they rolled the log from the dray, piled the tools on it, and took their way to camp. In the blue of the winter's sky was a single speck.

The speck grew. Soon it swooped. With a hoarse croak it lit on the snow at a wary distance, and began to strut back and forth. Presently, its suspicions at rest, the raven advanced, and with eager beak began its dreadful meal. By this time another, which had seen the first one's swoop, was in view through the ether; then another; then another. In an hour the brotherhood of ravens, thus telegraphically notified, was at feast.

CHAPTER EIGHT

FABIAN LAVEQUE elaborated the details of the catastrophe with volubility.

"Hee's not fonny dat she bre'ks t'rough," he said. "I 'ave see dem bre'k t'rough two, t'ree tam in de day, but nevaire dat she get drown! W'en dose dam-fool can't t'ink wit' hees haid—*sacrè Dieu!* eet is so easy, to chok' dat *cheval*—she make me cry wit' de eye!"

"I suppose it was a good deal my fault," commented Radway, doubtfully shaking his head, after Laveque had left the office. "I ought to have been surer about the ice."

"Eight inches is a little light, with so much snow atop," remarked the scaler carelessly.

By virtue of that same careless remark, however, Radway was so confirmed in his belief as to his own culpability that he quite overlooked Fabian's just contention—that the mere thinness of the ice was in reality no excuse for the losing of the horses. So Pat and Henrys were not discharged—were not instructed to "get their time." Fabian Laveque promptly demanded his.

"*Sacrè bleu!*" said he to old Jackson. "I no work wid dat dam-fool dat no t'ink wit' hees haid."

This deprived the camp at once of a teamster and a team. When you reflect that one pair of horses takes care of the exertions of a crew of sawyers, several swampers, and three or four cant-hook men, you will readily see what a serious derangement their loss would cause. And besides, the animals themselves are difficult to replace. They are big strong beasts, selected for their power, staying qualities, and intelligence, worth anywhere from three to six hundred dollars a pair. They must be shipped in from a distance. And, finally, they require a very careful and patient training before they are of value in co-operating with the nicely adjusted efforts necessary to place the saw-log where it belongs. Ready-trained horses are never for sale during the season.

Radway did his best. He took three days to search out a big team of farm horses. Then it became necessary to find a driver. After some deliberation he decided to advance Bob Stratton to the post, that " decker " having had more or less experience the year before. Erickson, the Swede, while not a star cant-hook man, was nevertheless sure and reliable. Radway placed him in Stratton's place. But now he must find a swamper. He remembered Thorpe.

So the young man received his first promotion toward the ranks of skilled labor. He gained at last a field of application for the accuracy he had so intelligently acquired while road-making, for now a false stroke marred a saw-log; and, besides, what was more to his taste, he found himself near the actual scene of operation, at the front, as it were. He had under his very eyes the process as far as it had been carried.

In his experience here he made use of the same searching analytical observation that had so quickly taught him the secret of the axe-swing. He knew that each of the things he saw, no matter how trivial, was either premeditated or the product of chance. If premeditated, he tried to find out its reason for being. If fortuitous, he wished to know the fact, and always attempted to figure out the possibility of its elimination.

So he learned why and when the sawyers threw a tree up or down hill; how much small standing timber they tried to fell it through; what consideration held for the cutting of different lengths of log; how the timber was skilfully decked on the skids in such a manner that the pile should not bulge and fall, and so that the scaler could easily determine the opposite ends of the same log;—in short, a thousand and one little details which ordinarily a man learns only as the exigencies arise to call in experience. Here, too, he first realized he was in the firing line.

Thorpe had assigned him as bunk mate the young fellow who assisted Tom Broadhead in the felling. Henry Paul was a fresh-complexioned, clear-eyed, quick-mannered young fellow with an air of steady responsibility about him. He came from the southern part of the State, where, during the summer, he worked on a little homestead farm of his own. After a few days he told Thorpe that he was married, and after a few days more he showed his bunk mate the photograph of a sweet-faced young woman who looked trustingly out of the picture.

"She's waitin' down there for me, and it ain't so very long till spring," said Paul wistfully. "She's the best little woman a man ever had, and there ain't nothin' too good for *her*, chummy!"

Thorpe, soul-sick after his recent experiences with the charity of the world, discovered a real pleasure in this fresh, clear passion. As he contemplated the abounding health, the upright carriage, the sparkling, bubbling spirits of the young woodsman, he could easily imagine the young girl and the young happiness, too big for a little backwoods farm.

Three days after the newcomer had started in at the swamping, Paul, during their early morning walk from camp to the scene of their operations, confided in him further.

"Got another letter, chummy," said he, "come in yesterday. She tells me," he hesitated with a blush, and then a happy laugh, "that they ain't going to be only two of us at the farm next year."

"You mean!" queried Thorpe.

"Yes," laughed Paul, "and if it's a girl she gets named after her mother, you bet."

The men separated. In a moment Thorpe found himself waist-deep in the pitchy aromatic top of an old bull-sap, clipping away at the projecting branches. After a time he heard Paul's gay halloo.

"Tim*ber*!" came the cry, and then the swish-sh-sh—*crash*! of the tree's fall.

Thorpe knew that now either Hank or Tom must be climbing with the long measuring pole along the prostrate trunk, marking by means of shallow axe-clips where the saw was to divide the logs. Then Tom shouted something unintelligible. The other men seemed to understand, however, for they dropped their work and ran hastily in the direction of the voice. Thorpe, after a moment's indecision, did the same. He arrived to find a group about a prostrate man. The man was Paul.

Two of the older woodsmen, kneeling, were conducting coolly a hasty examination. At the front every man is more or less of a surgeon.

"Is he hurt badly?" asked Thorpe; "what is it?"

"He's dead," answered one of the other men soberly.

With the skill of ghastly practice some of them wove a litter on which the body was placed. The pathetic little procession moved in the solemn, inscrutable forest.

When the tree had fallen it had crashed through the top of another, leaving suspended in the branches of the latter a long heavy limb. A slight breeze dislodged it. Henry Paul was impaled as by a javelin.

This is the chief of the many perils of the woods. Like crouching pumas the instruments of a man's destruction poise on the spring, sometimes for days. Then swiftly, silently, the leap is made. It is a danger unavoidable, terrible, ever-present. Thorpe, was destined in time to see men crushed and mangled in a hundred ingenious ways by the saw log, knocked into space and a violent death by the butts of trees, ground to powder in the mill of a jam, but never would he be more deeply impressed than by this ruthless silent taking of a life. The forces of nature are so tame, so simple, so obedient; and in the next instant so absolutely beyond human control or direction, so whirlingly contemptuous of puny human effort, that in time the wilderness shrouds itself to our eyes in the same impenetrable mystery as the sea.

That evening the camp was unusually quiet. Tallier let his fiddle hang. After supper Thorpe was approached by Purdy, the reptilian red-head with whom he had had the row some evenings before.

"You in, chummy?" he asked in a quiet voice. "It's a five apiece for Hank's woman."

"Yes," said Thorpe.

The men were earning from twenty to thirty dollars a month. They had, most of them, never seen

Hank Paul before this autumn. He had not, mainly because of his modest disposition, enjoyed any extraordinary degree of popularity. Yet these strangers cheerfully, as a matter of course, gave up the proceeds of a week's hard work, and that without expecting the slightest personal credit. The money was sent " from the boys." Thorpe later read a heart-broken letter of thanks to the unknown benefactors. It touched him deeply, and he suspected the other men of the same emotions, but by that time they had regained the independent, self-contained poise of the frontiersman. They read it with unmoved faces, and tossed it aside with a more than ordinarily rough joke or oath. Thorpe understood their reticence. It was a part of his own nature. He felt more than ever akin to these men.

As swamper he had more or less to do with a cant-hook in helping the teamsters roll the end of the log on the little " dray." He soon caught the knack. Toward Christmas he had become a fairly efficient cant-hook man, and was helping roll the great sticks of timber up the slanting skids. Thus always intelligence counts, especially that rare intelligence which resolves into the analytical and the minutely observing.

On Sundays Thorpe fell into the habit of accompanying old Jackson Hines on his hunting expeditions. The ancient had been raised in the woods. He seemed to know by instinct the haunts and habits of all the wild animals, just as he seemed to know by instinct when one of his horses was likely to be troubled by the colic. His woodcraft was really remarkable.

So the two would stand for hours in the early morning and late evening waiting for deer on the edges of the swamps. They haunted the runways during the middle of the day. On soft moccasined feet they stole about in the evening with a bull's-eye lantern fastened on the head of one of them for a " jack." Several times they surprised the wolves, and shone the animals' eyes like the scattered embers of a camp fire.

Thorpe learned to shoot at a deer's shoulders rather than his heart, how to tell when the animal had sustained a mortal hurt from the way it leaped and the white of its tail. He even made progress in the difficult art of still-hunting, where the man matches his senses against those of the creatures of the forest—and sometimes wins. He soon knew better than to cut the animal's throat, and learned from Hines that a single stab at a certain point of the chest was much better for the purposes of bleeding. And, what is more, he learned not to overshoot down-hill.

Besides these things Jackson taught him many other, minor, details of woodcraft. Soon the young man could interpret the thousands of signs, so insignificant in appearance and so important in reality, which tell the history of the woods. He acquired the knack of winter fishing.

These Sundays were perhaps the most nearly perfect of any of the days of that winter. In them the young man drew more directly face to face with the wilderness. He called a truce with the enemy; and in return that great inscrutable power poured into his heart a portion of her grandeur. His ambition grew; and, as always with him, his determination became the greater and the more secret. In proportion as his ideas increased, he took greater pains to shut them in from expression. For failure in great things would bring keener disappointment than failure in little.

He was getting just the experience and the knowledge he needed; but that was about all. His wages were twenty-five dollars a month, which his van bill would reduce to the double eagle. At the end of the winter he would have but a little over a hundred dollars to show for his season's work, and this could mean at most only fifty dollars for Helen. But the future was his. He saw now more plainly what he had dimly perceived before, that for the man who buys timber, and logs it well, a sure future is waiting. And in this camp he was beginning to learn from failure the conditions of success.

... occur, the season.

CHAPTER NINE

THEY finished cutting on section seventeen
during Thorpe's second week. It became necessary to begin on section fourteen, which lay two
miles to the east. In that direction the character of
the country changed somewhat.

The pine there grew thick on isolated "islands"
of not more than an acre or so in extent—little
knolls rising from the level of a marsh. In ordinary
conditions nothing would have been easier than to
have plowed roads across the frozen surface of this
marsh. The peculiar state of the weather interposed
tremendous difficulties.

The early part of autumn had been characterized
by a heavy snowfall immediately after a series of
mild days. A warm blanket of some thickness thus
overlaid the earth, effectually preventing the freezing which subsequent cold weather would have
caused. All the season Radway had contended with
this condition. Even in the woods, muddy swamp
and spring-holes caused endless difficulty and neces-
sitated a great deal of "corduroying," or the laying
of poles side by side to form an artificial bottom.
Here in the open some six inches of water and un-
limited mud awaited the first horse that should

break through the layer of snow and thin ice. Between each pair of islands a road had to be "tramped."

Thorpe and the rest were put at this disagreeable job. All day long they had to walk mechanically back and forth on diagonals between the marks set by Radway with his snowshoes. Early in the morning their feet were wet by icy water, for even the light weight of a man sometimes broke the frozen skin of the marsh. By night a road of trampled snow, of greater or less length, was marked out across the expanse. Thus the blanket was thrown back from the warm earth, and thus the cold was given a chance at the water beneath. In a day or so the road would bear a horse. A bridge of ice had been artificially constructed, on either side of which lay unsounded depths. This road was indicated by a row of firs stuck in the snow on either side.

It was very cold. All day long the restless wind swept across the shivering surface of the plains, and tore around the corners of the islands. The big woods are as good as an overcoat. The overcoat had been taken away.

When the lunch-sleigh arrived, the men huddled shivering in the lee of one of the knolls, and tried to eat with benumbed fingers before a fire that was but a mockery. Often it was nearly dark before their work had warmed them again. All of the skidways

had to be placed on the edges of the islands themselves, and the logs had to be travoyed over the
steep little knolls. A single misstep out onto the
plain meant a mired horse. Three times heavy
snows obliterated the roads, so that they had to be
plowed out before the men could go to work again.
It was a struggle.

Radway was evidently worried. He often paused
before a gang to inquire how they were " making
it." He seemed afraid they might wish to quit,
which was indeed the case, but he should never have
taken before them any attitude but that of absolute
confidence in their intentions. His anxiety was natural, however. He realized the absolute necessity
of skidding and hauling this job before the heavy
choking snows of the latter part of January should
make it impossible to keep the roads open. So insistent was this necessity that he had seized the first
respite in the phenomenal snowfall of the early
autumn to begin work. The cutting in the woods
could wait.

Left to themselves probably the men would never
have dreamed of objecting to whatever privations
the task carried with it. Radway's anxiety for their
comfort, however, caused them finally to imagine
that perhaps they might have some just grounds for
complaint after all. That is a great trait of the
lumber-jack.

But Dyer, the scaler, finally caused the outbreak.

Dyer was an efficient enough man in his way, but he loved his own ease. His habit was to stay in his bunk of mornings until well after daylight. To this there could be no objection—except on the part of the cook, who was supposed to attend to his business himself—for the scaler was active in his work, when once he began it, and could keep up with the skidding. But now he displayed a strong antipathy to the north wind on the plains. Of course he could not very well shirk the work entirely, but he did a good deal of talking on the very cold mornings.

"I don't pose for no tough son-of-a-gun," said he to Radway, "and I've got some respect for my ears and feet. She'll warm up a little by to-morrow, and perhaps the wind'll die. I can catch up on you fellows by hustling a little, so I guess I'll stay in and work on the books to-day."

"All right," Radway assented, a little doubtfully.

This happened perhaps two days out of the week. Finally Dyer hung out a thermometer, which he used to consult. The men saw it, and consulted it too. At once they felt much colder.

"She was stan' ten below," sputtered Baptiste Tallier, the Frenchman who played the fiddle. "He freeze t'rou to hees eenside. Dat is too cole for mak' de work."

"Them plains is sure a holy fright," assented Purdy.

" Th' old man knows it himself," agreed big Nolan; " did you see him rammin' around yesterday askin' us if we found her too cold? He knows damn well he ought not to keep a man out that sort o' weather."

" You'd shiver like a dog in a briar path on a warm day in July," said Jackson Hines contemptuously.

" Shut up! " said they. " You're barn-boss. You don't have to be out in th' cold."

This was true. So Jackson's intervention went for a little worse than nothing.

" It ain't lak' he has nuttin' besides," went on Baptiste. " He can mak' de cut in de meedle of de fores'."

" That's right," agreed Bob Stratton, " they's the west half of eight ain't been cut yet."

So they sent a delegation to Radway. Big Nolan was the spokesman.

" Boss," said he bluntly, " she's too cold to work on them plains to-day. She's the coldest day we had."

Radway was too old a hand at the business to make any promises on the spot.

" I'll see, boys," said he.

When the breakfast was over the crew were set to making skidways and travoy roads on eight. This was a precedent. In time the work on the plains was grumblingly done in any weather. However, as to this Radway proved firm enough. He was a good fighter when he knew he was being imposed on. A man could never cheat or defy him openly without collecting a little war that left him surprised at the jobber's belligerency. The doubtful cases, those on the subtle line of indecision, found him weak. He could be so easily persuaded that he was in the wrong. At times it even seemed that he was anxious to be proved at fault, so eager was he to catch fairly the justice of the other man's attitude. He held his men inexorably and firmly to their work on the indisputably comfortable days; but gave in often when an able-bodied woodsman should have seen in the weather no inconvenience, even. As the days slipped by, however, he tightened the reins. Christmas was approaching. An easy mathematical computation reduced the question of completing his contract with Morrison & Daly to a certain weekly quota. In fact he was surprised at the size of it. He would have to work diligently and steadily during the rest of the winter.

Having thus a definite task to accomplish in a definite number of days, Radway grew to be more of a taskmaster. His anxiety as to the completion of the work overlaid his morbidly sympathetic human interest. Thus he regained to a small degree the respect of his men. Then he lost it again.

One morning he came in from a talk with the supply-teamster, and woke Dyer, who was not yet up.

"I'm going down home for two or three weeks," he announced to Dyer, "you know my address. You'll have to take charge, and I guess you'd better let the scaling go. We can get the tally at the banking grounds when we begin to haul. Now we ain't got all the time there is, so you want to keep the boys at it pretty well."

Dyer twisted the little points of his mustache. "All right, sir," said he with his smile so inscrutably insolent that Radway never saw the insolence at all. He thought this a poor year for a man in Radway's position to spend Christmas with his family, but it was none of his business.

"Do as much as you can in the marsh, Dyer," went on the jobber. "I don't believe it's really necessary to lay off any more there on account of the weather. We've simply got to get that job in before the big snows."

"All right, sir," repeated Dyer.

The scaler did what he considered his duty. All day long he tramped back and forth from one gang of men to the other, keeping a sharp eye on the details of the work. His practical experience was sufficient to solve readily such problems of broken tackle, extra expedients, or facility which the days brought forth. The fact that in him was vested the power to discharge kept the men at work.

Dyer was in the habit of starting for the marsh an hour or so after sunrise. The crew, of course, were at work by daylight. Dyer heard them often through his doze, just as he heard the chore-boy come in to build the fire and fill the water pail afresh. After a time the fire, built of kerosene and pitchy jack pine, would get so hot that in self-defense he would arise and dress. Then he would breakfast leisurely.

Thus he incurred the enmity of the cook and cookee. Those individuals have to prepare food three times a day for a half hundred heavy eaters; besides which, on sleigh-haul, they are supposed to serve a breakfast at three o'clock for the loaders and a variety of lunches up to midnight for the sprinkler men. As a consequence, they resent infractions of the little system they may have been able to introduce.

Now the business of a foreman is to be up as soon as anybody. He does none of the work himself, but he must see that somebody else does it, and does it well. For this he needs actual experience at the work itself, but above all zeal and constant presence. He must know how a thing ought to be done, and he must be on hand unexpectedly to see how its accomplishment is progressing. Dyer should have been out of bed at first horn-blow.

One morning he slept until nearly ten o'clock. It was inexplicable! He hurried from his bunk, made a hasty toilet, and started for the dining-room to get some sort of a lunch to do him until dinner time.

As he stepped from the door of the office he caught sight of two men hurrying from the cook camp to the men's camp. He thought he heard the hum of conversation in the latter building. The cookee set hot coffee before him. For the rest, he took what he could find cold on the table.

On an inverted cracker box the cook sat reading an old copy of the *Police Gazette*. Various fifty-pound lard tins were bubbling and steaming on the range. The cookee divided his time between them and the task of sticking on the log walls pleasing patterns made of illustrations from cheap papers and the gaudy labels of canned goods. Dyer sat down, feeling, for the first time, a little guilty. This was not because of a sense of a dereliction in duty, but because he feared the strong man's contempt for inefficiency.

"I sort of pounded my ear a little long this morning," he remarked with an unwonted air of *bonhomie*.

The cook creased his paper with one hand and went on reading; the little action indicating at the same time that he had heard, but intended to vouchsafe no attention. The cookee continued his occupations.

"I suppose the men got out to the marsh on time," suggested Dyer, still easily.

The cook laid aside his paper and looked the scaler in the eye.

"You're the foreman; I'm the cook," said he. "You ought to know."

The cookee had paused, the paste brush in his hand.

Dyer was no weakling. The problem presenting, he rose to the emergency. Without another word he pushed back his coffee cup and crossed the narrow open passage to the men's camp.

When he opened the door a silence fell. He could see dimly that the room was full of lounging and smoking lumbermen. As a matter of fact, not a man had stirred out that morning. This was more for the sake of giving Dyer a lesson than of actually shirking the work, for a lumber-jack is honest in giving his time when it is paid for.

"How's this, men!" cried Dyer sharply; "why aren't you out on the marsh?"

No one answered for a minute. Then Baptiste:

"He mak' too tam cole for de marsh. Meester Radway he spik dat we kip off dat marsh w'en he mak' cole."

Dyer knew that the precedent was indisputable.

"Why didn't you cut on eight then?" he asked, still in peremptory tones.

"Didn't have no one to show us where to begin," drawled a voice in the corner.

Dyer turned sharp on his heel and went out.

"Sore as a boil, ain't he!" commented old Jackson Hines with a chuckle.

In the cook camp Dyer was saying to the cook, " Well, anyway, we'll have dinner early and get a good start for this afternoon."

The cook again laid down his paper. " I'm tending to this job of cook," said he, " and I'm getting the meals on time. Dinner will be on time to-day— not a minute early, and not a minute late."

Then he resumed his perusal of the adventures of ladies to whom the illustrations accorded magnificent calf-development.

The crew worked on the marsh that afternoon, and the subsequent days of the week. They labored conscientiously but not zealously. There is a deal of difference, and the lumber-jack's unaided conscience is likely to allow him a certain amount of conversation from the decks of skidways. The work moved slowly. At Christmas a number of the men " went out." Most of them were back again after four or five days, for, while men were not plenty, neither was work. The equilibrium was nearly exact.

But the convivial souls had lost to Dyer the days of their debauch, and until their thirst for recuperative " Pain Killer," " Hinckley " and Jamaica Ginger was appeased, they were not much good. Instead of keeping up to fifty thousand a day, as Radway had figured was necessary, the scale would not have exceeded thirty.

Dyer saw all this plainly enough, but was not

able to remedy it. That was not entirely his fault. He did not dare give the delinquents their time, for he would not have known where to fill their places. This lay in Radway's experience. Dyer felt that responsibilities a little too great had been forced on him, which was partly true. In a few days the young man's facile conscience had covered all his shortcomings with the blanket excuse. He conceived that he had a grievance against Radway!

CHAPTER TEN

R ADWAY returned to camp by the 6th of January. He went on snowshoes over the entire job; and then sat silently in the office smoking "Peerless" in his battered old pipe. Dyer watched him amusedly, secure in his grievance in case blame should be attached to him. The jobber looked older. The lines of dry good-humor about his eyes had subtly changed to an expression of pathetic anxiety. He attached no blame to anybody, but rose the next morning at horn-blow, and the men found they had a new master over them.

And now the struggle with the wilderness came to grapples. Radway was as one possessed by a burning fever. He seemed everywhere at once, always helping with his own shoulder and arm, hurrying eagerly. For once luck seemed with him. The marsh was cut over; the "eighty" on section eight was skidded without a break. The weather held cold and clear.

Now it became necessary to put the roads in shape for hauling. All winter the blacksmith, between his tasks of shoeing and mending, had occupied his time in fitting the iron-work on eight log-sleighs which the carpenter had hewed from solid sticks of

94

timber. They were tremendous affairs, these sleighs, with runners six feet apart, and bunks nine feet in width for the reception of logs. The bunks were so connected by two loosely coupled rods that, when emptied, they could be swung parallel with the road, so reducing the width of the sleigh. The carpenter had also built two immense tanks on runners, holding each some seventy barrels of water, and with holes so arranged in the bottom and rear that on the withdrawal of plugs the water would flood the entire width of the road. These sprinklers were filled by horse-power. A chain running through blocks attached to a solid upper framework, like the open belfry of an Italian monastery, dragged a barrel up a wooden track from the water hole to the opening in the sprinkler. When in action this formidable machine weighed nearly two tons and resembled a moving house. Other men had felled two big hemlocks, from which they had hewed beams for a V plow.

The V plow was now put in action. Six horses drew it down the road, each pair superintended by a driver. The machine was weighted down by a number of logs laid across the arms. Men guided it by levers, and by throwing their weight against the fans of the plow. It was a gay, animated scene this, full of the spirit of winter — the plodding, straining horses, the brilliantly dressed, struggling men, the sullen-yielding snow thrown to either side, the shouts, warnings, and commands. To right and left grew white banks of snow. Behind stretched a broad white path in which a scant inch hid the bare earth.

For some distance the way led along comparatively high ground. Then, skirting the edge of a lake, it plunged into a deep creek bottom between hills. Here, earlier in the year, eleven bridges had been constructed, each a labor of accuracy; and perhaps as many swampy places had been "corduroyed" by carpeting them with long parallel poles. Now the first difficulty began.

Some of the bridges had sunk below the level, and the approaches had to be corduroyed to a practicable grade. Others again were humped up like tom-cats, and had to be pulled apart entirely. In spots the "corduroy" had spread, so that the horses thrust their hoofs far down into leg-breaking holes. The experienced animals were never caught, however. As soon as they felt the ground giving way beneath one foot, they threw their weight on the other.

Still, that sort of thing was to be expected. A gang of men who followed the plow carried axes and cant-hooks for the purpose of repairing extemporaneously just such defects, which never would have been discovered otherwise than by the practical experience. Radway himself accompanied the plow. Thorpe, who went along as one of the "road monkeys," saw now why such care had been required of him in smoothing the way of stubs, knots, and hum-mocks.

Down the creek an accident occurred on this ac-count. The plow had encountered a drift. Three times the horses had plunged at it, and three times had been brought to a stand, not so much by the drag of the V plow as by the wallowing they them-selves had to do in the drift.

"No use, break her through, boys," said Radway.

So a dozen men hurled their bodies through, mak-ing an opening for the horses.

"Hi! *yup*!" shouted the three teamsters, gather-ing up their reins.

The horses put their heads down and plunged. The whole apparatus moved with a rush, men cling-ing, animals digging their hoofs in, snow flying. Suddenly there came a check, then a *crack*, and then the plow shot forward so suddenly and easily that the horses all but fell on their noses. The flanging arms of the V, forced in a place too narrow, had caught between heavy stubs. One of the arms had broken square off.

There was nothing for it but to fell another hem-lock and hew out another beam, which meant a day lost. Radway occupied his men with shovels in clearing the edge of the road, and started one of his sprinklers over the place already cleared. Water holes of suitable size had been blown in the creek bank by dynamite. There the machines were filled.

It was a slow process. Stratton attached his horse to the chain and drove him back and forth, hauling the barrel up and down the slideway. At the bottom it was capsized and filled by means of a long pole shackled to its bottom and manipulated by old man Heath. At the top it turned over by its own weight. Thus seventy-odd times.

Then Fred Green hitched his team on, and the four horses drew the creaking, cumbrous vehicle spouting down the road. Water gushed in fans from the openings on either side and beneath; and in streams from two holes behind. Not for an instant as long as the flow continued dared the teamsters breathe their horses, for a pause would freeze the runners tight to the ground. A tongue at either end obviated the necessity of turning around.

While the other men hewed at the required beam for the broken V plow, Heath, Stratton, and Green went over the cleared road length once. To do so required three sprinklerfuls. When the road should be quite free, and both sprinklers running, they would have to keep at it until after midnight.

And then silently the wilderness stretched forth her hand and pushed these struggling atoms back to their place.

That night it turned warmer. The change was heralded by a shift of wind. Then some blue-jays appeared from nowhere and began to scream at their more silent brothers, the whiskey jacks.

"She's goin' to rain," said old Jackson. "The air is kind o' holler."

"Hollow?" said Thorpe, laughing. "How is that?"

"I don' no," confessed Hines, "but she is. She jest *feels* that way."

In the morning the icicles dripped from the roof, and although the snow did not appreciably melt, it shrank into itself and became pockmarked on the surface.

Radway was down looking at the road.

"She's holdin' her own," said he, "but there ain't any use putting more water on her. She ain't freezing a mite. We'll plow her out."

So they finished the job, and plowed her out, leaving exposed the wet, marshy surface of the creek-bottom, on which at night a thin crust formed. Across the marsh the old tramped road held up the horses, and the plow swept clear a little wider swath.

"She'll freeze a little to-night," said Radway hopefully. "You sprinkler boys get at her and wet her down."

Until two o'clock in the morning the four teams and the six men creaked back and forth spilling hardly gathered water — weird, unearthly, in the flickering light of their torches. Then they crept in and ate sleepily the food that a sleepy cookee set out for them.

By morning the mere surface of this sprinkled water had frozen, the remainder beneath had drained away, and so Radway found in his road considerable patches of shell ice, useless, crumbling. He looked in despair at the sky. Dimly through the gray he caught the tint of blue.

The sun came out. Nuthatches and woodpeckers ran gayly up the warming trunks of the trees. Blue-jays fluffed and perked and screamed in the hard-wood tops. A covey of grouse ventured from the swamp and strutted vainly, a pause of contemplation between each step. Radway, walking out on the tramped road of the marsh, cracked the artificial skin and thrust his foot through into icy water. That night the sprinklers stayed in.

The devil seemed in it. If the thaw would only cease before the ice bottom so laboriously constructed was destroyed! Radway vibrated between the office and the road. Men were lying idle; teams were doing the same. Nothing went on but the days of the year; and four of them had already ticked off the calendar. The deep snow of the unusually cold autumn had now disappeared from the tops of the stumps. Down in the swamp the covey of partridges were beginning to hope that in a few days more they might discover a bare spot in the burnings. It even stopped freezing during the night. At times Dyer's little thermometer marked as high as forty degrees.

" I often heard this was a sort 'v summer resort," observed Tom Broadhead, " but danged if I knew it was a summer resort all the year 'round."

The weather got to be the only topic of conversation. Each had his say, his prediction. It became maddening. Toward evening the chill of melting snow would deceive many into the belief that a cold snap was beginning.

" She'll freeze before morning, sure," was the hopeful comment.

And then in the morning the air would be more balmily insulting than ever.

" Old man is as blue as a whetstone," commented Jackson Hines, " an' I don't blame him. This weather'd make a man mad enough to eat the devil with his horns left on."

By and by it got to be a case of looking on the bright side of the affair from pure reaction.

" I don't know," said Radway, " it won't be so bad after all. A couple of days of zero weather, with all this water lying around, would fix things up in pretty good shape. If she only freezes tight, we'll have a good solid bottom to build on, and that'll be quite a good rig out there on the marsh."

The inscrutable goddess of the wilderness smiled, and calmly, relentlessly, moved her next pawn.

It was all so unutterably simple, and yet so effective. Something there was in it of the calm inevitability of fate. It snowed.

All night and all day the great flakes zigzagged softly down through the air. Radway plowed away two feet of it. The surface was promptly covered by a second storm. Radway doggedly plowed it out again.

This time the goddess seemed to relent. The ground froze solid. The sprinklers became assiduous in their labor. Two days later the road was ready for the first sleigh, its surface of thick, glassy ice, beautiful to behold; the ruts cut deep and true; the grades sanded, or sprinkled with retarding hay on the descents. At the river the banking ground proved solid. Radway breathed again, then sighed. Spring was eight days nearer. He was eight days more behind.

CHAPTER ELEVEN

A S soon as loading began, the cook served breakfast at three o'clock. The men worked by the light of torches, which were often merely catsup jugs with wicking in the necks. Nothing could be more picturesque than a teamster conducting one of his great pyramidical loads over the little inequalities of the road, in the ticklish places standing atop with the bent knee of the Roman charioteer, spying and forestalling the chances of the way with a fixed eye and an intense concentration that relaxed not one inch in the miles of the haul. Thorpe had become a full-fledged cant-hook man.

He liked the work. There is about it a skill that fascinates. A man grips suddenly with the hook of his strong instrument, stopping one end that the other may slide; he thrusts the short, strong stock between the log and the skid, allowing it to be overrun; he stops the roll with a sudden sure grasp applied at just the right moment to be effective. Sometimes he allows himself to be carried up bodily, clinging to the cant-hook like an acrobat to a bar, until the log has rolled once; when, his weapon loosened, he drops lightly, easily to the ground. And it is exciting to pile the logs on the sleigh, first a layer of five, say; then one of six smaller; of but three; of two; until, at the very apex, the last is dragged slowly up the skids, poised, and, just as it is about to plunge down the other side, is gripped and held inexorably by the little men in blue flannel shirts.

Chains bind the loads. And if ever, during the loading, or afterward when the sleigh is in motion, the weight of the logs causes the pyramid to break down and squash out;—then woe to the driver, or whoever happens to be near! A saw log does not make a great deal of fuss while falling, but it falls through anything that happens in its way, and a man who gets mixed up in a load of twenty-five or thirty of them obeying the laws of gravitation from a height of some fifteen to twenty feet, can be crushed into strange shapes and fragments. For this reason the loaders are picked and careful men.

At the banking grounds, which lie in and about the bed of the river, the logs are piled in a gigantic skidway to await the spring freshets, which will carry them down stream to the " boom." In that enclosure they remain until sawed in the mill.

Such is the drama of the saw log, a story of grit, resourcefulness, adaptability, fortitude and ingenuity hard to match. Conditions never repeat themselves in the woods as they do in the factory. The wilderness offers ever new complications to solve, difficulties to overcome. A man must think of everything, figure on everything, from the grand sweep of the country at large to the pressure on a king-bolt. And where another possesses the boundless resources of a great city, he has to rely on the material stored in one corner of a shed. It is easy to build a palace with men and tools; it is difficult to build a log cabin with nothing but an axe. His wits must help him where his experience fails; and his experience must push him mechanically along the track of habit when successive buffetings have beaten his wits out of his head. In a day he must construct elaborate engines, roads, and implements which old civilization considers the works of leisure. Without a thought of expense he must abandon as temporary, property which other industries cry out at being compelled to acquire as permanent. For this reason he becomes in time different from his fellows. The wilderness leaves something of her mystery in his eyes, that mystery of hidden, unknown but guessed, power. Men look after him on the street, as they would look after any other pioneer, in vague admiration of a scope more virile than their own.

Thorpe, in common with the other men, had thought Radway's vacation at Christmas time a mistake. He could not but admire the feverish animation that now characterized the jobber. Every mischance was as quickly repaired as aroused expedient could do the work.

The marsh received first attention. There the restless snow drifted uneasily before the wind. Nearly every day the road had to be plowed, and the sprinklers followed the teams almost constantly. Often it was bitter cold, but no one dared to suggest to the determined jobber that it might be better to remain indoors. The men knew as well as he that the heavy February snows would block traffic beyond hope of extrication.

As it was, several times an especially heavy fall clogged the way. The snow-plow, even with extra teams, could hardly force its path through. Men with shovels helped. Often but a few loads a day, and they small, could be forced to the banks by the utmost exertions of the entire crew. *Esprit de corps* awoke. The men sprang to their tasks with alacrity, gave more than an hour's exertion to each of the twenty-four, took a pride in repulsing the assaults of the great enemy, whom they personified under the generic "She." Mike McGovern raked up a saint somewhere whom he apostrophized in a personal and familiar manner.

He hit his head against an overhanging branch.

"You're a nice wan, now ain't ye?" he cried angrily at the unfortunate guardian of his soul. "Dom if Oi don't quit ye! Ye see!"

"Be the gate of Hivin!" he shouted, when he opened the door of mornings and discovered another six inches of snow, "Ye're a burrd! If Oi couldn't make out to be more of a saint than that, Oi'd quit the biznis! Move yor pull, an' get us some dacint weather! Ye awt t' be road monkeyin' on th' golden streets, thot's what ye awt to be doin'! "

Jackson Hines was righteously indignant, but with the shrewdness of the old man, put the blame partly where it belonged.

" I ain't sayin'," he observed judicially, " that this weather ain't hell. It's hell and repeat. But a man sort've got to expec' weather. He looks for it, and he oughta be ready for it. The trouble is we got behind Christmas. It's that Dyer. He's about as mean as they make 'em. The only reason he didn't die long ago is becuz th' Devil's thought him too mean to pay any 'tention to. If ever he should die an' go to Heaven he'd pry up th' golden streets an' use the infernal pit for a smelter."

With this magnificent bit of invective, Jackson seized a lantern and stumped out to see that the teamsters fed their horses properly.

" Didn't know you were a miner, Jackson," called Thorpe, laughing.

" Young feller," replied Jackson at the door, " it's a lot easier to tell what I *ain't* been."

So floundering, battling, making a little progress every day, the strife continued.

One morning in February, Thorpe was helping load a big butt log. He was engaged in " sending up "; that is, he was one of the two men who stand at either side of the skids to help the ascending log keep straight and true to its bed on the pile. His assistant's end caught on a sliver, ground for a second, and slipped back. Thus the log ran slanting across the skids instead of perpendicular to them. To rectify the fault, Thorpe dug his cant-hook into the timber and threw his weight on the stock. He hoped in this manner to check correspondingly the ascent of his end. In other words, he took the place, on his side, of the preventing sliver, so equalizing the pressure and forcing the timber to its proper position. Instead of rolling, the log slid. The stock of the cant-hook was jerked from his hands. He fell back, and the cant-hook, after clinging for a moment to the rough bark, snapped down and hit him a crushing blow on the top of the head.

Had a less experienced man than Jim Gladys been stationed at the other end, Thorpe's life would have ended there. A shout of surprise or horror would have stopped the horse pulling on the decking chain; the heavy stick would have slid back on the prostrate young man, who would have thereupon been ground to atoms as he lay. With the utmost coolness Gladys swarmed the slanting face of the load; interposed the length of his cant-hook stock between the log and it; held it exactly long enough to straighten the timber, but not so long as to crush his own head and arm; and ducked, just as the great piece of wood rumbled over the end of the skids and dropped with a thud into the place Norton, the " top " man, had prepared for it.

It was a fine deed, quickly thought, quickly dared. No one saw it. Jim Gladys was a hero, but a hero without an audience.

They took Thorpe up and carried him in, just as they had carried Hank Paul before. Men who had not spoken a dozen words to him in as many days gathered his few belongings and stuffed them awkwardly into his satchel. Jackson Hines prepared the bed of straw and warm blankets in the bottom of the sleigh that was to take him out.

" He would have made a good boss," said the old fellow. " He's a hard man to nick."

Thorpe was carried in from the front, and the battle went on without him.

CHAPTER TWELVE

THORPE never knew how carefully he was carried to camp, nor how tenderly the tote teamster drove his hay-couched burden to Beeson Lake. He had no consciousness of the jolting train, in the baggage car of which Jimmy, the little brakeman, and Bud, and the baggage man spread blankets, and altogether put themselves to a great deal of trouble. When finally he came to himself, he was in a long, bright, clean room, and the sunset was throwing splashes of light on the ceiling over his head.

He watched them idly for a time; then turned on his pillow. At once he perceived a long, double row of clean white-painted iron beds, on which lay or sat figures of men. Other figures, of women, glided here and there noiselessly. They wore long, spreading dove-gray clothes, with a starched white kerchief drawn over the shoulders and across the breast. Their heads were quaintly white-garbed in stiff wing-like coifs, fitting close about the oval of the face. Then Thorpe sighed comfortably, and closed his eyes and blessed the chance that he had bought a hospital ticket of the agent who had visited camp the month before. For these were Sisters, and the young man lay in the Hospital of St. Mary.

Time was when the lumber-jack who had the misfortune to fall sick or to meet with an accident was in a sorry plight indeed. If he possessed a " stake," he would receive some sort of unskilled attention in one of the numerous and fearful lumberman's boarding-houses—just so long as his money lasted, not one instant more. Then he was bundled brutally into the street, no matter what his condition might be. Penniless, without friends, sick, he drifted naturally to the county poorhouse. There he was patched up quickly and sent out half-cured. The authorities were not so much to blame. With the slender appropriations at their disposal, they found difficulty in taking care of those who came legitimately under their jurisdiction. It was hardly to be expected that they would welcome with open arms a vast army of crippled and diseased men temporarily from the woods. The poor lumber-jack was often left broken in mind and body from causes which a little intelligent care would have rendered unimportant.

With the establishment of the first St. Mary's hospital, I think at Bay City, all this was changed. Now, in it and a half dozen others conducted on the same principles, the woodsman receives the best of medicines, nursing, and medical attendance. From one of the numerous agents who periodically visit the camps, he purchases for eight dollars a ticket which admits him at any time during the year to the hospital, where he is privileged to remain free of further charge until convalescent. So valuable are these institutions, and so excellently are they maintained by the Sisters, that a hospital agent is always welcome, even in those camps from which ordinary peddlers and insurance men are rigidly excluded. Like a great many other charities built on a common-sense self-supporting rational basis, the woods hospitals are under the Roman Catholic Church.

In one of these hospitals Thorpe lay for six weeks suffering from a severe concussion of the brain. At the end of the fourth, his fever had broken, but he was pronounced as yet too weak to be moved.

His nurse was a red-cheeked, blue-eyed, homely little Irish girl, brimming with motherly good-humor. When Thorpe found strength to talk, the two became friends. Through her influence he was moved to a bed about ten feet from the window. Thence his privileges were three roofs and a glimpse of the distant river.

The roofs were covered with snow. One day Thorpe saw it sink into itself and gradually run away. The *tinkle tinkle tank tank* of drops sounded from his own eaves. Down the far-off river, sluggish reaches of ice drifted. Then in a night the blue disappeared from the stream. It became a menacing gray, and even from his distance Thorpe could catch the swirl of its rising waters. A day or two later dark masses drifted or shot across the field of his vision, and twice he thought he distinguished men standing upright and bold on single logs as they rushed down the current.

"What is the date?" he asked of the Sister.

"The elevent' of March."

"Isn't it early for the thaw?"

"Listen to 'im!" exclaimed the Sister delightedly. "Early is it! Sure th' freshet co't thim all. Look, darlint, ye kin see th' drive from here."

"I see," said Thorpe wearily, "when can I get out?"

"Not for wan week," replied the Sister decidedly.

At the end of the week Thorpe said good-by to his attendant, who appeared as sorry to see him go as though the same partings did not come to her a dozen times a year; he took two days of tramping the little town to regain the use of his legs, and boarded the morning train for Beeson Lake. He did not pause in the village, but bent his steps to the river trail.

CHAPTER THIRTEEN

THORPE found the woods very different from when he had first traversed them. They were full of patches of wet earth and of sunshine; of dark pine, looking suddenly worn, and of fresh green shoots of needles, looking deliciously spring-like. This was the contrast everywhere—stern, earnest, purposeful winter, and gay, laughing, careless spring. It was impossible not to draw in fresh spirits with every step.

He followed the trail by the river. Butterballs and scoters paddled up at his approach. Bits of rotten ice occasionally swirled down the diminishing stream. The sunshine was clear and bright, but silvery rather than golden, as though a little of the winter's snow—a last ethereal incarnation—had lingered in its substance. Around every bend Thorpe looked for some of Radway's crew "driving" the logs down the current. He knew from chance encounters with several of the men in Bay City that Radway was still in camp; which meant, of course, that the last of the season's operations were not yet finished. Five miles farther Thorpe began to wonder whether this last conclusion might not be erroneous. The Cass Branch had shrunken almost to its original limits. Only here and there a little *bayou* or marsh attested recent freshets. The drive must have been finished, even this early, for the stream in its present condition would hardly float saw logs, certainly not in quantity.

Thorpe, puzzled, walked on. At the banking ground he found empty skids. Evidently the drive was over. And yet even to Thorpe's ignorance, it seemed incredible that the remaining million and a half of logs had been hauled, banked and driven during the short time he had lain in the Bay City hospital. More to solve the problem than in any hope of work, he set out up the logging road.

Another three miles brought him to camp. It looked strangely wet and sodden and deserted. In fact, Thorpe found a bare half dozen people in it— Radway, the cook, and four men who were helping to pack up the movables, and who later would drive out the wagons containing them. The jobber showed strong traces of the strain he had undergone, but greeted Thorpe almost jovially. He seemed able to show more of his real nature now that the necessity of authority had been definitely removed.

"Hullo, young man," he shouted at Thorpe's mud-splashed figure, "come back to view the remains? All well again, heigh? That's good!"

He strode down to grip the young fellow heartily

by the hand. It was impossible not to be charmed by the sincere cordiality of his manner.

" I didn't know you were through," explained Thorpe, " I came to see if I could get a job."

" Well now I *am* sorry ! " cried Radway, " you can turn in and help though, if you want to."

Thorpe greeted the cook and old Jackson Hines, the only two whom he knew, and set to work to tie up bundles of blankets, and to collect axes, peavies, and tools of all descriptions. This was evidently the last wagon-trip, for little remained to be done.

" I ought by rights to take the lumber of the roofs and floors," observed Radway thoughtfully, " but I guess she don't matter."

Thorpe had never seen him in better spirits. He ascribed the older man's hilarity to relief over the completion of a difficult task. That evening the seven dined together at one end of the long table. The big room exhaled already the atmosphere of desertion.

" Not much like old times, is she? " laughed Radway. " Can't you just shut your eyes and hear Baptiste say, ' Mak' heem de soup one tam more for me ' ? She's pretty empty now."

Jackson Hines looked whimsically down the bare board. " More room than God made for geese in Ireland," was his comment.

After supper they even sat outside for a little time to smoke their pipes, chair-tilted against the logs of the cabins, but soon the chill of melting snow drove them indoors. The four teamsters played seven-up in the cook camp by the light of a barn lantern, while Thorpe and the cook wrote letters. Thorpe's was to his sister.

"I have been in the hospital for about a month," he wrote. "Nothing serious—a crack on the head, which is all right now. But I cannot get home this summer, nor, I am afraid, can we arrange about the school this year. I am about seventy dollars ahead of where I was last fall, so you see it is slow business. This summer I am going into a mill, but the wages for green labor are not very high there either," and so on.

When Miss Helen Thorpe, aged seventeen, received this document she stamped her foot almost angrily. "You'd think he was a day-laborer!" she cried. "Why doesn't he try for a clerkship or something in the city where he'd have a chance to use his brains!"

The thought of her big, strong, tanned brother chained to a desk rose to her, and she smiled a little sadly.

"I know," she went on to herself, "he'd rather be a common laborer in the woods than railroad manager in the office. He loves his out-of-doors."

"Helen!" called a voice from below, "if you're through up there, I wish you'd come down and help me carry this rug out."

The girl's eyes cleared with a snap.

"So do I!" she cried defiantly, "so do I love out-of-doors! I like the woods and the fields and the trees just as much as he does, only differently; but *I* don't get out!"

And thus she came to feeling rebelliously that her brother had been a little selfish in his choice of an occupation, that he sacrificed her inclinations to his own. She did not guess—how could she?—his dreams for her. She did not see the future through his thoughts, but through his words. A negative hopelessness settled down on her, which soon her strong spirit, worthy counterpart of her brother's, changed to more positive rebellion. Thorpe had aroused antagonism where he craved only love. The knowledge of that fact would have surprised and hurt him, for he was entirely without suspicion of it. He lived subjectively to so great a degree that his thoughts and aims took on a certain tangible objectivity—they became so real to him that he quite overlooked the necessity of communication to make them as real to others. He assumed unquestioningly that the other must know. So entirely had he thrown himself into his ambition of making a suitable position for Helen, so continually had he dwelt on it in his thoughts, so earnestly had he striven for it in every step of the great game he was beginning to play, that it never occurred to him he should also concede a definite outward manifestation of his feeling in order to assure its acceptance. Thorpe believed that he had sacrificed every thought and effort to his sister. Helen was becoming convinced that he had considered only himself.

After finishing the letter which gave occasion to this train of thought, Thorpe lit his pipe and strolled out into the darkness. Opposite the little office he stopped amazed.

Through the narrow window he could see Radway seated in front of the stove. Every attitude of the man denoted the most profound dejection. He had sunk down into his chair until he rested on almost the small of his back, his legs were struck straight out in front of him, his chin rested on his breast, and his two arms hung listless at his side, a pipe half falling from the fingers of one hand. All the facetious lines had turned to pathos. In his face sorrowed the anxious, questing, wistful look of the St. Bernard that does not understand.

" What's the matter with the boss, anyway? " asked Thorpe in a low voice of Jackson Hines, when the seven-up game was finished.

" H'aint ye heard? " inquired the old man in surprise.

" Why, no. What? "

" Busted," said the old man sententiously.

" How? What do you mean? "

" What I say. He's busted. That freshet caught him too quick. They's more'n a million and a half logs left in the woods that can't be got out this year, and as his contract calls for a finished job, he don't get nothin' for what he's done."

"That's a queer rig," commented Thorpe. "He's done a lot of valuable work here—the timber's cut and skidded, anyway; and he's delivered a good deal of it to the main drive. The M. & D. outfit get all the advantage of that."

"They do, my son. When old Daly's hand gets near anything, it cramps. I don't know how the old man come to make such a contrac', but he did. Result is, he's out his expenses and time."

To understand exactly the catastrophe that had occurred, it is necessary to follow briefly an outline of the process after the logs have been piled on the banks. There they remain until the break-up attendant on spring shall flood the stream to a freshet. The rollways are then broken, and the saw logs floated down the river to the mill where they are to be cut into lumber.

If for any reason this transportation by water is delayed until the flood goes down, the logs are stranded or left in pools. Consequently every logger puts into the two or three weeks of freshet water a feverish activity which shall carry his product through before the ebb.

The exceptionally early break-up of this spring, combined with the fact that, owing to the series of incidents and accidents already sketched, the actual cutting and skidding had fallen so far behind, caught Radway unawares. He saw his rollways breaking out while his teams were still hauling in the woods. In order to deliver to the mouth of the Cass Branch the three million already banked, he was forced to drop everything else and attend strictly to the drive. This left still, as has been stated, a million and a half on skidways, which Radway knew he would be unable to get out that year.

In spite of the jobber's certainty that his claim was thus annulled, and that he might as well abandon the enterprise entirely for all he would ever get out of it, he finished the " drive " conscientiously and saved to the Company the logs already banked. Then he had interviewed Daly. The latter refused to pay him one cent. Nothing remained but to break camp and grin as best he might over the loss of his winter's work and expenses.

The next day Radway and Thorpe walked the ten miles of the river trail together, while the teamsters and the cook drove down the five teams. Under the influence of the solitude and a certain sympathy which Thorpe manifested, Radway talked—a very little.

" I got behind; that's all there is to it," he said. " I s'pose I ought to have driven the men a little; but still, I don't know. It gets pretty cold on the plains. I guess I bit off more than I could chew."

His eye followed listlessly a frenzied squirrel swinging from the tops of poplars.

" I wouldn't 'a done it for myself," he went on. " I don't like the confounded responsibility. They's too much worry connected with it all. I had a good snug little stake—mighty nigh six thousand. She's all gone now. That'd have been enough for me—I ain't a drinkin' man. But then there was the woman and the kid. This ain't no country for woman-folks, and I wanted t' take little Lida out o' here. I had lots of experience in the woods, and I've seen men make big money time and again, who didn't know as much about it as I do. But they got there, somehow. Says I, I'll make a stake this year—I'd 'a had twelve thousand in th' bank, if things'd have gone right—and then we'll jest move down around Detroit an' I'll put Lida in school."

Thorpe noticed a break in the man's voice, and glancing suddenly toward him was astounded to catch his eyes brimming with tears. Radway perceived the surprise.

" You know when I left Christmas?" he asked.

" Yes."

" I was gone two weeks, and them two weeks done me. We was going slow enough before, God knows, but even with the rank weather and all, I think we'd have won out, if we could have held the same gait."

Radway paused. Thorpe was silent.

"The boys thought it was a mighty poor rig, my leaving that way."

He paused again in evident expectation of a reply. Again Thorpe was silent.

"Didn't they?" Radway insisted.

"Yes, they did," answered Thorpe.

The older man sighed. "I thought so," he went on. "Well, I didn't go to spend Christmas. I went because Jimmy brought me a telegram that Lida was sick with diphtheria. I sat up nights with her for 'leven days."

"No bad after-effects, I hope?" inquired Thorpe.

"She died," said Radway simply.

The two men tramped stolidly on. This was too great an affair for Thorpe to approach except on the knees of his spirit. After a long interval, during which the waters had time to still, the young man changed the subject.

"Aren't you going to get anything out of M. & D.?" he asked.

"No. Didn't earn nothing. I left a lot of their saw logs hung up in the woods, where they'll deteriorate from rot and worms. This is their last season in this district."

"Got anything left?"

"Not a cent."

"What are you going to do?"

"Do!" cried the old woodsman, the fire springing to his eye. "Do! I'm going into the woods, by

God! I'm going to work with my hands, and be happy! I'm going to do other men's work for them and take other men's pay. Let them do the figuring and worrying. I'll boss their gangs and make their roads and see to their logging for 'em, but it's got to be *theirs*. Do! I'm going to be a free man by the G. jumping Moses!"

CHAPTER FOURTEEN

THORPE dedicated a musing instant to the incongruity of rejoicing over a freedom gained by ceasing to be master and becoming servant.

"Radway," said he suddenly, "I need money and I need it bad. I think you ought to get something out of this job of the M. & D.—not much, but something. Will you give me a share of what I can collect from them?"

"Sure!" agreed the jobber readily, with a laugh. "Sure! But you won't get anything. I'll give you ten per cent. quick."

"Good enough!" cried Thorpe.

"But don't be too sure you'll earn day wages doing it," warned the other. "I saw Daly when I was down here last week."

"My time's not valuable," replied Thorpe. "Now when we get to town I want your power of attorney and a few figures, after which I will not bother you again."

The next day the young man called for the second time at the little red-painted office under the shadow of the mill, and for the second time stood before the bulky power of the junior member of the firm.

"Well, young man, what can I do for you?" asked the latter.

"I have been informed," said Thorpe without preliminary, "that you intend to pay John Radway nothing for the work done on the Cass Branch this winter. Is that true?"

Daly studied his antagonist meditatively. "If it is true, what is it to you?" he asked at length.

"I am acting in Mr. Radway's interest."

"You are one of Radway's men?"

"Yes."

"In what capacity have you been working for him?"

"Cant-hook man," replied Thorpe briefly.

"I see," said Daly slowly. Then suddenly, with an intensity of energy that startled Thorpe, he cried: "Now you get out of here! Right off! Quick!"

The younger man recognized the compelling and autocratic boss addressing a member of the crew.

"I shall do nothing of the kind!" he replied with a flash of fire.

The mill-owner leaped to his feet every inch a leader of men. Thorpe did not wish to bring about an actual scene of violence. He had attained his object, which was to fluster the other out of his judicial calm.

"I have Radway's power of attorney," he added.

Daly sat down, controlled himself with an effort, and growled out, "Why didn't you say so?"

"Now I would like to know your position," went on Thorpe. "I am not here to make trouble, but as an associate of Mr. Radway, I have a right to understand the case. Of course I have his side of the story——," he suggested, as though convinced that a detailing of the other side might change his views.

Daly considered carefully, fixing his flint-blue eyes unswervingly on Thorpe's face. Evidently his scrutiny advised him that the young man was a force to be reckoned with.

"It's like this," said he abruptly, "we contracted last fall with this man Radway to put in five million feet of our timber, delivered to the main drive at the mouth of the Cass Branch. In this he was to act independently except as to the matter of provisions. Those he drew from our van, and was debited with the amount of the same. Is that clear?"

"Perfectly," replied Thorpe.

"In return we were to pay him, merchantable scale, four dollars a thousand. If, however, he failed to put in the whole job, the contract was void."

"That's how I understand it," commented Thorpe. "Well?"

"Well, he didn't get in the five million. There's a million and a half hung up in the woods."

"But you have in your hands three million and a

half, which under the present arrangement you get free of any charge whatever."

"And we ought to get it," cried Daly. "Great guns! Here we intend to saw this summer and quit. We want to get in every stick of timber we own so as to be able to clear out of here for good and all at the close of the season; and now this condigned jobber ties us up for a million and a half."

"It is exceedingly annoying," conceded Thorpe, "and it is a good deal of Radway's fault, I am willing to admit, but it's your fault too."

"To be sure," replied Daly with the accent of sarcasm.

"You had no business entering into any such contract. It gave him no show."

"I suppose that was mainly his lookout, wasn't it? and as I already told you, we had to protect ourselves."

"You should have demanded security for the completion of the work. Under your present agreement, if Radway got in the timber, you were to pay him a fair price. If he didn't, you appropriated everything he had already done. In other words, you made him a bet."

"I don't care what you call it," answered Daly, who had recovered his good-humor in contemplation of the security of his position. "The fact stands all right."

"It does," replied Thorpe unexpectedly, "and

128

I'm glad of it. Now let's examine a few figures. You owned five million feet of timber, which at the price of stumpage " (standing trees) " was worth ten thousand dollars."

" Well."

" You come out at the end of the season with three million and a half of saw logs, which with the four dollars' worth of logging added, are worth twenty-one thousand dollars."

" Hold on! " cried Daly, " we paid Radway four dollars; we could have done it ourselves for less."

" You could not have done it for one cent less than four-twenty in that country," replied Thorpe, " as any expert will testify."

" Why did we give it to Radway at four, then? "

" You saved the expense of a salaried overseer, and yourselves some bother," replied Thorpe. " Radway could do it for less, because, for some strange reason which you yourself do not understand, a jobber can always log for less than a company."

" We could have done it for four," insisted Daly stubbornly, " but get on. What are you driving at? My time's valuable."

" Well, put her at four, then," agreed Thorpe. " That makes your saw logs worth over twenty thousand dollars. Of this value Radway added thirteen thousand. You have appropriated that much of his without paying him one cent."

Daly seemed amused. "How about the million and a half feet of ours *he* appropriated?" he asked quietly.

"I'm coming to that. Now for your losses. At the stumpage rate your million and a half which Radway 'appropriated' would be only three thousand. But for the sake of argument, we'll take the actual sum you'd have received for saw logs. Even then the million and a half would only have been worth between eight and nine thousand. Deducting this purely theoretical loss, Radway has occasioned you, from the amount he has gained for you, you are still some four or five thousand ahead of the game. For that you paid him nothing."

"That's Radway's lookout."

"In justice you should pay him that amount. He is a poor man. He has sunk all he owned in this venture, some twelve thousand dollars, and he has nothing to live on. Even if you pay him five thousand, he has lost considerable, while you have gained."

"How have we gained by this bit of philanthropy?"

"Because you originally paid in cash for all that timber on the stump just ten thousand dollars and you get from Radway saw logs to the value of twenty," replied Thorpe sharply. "Besides you still own the million and a half which, if you do not

care to put them in yourself, you can sell for something on the skids."

"Don't you know, young man, that white pine
logs on skids will spoil utterly in a summer?
Worms get into 'em."

"I do," replied Thorpe, "unless you bark them;
which process will cost you about one dollar a thousand. You can find any amount of small purchasers
at reduced price. You can sell them easily at three
dollars. That nets you for your million and a half
a little over four thousand dollars more. Under the
circumstances, I do not think that my request for
five thousand is at all exorbitant."

Daly laughed. "You are a shrewd figurer, and
your remarks are interesting," said he.

"Will you give five thousand dollars?" asked
Thorpe.

"I will not," replied Daly, then with a sudden
change of humor, "and now I'll do a little talking.
I've listened to you just as long as I'm going to. I
have Radway's contract in that safe and I live up to
it. I'll thank you to go plumb to hell!"

"That's your last word, is it?" asked Thorpe,
rising.

"It is."

"Then," said he slowly and distinctly, "I'll tell
you what *I'll* do. I intend to collect in full the four
dollars a thousand for the three million and a half
Mr. Radway has delivered to vou. In return Mr.

Radway will purchase of you at the stumpage rates of two dollars a thousand the million and a half he failed to put in. That makes a bill against you, if my figuring is correct, of just eleven thousand dollars. You will pay that bill, and I will tell you why: your contract will be classed in any court as a gambling contract for lack of consideration. You have no legal standing in the world. I call your bluff, Mr. Daly, and I'll fight you from the drop of the hat through every court in Christendom."

"Fight ahead," advised Daly sweetly, who knew perfectly well that Thorpe's law was faulty. As a matter of fact the young man could have collected on other grounds, but neither was aware of that.

"Furthermore," pursued Thorpe in addition, "I'll repeat my offer before witnesses; and if I win the first suit, I'll sue you for the money we could have made by purchasing the extra million and a half before it had a chance to spoil."

This statement had its effect, for it forced an immediate settlement before the pine on the skids should deteriorate. Daly lounged back with a little more deadly carelessness.

"And, lastly," concluded Thorpe, playing his trump card, "the suit from start to finish will be published in every important paper in this country. If you do not believe I have the influence to do this, you are at liberty to doubt the fact."

Daly was cogitating many things. He knew that

publicity was the last thing to be desired. Thorpe's
statement had been made in view of the fact that
much of the business of a lumber firm is done on
credit. He thought that perhaps a rumor of a big
suit going against the firm might weaken confidence.
As a matter of fact, this consideration had no weight
whatever with the older man, although the threat
of publicity actually gained for Thorpe what he demanded. The lumberman feared the noise of an
investigation solely and simply because his firm, like
so many others, was engaged at the time in stealing
government timber in the upper peninsula. He did
not call it stealing; but that was what it amounted
to. Thorpe's shot in the air hit full.

"I think we can arrange a basis of settlement,"
he said finally. "Be here to-morrow morning at ten
with Radway."

"Very well," said Thorpe.

"By the way," remarked Daly, "I don't believe
I know your name?"

"Thorpe," was the reply.

"Well, Mr. Thorpe," said the lumberman with
cold anger, "if at any time there is anything within
my power or influence that you want—I'll see that
you don't get it."

CHAPTER FIFTEEN

THE whole affair was finally compromised for nine thousand dollars. Radway, grateful beyond expression, insisted on Thorpe's acceptance of an even thousand of it. With this money in hand, the latter felt justified in taking a vacation for the purpose of visiting his sister, so in two days after the signing of the check he walked up the straight garden path that led to Renwick's home.

It was a little painted frame house, back from the street, fronted by a precise bit of lawn, with a willow bush at one corner. A white picket fence effectually separated it from a broad, shaded, not unpleasing street. An osage hedge and a board fence respectively bounded the side and back.

Under the low porch Thorpe rang the bell at a door flanked by two long, narrow strips of imitation stained glass. He entered then a little dark hall from which the stairs rose almost directly at the door, containing with difficulty a hat-rack and a table on which rested a card tray with cards. In the course of greeting an elderly woman, he stepped into the parlor. This was a small square apartment carpeted in dark Brussels, and stuffily glorified in the bourgeois manner by a white marble mantel-

134

piece, several pieces of mahogany furniture upholstered in haircloth, a table on which reposed a
number of gift books in celluloid and other fancy
bindings, an old-fashioned piano with a doily and a
bit of china statuary, a cabinet or so containing such
things as ore specimens, dried seaweed and coins, and
a spindle-legged table or two upholding glass cases
garnished with stuffed birds and wax flowers. The
ceiling was so low that the heavy window hangings
depended almost from the angle of it and the walls.

Thorpe, by some strange freak of psychology, suddenly recalled a wild, windy day in the forest. He
had stood on the top of a height. He saw again the
sharp puffs of snow, exactly like the smoke from
bursting shells, where a fierce swoop of the storm
struck the laden tops of pines; the dense swirl, again
exactly like smoke but now of a great fire, that
marked the lakes. The picture superimposed itself
silently over this stuffy bourgeois respectability, like
the shadow of a dream. He heard plainly enough
the commonplace drawl of the woman before him
offering him the platitudes of her kind.

" You *are* lookin' real well, Mr. Thorpe," she was
saying, " an' I just know Helen will be glad to see
you. She had a hull afternoon out to-day and won't
be back to tea. Dew set and tell me about what
you've been a-doin' and how you're a-gettin' along."

" No, thank you, Mrs. Renwick," he replied, " I'll
come back later. How is Helen? "

"She's purty well; and sech a nice girl. I think she's getting right handsome."

"Can you tell me where she went?"

But Mrs. Renwick did not know. So Thorpe wandered about the maple-shaded streets of the little town.

For the purposes he had in view five hundred dollars would be none too much. The remaining five hundred he had resolved to invest in his sister's comfort and happiness. He had thought the matter over and come to his decision in that secretive, careful fashion so typical of him, working over every logical step of his induction so thoroughly that it ended by becoming part of his mental fibre. So when he reached the conclusion it had already become to him an axiom. In presenting it as such to his sister, he never realized that she had not followed with him the logical steps, and so could hardly be expected to accept the conclusion out-of-hand.

Thorpe wished to give his sister the best education possible in the circumstances. She was now nearly eighteen years old. He knew likewise that he would probably experience a great deal of difficulty in finding another family which would afford the young girl quite the same equality coupled with so few disadvantages. Admitted that its level of intellect and taste was not high, Mrs. Renwick was on the whole a good influence. Helen had not in the least the position of servant, but of a daughter. She helped around the house; and in return she was fed, lodged and clothed for nothing.

So though the money might have enabled Helen to live independently in a modest way for a year or so, Thorpe preferred that she remain where she was. His game was too much a game of chance. He might find himself at the end of the year without further means. Above all things he wished to assure Helen's material safety until such time as he should be quite certain of himself.

In pursuance of this idea he had gradually evolved what seemed to him an excellent plan. He had already perfected it by correspondence with Mrs. Renwick. It was, briefly, this: he, Thorpe, would at once hire a servant girl, who would make anything but supervision unnecessary in so small a household. The remainder of the money he had already paid for a year's tuition in the Seminary of the town. Thus Helen gained her leisure and an opportunity for study; and still retained her home in case of reverse.

Thorpe found his sister already a young lady. After the first delight of meeting had passed, they sat side by side on the haircloth sofa and took stock of each other.

Helen had developed from the school child to the woman. She was a handsome girl, possessed of a slender, well-rounded form, deep hazel eyes with the level gaze of her brother, a clean-cut patrician face, and a thoroughbred neatness of carriage that advertised her good blood. Altogether a figure rather aloof, a face rather impassive; but with the possibility of passion and emotion, and a will to back them.

"Oh, but you're tanned and—and *big*!" she cried, kissing her brother. "You've had such a strange winter, haven't you?"

"Yes," he replied absently.

Another man would have struck her young imagination with the wild, free thrill of the wilderness. Thus he would have gained her sympathy and understanding. Thorpe was too much in earnest.

"Things came a little better than I thought they were going to, toward the last," said he, "and I made a little money."

"Oh, I'm so glad!" she cried. "Was it much?"

"No, not much," he answered. The actual figures would have been so much better! "I've made arrangements with Mrs. Renwick to hire a servant girl, so you will have all your time free; and I have paid a year's tuition for you in the Seminary."

"Oh!" said the girl, and fell silent.

After a time, "Thank you very much, Harry dear." Then after another interval, "I think I'll go get ready for supper."

Instead of getting ready for supper, she paced excitedly up and down her room.

"Oh, why *didn't* he say what he was about?" she cried to herself. "Why didn't he! Why didn't he!"

Next morning she opened the subject again.

"Harry, dear," said she, "I have a little scheme, and I want to see if it is not feasible. How much will the girl and the Seminary cost?"

"About four hundred dollars."

"Well now, see, dear. With four hundred dollars I can live for a year very nicely by boarding with some girls I know who live in a sort of a club; and I could learn much more by going to the High School and continuing with some other classes I am interested in now. Why see, Harry!" she cried, all interest. "We have Professor Carghill come twice a week to teach us English, and Professor Johns, who teaches us history, and we hope to get one or two more this winter. If I go to the Seminary, I'll have to miss all that. And Harry, really I don't *want* to go to the Seminary. I don't think I should like it. I *know* I shouldn't."

"But why not live here, Helen?" he asked.

"Because I'm *tired* of it!" she cried; "sick to the soul of the stuffiness, and the glass cases, and the— the *goodness* of it!"

Thorpe remembered his vision of the wild, wind-tossed pines, and sighed. He wanted very, very much to act in accordance with his sister's desires, although he winced under the sharp hurt pang of the sensitive man whose intended kindness is not appreciated. The impossibility of complying, however, reacted to shut his real ideas and emotions the more inscrutably within him.

"I'm afraid you would not find the girls' boarding-club scheme a good one, Helen," said he. "You'd find it would work better in theory than in practice."

"But it has worked with the other girls!" she cried.

"I think you would be better off here."

Helen bravely choked back her disappointment.

"I might live here, but let the Seminary drop, anyway. That would save a good deal," she begged. "I'd get quite as much good out of my work outside, and then we'd have all that money besides."

"I don't know; I'll see," replied Thorpe. "The mental discipline of class-room work might be a good thing."

He had already thought of this modification himself, but with his characteristic caution, threw cold water on the scheme until he could ascertain definitely whether or not it was practicable. He had already paid the tuition for the year, and was in doubt as to its repayment. As a matter of fact, the negotiation took about two weeks.

During that time Helen Thorpe went through her disappointment and emerged on the other side. Her nature was at once strong and adaptable. One by one she grappled with the different aspects of the case, and turned them the other way. By a *tour de force* she actually persuaded herself that her own plan was not really attractive to her. But what heart-breaks and tears this cost her, only those who in their youth have encountered such absolute negations of cherished ideas can guess.

Then Thorpe told her.

" I've fixed it, Helen," said he. " You can attend the High School and the classes, if you please. I have put the two hundred and fifty dollars out at interest for you."

" Oh, Harry! " she cried reproachfully. " Why didn't you tell me before! "

He did not understand; but the pleasure of it had all faded. She no longer felt enthusiasm, nor gratitude, nor anything except a dull feeling that she had been unnecessarily discouraged. And on his side, Thorpe was vaguely wounded.

The days, however, passed in the main pleasurably for them both. They were fond of one another. The barrier slowly rising between them was not yet cemented by lack of affection on either side, but rather by lack of belief in the other's affection. Helen imagined Thorpe's interest in her becoming daily more perfunctory. Thorpe fancied his sister cold, unreasoning, and ungrateful. As yet this was but the vague dust of a cloud. They could not forget that, but for each other, they were alone in the world. Thorpe delayed his departure from day to day, making all the preparations he possibly could at home.

Finally Helen came on him busily unpacking a box which a dray had left at the door. He unwound and laid one side a Winchester rifle, a variety of fishing tackle, and some other miscellanies of the woodsman. Helen was struck by the beauty of the sporting implements.

"Oh, Harry!" she cried, "aren't they fine! What are you going to do with them?"

"Going camping," replied Thorpe, his head in the excelsior.

"When?"

"This summer."

Helen's eyes lit up with a fire of delight. "How nice! May I go with you?" she cried.

Thorpe shook his head.

"I'm afraid not, little girl. It's going to be a hard trip a long ways from anywhere. You couldn't stand it."

"I'm sure I could. Try me."

"No," replied Thorpe. "I know you couldn't. We'll be sleeping on the ground and going on foot through much extremely difficult country."

"I wish you'd take me somewhere," pursued Helen. "I can't get away this summer unless you do. Why don't you camp somewhere nearer home, so I can go?"

Thorpe arose and kissed her tenderly. He was extremely sorry that he could not spend the summer with his sister, but he believed likewise that their future depended to a great extent on this very trip. But he did not say so.

" I can't, little girl; that's all. We've got our way to make."

She understood that he considered the trip too expensive for them both. At this moment a paper fluttered from the excelsior. She picked it up. A glance showed her a total of figures that made her gasp.

" Here is your bill," she said with a strange choke in her voice, and left the room.

" He can spend sixty dollars on his old guns; but he can't afford to let me leave this hateful house," she complained to the apple tree. " He can go 'way off camping somewhere to have a good time, but he leaves me sweltering in this miserable little town all summer. I don't care if he *is* supporting me. He ought to. He's my brother. Oh, I wish I were a man; I wish I were dead! "

Three days later Thorpe left for the north. He was reluctant to go. When the time came, he attempted to kiss Helen good-by. She caught sight of the rifle in its new leather and canvas case, and on a sudden impulse which she could not explain to herself, she turned away her face and ran into the house. Thorpe, vaguely hurt, a little resentful, as the genuinely misunderstood are apt to be, hesitated a moment, then trudged down the street. Helen too paused at the door, choking back her grief.

"Harry! Harry!" she cried wildly; but it was too late.

Both felt themselves to be in the right. Each realized this fact in the other. Each recognized the impossibility of imposing his own point of view over the other's.

PART II
THE LANDLOOKER

CHAPTER SIXTEEN

IN every direction the woods. Not an opening of any kind offered the mind a breathing place under the free sky. Sometimes the pine groves—vast, solemn, grand, with the patrician aloofness of the truly great; sometimes the hardwood—bright, mysterious, full of life; sometimes the swamps—dark, dank, speaking with the voices of the shyer creatures; sometimes the spruce and balsam thickets—aromatic, enticing. But never the clear, open sky.

And always the woods creatures, in startling abundance and tameness. The solitary man with the pack-straps across his forehead and shoulders had never seen so many of them. They withdrew silently before him as he advanced. They accompanied him on either side, watching him with intelligent, bright eyes. They followed him stealthily for a little distance, as though escorting him out of their own particular territory. Dozens of times a day the traveller glimpsed the flaunting white flags of deer. Often the creatures would take but a few hasty jumps, and then would wheel, the beautiful embodiments of the picture deer, to snort and paw the leaves. Hundreds of birds, of which he did not

147

know the name, stooped to his inspection, whirred away at his approach, or went about their business with hardy indifference under his very eyes. Blasé porcupines trundled superbly from his path. Once a mother-partridge simulated a broken wing, fluttering painfully. Early one morning the traveller ran plump on a fat lolling bear, taking his ease from the new sun, and his meal from a panic-stricken army of ants. As beseemed two innocent wayfarers they honored each other with a salute of surprise, and went their way. And all about and through, weaving, watching, moving like spirits, were the forest multitudes which the young man never saw, but which he divined, and of whose movements he sometimes caught for a single instant the faintest patter or rustle. It constituted the mystery of the forest, that great fascinating, lovable mystery which, once it steals into the heart of a man, has always a hearing and a longing when it makes its voice heard.

The young man's equipment was simple in the extreme. Attached to a heavy leather belt of cartridges hung a two-pound axe and a sheath knife. In his pocket reposed a compass, an air - tight tin of matches, and a map drawn on oiled paper of a district divided into sections. Some few of the sections were colored, which indicated that they belonged to private parties. All the rest was State or Government land. He carried in his hand a repeating rifle. The pack, if opened, would have been found to contain a woolen and a rubber blanket, fishing tackle, twenty pounds or so of flour, a package of tea, sugar, a slab of bacon carefully wrapped in oiled cloth, salt, a suit of underwear, and several extra pairs of thick stockings. To the outside of the pack had been strapped a frying pan, a tin pail, and a cup.

For more than a week Thorpe had journeyed through the forest without meeting a human being, or seeing any indications of man, excepting always the old blaze of the government survey. Many years before, officials had run careless lines through the country along the section-boundaries. At this time the blazes were so weather-beaten that Thorpe often found difficulty in deciphering the indications marked on them. These latter stated always the section, the township, and the range east or west by number. All Thorpe had to do was to find the same figures on his map. He knew just where he was. By means of his compass he could lay his course to any point that suited his convenience.

The map he had procured at the United States Land Office in Detroit. He had set out with the scanty equipment just described for the purpose of " looking " a suitable bunch of pine in the northern peninsula, which, at that time, was practically untouched. Access to its interior could be obtained only on foot or by river. The South Shore Railroad was already engaged in pushing a way through the virgin forest, but it had as yet penetrated only as far

as Seney; and after all, had been projected more
with the idea of establishing a direct route to Duluth
and the copper districts than to aid the lumber industry. Marquette, Menominee, and a few smaller
places along the coast were lumbering near at home;
but they shipped entirely by water. Although the
rest of the peninsula also was finely wooded, a general impression obtained among the craft that it
would prove too inaccessible for successful operation.

Furthermore, at that period, a great deal of talk
was believed as to the inexhaustibility of Michigan
pine. Men in a position to know what they were
talking about stated dogmatically that the forests of
the southern peninsula would be adequate for a great
many years to come. Furthermore, the magnificent
timber of the Saginaw, Muskegon, and Grand River
valleys in the southern peninsula occupied entire attention. No one cared to bother about property at
so great a distance from home. As a consequence,
few as yet knew even the extent of the resources so
far north.

Thorpe, however, with the far-sightedness of the
born pioneer, had perceived that the exploitation of
the upper country was an affair of a few years only.
The forests of southern Michigan were vast, but not
limitless; and they had all passed into private own-
ership. The north, on the other hand, would not
prove as inaccessible as it now seemed, for the carry-

ing trade would some day realize that the entire waterway of the Great Lakes offered an unrivalled outlet. With that elementary discovery would begin a rush to the new country. Tiring of a profitless employment farther south he resolved to anticipate it, and by acquiring his holdings before general attention should be turned that way, to obtain of the best.

He was without money, and practically without friends; while Government and State lands cost respectively two dollars and a half and a dollar and a quarter an acre, cash down. But he relied on the good sense of capitalists to perceive, from the statistics which his explorations would furnish, the wonderful advantage of logging a new country with the chain of Great Lakes as shipping outlet at its very door. In return for his information, he would expect a half interest in the enterprise. This is the usual method of procedure adopted by landlookers everywhere.

We have said that the country was quite new to logging, but the statement is not strictly accurate. Thorpe was by no means the first to see the money in northern pine. Outside the big mill districts already named, cuttings of considerable size were already under way, the logs from which were usually sold to the mills of Marquette or Menominee. Here and there along the best streams, men had already begun operations.

151

But they worked on a small scale and with an eye to the immediate present only; bending their efforts to as large a cut as possible each season rather than to the acquisition of holdings for future operations. This they accomplished naïvely by purchasing one forty and cutting a dozen. Thorpe's map showed often near the forks of an important stream a section whose coloring indicated private possession. Legally the owners had the right only to the pine included in the marked sections; but if any one had taken the trouble to visit the district, he would have found operations going on for miles up and down stream. The colored squares would prove to be nothing but so many excuses for being on the ground. The bulk of the pine of any season's cut he would discover had been stolen from unbought State or Government land.

This in the old days was a common enough trick. One man, at present a wealthy and respected citizen, cut for six years, and owned just one forty-acres! Another logged nearly fifty million feet from an eighty! In the State to-day live prominent business men, looked upon as models in every way, good fellows, good citizens, with sons and daughters proud of their social position, who, nevertheless, made the bulk of their fortunes by stealing Government pine.

"What you want to-day, old man?" inquired a wholesale lumber dealer of an individual whose name now stands for domestic and civic virtue.

" I'll have five or six million saw logs to sell you in the spring, and I want to know what you'll give for them."

" Go on!" expostulated the dealer with a laugh, " ain't you got that forty all cut yet?"

" She holds out pretty well," replied the other with a grin.

An official, called the Inspector, is supposed to report such stealings, after which another official is to prosecute. Aside from the fact that the danger of discovery is practically zero in so wild and distant a country, it is fairly well established that the old-time logger found these two individuals susceptible to the gentle art of " sugaring." The officials, as well as the lumberman, became rich. If worst came to worst, and investigation seemed imminent, the operator could still purchase the land at legal rates, and so escape trouble. But the intention to appropriate was there, and, to confess the truth, the whitewashing by purchase needed but rarely to be employed. I have time and again heard landlookers assert that the old Land Offices were rarely " on the square," but as to that I cannot, of course, venture an opinion.

Thorpe was perfectly conversant with this state of affairs. He knew, also, that in all probability many of the colored districts on his map represented firms engaged in steals of greater or less magnitude. He was further aware that most of the concerns stole the timber because it was cheaper to steal than to buy; but that they would buy readily enough if forced to do so in order to prevent its acquisition by another. This other might be himself. In his exploration, therefore, he decided to employ the utmost circumspection. As much as possible he purposed to avoid other men; but if meetings became inevitable, he hoped to mask his real intentions. He would pose as a hunter and fisherman.

During the course of his week in the woods, he discovered that he would be forced eventually to resort to this expedient. He encountered quantities of fine timber in the country through which he travelled, and some day it would be logged, but at present the difficulties were too great. The streams were shallow, or they did not empty into a good shipping port. Investors would naturally look first for holdings along the more practicable routes.

A cursory glance sufficed to show that on such waters the little red squares had already blocked a foothold for other owners. Thorpe surmised that he would undoubtedly discover fine unbought timber along their banks, but that the men already engaged in stealing it would hardly be likely to allow him peaceful acquisition.

For a week, then, he journeyed through magnificent timber without finding what he sought, working always more and more to the north, until finally he stood on the shores of Superior. Up to now the streams had not suited him. He resolved to follow the shore west to the mouth of a fairly large river called the Ossawinamakee.* It showed, in common with most streams of its size, land already taken, but Thorpe hoped to find good timber nearer the mouth. After several days' hard walking with this object in view, he found himself directly north of a bend in the river; so, without troubling to hunt for its outlet into Superior, he turned through the woods due south, with the intention of striking in on the stream. This he succeeded in accomplishing some twenty miles inland, where also he discovered a well-defined and recently used trail leading up the river. Thorpe camped one night at the bend, and then set out to follow the trail.

It led him for upward of ten miles nearly due south, sometimes approaching, sometimes leaving the river, but keeping always in its direction. The country in general was rolling. Low parallel ridges of gentle declivity glided constantly across his way, their valleys sloping to the river. Thorpe had never seen a grander forest of pine than that which clothed them.

For almost three miles, after the young man had passed through a preliminary jungle of birch, cedar, spruce, and hemlock, it ran without a break, clear, clean, of cloud-sweeping altitude, without underbrush. Most of it was good bull-sap, which is

* Accent the last syllable.

known by the fineness of the bark, though often in the hollows it shaded gradually into the rough-skinned cork pine. In those days few people paid any attention to the Norway, and hemlock was not even thought of. With every foot of the way Thorpe became more and more impressed.

At first the grandeur, the remoteness, the solemnity of the virgin forest fell on his spirit with a kind of awe. The tall, straight trunks lifted directly upward to the vaulted screen through which the sky seemed as remote as the ceiling of a Roman church. Ravens wheeled and croaked in the blue, but infinitely far away. Some lesser noises wove into the stillness without breaking the web of its splendor, for the pine silence laid soft, hushing fingers on the lips of those who might waken the sleeping sunlight.

Then the spirit of the pioneer stirred within his soul. The wilderness sent forth its old-time challenge to the hardy. In him awoke that instinct which, without itself perceiving the end on which it is bent, clears the way for the civilization that has been ripening in old-world hot-houses during a thousand years. Men must eat; and so the soil must be made productive. We regret, each after his manner, the passing of the Indian, the buffalo, the great pine forests, for they are of the picturesque; but we live gladly on the product of the farms that have taken their places. Southern Michigan was once a pine forest: now the twisted stump-fences about the most fertile farms of the north alone break the expanse of prairie and of trim " wood-lots."

Thorpe knew little of this, and cared less. These feathered trees, standing close-ranked and yet each isolate in the dignity and gravity of a sphinx of stone, set to dancing his blood of the frontiersman. He spread out his map to make sure that so valuable a clump of timber remained still unclaimed. A few sections lying near the headwaters were all he found marked as sold. He resumed his tramp light-heartedly.

At the ten-mile point he came upon a dam. It was a crude dam—built of logs—whose face consisted of strong buttresses slanted up-stream, and whose sheer was made of unbarked timbers laid smoothly side by side at the required angle. At present its gate was open. Thorpe could see that it was an unusually large gate, with a powerful apparatus for the raising and the lowering of it.

The purpose of the dam in this new country did not puzzle him in the least, but its presence bewildered him. Such constructions are often thrown across logging streams at proper intervals in order that the operator may be independent of the spring freshets. When he wishes to " drive " his logs to the mouth of the stream, he first accumulates a head of water behind his dams, and then, by lifting the gates, creates an artificial freshet sufficient to float his timber to the pool formed by the next dam below. The device is common enough; but it is expensive. People do not build dams except in the certainty of some years of logging, and quite extensive logging at that. If the stream happens to be navigable, the promoter must first get an Improvement Charter from a board of control appointed by the State. So Thorpe knew that he had to deal, not with a hand-to-mouth-timber-thief, but with a great company preparing to log the country on a big scale.

He continued his journey. At noon he came to another and similar structure. The pine forest had yielded to knolls of hardwood separated by swampholes of blackthorn. Here he left his pack and pushed ahead in light marching order. About eight miles above the first dam, and eighteen from the bend of the river, he ran into a " slashing " of the year before. The decapitated stumps were already beginning to turn brown with weather, the tangle of tops and limbs was partially concealed by poplar growths and wild raspberry vines. Parenthetically, it may be remarked that the promptitude with which these growths succeed the cutting of the pine is an inexplicable marvel. Clear forty acres at random in the very centre of a pine forest, without a tract of poplar within an hundred miles; the next season will bring up the fresh shoots. Some claim that blue-jays bring the seeds in their crops. Others incline to the theory that the creative elements lie dormant in the soil, needing only the sun to start them to life. Final speculation is impossible, but the fact stands.

To Thorpe this particular clearing became at once of the greatest interest. He scrambled over and through the ugly *débris* which for a year or two after logging operations cumbers the ground. By a rather prolonged search he found what he sought— the "section corners" of the tract, on which the government surveyor had long ago marked the "descriptions." A glance at the map confirmed his suspicions. The slashing lay some two miles north of the sections designated as belonging to private parties. It was Government land.

Thorpe sat down, lit a pipe, and did a little thinking.

As an axiom it may be premised that the shorter the distance logs have to be transported, the less it costs to get them in. Now Thorpe had that very morning passed through beautiful timber lying much nearer the mouth of the river than either this, or the sections farther south. Why had these men deliberately ascended the stream? Why had they stolen timber eighteen miles from the bend, when they could equally well have stolen just as good fourteen miles nearer the terminus of their drive?

Thorpe ruminated for some time without hitting upon a solution. Then suddenly he remembered the two dams, and his idea that the men in charge of the river must be wealthy and must intend operating on a large scale. He thought he glimpsed it. After another pipe, he felt sure.

The Unknowns were indeed going in on a large scale. They intended eventually to log the whole of the Ossawinamakee basin. For this reason they had made their first purchase, planted their first foothold, near the headwaters. Furthermore, located as they were far from a present or an immediately future civilization, they had felt safe in leaving for the moment their holdings represented by the three sections already described. Some day they would buy all the standing Government pine in the basin; but in the meantime they would steal all they could at a sufficient distance from the lake to minimize the danger of discovery. They had not dared to appropriate the three-mile tract Thorpe had passed through, because in that locality the theft would probably be remarked, so they intended eventually to buy it. Until that should become necessary, however, every stick cut meant so much less to purchase.

"They're going to cut, and keep on cutting, working down river as fast as they can," argued Thorpe. "If anything happens so they *have* to, they'll buy in the pine that is left; but if things go well with them, they'll take what they can for nothing. They're getting this stuff out up-river first, because they can steal safer while the country is still unsettled; and

even when it does fill up, there will not be much
likelihood of an investigation so far in-country—at
least until after they have folded their tents"

It seems to us who are accustomed to the accurate
policing of our twentieth century, almost incredible
that such wholesale robberies should have gone on
with so little danger of detection. Certainly detection was a matter of sufficient simplicity. Some one
happens along, like Thorpe, carrying a Government
map in his pocket. He runs across a parcel of unclaimed land already cut over. It would seem easy
to lodge a complaint, institute a prosecution against
the men known to have put in the timber. *But it is
almost never done.*

Thorpe knew that men occupied in so precarious
a business would be keenly on the watch. At the
first hint of rivalry, they would buy in the timber
they had selected. But the situation had set his
fighting blood to racing. The very fact that these
men were thieves on so big a scale made him the
more obstinately determined to thwart them. They
undoubtedly wanted the tract down river. Well,
so did he!

He purposed to look it over carefully, to ascertain
its exact boundaries and what sections it would be
necessary to buy in order to include it, and perhaps
even to estimate it in a rough way. In the accomplishment of this he would have to spend the summer, and perhaps part of the fall, in that district.

He could hardly expect to escape notice. By the indications on the river, he judged that a crew of men had shortly before taken out a drive of logs. After the timber had been rafted and towed to Marquette, they would return. He might be able to hide in the forest, but sooner or later, he was sure, one of the company's landlookers or hunters would stumble on his camp. Then his very concealment would tell them what he was after. The risk was too great. For above all things Thorpe needed time. He had, as has been said, to ascertain what he could offer. Then he had to offer it. He would be forced to interest capital, and that is a matter of persuasior and leisure.

Finally his shrewd, intuitive good-sense flashed the solution on him. He returned rapidly to his pack, assumed the straps, and arrived at the first dam about dark of the long summer day.

There he looked carefully about him. Some fifty feet from the water's edge a birch knoll supported, besides the birches, a single big hemlock. With his belt axe, Thorpe cleared away the little white trees. He stuck the sharpened end of one of them in the bark of the shaggy hemlock, fastened the other end in a crotch eight or ten feet distant, slanted the rest of the saplings along one side of this ridge pole, and turned in, after a hasty supper, leaving the completion of his permanent camp to the morrow.

CHAPTER SEVENTEEN

IN the morning he thatched smooth the roof of
the shelter, using for the purpose the thick
branches of hemlocks; placed two green spruce logs
side by side as cooking range; slung his pot on a
rod across two forked sticks; cut and split a quantity of wood; spread his blankets; and called himself established. His beard was already well grown,
and his clothes had become worn by the brush and
faded by the sun and rain. In the course of the
morning he lay in wait very patiently near a spot
overflowed by the river, where, the day before, he
had noticed lily-pads growing. After a time a doe
and a spotted fawn came and stood ankle-deep in
the water, and ate of the lily-pads. Thorpe lurked
motionless behind his screen of leaves; and as he
had taken the precaution so to station himself that
his hiding-place lay down-wind, the beautiful animals were unaware of his presence.

By and by a prong-buck joined them. He was a
two-year-old, young, tender, with the velvet just off
his antlers. Thorpe aimed at his shoulder, six inches
above the belly-line, and pressed the trigger. As
though by enchantment the three woods creatures

disappeared. But the hunter had noticed that, whereas the doe and fawn flourished bravely the broad white flags of their tails, the buck had seemed but a streak of brown. By this he knew he had hit.

Sure enough, after two hundred yards of following the prints of sharp hoofs and occasional gobbets of blood on the leaves, he came upon his prey dead. It became necessary to transport the animal to camp. Thorpe stuck his hunting knife deep into the front of the deer's chest, where the neck joins, which allowed most of the blood to drain away. Then he fastened wild grape vines about the antlers, and, with a little exertion drew the body after him as though it had been a toboggan.

It slid more easily than one would imagine, along the grain; but not as easily as by some other methods with which Thorpe was unfamiliar.

At camp he skinned the deer, cut most of the meat into thin strips which he salted and placed in the sun to dry, and hung the remainder in a cool arbor of boughs. The hide he suspended over a pole.

All these things he did hastily, as though he might be in a hurry; as indeed he was.

At noon he cooked himself a venison steak and some tea. Then with his hatchet he cut several small pine poles, which he fashioned roughly in a number of shapes and put aside for the future. The brains of the deer, saved for the purpose, he boiled with

water in his tin pail, wishing it were larger. With
the liquor thus obtained he intended later to remove
the hair and grain from the deer hide. Toward
evening he caught a dozen trout in the pool below
the dam. These he ate for supper.

Next day he spread the buck's hide out on the
ground and drenched it liberally with the product of
deer-brains. Later the hide was soaked in the river,
after which, by means of a rough two-handled
spatula, Thorpe was enabled after much labor to
scrape away entirely the hair and grain. He cut
from the edge of the hide a number of long strips of
raw-hide, but anointed the body of the skin liberally
with the brain liquor.

"Glad I don't have to do that every day!" he
commented, wiping his brow with the back of his
wrist.

As the skin dried he worked and kneaded it to
softness. The result was a fair quality of white
buckskin, the first Thorpe had ever made. If
wetted, it would harden dry and stiff. Thorough
smoking in the fumes of punk maple would obviate
this, but that detail Thorpe left until later.

"I don't know whether it's all necessary," he said
to himself doubtfully, "but if you're going to assume a disguise, let it be a good one."

In the meantime, he had bound together with his
rawhide thongs several of the oddly shaped pine
timbers to form a species of dead-fall trap. It was

slow work, for Thorpe's knowledge of such things was theoretical. He had learned his theory well, however, and in the end arrived.

All this time he had made no effort to look over the pine, nor did he intend to begin until he could be sure of doing so in safety. His object now was to give his knoll the appearances of a trapper's camp.

Toward the end of the week he received his first visit. Evening was drawing on, and Thorpe was busily engaged in cooking a panful of trout, resting the frying pan across the two green spruce logs between which glowed the coals. Suddenly he became aware of a presence at his side. How it had reached the spot he could not imagine, for he had heard no approach. He looked up quickly.

"How do," greeted the newcomer gravely.

The man was an Indian, silent, solemn, with the straight, unwinking gaze of his race.

"How do," replied Thorpe.

The Indian without further ceremony threw his pack to the ground, and, squatting on his heels, watched the white man's preparations. When the meal was cooked, he coolly produced a knife, selected a clean bit of hemlock bark, and helped himself. Then he lit a pipe, and gazed keenly about him. The buckskin interested him.

"No good," said he, feeling of its texture.

Thorpe laughed. "Not very," he confessed.

"Good," continued the Indian, touching lightly his own moccasins.

"What you do?" he inquired after a long silence, punctuated by the puffs of tobacco.

"Hunt; trap; fish," replied Thorpe with equal sententiousness.

"Good," concluded the Indian, after a ruminative pause.

That night he slept on the ground. Next day he made a better shelter than Thorpe's in less than half the time; and was off hunting before the sun was an hour high. He was armed with an old-fashioned smooth-bore muzzle-loader; and Thorpe was astonished, after he had become better acquainted with his new companion's methods, to find that he hunted deer with fine bird shot. The Indian never expected to kill or even mortally wound his game; but he would follow for miles the blood drops caused by his little wounds, until the animals in sheer exhaustion allowed him to approach close enough for a dispatching blow. At two o'clock he returned with a small buck, tied scientifically together for toting, with the waste parts cut away, but every ounce of utility retained.

"I show," said the Indian:—and he did. Thorpe learned the Indian tan; of what use are the hollow shank bones; how the spinal cord is the toughest, softest, and most pliable sewing-thread known.

The Indian appeared to intend making the birch-knoll his permanent headquarters. Thorpe was at first a little suspicious of his new companion, but the man appeared scrupulously honest, was never intrusive, and even seemed genuinely desirous of teaching the white little tricks of the woods brought to their perfection by the Indian alone. He ended by liking him. The two rarely spoke. They merely sat near each other, and smoked. One evening the Indian suddenly remarked:

"You look 'um tree."

"What's that?" cried Thorpe, startled.

"You no hunter, no trapper. You look 'um tree, for make 'um lumber."

The white had not begun as yet his explorations. He did not dare until the return of the logging crew or the passing of some one in authority at the up-river camp, for he wished first to establish in their minds the innocence of his intentions.

"What makes you think that, Charley?" he asked.

"You good man in woods," replied Injin Charley sententiously, "I tell by way you look at him pine."

Thorpe ruminated.

"Charley," said he, "why are you staying here with me?"

"Big frien'," replied the Indian promptly.

"Why are you my friend? What have I ever done for you?"

"You gottum chief's eye," replied his companion with simplicity.

Thorpe looked at the Indian again. There seemed to be only one course.

"Yes, I'm a lumberman," he confessed, "and I'm looking for pine. But, Charley, the men up the river must not know what I'm after."

"They gettum pine," interjected the Indian like a flash.

"Exactly," replied Thorpe, surprised afresh at the other's perspicacity.

"Good!" ejaculated Injin Charley, and fell silent.

With this, the longest conversation the two had attempted in their peculiar acquaintance, Thorpe was forced to be content. He was, however, ill at ease over the incident. It added an element of uncertainty to an already precarious position.

Three days later he was intensely thankful the conversation had taken place.

After the noon meal he lay on his blanket under the hemlock shelter, smoking and lazily watching Injin Charley busy at the side of the trail. The Indian had terminated a long two days' search by toting from the forest a number of strips of the outer bark of white birch, in its green state pliable as cotton, thick as leather, and light as air. These he had cut into arbitrary patterns known only to himself, and was now sewing as a long shapeless sort of bag or sac to a slender beech-wood oval. Later it was to become a birch-bark canoe, and the beech-wood oval would be the gun-wale.

So idly intent was Thorpe on this piece of construction that he did not notice the approach of two men from the down-stream side. They were short, alert men, plodding along with the knee-bent persistency of the woods-walker, dressed in broad hats, flannel shirts, coarse trousers tucked in high laced " cruisers "; and carrying each a bulging meal sack looped by a cord across the shoulders and chest. Both were armed with long slender scaler's rules. The first intimation Thorpe received of the presence of these two men was the sound of their voices addressing Injin Charley.

" Hullo Charley," said one of them, " what you doing here? Ain't seen you since th' Sturgeon district."

" Mak' 'um canoe," replied Charley rather obviously.

" So I see. But what you expect to get in this God-forsaken country? "

" Beaver, muskrat, mink, otter."

" Trapping, eh? " The man gazed keenly at Thorpe's recumbent figure. " Who's the other fellow? "

Thorpe held his breath; then exhaled it in a long sigh of relief.

"Him white man," Injin Charley was replying, "him hunt too. He mak' 'um buckskin."

The landlooker arose lazily and sauntered toward the group. It was part of his plan to be well recognized so that in the future he might arouse no suspicions.

"Howdy," he drawled, "got any smokin'?"

"How are you," replied one of the scalers, eying him sharply, and tendering his pouch. Thorpe filled his pipe deliberately, and returned it with a heavy-lidded glance of thanks. To all appearances he was one of the lazy, shiftless white hunters of the backwoods. Seized with an inspiration, he said, "What sort of chances is they at your camp for a little flour? Me and Charley's about out. I'll bring you meat; or I'll make you boys moccasins. I got some good buckskin."

It was the usual proposition.

"Pretty good, I guess. Come up and see," advised the scaler. "The crew's right behind us."

"I'll send up Charley," drawled Thorpe, "I'm busy now makin' traps," he waved his pipe, calling attention to the pine and rawhide dead-falls.

They chatted a few moments, practically and with an eye to the strict utility of things about them, as became woodsmen. Then two wagons creaked lurching by, followed by fifteen or twenty men. The last of these, evidently the foreman, was joined by the two scalers.

"What's that outfit?" he inquired with the sharpness of suspicion.

"Old Injin Charley—you remember, the old boy that tanned that buck for you down on Cedar Creek."

"Yes, but the other fellow."

"Oh, a hunter," replied the scaler carelessly.

"Sure?"

The man laughed. "Couldn't be nothin' else," he asserted with confidence. "Regular old backwoods mossback."

At the same time Injin Charley was setting about the splitting of a cedar log.

"You see," he remarked, "I big frien'."

CHAPTER EIGHTEEN

IN the days that followed, Thorpe cruised about the great woods. It was slow business, but fascinating. He knew that when he should embark on his attempt to enlist considerable capital in an "unsight unseen" investment, he would have to be well supplied with statistics. True, he was not much of a timber estimator, nor did he know the methods usually employed, but his experience, observation, and reading had developed a latent sixth sense by which he could appreciate quality, difficulties of logging, and such kindred practical matters.

First of all he walked over the country at large, to find where the best timber lay. This was a matter of tramping; though often on an elevation he succeeded in climbing a tall tree whence he caught bird's-eye views of the country at large. He always carried his gun with him, and was prepared at a moment's notice to seem engaged in hunting—either for game or for spots in which later to set his traps. The expedient was, however, unnecessary.

Next he ascertained the geographical location of the different clumps and forests, entering the sections, the quarter-sections, even the separate forties in his note-book; taking in only the " descriptions " containing the best pine.

Finally he wrote accurate notes concerning the topography of each and every pine district—the lay of the land; the hills, ravines, swamps, and valleys; the distance from the river; the character of the soil. In short, he accumulated all the information he could by which the cost of logging might be estimated.

The work went much quicker than he had anticipated, mainly because he could give his entire attention to it. Injin Charley attended to the commissary, with a delight in the process that removed it from the category of work. When it rained, an infrequent occurrence, the two hung Thorpe's rubber blankets before the opening of the driest shelter, and waited philosophically for the weather to clear. Injin Charley had finished the first canoe, and was now leisurely at work on another. Thorpe had filled his note-book with the class of statistics just described. He decided now to attempt an estimate of the timber.

For this he had really too little experience. He knew it, but determined to do his best. The weak point of his whole scheme lay in that it was going to be impossible for him to allow the prospective purchaser a chance of examining the pine. That difficulty Thorpe hoped to overcome by inspiring personal confidence in himself. If he failed to do so, he might return with a landlooker whom the investor trusted, and the two could re-enact the comedy of this summer. Thorpe hoped, however, to avoid the necessity. It would be too dangerous. He set about a rough estimate of the timber.

Injin Charley intended evidently to work up a trade in buckskin during the coming winter. Although the skins were in poor condition at this time of the year, he tanned three more, and smoked them. In the day-time he looked the country over as carefully as did Thorpe. But he ignored the pines, and paid attention only to the hardwood and the beds of little creeks. Injin Charley was in reality a trapper, and he intended to get many fine skins in this promising district. He worked on his tanning and his canoe-making late in the afternoon.

One evening just at sunset Thorpe was helping the Indian shape his craft. The loose sac of birch-bark sewed to the long beech oval was slung between two tripods. Injin Charley had fashioned a number of thin, flexible cedar strips of certain arbitrary lengths and widths. Beginning with the smallest of these, Thorpe and his companion were catching one end under the beech oval, bending the strip bow-shape inside the sac, and catching again the other side of the oval. Thus the spring of the bent cedar, pressing against the inside of the birch-bark sac, distended it tightly. The cut of the sac and the length of the cedar strips gave to the canoe its graceful shape.

The two men bent there at their task, the dull glow of evening falling upon them. Behind them the knoll stood out in picturesque relief against the darker pine—the little shelters, the fire-places of green spruce, the blankets, the guns, a deer's carcass suspended by the feet from a cross pole, the drying buckskin on either side. The river rushed by with a never-ending roar and turmoil. Through its shouting one perceived, as through a mist, the still lofty peace of evening.

A young fellow, hardly more than a boy, exclaimed with keen delight of the picturesque as his canoe shot around the bend into sight of it.

The canoe was large and powerful, but well filled. An Indian knelt in the stern; amidships was well laden with duffle of all descriptions; then the young fellow sat in the bow. He was a bright-faced, eager-eyed, curly-haired young fellow, all enthusiasm and fire. His figure was trim and clean, but rather slender; and his movements were quick but nervous. When he stepped carefully out on the flat rock to which his guide brought the canoe with a swirl of the paddle, one initiated would have seen that his clothes, while strong and serviceable, had been bought from a sporting catalogue. There was a trimness, a neatness, about them.

"This is a good place," he said to the guide,

" we'll camp here." Then he turned up the steep bank without looking back.

" Hullo! " he called in a cheerful, unembarrassed fashion to Thorpe and Charley. " How are you? Care if I camp here? What you making? By Jove! I never saw a canoe made before. I'm going to watch you. Keep right at it."

He sat on one of the outcropping boulders and took off his hat.

" Say! you've got a great place here! You here all summer? Hullo! you've got a deer hanging up. Are there many of 'em around here? I'd like to kill a deer first rate. I never have. It's sort of out of season now, isn't it? "

" We only kill the bucks," replied Thorpe.

" I like fishing, too," went on the boy; " are there any here? In the pool? John," he called to his guide, " bring me my fishing tackle."

In a few moments he was whipping the pool with long, graceful drops of the fly. He proved to be adept. Thorpe and Injin Charley stopped work to watch him. At first the Indian's stolid countenance seemed a trifle doubtful. After a time it cleared.

" Good! " he grunted.

" You do that well," Thorpe remarked. " Is it difficult? "

" It takes practice," replied the boy. " See that riffle? " He whipped the fly lightly within six inches of a little suction hole; a fish at once rose and struck.

The others had been little fellows and easily handled. At the end of fifteen minutes the new-comer landed a fine two-pounder.

"That must be fun," commented Thorpe. "I never happened to get in with fly-fishing. I'd like to try it sometime."

"Try it now!" urged the boy, enchanted that he could teach a woodsman anything.

"No," Thorpe declined, "not to-night, to-morrow perhaps."

The other Indian had by now finished the erection of a tent, and had begun to cook supper over a little sheet-iron camp stove. Thorpe and Charley could smell ham.

"You've got quite a pantry," remarked Thorpe.

"Won't you eat with me?" proffered the boy hospitably.

But Thorpe declined. He could, however, see canned goods, hard tack, and condensed milk.

In the course of the evening the boy approached the older man's camp, and, with a charming dif-fidence, asked permission to sit a while at their fire.

He was full of delight over everything that savored of the woods, or woodscraft. The most trivial and everyday affairs of the life interested him. His eager questions, so frankly proffered, aroused even the taciturn Charley to eloquence. The construction of the shelter, the cut of a deer's hide, the simple process of " jerking " venison—all these awakened his enthusiasm.

" It must be good to live in the woods," he said with a sigh, " to do all things for yourself. It's so free! "

The men's moccasins interested him. He asked a dozen questions about them—how they were cut, whether they did not hurt the feet, how long they would wear. He seemed surprised to learn that they are excellent in cold weather.

" I thought *any* leather would wet through in the snow! " he cried. " I wish I could get a pair somewhere! " he exclaimed. " You don't know where I could buy any, do you? " he asked of Thorpe.

" I don't know," answered he, " perhaps Charley here will make you a pair."

" *Will* you, Charley? " cried the boy.

" I mak' him," replied the Indian stolidly.

The many-voiced night of the woods descended close about the little camp fire, and its soft breezes wafted stray sparks here and there like errant stars. The newcomer, with shining eyes, breathed deep in satisfaction. He was keenly alive to the romance, the grandeur, the mystery, the beauty of the littlest things, seeming to derive a deep and solid contentment from the mere contemplation of the woods and its ways and creatures.

" I just *do* love this! " he cried again and again.

"Oh, it's great, after all that fuss down there!" and he cried it so fervently that the other men present smiled; but so genuinely that the smile had in it nothing but kindliness.

"I came out for a month," said he suddenly, "and I guess I'll stay the rest of it right here. You'll let me go with you sometimes hunting, won't you?" he appealed to them with the sudden openheartedness of a child. "I'd like first rate to kill a deer."

"Sure," said Thorpe, "glad to have you."

"My name is Wallace Carpenter," said the boy with a sudden unmistakable air of good-breeding.

"Well," laughed Thorpe, "two old woods loafers like us haven't got much use for names. Charley here is called Geezigut, and mine's nearly as bad; but I guess plain Charley and Harry will do."

"All right, Harry," replied Wallace.

After the young fellow had crawled into the sleeping bag which his guide had spread for him over a fragrant layer of hemlock and balsam, Thorpe and his companion smoked one more pipe. The whippoor-wills called back and forth across the river. Down in the thicket, fine, clear, beautiful, like the silver thread of a dream, came the notes of the white-throat—the nightingale of the North. Injin Charley knocked the last ashes from his pipe.

"Him nice boy!" said he.

180

CHAPTER NINETEEN

THE young fellow stayed three weeks, and was a constant joy to Thorpe. His enthusiasms were so whole-souled; his delight so perpetual; his interest so fresh! The most trivial expedients of woods lore seemed to him wonderful. A dozen times a day he exclaimed in admiration or surprise over some bit of woodcraft practiced by Thorpe or one of the Indians.

"Do you mean to say you have lived here six weeks and only brought in what you could carry on your backs!" he cried.

"Sure," Thorpe replied.

"Harry, you're wonderful! I've got a whole canoe load, and imagined I was travelling light and roughing it. You beat Robinson Crusoe! He had a whole ship to draw from."

"My man Friday helps me out," answered Thorpe, laughingly indicating Injin Charley.

Nearly a week passed before Wallace managed to kill a deer. The animals were plenty enough; but the young man's volatile and eager attention stole his patience. And what few running shots offered, he missed, mainly because of buck fever. Finally, by a lucky chance, he broke a four-year-old's neck,

dropping him in his tracks. The hunter was de-
lighted. He insisted on doing everything for himself—cruel hard work it was too—including the
toting and skinning. Even the tanning he had a
share in. At first he wanted the hide cured, " with
the hair on." Injin Charley explained that the fur
would drop out. It was the wrong season of the
year for pelts.

" Then we'll have buckskin and I'll get a buckskin shirt out of it," suggested Wallace.

Injin Charley agreed. One day Wallace returned
from fishing in the pool to find that the Indian had
cut out the garment, and was already sewing it together.

" Oh! " he cried, a little disappointed, " I wanted
to see it done! "

Injin Charley merely grunted. To make a buckskin shirt requires the hides of three deer. Charley
had supplied the other two, and wished to keep the
young man from finding it out.

Wallace assumed the woods life as a man would
assume an unaccustomed garment. It sat him well,
and he learned fast, but he was always conscious of
it. He liked to wear moccasins, and a deer knife;
he liked to cook his own supper, or pluck the fragrant
hemlock browse for his pillow. Always he seemed
to be trying to realize and to savor fully the charm,
the picturesqueness, the romance of all that he was
doing and seeing. To Thorpe these things were a

part of everyday life; matters of expedient or necessity. He enjoyed them, but subconsciously, as one
enjoys an environment. Wallace trailed the cloak
of his glories in frank admiration of their splendor.

This double point of view brought the men very
close together. Thorpe liked the boy because he was
open-hearted, free from affectation, assumptive of
no superiority—in short, because he was direct and
sincere, although in a manner totally different from
Thorpe's own directness and sincerity. Wallace, on
his part, adored in Thorpe the free, open-air life, the
adventurous quality, the quiet hidden power, the resourcefulness and self-sufficiency of the pioneer.
He was too young as yet to go behind the picturesque
or romantic; so he never thought to inquire of himself what Thorpe did there in the wilderness, or indeed if he did anything at all. He accepted Thorpe
for what he thought him to be, rather than for what
he might think him to be. Thus he reposed un-
bounded confidence in him.

After a while, observing the absolute ingenuous-
ness of the boy, Thorpe used to take him from time
to time on some of his daily trips to the pines.
Necessarily he explained partially his position and
the need of secrecy. Wallace was immensely excited and important at learning a secret of such
moment, and deeply flattered at being entrusted
with it.

Some may think that here, considering the magnitude of the interests involved, Thorpe committed an indiscretion. It may be; but if so, it was practically an inevitable indiscretion. Strong, reticent characters like Thorpe's prove the need from time to time of violating their own natures, of running counter to their ordinary habits of mind and deed. It is a necessary relaxation of the strenuous, a debauch of the soul. Its analogy in the lower plane is to be found in the dissipations of men of genius; or still lower in the orgies of fighters out of training. Sooner or later Thorpe was sure to emerge for a brief space from that iron-bound silence of the spirit, of which he himself was the least aware. It was not so much a hunger for affection, as the desire of a strong man temporarily to get away from his strength. Wallace Carpenter became in his case the exception to prove the rule.

Little by little the eager questionings of the youth extracted a full statement of the situation. He learned of the timber-thieves up the river, of their present operations; and their probable plans; of the valuable pine lying still unclaimed; of Thorpe's stealthy raid into the enemy's country. It looked big to him—epic! These were tremendous forces in motion, here was intrigue, here was direct practical application of the powers he had been playing with.

"Why, it's great! It's better than any book I ever read!"

He wanted to know what he could do to help.

"Nothing except keep quiet," replied Thorpe, already uneasy, not lest the boy should prove unreliable, but lest his very eagerness to seem unconcerned should arouse suspicion. "You mustn't try to act any different. If the men from up-river come by, be just as cordial to them as you can, and don't act mysterious and important."

"All right," agreed Wallace, bubbling with excitement. "And then what do you do—after you get the timber estimated?"

"I'll go South and try, quietly, to raise some money. That will be difficult, because, you see, people don't know me; and I am not in a position to let them look over the timber. Of course it will be merely a question of my judgment. They can go themselves to the Land Office and pay their money. There won't be any chance of my making way with that. The investors will become possessed of certain 'descriptions' lying in this country, all right enough. The rub is, will they have enough confidence in me and my judgment to believe the timber to be what I represent it?"

"I see," commented Wallace, suddenly grave.

That evening Injin Charley went on with his canoe building. He melted together in a pot, resin and pitch. The proportion he determined by experiment, for the mixture had to be neither hard enough to crack nor soft enough to melt in the sun.

Then he daubed the mess over all the seams. Wallace superintended the operation for a time in silence.

"Harry," he said suddenly with a crisp decision new to his voice, "will you take a little walk with me down by the dam. I want to talk with you."

They strolled to the edge of the bank and stood for a moment looking at the swirling waters.

"I want you to tell me all about logging," began Wallace. "Start from the beginning. Suppose, for instance, you had bought this pine here we were talking about—what would be your first move?"

They sat side by side on a log, and Thorpe explained. He told of the building of the camps, the making of the roads; the cutting, swamping, travoying, skidding; the banking and driving. Unconsciously a little of the battle clang crept into his narrative. It became a struggle, a gasping tug and heave for supremacy between the man and the wilderness. The excitement of war was in it. When he had finished, Wallace drew a deep breath.

"When I am home," said he simply, "I live in a big house on the Lake Shore Drive. It is heated by steam and lighted by electricity. I touch a button or turn a screw, and at once I am lighted and warmed. At certain hours meals are served me. I don't know how they are cooked, or where the materials come from. Since leaving college I have spent a little time down town every day; and then I've played golf or tennis or ridden a horse in the park. The only real thing left is the sailing. The wind blows just as hard and the waves mount just as high to-day as they did when Drake sailed. All the rest is tame. We do little imitations of the real thing with blue ribbons tied to them, and think we are camping or roughing it. This life of yours is glorious, is vital, it means something in the march of the world;—and I doubt whether ours does. You are subduing the wilderness, extending the frontier. After you will come the backwoods farmer to pull up the stumps; and after him the big farmer and the cities."

The young fellow spoke with unexpected swiftness and earnestness. Thorpe looked at him in surprise.

"I know what you are thinking," said the boy, flushing. "You are surprised that I can be in earnest about anything. I'm out of school up here. Let me shout and play with the rest of the children."

Thorpe watched him with sympathetic eyes, but with lips that obstinately refused to say one word. A woman would have felt rebuffed. The boy's admiration, however, rested on the foundation of the more manly qualities he had already seen in his friend. Perhaps this very aloofness, this very silent, steady-eyed power appealed to him.

"I left college at nineteen because my father died," said he. "I am now just twenty-one. A large estate descended to me, and I have had to care for its investments all alone. I have one sister—that is all."

" So have I," cried Thorpe, and stopped.

" The estates have not suffered," went on the boy simply. " I have done well with them. But," he cried fiercely, " I *hate* it! It is petty and mean and worrying and nagging! That's why I was so glad to get out in the woods."

He paused.

" Have some tobacco," said Thorpe.

Wallace accepted with a nod.

" Now, Harry, I have a proposal to make to you. It is this; you need thirty thousand dollars to buy your land. Let me supply it, and come in as half partner."

An expression of doubt crossed the landlooker's face.

" Oh *please*! " cried the boy, " I do want to get in something real! It will be the making of me! "

" Now see here," interposed Thorpe suddenly, " you don't even know my name."

" I know *you*," replied the boy.

" My name is Harry Thorpe," pursued the other. " My father was Henry Thorpe, an embezzler."

" Harry," replied Wallace soberly, " I am sorry I made you say that. I do not care for your name—except perhaps to put it in the articles of partnership—and I have no concern with your ancestry. I tell you it is a favor to let me in on this deal. I don't know anything about lumbering, but I've got eyes. I can see that big timber standing up thick and tall, and I know people make profits in the business. It isn't a question of the raw material surely, and you have experience."

"Not so much as you think," interposed Thorpe.

"There remains," went on Wallace without attention to Thorpe's remark, "only the question of——"

"My honesty," interjected Thorpe grimly.

"No!" cried the boy hotly, "of your letting me in on a good thing!"

Thorpe considered a few moments in silence.

"Wallace," he said gravely at last, "I honestly do think that whoever goes into this deal with me will make money. Of course there's always chances against it. But I am going to do my best. I've seen other men fail at it, and the reason they've failed is because they did not demand success of others and of themselves. That's it; success! When a general commanding troops receives a report on something he's ordered done, he does not trouble himself with excuses;—he merely asks whether or not the thing was accomplished. Difficulties don't count. It is a soldier's duty to perform the impossible. Well, that's the way it ought to be with us. A man has no right to come to me and say, 'I failed because such and such things happened.' Either he should succeed in spite of it all; or he should step up and take his medicine without whining. Well, I'm going to succeed!"

The man's accustomed aloofness had gone. His eye flashed, his brow frowned, the muscles of his cheeks contracted under his beard. In the bronze light of evening he looked like a fire-breathing statue to that great ruthless god he had himself invoked—Success.

Wallace gazed at him with fascinated admiration.

"Then you will?" he asked tremulously.

"Wallace," he replied again, "they'll say you have been the victim of an adventurer, but the result will prove them wrong. If I weren't perfectly sure of this, I wouldn't think of it, for I like you, and I know you want to go into this more out of friendship for me and because your imagination is touched, than from any business sense. But I'll accept, gladly. And I'll do my best!"

"Hooray!" cried the boy, throwing his cap up in the air. "We'll do 'em up in the first round!"

At last when Wallace Carpenter reluctantly quitted his friends on the Ossawinamakee, he insisted on leaving with them a variety of the things he had brought.

"I'm through with them," said he. "Next time I come up here we'll have a camp of our own, won't we, Harry? And I do feel that I am awfully in you fellows' debt. You've given me the best time

I have ever had in my life, and you've refused payment for the moccasins and things you've made for me. I'd feel much better if you'd accept them—just as keepsakes."

"All right, Wallace," replied Thorpe, "and much obliged."

"Don't forget to come straight to me when you get through estimating, now, will you? Come to the house and stay. Our compact holds now, honest Injin; doesn't it?" asked the boy anxiously.

"Honest Injin," laughed Thorpe. "Good-by."

The little canoe shot away down the current. The last Injin Charley and Thorpe saw of the boy was as he turned the curve. His hat was off and waving in his hand, his curls were blowing in the breeze, his eyes sparkled with bright good-will, and his lips parted in a cheery halloo of farewell.

"Him nice boy," repeated Injin Charley, turning to his canoe.

CHAPTER TWENTY

THUS Thorpe and the Indian unexpectedly found themselves in the possession of luxury. The outfit had not meant much to Wallace Carpenter, for he had bought it in the city, where such things are abundant and excite no remark; but to the woodsman each article possessed a separate and particular value. The tent, an iron kettle, a side of bacon, oatmeal, tea, matches, sugar, some canned goods, a box of hard-tack—these, in the woods, represented wealth. Wallace's rifle chambered the .38 Winchester cartridge, which was unfortunate, for Thorpe's .44 had barely a magazineful left.

The two men settled again into their customary ways of life. Things went much as before, except that the flies and mosquitoes became thick. To men as hardened as Thorpe and the Indian, these pests were not as formidable as they would have been to any one directly from the city, but they were sufficiently annoying. Thorpe's old tin pail was pressed into service as a smudge-kettle. Every evening about dusk, when the insects first began to emerge from the dark swamps, Charley would build a tiny smoky fire in the bottom of the pail, feeding it with peat, damp moss, punk maple, and other inflammable smoky fuel. This censer swung twice or thrice about the tent, effectually cleared it. Besides, both men early established on their cheeks an invulnerable glaze of a decoction of pine tar, oil, and a pungent herb. Toward the close of July, however, the insects began sensibly to diminish, both in numbers and persistency.

Up to the present Thorpe had enjoyed a clear field. Now two men came down from above and established a temporary camp in the woods half a mile below the dam. Thorpe soon satisfied himself that they were picking out a route for the logging road. Plenty which could be cut and travoyed directly to the banking ground lay exactly along the bank of the stream; but every logger possessed of a tract of timber tries each year to get in some that is easy to handle and some that is difficult. Thus the average of expense is maintained.

The two men, of course, did not bother themselves with the timber to be travoyed, but gave their entire attention to that lying farther back. Thorpe was enabled thus to avoid them entirely. He simply transferred his estimating to the forest by the stream. Once he met one of the men; but was fortunately in a country that lent itself to his pose of hunter. The other he did not see at all.

But one day he heard him. The two up-river men were following carefully but noisily the bed of a little creek. Thorpe happened to be on the side-hill, so he seated himself quietly until they should have moved on down. One of the men shouted to the other, who, crashing through a thicket, did not hear. "Ho-o-o! *Dyer!*" the first repeated. "Here's that infernal comer; over here!"

"Yop," assented the other. "Coming!"

Thorpe recognized the voice instantly as that of Radway's scaler. His hand crisped in a gesture of disgust. The man had always been obnoxious to him.

Two days later he stumbled on their camp. He paused in wonder at what he saw.

The packs lay open, their contents scattered in every direction. The fire had been hastily extinguished with a bucket of water, and a frying pan lay where it had been overturned. If the thing had been possible, Thorpe would have guessed at a hasty and unpremeditated flight.

He was about to withdraw carefully lest he be discovered, when he was startled by a touch on his elbow. It was Injin Charley.

"Dey go up river," he said. "I come see what de row."

The Indian examined rapidly the condition of the little camp.

"Dey look for somethin'," said he, making his hand revolve as though rummaging, and indicating the packs.

"I t'ink dey see you in de woods," he concluded. "Dey go camp gettum boss. Boss he gone on river trail two t'ree hour."

"You're right, Charley," replied Thorpe, who had been drawing his own conclusions. "One of them knows me. They've been looking in their packs for their note-books with the descriptions of these sections in them. Then they piled out for the boss. If I know anything at all, the boss'll make tracks for Detroit."

"W'ot you do?" asked Injin Charley curiously.

"I got to get to Detroit before they do; that's all."

Instantly the Indian became all action.

"You come," he ordered, and set out at a rapid pace for camp.

There, with incredible deftness, he packed together about twelve pounds of the jerked venison and a pair of blankets, thrust Thorpe's waterproof match safe in his pocket, and turned eagerly to the young man.

"You come," he repeated.

Thorpe hastily unearthed his " descriptions " and wrapped them up. The Indian, in silence, rearranged the displaced articles in such a manner as to relieve the camp of its abandoned air.

It was nearly sundown. Without a word the two men struck off into the forest, the Indian in the lead. Their course was southeast, but Thorpe asked no questions. He followed blindly. Soon he found that if he did even that adequately, he would have little attention left for anything else. The Indian walked with long, swift strides, his knees always slightly bent, even at the finish of the step, his back hollowed, his shoulders and head thrust forward. His gait had a queer sag in it, up and down in a long curve from one rise to the other. After a time Thorpe became fascinated in watching before him this easy, untiring lope, hour after hour, without the variation of a second's fraction in speed nor an inch in length. It was as though the Indian were made of steel springs. He never appeared to hurry; but neither did he ever rest.

At first Thorpe followed him with comparative ease, but at the end of three hours he was compelled to put forth decided efforts to keep pace. His walking was no longer mechanical, but conscious. When it becomes so, a man soon tires. Thorpe resented the inequalities, the stones, the roots, the patches of soft ground which lay in his way. He felt dully that they were not fair. He could negotiate the distance; but anything else was a gratuitous insult.

Then suddenly he gained his second wind. He felt better and stronger and moved freer. For second wind is only to a very small degree a question of the breathing power. It is rather the response of the vital forces to a will that refuses to heed their first grumbling protests. Like dogs by the fire they

do their utmost to convince their master that the
limit of freshness is reached; but at last, under the
whip, spring to their work.

At midnight Injin Charley called a halt. He
spread his blanket, leaned on one elbow long enough
to eat a strip of dried meat, and fell asleep. Thorpe
imitated his example. Three hours later the Indian
roused his companion, and the two set out again.

Thorpe had walked a leisurely ten days through
the woods far to the north. In that journey he had
encountered many difficulties. Sometimes he had
been tangled for hours at a time in a dense and
almost impenetrable thicket. Again he had spent
a half day in crossing a treacherous swamp. Or
there had interposed in his trail abattises of down
timber a quarter of a mile wide over which it had
been necessary to pick a precarious way eight or ten
feet from the ground.

This journey was in comparison easy. Most of
the time the travellers walked along high beech
ridges or through the hardwood forests. Occasionally they were forced to pass into the lowlands, but
always little saving spits of highland reaching out
toward each other abridged the necessary wallowing. Twice they swam rivers.

At first Thorpe thought this was because the
country was more open; but as he gave better attention to their route, he learned to ascribe it entirely
to the skill of his companion. The Indian seemed

by a species of instinct to select the most practicable routes. He seemed to know how the land ought to lie, so that he was never deceived by appearances into entering a *cul de sac*. His beech ridges always led to other beech ridges; his hardwood never petered out into the terrible black swamps. Sometimes Thorpe became sensible that they had commenced a long detour; but it was never an abrupt detour, unforeseen and blind.

From three o'clock until eight they walked continually without a pause, without an instant's breathing spell. Then they rested a half hour, ate a little venison, and smoked a pipe.

An hour after noon they repeated the rest. Thorpe rose with a certain physical reluctance. The Indian seemed as fresh—or as tired—as when he started. At sunset they took an hour. Then forward again by the dim intermittent light of the moon and stars through the ghostly haunted forest, until Thorpe thought he would drop with weariness, and was mentally incapable of contemplating more than a hundred steps in advance.

"When I get to that square patch of light, I'll quit," he would say to himself, and struggle painfully the required twenty rods.

"No, I won't quit here," he would continue, "I'll make it that birch. Then I'll lie down and die."

And so on. To the actual physical exhaustion of Thorpe's muscles was added that immense mental weariness which uncertainty of the time and distance inflicts on a man. The journey might last a week, for all he knew. In the presence of an emergency these men of action had actually not exchanged a dozen words. The Indian led; Thorpe followed.

When the halt was called, Thorpe fell into his blanket too weary even to eat. Next morning sharp, shooting pains, like the stabs of swords, ran through his groin.

"You come," repeated the Indian, stolid as ever.

When the sun was an hour high the travellers suddenly ran into a trail, which as suddenly dived into a spruce thicket. On the other side of it Thorpe unexpectedly found himself in an extensive clearing, dotted with the blackened stumps of pines. Athwart the distance he could perceive the wide blue horizon of Lake Michigan. He had crossed the Upper Peninsula on foot!

"Boat come by to-day," said Injin Charley, indicating the tall stacks of a mill. "Him no stop. You mak' him stop take you with him. You get train Mackinaw City to-night. Dose men, dey on dat train."

Thorpe calculated rapidly. The enemy would require, even with their teams, a day to cover the thirty miles to the fishing village of Munising, whence the stage ran each morning to Seney, the present terminal of the South Shore Railroad. He,

Thorpe, on foot and three hours behind, could never have caught the stage. But from Seney only one train a day was despatched to connect at Mackinaw City with the Michigan Central, and on that one train, due to leave this very morning, the up-river man was just about pulling out. He would arrive at Mackinaw City at four o'clock of the afternoon, where he would be forced to wait until eight in the evening. By catching a boat at the mill to which Injin Charley had led him, Thorpe could still make the same train. Thus the start in the race for Detroit's Land Office would be fair.

"All right," he cried, all his energy returning to him. "Here goes! We'll beat him out yet!"

"You come back?" inquired the Indian, peering with a certain anxiety into his companion's eyes.

"Come back!" cried Thorpe. "You bet your hat!"

"I wait," replied the Indian, and was gone.

"Oh, Charley!" shouted Thorpe in surprise. "Come on and get a square meal, anyway."

But the Indian was already on his way back to the distant Ossawinamakee.

Thorpe hesitated in two minds whether to follow and attempt further persuasion, for he felt keenly the interest the other had displayed. Then he saw, over the headland to the east, a dense trail of black smoke. He set off on a stumbling run toward the mill.

CHAPTER TWENTY-ONE

HE arrived out of breath in a typical little mill town consisting of the usual unpainted houses, the saloons, mill, office, and general store. To the latter he addressed himself for information.

The proprietor, still sleepy, was mopping out the place.

" Does that boat stop here? " shouted Thorpe across the suds.

" Sometimes," replied the man somnolently.

" Not always? "

" Only when there's freight for her."

" Doesn't she stop for passengers? "

" Nope."

" How does she know when there's freight? "

" Oh, they signal her from the mill—" but Thorpe was gone.

At the mill Thorpe dove for the engine room. He knew that elsewhere the clang of machinery and the hurry of business would leave scant attention to him. And besides, from the engine room the signals would be given. He found, as is often the case in north-country sawmills, a Scotchman in charge.

" Does the boat stop here this morning? " he inquired.

"Weel," replied the engineer with fearful deliberation, "I canna say. But I hae received na orders to that effect."

"Can't you whistle her in for me?" asked Thorpe.

"I canna," answered the engineer, promptly enough this time.

"Why not?"

"Ye're na what a body might call freight."

"No other way out of it?"

"Na."

Thorpe was seized with an idea.

"Here!" he cried. "See that boulder over there? I want to ship that to Mackinaw City by freight on this boat."

The Scotchman's eyes twinkled appreciatively.

"I'm dootin' ye hae th' freight-bill from the office," he objected simply.

"See here," replied Thorpe, "I've just got to get that boat. It's worth twenty dollars to me, and I'll square it with the captain. There's your twenty."

The Scotchman deliberated, looking aslant at the ground and thoughtfully oiling a cylinder with a greasy rag.

"It'll na be a matter of life and death?" he asked hopefully. "She aye stops for life and death."

"No," replied Thorpe reluctantly. Then with

an explosion, "Yes, by God, it is! If I don't make that boat, I'll kill *you*."

The Scotchman chuckled and pocketed the money. "I'm dootin' that's in order," he replied. " I'll no be party to any such proceedin's. I'm goin' noo for a fresh pail of watter," he remarked, pausing at the door, "but as a wee item of information: yander's th' wheestle rope; and a mon wheestles one short and one long for th' boat."

He disappeared. Thorpe seized the cord and gave the signal. Then he ran hastily to the end of the long lumber docks, and peered with great eagerness in the direction of the black smoke.

The steamer was as yet concealed behind a low spit of land which ran out from the west to form one side of the harbor. In a moment, however, her bows appeared, headed directly down toward the Straits of Mackinaw. When opposite the little bay Thorpe confidently looked to see her turn in, but to his consternation she held her course. He began to doubt whether his signal had been heard. Fresh black smoke poured from the funnel; the craft seemed to gather speed as she approached the eastern point. Thorpe saw his hopes sailing away. He wanted to stand up absurdly and wave his arms to attract attention at that impossible distance. He wanted to sink to the planks in apathy. Finally he sat down, and with dull eyes watched the distance widen between himself and his aims.

And then with a grand free sweep she turned and headed directly for him.

Other men might have wept or shouted. Thorpe merely became himself, imperturbable, commanding, apparently cold. He negotiated briefly with the captain, paid twenty dollars more for speed and the privilege of landing at Mackinaw City. Then he slept for eight hours on end and was awakened in time to drop into a small boat which deposited him on the broad sand beach of the lower peninsula.

CHAPTER TWENTY-TWO

THE train was just leisurely making up for departure. Thorpe, dressed as he was in old "pepper and salt" garments patched with buckskin, his hat a flopping travesty on headgear, his moccasins, worn and dirty, his face bearded and bronzed, tried as much as possible to avoid attention. He sent an instant telegram to Wallace Carpenter conceived as follows:

"Wire thirty thousand my order care Land Office, Detroit, before nine o'clock to-morrow morning. Do it if you have to rustle all night. Important."

Then he took a seat in the baggage car on a pile of boxes and philosophically waited for the train to start. He knew that sooner or later the man, provided he were on the train, would stroll through the car, and he wanted to be out of the way. The baggage man proved friendly, so Thorpe chatted with him until after bedtime. Then he entered the smoking car and waited patiently for morning.

So far the affair had gone very well. It had depended on personal exertions, and he had made it go. Now he was forced to rely on outward circumstances. He argued that the up-river man would have first to make his financial arrangements before he could buy in the land, and this would give the landlooker a chance to get in ahead at the office. There would probably be no difficulty about that. The man suspected nothing. But Thorpe had to confess himself fearfully uneasy about his own financial arrangements. That was the rub. Wallace Carpenter had been sincere enough in his informal striking of partnership, but had he retained his enthusiasm? Had second thought convicted him of folly? Had conservative business friends dissuaded him? Had the glow faded in the reality of his accustomed life? And even if his good-will remained unimpaired, would he be able, at such short notice, to raise so large a sum? Would he realize from Thorpe's telegram the absolute necessity of haste?

At the last thought, Thorpe decided to send a second message from the next station. He did so. It read: " Another buyer of timber on same train with me. Must have money at nine o'clock or lose land." He paid day rates on it to insure immediate delivery. Suppose the boy should be away from home!

Everything depended on Wallace Carpenter; and Thorpe could not but confess the chance slender. One other thought made the night seem long. Thorpe had but thirty dollars left.

Morning came at last, and the train drew in and stopped. Thorpe, being in the smoking car, dropped off first and stationed himself near the exit where he could look over the passengers without being seen. They filed past. Two only he could accord the rôle of master lumbermen — all the rest were plainly drummers or hayseeds. And in these two Thorpe recognized Daly and Morrison themselves. They passed within ten feet of him, talking earnestly together. At the curb they hailed a cab and drove away. Thorpe with satisfaction heard them call the name of a hotel.

It was still two hours before the Land Office would be open. Thorpe ate breakfast at the depot and wandered slowly up Jefferson Avenue to Woodward, a strange piece of our country's medievalism in modern surroundings. He was so occupied with his own thoughts that for some time he remained unconscious of the attention he was attracting. Then, with a start, he felt that every one was staring at him. The hour was early, so that few besides the working classes were abroad, but he passed one lady driving leisurely to an early train whose frank scrutiny brought him to himself. He became conscious that his broad hat was weather-soiled and limp, that his flannel shirt was faded, that his " pepper and salt " trousers were patched, that moccasins must seem as anachronistic as chain mail. It abashed him. He could not know that it was all wild and picturesque, that his straight and muscular figure moved with a grace quite its own and the woods', that the bronze of his skin contrasted splendidly with the clearness of his eye, that his whole bearing expressed the serene power that comes only from the confidence of battle. The woman in the carriage saw it, however.

" He is magnificent! " she cried. " I thought such men had died with Cooper! "

Thorpe whirled sharp on his heel and returned at once to a boarding-house off Fort Street, where he had " outfitted " three months before. There he reclaimed his valise, shaved, clothed himself in linen and cheviot once more, and sauntered slowly over to the Land Office to await its opening.

CHAPTER TWENTY-THREE

A T nine o'clock neither of the partners had appeared. Thorpe entered the office and approached the desk.

"Is there a telegram here for Harry Thorpe?" he inquired.

The clerk to whom he addressed himself merely motioned with his head toward a young fellow behind the railing in a corner. The latter, without awaiting the question, shifted comfortably and replied:

"No."

At the same instant steps were heard in the corridor, the door opened, and Mr. Morrison appeared on the sill. Then Thorpe showed the stuff of which he was made.

"Is this the desk for buying Government lands?" he asked hurriedly.

"Yes," replied the clerk.

"I have some descriptions I wish to buy in."

"Very well," replied the clerk, "what township?"

Thorpe detailed the figures, which he knew by heart, the clerk took from a cabinet the three books containing them, and spread them out on the counter. At this moment the bland voice of Mr. Morrison made itself heard at Thorpe's elbow.

"Good morning, Mr. Smithers," it said with the deliberation of the consciously great man. "I have a few descriptions I would like to buy in the northern peninsula."

"Good morning, Mr. Morrison. Archie there will attend to you. Archie, see what Mr. Morrison wishes."

The lumberman and the other clerk consulted in a low voice, after which the official turned to fumble among the records. Not finding what he wanted, he approached Smithers. A whispered consultation ensued between these two. Then Smithers called:

"Take a seat, Mr. Morrison. This gentleman is looking over these townships, and will have finished in a few minutes."

Morrison's eye suddenly became uneasy.

"I am somewhat busy this morning," he objected with a shade of command in his voice.

"If this gentleman—?" suggested the clerk delicately.

"I am sorry," put in Thorpe with brevity, "my time, too, is valuable."

Morrison looked at him sharply.

"My deal is a big one," he snapped. "I can probably arrange with this gentleman to let him have his farm."

"I claim precedence," replied Thorpe calmly.

"Well," said Morrison swift as light, "I'll tell you, Smithers. I'll leave my list of descriptions and a check with you. Give me a receipt, and mark my lands off after you've finished with this gentleman."

Now Government and State lands are the property of the man who pays for them. Although the clerk's receipt might not give Morrison a valid claim; nevertheless it would afford basis for a lawsuit. Thorpe saw the trap, and interposed.

"Hold on," he interrupted, "I claim precedence. You can give no receipt for any land in these townships until after my business is transacted. I have reason to believe that this gentleman and myself are both after the same descriptions."

"What!" shouted Morrison, assuming surprise.

"You will have to await your turn, Mr. Morrison," said the clerk, virtuous before so many witnesses.

The business man was in a white rage of excitement.

"I insist on my application being filed at once!" he cried waving his check. "I have the money right here to pay for every acre of it; and if I know the law, the first man to pay takes the land."

He slapped the check down on the rail, and hit it a number of times with the flat of his hand. Thorpe turned and faced him with a steel look in his level eyes.

" Mr. Morrison," he said, " you are quite right. The first man who pays gets the land; but I have won the first chance to pay. You will kindly step one side until I finish my business with Mr. Smithers here."

" I suppose you have the amount actually with you," said the clerk, quite respectfully, " because if you have not, Mr. Morrison's claim will take pre-cedence."

" I would hardly have any business in a land office, if I did not know that," replied Thorpe, and began his dictation of the description as calmly as though his inside pocket contained the required amount in bank bills.

Thorpe's hopes had sunk to zero. After all, look-ing at the matter dispassionately, why should he ex-pect Carpenter to trust him, a stranger, with so large a sum? It had been madness. Only the blind con-fidence of the fighting man led him further into the struggle. Another would have given up, would have stepped aside from the path of this bona-fide purchaser with the money in his hand.

But Thorpe was of the kind that hangs on until the last possible second, not so much in the expecta-tion of winning, as in sheer reluctance to yield. Such men shoot their last cartridge before surrender-ing, swim the last ounce of strength from their arms before throwing them up to sink, search coolly until the latest moment for a way from the burning building — and sometimes come face to face with miracles.

Thorpe's descriptions were contained in the battered little note-book he had carried with him in the woods. For each piece of land first there came the township described by latitude and east-and-west range. After this generic description followed another figure representing the section of that particular district. So 49 — 17 W — 8, meant section 8, of the township on range 49 north, 17 west. If Thorpe wished to purchase the whole section, that description would suffice. On the other hand, if he wished to buy only one forty, he described its position in the quarter-section. Thus SW — NW 49 — 17 — 8, meant the southwest forty of the northwest quarter of section 8 in the township already described.

The clerk marked across each square of his map as Thorpe read them, the date and the purchaser's name.

In his note-book Thorpe had, of course, entered the briefest description possible. Now, in dictating to the clerk, he conceived the idea of specifying each subdivision. This gained some time. Instead of saying simply, " Northwest quarter of section 8," he made of it four separate descriptions, as follows:—Northwest quarter of northwest quarter; northeast of northwest quarter; southwest of northwest quarter; and southeast of northwest quarter.

He was not so foolish as to read the descriptions in succession, but so scattered them that the clerk, putting down the figures mechanically, had no idea of the amount of unnecessary work he was doing. The minute hands of the clock dragged around. Thorpe droned down the long column. The clerk scratched industriously, repeating in a half voice each description as it was transcribed.

At length the task was finished. It became necessary to type duplicate lists of the descriptions. While the somnolent youth finished this task, Thorpe listened for the messenger boy on the stairs.

A faint slam was heard outside the rickety old building. Hasty steps sounded along the corridor. The landlooker merely stopped the drumming of his fingers on the broad arm of the chair. The door flew open, and Wallace Carpenter walked quickly to him.

Thorpe's face lighted up as he rose to greet his partner. The boy had not forgotten their compact after all.

" Then it's all right? " queried the latter breathlessly.

" Sure," answered Thorpe heartily, " got 'em in good shape."

At the same time he was drawing the youth beyond the vigilant watchfulness of Mr. Morrison.

" You're just in time," he said in an undertone. " Never had so close a squeak. I suppose you have cash or a certified check: that's all they'll take here."

"What do you mean?" asked Carpenter blankly.

"Haven't you that money?" returned Thorpe quick as a hawk.

"For Heaven's sake, isn't it here?" cried Wallace in consternation. "I wired Duncan, my banker, here last night, and received a reply from him. He answered that he'd see to it. Haven't you seen him?"

"No," repeated Thorpe in his turn.

"What can we do?"

"Can you get your check certified here near at hand?"

"Yes."

"Well, go do it. And get a move on you. You have precisely until that boy there finishes clicking that machine. Not a second longer."

"Can't you get them to wait a few minutes?"

"Wallace," said Thorpe, "do you see that white-whiskered old lynx in the corner? That's Morrison, the man who wants to get our land. If I fail to plank down the cash the very instant it is demanded, he gets his chance. And he'll take it. Now, go. Don't hurry until you get beyond the door: then *fly!*"

Thorpe sat down again in his broad-armed chair and resumed his drumming. The nearest bank was six blocks away. He counted over in his mind the steps of Carpenter's progress; now to the door, now in the next block, now so far beyond. He had just escorted him to the door of the bank, when the clerk's voice broke in on him.

"Now," Smithers was saying, "I'll give you a receipt for the amount, and later will send to your address the title deeds of the descriptions."

Carpenter had yet to find the proper official, to identify himself, to certify the check, and to return. It was hopeless. Thorpe dropped his hands in surrender.

Then he saw the boy lay the two typed lists before his principal, and dimly he perceived that the youth, shamefacedly, was holding something bulky toward himself.

"Wh—what is it?" he stammered, drawing his hand back as though from a red-hot iron.

"You asked me for a telegram," said the boy stubbornly, as though trying to excuse himself, "and I didn't just catch the name, anyway. When I saw it on those lists I had to copy, I thought of this here."

"Where'd you get it?" asked Thorpe breathlessly.

"A fellow came here early and left it for you while I was sweeping out," explained the boy. "Said he had to catch a train. It's yours all right, ain't it?"

"Oh, yes," replied Thorpe.

He took the envelope and walked uncertainly to the tall window. He looked out at the chimneys. After a moment he tore open the envelope.

"I hope there's no bad news, sir?" said the clerk, startled at the paleness of the face Thorpe turned to the desk.

"No," replied the landlooker. "Give me a receipt. There's a certified check for your money!"

THE LANDLOOKER

CHAPTER TWENTY-FOUR

NOW that the strain was over, Thorpe experienced a great weariness. The long journey through the forest, his sleepless night on the train, the mental alertness of playing the game with shrewd foes—all these stretched his fibres out one by one and left them limp. He accepted stupidly the clerk's congratulations on his success, left the name of the little hotel off Fort Street as the address to which to send the deeds, and dragged himself off with infinite fatigue to his bedroom. There he fell at once into profound unconsciousness.

He was awakened late in the afternoon by the sensation of a strong pair of young arms around his shoulders, and the sound of Wallace Carpenter's fresh voice crying in his ears:

"Wake up, wake up! you Indian! You've been asleep all day, and I've been waiting here all that time. I want to hear about it. Wake up, I say!"

Thorpe rolled to a sitting posture on the edge of the bed, and smiled uncertainly. Then as the sleep drained from his brain, he reached out his hand.

"You bet we did 'em, Wallace," said he, "but it looked like a hard proposition for a while."

"How was it? Tell me about it!" insisted the boy eagerly. "You don't know how impatient I've been. The clerk at the Land Office merely told me it was all right. How did you fix it?"

While Thorpe washed and shaved and leisurely freshened himself, he detailed his experiences of the last week.

"And," he concluded gravely, "there's only one man I know or ever heard of to whom I would have considered it worth while even to think of sending that telegram, and you are he. Somehow I knew you'd come to the scratch."

"It's the most exciting thing I ever heard of," sighed Wallace drawing a full breath, "and I wasn't in it! It's the sort of thing I long for. If I'd only waited another two weeks before coming down!"

"In that case we couldn't have gotten hold of the money, remember," smiled Thorpe.

"That's so." Wallace brightened. "I did count, didn't I?"

"I thought so about ten o'clock this morning," Thorpe replied.

"Suppose you hadn't stumbled on their camp; suppose Injin Charley hadn't seen them go up-river; suppose you hadn't struck that little mill town *just* at the time you did!" marvelled Wallace.

"That's always the way," philosophized Thorpe in reply. "It's the old story of 'if the horseshoe nail hadn't been lost,' you know. But we got there; and that's the important thing."

"We did!" cried the boy, his enthusiasm re-kindling, "and to-night we'll celebrate with the best dinner we can buy in town!"

Thorpe was tempted, but remembered the thirty dollars in his pocket, and looked doubtful.

Carpenter possessed, as part of his volatile enthusiastic temperament, keen intuitions.

"Don't refuse!" he begged. "I've set my heart on giving my senior partner a dinner. Surely you won't refuse to be my guest here, as I was yours in the woods!"

"Wallace," said Thorpe, "I'll go you. I'd like to dine with you; but moreover, I'll confess, I should like to eat a good dinner again. It's been more than a year since I've seen a salad, or heard of after-dinner coffee."

"Come on then," cried Wallace.

Together they sauntered through the lengthening shadows to a certain small restaurant near Woodward Avenue, then much in vogue among Detroit's epicures. It contained only a half dozen tables, but was spotlessly clean, and its cuisine was unrivalled. A large fireplace near the centre of the room robbed it of half its restaurant air; and a thick carpet on the floor took the rest. The walls were decorated in dark colors after the German style. Several easy chairs grouped before the fireplace, and a light wicker table heaped with magazines and papers invited the guests to lounge while their orders were being prepared.

Thorpe was not in the least Sybaritic in his tastes, but he could not stifle a sigh of satisfaction at sinking so naturally into the unobtrusive little comforts which the ornamental life offers to its votaries. They rose up around him and pillowed him, and were grateful to the tired fibres of his being. His remoter past had enjoyed these things as a matter of course. They had framed the background to his daily habit. Now that the background had again slid into place on noiseless grooves, Thorpe for the first time became conscious that his strenuous life had indeed been in the open air, and that the winds of earnest endeavor, while bracing, had chilled. Wallace Carpenter, with the poet's insight and sympathy, saw and understood this feeling.

" I want you to order this dinner," said he, handing over to Thorpe the card which an impossibly correct waiter presented him. " And I want it a good one. I want you to begin at the beginning and skip nothing. Pretend you are ordering just the dinner you would like to offer your sister," he suggested on a sudden inspiration. " I assure you I'll try to be just as critical and exigent as she would be."

Thorpe took up the card dreamily.

" There are no oysters and clams now," said he,

"so we'll pass right on to the soup. It seems to me a desecration to pretend to replace them. We'll have a *bisque*," he told the waiter, "rich and creamy. Then planked whitefish, and have them just a light crisp brown. You can bring some celery, too, if you have it fresh and good. And for *entree* tell your cook to make some *macaroni au gratin*, but the inside must be soft and very creamy, and the outside very crisp. I know it's a queer dish for a formal dinner like ours," he addressed Wallace with a little laugh, "but it's very, very good. We'll have roast beef, rare and juicy—if you bring it any way but a *cooked* red, I'll send it back—and potatoes roasted with the meat, and brown gravy. Then the breast of chicken with the salad, in the French fashion. And I'll make the dressing. We'll have an ice and some fruit for dessert. Black coffee."

"Yes, sir," replied the waiter, his pencil poised. "And the wines?"

Thorpe ruminated sleepily.

"A rich red Burgundy," he decided, "for all the dinner. If your cellar contains a very good smooth Beaune, we'll have that."

"Yes, sir," answered the waiter, and departed.

Thorpe sat and gazed moodily into the wood fire. Wallace respected his silence. It was yet too early for the fashionable world, so the two friends had the place to themselves. Gradually the twilight fell; strange shadows leaped and died on the wall. A boy dressed all in white turned on the lights. By and by the waiter announced that their repast awaited them.

Thorpe ate, his eyes half closed, in somnolent satisfaction. Occasionally he smiled contentedly across at Wallace, who smiled in response. After the coffee he had the waiter bring cigars. They went back between the tables to a little upholstered smoking-room, where they sank into the depths of leather chairs, and blew the gray clouds of smoke toward the ceiling. About nine o'clock Thorpe spoke the first word.

"I'm stupid this evening, I'm afraid," said he, shaking himself. "Don't think on that account I am not enjoying your dinner. I believe," he asserted earnestly, "that I never had such an altogether comfortable, happy evening before in my life."

"I know," replied Wallace sympathetically.

"It seems just now," went on Thorpe, sinking more luxuriously into his armchair, "that this alone is living—to exist in an environment exquisitely toned; to eat, to drink, to smoke the best, not like a gormand, but delicately as an artist would. It is the flower of our civilization."

Wallace remembered the turmoil of the wilderness brook; the little birch knoll, yellow in the evening glow; the mellow voice of the summer night crooning through the pines. But he had the rare tact to say nothing.

"Did it ever occur to you that what you needed, when sort of tired out this way," he said abruptly after a moment, "is a woman to understand and sympathize? Wouldn't it have made this evening perfect to have seen opposite you a being whom you loved, who understood your moments of weariness, as well as your moments of strength?"

"No," replied Thorpe, stretching his arms over his head, "a woman would have talked. It takes a friend and a man to know when to keep silent for three straight hours."

The waiter brought the bill on a tray, and Carpenter paid it.

"Wallace," said Thorpe suddenly after a long interval, "we'll borrow enough by mortgaging our land to supply the working expenses. I suppose capital will have to investigate, and that'll take time; but I can begin to pick up a crew and make arrangements for transportation and supplies. You can let me have a thousand dollars on the new Company's note for initial expenses. We'll draw up articles of partnership to-morrow."

CHAPTER TWENTY-FIVE

NEXT day the articles of partnership were drawn; and Carpenter gave his note for the necessary expenses. Then in answer to a pencilled card which Mr. Morrison had evidently left at Thorpe's hotel in person, both young men called at the lumberman's place of business. They were ushered immediately into the private office.

Mr. Morrison was a smart little man with an ingratiating manner and a fishy eye. He greeted Thorpe with marked geniality.

"My opponent of yesterday!" he cried jocularly. "Sit down, Mr. Thorpe! Although you did me out of some land I had made every preparation to purchase, I can't but admire your grit and resourcefulness. How did you get here ahead of us?"

"I walked across the upper peninsula, and caught a boat," replied Thorpe briefly.

"Indeed, *indeed*!" replied Mr. Morrison, placing the tips of his fingers together. "Extraordinary! Well, Mr. Thorpe, you overreached us nicely; and I suppose we must pay for our carelessness. We must have that pine, even though we pay stumpage on it. Now what would you consider a fair price for it?"

"It is not for sale," answered Thorpe.

"We'll waive all that. Of course it is to your interest to make difficulties and run the price up as high as you can. But my time is somewhat occupied just at present, so I would be very glad to hear your top price—we will come to an agreement afterward."

"You do not understand me, Mr. Morrison. I told you the pine is not for sale, and I mean it."

"But surely— What did you buy it for, then?" cried Mr. Morrison, with evidences of a growing excitement.

"We intend to manufacture it."

Mr. Morrison's fishy eyes nearly popped out of his head. He controlled himself with an effort.

"Mr. Thorpe," said he, "let us try to be reasonable. Our case stands this way. We have gone to a great deal of expense on the Ossawinamakee in expectation of undertaking very extensive operations there. To that end we have cleared the stream, built three dams, and have laid the foundations of a harbor and boom. This has been very expensive. Now your purchase includes most of what we had meant to log. You have, roughly speaking, about three hundred millions in your holding, in addition to which there are several millions scattering near it, which would pay nobody but yourself to get in.

Our holdings are further up stream, and comprise only about the equal of yours."

" Three hundred millions are not to be sneezed at," replied Thorpe.

" Certainly not," agreed Morrison, suavely, gaining confidence from the sound of his own voice. " Not in this country. But you must remember that a man goes into the northern peninsula only because he can get something better there than here. When the firm of Morrison & Daly establishes itself now, it must be for the last time. We want enough timber to do us for the rest of the time we are in business."

" In that case, you will have to hunt up another locality," replied Thorpe calmly.

Morrison's eyes flashed. But he retained his appearance of geniality, and appealed to Wallace Carpenter.

" Then you will retain the advantage of our dams and improvements," said he. " Is that fair? "

" No, not on the face of it," admitted Thorpe. " But you did your work in a navigable stream for private purposes, without the consent of the Board of Control. Your presence on the river is illegal. You should have taken out a charter as an Improvement Company. Then, as long as you 'tended to business and kept the concern in repair, we'd have paid you a toll per thousand feet. As soon as you let it slide, however, the works would revert to the

State. I won't hinder your doing that yet; although I might. Take out your charter and fix your rate of toll."

"In other words, you force us to stay there and run a little two-by-four Improvement Company for your benefit, or else lose the value of our improvements?"

"Suit yourself," answered Thorpe carelessly. "You can always log your present holdings."

"Very well," cried Morrison, so suddenly in a passion that Wallace started back. "It's war! And let me tell you this, young man; you're a new concern and we're an old one. We'll crush you like *that*!" He crisped an envelope vindictively, and threw it in the waste-basket.

"Crush ahead," replied Thorpe with great good humor. "Good-day, Mr. Morrison," and the two went out.

Wallace was sputtering and trembling with nervous excitement. His was one of those temperaments which require action to relieve the stress of a stormy interview. He was brave enough, but he would always tremble in the presence of danger until the moment for striking arrived. He wanted to do something at once.

"Hadn't we better see a lawyer?" he asked. "Oughtn't we to look out that they don't take some of our pine? Oughtn't we———"

"You just leave all that to me," replied Thorpe.

228

" The first thing we want to do is to rustle some money."

" And you can leave *that* to *me*," echoed Wallace. " I know a little of such things, and I have business connections who know more. You just get the camp running."

" I'll start for Bay City to-night," submitted Thorpe. " There ought to be a good lot of lumberjacks lying around idle at this time of year; and it's a good place to outfit from because we can probably get freight rates direct by boat. We'll be a little late in starting, but we'll get in *some* logs this winter, anyway."

PART III

THE BLAZING OF THE TRAIL

CHAPTER TWENTY-SIX

A LUMBERING town after the drive is a fearful thing. Men just off the river draw a deep breath, and plunge into the wildest reactionary dissipation. In droves they invade the cities—wild, picturesque, lawless. As long as the money lasts, they blow it in.

" Hot money! " is the cry. " She's burnt holes in all my pockets already! "

The saloons are full, the gambling houses overflow, all the places of amusement or crime run full blast. A chip rests lightly on every one's shoulder. Fights are as common as raspberries in August. Often one of these formidable men, his muscles toughened and quickened by the active, strenuous river work, will set out to " take the town apart." For a time he leaves rack and ruin, black eyes and broken teeth behind him, until he meets a more redoubtable " knocker " and is pounded and kicked into unconsciousness. Organized gangs go from house to house forcing the peaceful inmates to drink from their bottles. Others take possession of certain sections of the street and resist *à l'outrance* the attempts of others to pass. Inoffensive citizens are stood on their heads, or shaken upside down until the contents of their pockets rattle on the street. Parenthetically, these contents are invariably returned to their owners. The riverman's object is fun, not robbery.

And if rip-roaring, swashbuckling, drunken glory is what he is after, he gets it. The only trouble is, that a whole winter's hard work goes in two or three weeks. The only redeeming feature is, that he is never, in or out of his cups, afraid of anything that walks the earth.

A man comes out of the woods or off the drive with two or three hundred dollars, which he is only too anxious to throw away by the double handful. It follows naturally that a crew of sharpers are on hand to find out who gets it. They are a hard lot. Bold, unprincipled men, they too are afraid of nothing; not even a drunken lumber-jack, which is one of the dangerous wild animals of the American fauna. Their business is to relieve the man of his money as soon as possible. They are experts at their business.

The towns of Bay City and Saginaw alone in 1878 supported over fourteen hundred tough characters. Block after block was devoted entirely to saloons. In a radius of three hundred feet from the famous old Catacombs could be numbered forty saloons, where drinks were sold by from three to ten " pretty waiter girls." When the boys struck town.

the proprietors and waitresses stood in their door-
ways to welcome them.

"Why, Jack!" one would cry, "when did you
drift in? Tickled to death to see you! Come in an'
have a drink. That your chum? Come in, old man,
and have a drink. Never mind the pay; that's all
right."

And after the first drink, Jack, of course, had to
treat, and then the chum.

Or if Jack resisted temptation and walked resolutely on, one of the girls would remark audibly to
another:

"He ain't no lumber-jack! You can see that
easy 'nuff! He's jest off th' hay-trail!"

Ten to one that brought him, for the woodsman
is above all things proud and jealous of his craft.

In the centre of this whirlpool of iniquity stood
the Catacombs as the hub from which lesser spokes
in the wheel radiated. Any old logger of the Saginaw Valley can tell you of the Catacombs, just as
any old logger of any other valley will tell you of
the "Pen," the "White Row," the "Water
Streets" of Alpena, Port Huron, Ludington, Muskegon, and a dozen other lumber towns.

The Catacombs was a three-story building. In
the basement were vile, ill-smelling, ill-lighted dens,
small, isolated, dangerous. The shanty boy with a
small stake, far gone in drunkenness, there tasted the
last drop of wickedness, and thence was flung uncon-

scious and penniless on the streets. A trap-door directly into the river accommodated those who were inconsiderate enough to succumb under rough treatment.

The second story was given over to drinking. Polly Dickson there reigned supreme, an anomaly. She was as pretty and fresh and pure-looking as a child; and at the same time was one of the most ruthless and unscrupulous of the gang. She could at will exercise a fascination the more terrible in that it appealed at once to her victim's nobler instincts of reverence, his capacity for what might be called æsthetic fascination, as well as his passions. When she finally held him, she crushed him as calmly as she would a fly.

Four bars supplied the drinkables. Dozens of "pretty waiter girls" served the customers. A force of professional fighters was maintained by the establishment to preserve that degree of peace which should look to the preservation of mirrors and glassware.

The third story contained a dance hall and a theatre. The character of both would better be left to the imagination.

Night after night during the season, this den ran at top-steam.

By midnight, when the orgy was at its height, the windows brilliantly illuminated, the various bursts of music, laughing, cursing, singing, shouting, fighting, breaking in turn or all together from its open windows, it was, as Jackson Hines once expressed it to me, like hell let out for noon.

The respectable elements of the towns were powerless. They could not control the elections. Their police would only have risked total annihilation by attempting a raid. At the first sign of trouble they walked straightly in the paths of their own affairs, awaiting the time soon to come when, his stake "blown-in," the last bitter dregs of his pleasure gulped down, the shanty boy would again start for the woods.

CHAPTER TWENTY-SEVEN

NOW in August, however, the first turmoil had died. The "jam" had boiled into town, "taken it apart," and left the inhabitants to piece it together again as they could; the "rear" had not yet arrived. As a consequence, Thorpe found the city comparatively quiet.

Here and there swaggered a strapping riverman, his small felt hat cocked aggressively over one eye, its brim curled up behind; a cigar stump protruding at an angle from beneath his sweeping mustache; his hands thrust into the pockets of his trousers, "stagged" off at the knee; the spikes of his river boots cutting little triangular pieces from the wooden sidewalk. His eye was aggressively humorous, and the smile of his face was a challenge.

For in the last month he had faced almost certain death a dozen times a day. He had ridden logs down the rapids where a loss of balance meant in one instant a ducking and in the next a blow on the back from some following battering-ram; he had tugged and strained and jerked with his peavey under a sheer wall of tangled timber twenty feet high—behind which pressed the full power of the freshet—only to jump with the agility of a cat from one bit of unstable footing to another when the first sharp *crack* warned him that he had done his work, and that the whole mass was about to break down on him like a wave on the shore; he had worked fourteen hours a day in ice-water, and had slept damp; he had pried at the key log in the rollways on the bank until the whole pile had begun to rattle down into the river like a cascade, and had jumped, or ridden, or even dived out of danger at the last second. In a hundred passes he had juggled with death as a child plays with a rubber balloon. No wonder that he has brought to the town and his vices a little of the lofty bearing of an heroic age. No wonder that he fears no man, since nature's most terrible forces of the flood have hurled a thousand weapons at him in vain. His muscles have been hardened, his eye is quiet and sure, his courage is undaunted, and his movements are as quick and accurate as a panther's. Probably nowhere in the world is a more dangerous man of his hands than the riverman. He would rather fight than eat, especially when he is drunk, as, like the cowboy, he usually is when he gets into town. A history could be written of the feuds, the wars, the raids instituted by one camp or one town against another.

The men would go in force sometimes to another city with the avowed purpose of cleaning it out. One battle I know of lasted nearly all night. Deadly weapons were almost never resorted to, unless indeed a hundred and eighty pounds of muscle behind a fist hard as iron might be considered a deadly weapon. A man hard pressed by numbers often resorted to a billiard cue, or an axe, or anything else that happened to be handy, but that was an expedient called out by necessity. Knives or six-shooters implied a certain premeditation which was discountenanced.

On the other hand, the code of fair fighting obtained hardly at all. The long spikes of river-boots made an admirable weapon in the straight kick. I have seen men whose faces were punctured as thickly as though by smallpox, where the steel points had penetrated. In a free-for-all knock-down-and-drag-out, kicking, gouging, and biting are all legitimate. Anything to injure the other man, provided always you do not knife him. And when you take a half dozen of these enduring, active, muscular, and fiery men, not one entertaining in his innermost heart the faintest hesitation or fear, and set them at each other with the lightning tirelessness of so many wild-cats, you get as hard a fight as you could desire. And they seem to like it.

One old fellow, a good deal of a character in his way, used to be on the " drive " for a firm lumbering near Six Lakes. He was intensely loyal to his " Old Fellows," and every time he got a little " budge " in him he instituted a raid on the town owned by a rival firm. So frequent and so severe did these battles become that finally the men were informed that another such expedition would mean instant discharge. The rule had its effect. The raids ceased.

But one day old Dan visited the saloon once too often. He became very warlike. The other men merely laughed, for they were strong enough themselves to recognize firmness in others, and it never occurred to them that they could disobey so absolute a command. So finally Dan started out quite alone.

He invaded the enemy's camp, attempted to clean out the saloon with a billiard cue single-handed, was knocked down, and would have been kicked to death as he lay on the floor if he had not succeeded in rolling under the billiard table where the men's boots could not reach him. As it was, his clothes were literally torn to ribbons, one eye was blacked, his nose broken, one ear hung to its place by a mere shred of skin, and his face and flesh were ripped and torn everywhere by the " corks " on the boots. Any but a riverman would have qualified for the hospital. Dan rolled to the other side of the table, made a sudden break, and escaped.

But his fighting blood was not all spilled. He raided the butcher-shop, seized the big carving knife, and returned to the battlefield.

The enemy decamped—rapidly—some of them through the window. Dan managed to get in but one blow. He ripped the coat down the man's back as neatly as though it had been done with shears, one clean straight cut from collar to bottom seam. A quarter of an inch nearer would have split the fellow's backbone. As it was, he escaped without even a scratch.

Dan commandered two bottles of whiskey, and, gory and wounded as he was, took up the six-mile tramp home, bearing the knife over his shoulder as a banner of triumph.

Next morning, weak from the combined effects of war and whiskey, he reported to headquarters.

" What is it, Dan? " asked the Old Fellow without turning.

" I come to get my time," replied the riverman humbly.

" What for? " inquired the lumberman.

" I have been over to Howard City," confessed Dan.

The owner turned and looked him over.

" They sort of got ahead of me a little," explained Dan sheepishly.

The lumberman took stock of the old man's cuts and bruises, and turned away to hide a smile.

" I guess I'll let you off this trip," said he. " Go to work—when you can. I don't believe you'll go back there again."

" No, sir," replied Dan humbly.

And so the life of alternate work and pleasure.

both full of personal danger, develops in time a class of men whose like is to be found only among the cowboys, scouts, trappers, and Indian fighters of our other frontiers. The moralists will always hold up the hands of horror at such types; the philosopher will admire them as the last incarnation of the heroic age, when the man is bigger than his work. Soon the factories, the machines, the mechanical structures and constructions, the various branches of co-operation will produce quasi-automatically institutions evidently more important than the genius or force of any one human being. The personal element will have become nearly eliminated. In the woods and on the frontier still are many whose powers are greater than their works; whose fame is greater than their deeds. They are men, powerful, virile, even brutal at times, but magnificent with the strength of courage and resource.

All this may seem a digression from the thread of our tale, but as a matter of fact it is necessary that you understand the conditions of the time and place in which Harry Thorpe had set himself the duty of success.

He had seen too much of incompetent labor to be satisfied with anything but the best. Although his ideas were not as yet formulated, he hoped to be able to pick up a crew of first-class men from those who had come down with the advance, or " jam," of the spring's drive. They should have finished their orgies by now, and, empty of pocket, should be found hanging about the boarding-houses and the quieter saloons. Thorpe intended to offer good wages for good men. He would not need more than twenty at first, for during the approaching winter he purposed to log on a very small scale indeed. The time for expansion would come later.

With this object in view he set out from his hotel about half-past seven on the day of his arrival, to cruise about in the lumber-jack district already described. The hotel clerk had obligingly given him the names of a number of the quieter saloons, where the boys " hung out " between bursts of prosperity. In the first of these Thorpe was helped materially in his vague and uncertain quest by encountering an old acquaintance.

From the sidewalk he heard the vigorous sounds of a one-sided altercation punctuated by frequent, bursts of quickly silenced laughter. Evidently some one was very angry, and the rest amused. After a moment Thorpe imagined he recognized the excited voice. So he pushed open the swinging screen door and entered.

The place was typical. Across one side ran the hardwood bar with foot-rest and little towels hung in metal clasps under its edge. Behind it was a long mirror, a symmetrical pile of glasses, a number of plain or ornamental bottles, and a miniature keg or so of porcelain containing the finer whiskeys and brandies. The barkeeper drew beer from two pumps immediately in front of him, and rinsed glasses in some sort of a sink under the edge of the bar. The centre of the room was occupied by a tremendous stove capable of burning whole logs of cordwood. A stovepipe led from the stove here and there in wire suspension to a final exit near the other corner. On the wall were two sporting chromos, and a good variety of lithographed calendars and illuminated tin signs advertising beers and spirits. The floor was liberally sprinkled with damp sawdust, and was occupied, besides the stove, by a number of wooden chairs and a single round table.

The latter, a clumsy heavy affair beyond the strength of an ordinary man, was being deftly interposed between himself and the attacks of the possessor of the angry voice by a gigantic young riverman in the conventional stagged (*i.e.*, chopped off) trousers, " cork " shoes, and broad belt typical of his craft. In the aggressor Thorpe recognized old Jackson Hines.

" Damn you! " cried the old man, qualifying the oath, " let me get at you, you great big sock-stealer, I'll make you hop high! I'll snatch you bald-headed so quick that you'll think you never had any hair! "

" I'll settle with you in the morning, Jackson," laughed the riverman.

" You want to eat a good breakfast, then, because you won't have no appetite for dinner."

The men roared, with encouraging calls. The riverman put on a ludicrous appearance of offended dignity.

"Oh, you needn't swell up like a poisoned pup!" cried old Jackson plaintively, ceasing his attacks from sheer weariness. "You know you're as safe as a cow tied to a brick wall behind that table."

Thorpe seized the opportunity to approach.

"Hello, Jackson," said he.

The old man peered at him out of the blur of his excitement.

"Don't you know me?" inquired Thorpe.

"Them lamps gives 'bout as much light as a piece of chalk," complained Jackson testily. "Knows you? You bet I do! How are you, Harry? Where you been keepin' yourself? You look 'bout as fat as a stall-fed knittin' needle."

"I've been landlooking in the upper peninsula," explained Thorpe, "on the Ossawinamakee, up in the Marquette country."

"Sho'!" commented Jackson in wonder, "way up there where the moon changes!"

"It's a fine country," went on Thorpe so every one could hear, "with a great cutting of white pine. It runs as high as twelve hundred thousand to the forty sometimes."

"Trees clean an' free of limbs?" asked Jackson.

"They're as good as the stuff over on seventeen; you remember that."

"Clean as a baby's leg," agreed Jackson.

"Have a glass of beer?" asked Thorpe.

"Dry as a tobacco box," confessed Hines.

"Have something, the rest of you?" invited Thorpe.

So they all drank.

On a sudden inspiration Thorpe resolved to ask the old man's advice as to crew and horses. It might not be good for much, but it would do no harm.

Jackson listened attentively to the other's brief recital.

"Why don't you see Tim Shearer? He ain't doin' nothin' since the jam came down," was his comment.

"Isn't he with the M. & D. people?" asked Thorpe.

"Nope. Quit."

"How's that?"

"'Count of Morrison. Morrison he comes up to run things some. He does. Tim he's getting the drive in shape, and he don't want to be bothered, but old Morrison he's as busy as hell beatin' tanbark. Finally Tim, he calls him. "'Look here, Mr. Morrison,' says he, 'I'm runnin' this drive. If I don't get her there, all right; you can give me my time. 'Till then you ain't got nothin' to say.'

"Well, that makes the Old Fellow as sore as a scalded pup. He's used to bossin' clerks and such things, and don't have much of an idea of lumber-jacks. He has big ideas of respect, so he 'calls' Tim dignified like.

"Tim didn't hit him; but I guess he felt like th' man who met the bear without any weapon—even a newspaper would 'a' come handy. He hands in his time t' once and quits. Sence then he's been as mad as a bar-keep with a lead quarter, which ain't usual for Tim. He's been filin' his teeth for M. & D. right along. Somethin's behind it all, I reckon."

"Where'll I find him?" asked Thorpe.

Jackson gave the name of a small boarding-house. Shortly after, Thorpe left him to amuse the others with his unique conversation, and hunted up Shearer's stopping-place.

CHAPTER TWENTY-EIGHT

THE boarding-house proved to be of the typical lumber-jack class—a narrow " stoop," a hallway and stairs in the centre, and an office and bar on either side. Shearer and a half dozen other men about his own age sat, their chairs on two legs and their " cork " boots on the rounds of the chairs, smoking placidly in the tepid evening air. The light came from inside the building, so that while Thorpe was in plain view, he could not make out which of the dark figures on the piazza was the man he wanted. He approached, and attempted an identifying scrutiny. The men, with the taciturnity of their class in the presence of a stranger, said nothing.

" Well, bub," finally drawled a voice from the corner, " blowed that stake you made out of Radway, yet? "

" That you, Shearer? " inquired Thorpe advancing. " You're the man I'm looking for."

" You've found me," replied the old man dryly.

Thorpe was requested elaborately to " shake hands " with the owners of six names. Then he had a chance to intimate quietly to Shearer that he wanted a word with him alone. The riverman rose silently and led the way up the straight, uncarpeted stairs, along a narrow, uncarpeted hall, to a square, uncarpeted bedroom. The walls and ceiling of this apartment were of unpainted planed pine. It contained a cheap bureau, one chair, and a bed and washstand to match the bureau. Shearer lit the lamp and sat on the bed.

" What is it? " he asked.

" I have a little pine up in the northern peninsula within walking distance of Marquette," said Thorpe, " and I want to get a crew of about twenty men. It occurred to me that you might be willing to help me."

The riverman frowned steadily at his interlocutor from under his bushy brows.

" How much pine you got? " he asked finally.

" About three hundred millions," replied Thorpe quietly.

The old man's blue eyes fixed themselves with unwavering steadiness on Thorpe's face.

" You're jobbing some of it, eh? " he submitted finally as the only probable conclusion. " Do you think you know enough about it? Who does it belong to? "

" It belongs to a man named Carpenter and myself."

The riverman pondered this slowly for an appreciable interval, and then shot out another question.

" How'd you get it? "

Thorpe told him simply, omitting nothing except the name of the firm up-river. When he had finished, Shearer evinced no astonishment nor approval.

"You done well," he commented finally. Then after another interval:

"Have you found out who was the men stealin' the pine?"

"Yes," replied Thorpe quietly, "it was Morrison & Daly."

The old man flickered not an eyelid. He slowly filled his pipe and lit it.

"I'll get you a crew of men," said he, "if you'll take me as foreman."

"But it's a little job at first," protested Thorpe. "I only want a camp of twenty. It wouldn't be worth your while."

"That's my look-out. I'll take th' job," replied the logger grimly. "You got three hundred million there, ain't you? And you're goin' to cut it? It ain't such a small job."

Thorpe could hardly believe his good-fortune in having gained so important a recruit. With a practical man as foreman, his mind would be relieved of a great deal of worry over unfamiliar detail. He saw at once that he would himself be able to perform all the duties of scaler, keep in touch with the needs of the camp, and supervise the campaign. Nevertheless he answered the older man's glance with one as keen, and said:

251

"Look here, Shearer, if you take this job, we may as well understand each other at the start. This is going to be my camp, and I'm going to be boss. I don't know much about logging, and I shall want you to take charge of all that, but I shall want to know just why you do each thing, and if my judgment advises otherwise, my judgment goes. If I want to discharge a man, he *walks* without any question. I know about what I shall expect of each man; and I intend to get it out of him. And in questions of policy mine is the say-so every trip. Now I know you're a good man—one of the best there is—and I presume I shall find your judgment the best, but I don't want any mistakes to start with. If you want to be my foreman on those terms, just say so, and I'll be tickled to death to have you."

For the first time the lumberman's face lost, during a single instant, its mask of immobility. His steel-blue eyes flashed, his mouth twitched with some strong emotion. For the first time, too, he spoke without his contemplative pause of preparation.

"That's th' way to talk!" he cried. "Go with you? Well I should rise to remark! You're the boss; and I always said it. I'll get you a gang of bully boys that will roll logs till there's skating in hell!"

Thorpe left, after making an appointment at his

own hotel for the following day, more than pleased with his luck. Although he had by now fairly good and practical ideas in regard to the logging of a bunch of pine, he felt himself to be very deficient in the details. In fact, he anticipated his next step with shaky confidence. He would now be called upon to buy four or five teams of horses, and enough feed to last them the entire winter; he would have to arrange for provisions in abundance and variety for his men; he would have to figure on blankets, harness, cook-camp utensils, stoves, blacksmith tools, iron, axes, chains, cant-hooks, van-goods, pails, lamps, oil, matches, all sorts of hardware—in short, all the thousand and one things, from needles to court-plaster, of which a self-sufficing community might come in need. And he would have to figure out his requirements for the entire winter. After navigation closed, he could import nothing more.

How could he know what to buy—how many barrels of flour, how much coffee, raisins, baking powder, soda, pork, beans, dried apples, sugar, nutmeg, pepper, salt, crackers, molasses, ginger, lard, tea, corned beef, catsup, mustard—to last twenty men five or six months? How could he be expected to think of each item of a list of two hundred, the lack of which meant measureless bother, and the desirability of which suggested itself only when the necessity arose? It is easy, when the mind is occupied with multitudinous detail, to forget simple things, like brooms or iron shovels. With Tim Shearer to help his inexperience, he felt easy. He knew he could attend to advantageous buying, and to making arrangements with the steamship line to Marquette for the landing of his goods at the mouth of the Ossawinamakee.

Deep in these thoughts, he wandered on at random. He suddenly came to himself in the toughest quarter of Bay City.

Through the summer night shrilled the sound of cachinations painted to the colors of mirth. A cheap piano rattled and thumped through an open window. Men's and women's voices mingled in rising and falling gradations of harshness. Lights streamed irregularly across the dark.

Thorpe became aware of a figure crouched in the doorway almost at his feet. The sill lay in shadow so the bulk was lost, but the flickering rays of a distant street lamp threw into relief the high-lights of a violin, and a head. The face upturned to him was thin and white and wolfish under a broad white brow. Dark eyes gleamed at him with the expression of a fierce animal. Across the forehead ran a long but shallow cut from which blood dripped. The creature clasped both arms around a violin. He crouched there and stared up at Thorpe, who stared down at him.

" What's the matter? " asked the latter finally.

The creature made no reply, but drew his arms

closer about his instrument, and blinked his wolf eyes.

Moved by some strange, half-tolerant whim of compassion, Thorpe made a sign to the unknown to rise.

"Come with me," said he, "and I'll have your forehead attended to."

The wolf eyes gleamed into his with a sudden savage concentration. Then their owner obediently arose.

Thorpe now saw that the body before him was of a cripple, short-legged, hunch-backed, long-armed, pigeon-breasted. The large head sat strangely top-heavy between even the broad shoulders. It confirmed the hopeless but sullen despair that brooded on the white countenance.

At the hotel Thorpe, examining the cut, found it more serious in appearance than in reality. With a few pieces of sticking plaster he drew its edges together.

Then he attempted to interrogate his find.

"What is your name?" he asked.

"Phil."

"Phil what?"

Silence.

"How did you get hurt?"

No reply.

"Were you playing your fiddle in one of those houses?"

The cripple nodded slowly.

"Are you hungry?" asked Thorpe, with a sudden thoughtfulness.

"Yes," replied the cripple, with a lightning gleam in his wolf eyes.

Thorpe rang the bell. To the boy who answered it he said:

"Bring me half a dozen beef sandwiches and a glass of milk, and be quick about it."

"Do you play the fiddle much?" continued Thorpe.

The cripple nodded again.

"Let's hear what you can do."

"They cut my strings!" cried Phil with a passionate wail.

The cry came from the heart, and Thorpe was touched by it. The price of strings was evidently a big sum.

"I'll get you more in the morning," said he. "Would you like to leave Bay City?"

"Yes!" cried the boy with passion.

"You would have to work. You would have to be chore-boy in a lumber camp, and play fiddle for the men when they wanted you to."

"I'll do it," said the cripple.

"Are you sure you could? You will have to split all the wood for the men, the cook, and the office; you will have to draw the water, and fill the lamps, and keep the camps clean. You will be paid for it, but it is quite a job. And you would have to do it well. If you did not do it well, I would discharge you."

"I will do it!" repeated the cripple with a shade more earnestness.

"All right, then I'll take you," replied Thorpe.

The cripple said nothing, nor moved a muscle of his face, but the gleam of the wolf faded to give place to the soft, affectionate glow seen in the eyes of a setter dog. Thorpe was startled at the change.

A knock announced the sandwiches and milk. The cripple fell upon them with both hands in a sudden ecstasy of hunger. When he had finished, he looked again at Thorpe, and this time there were tears in his eyes.

A little later Thorpe interviewed the proprietor of the hotel.

"I wish you'd give this boy a good cheap room and charge his keep to me," said he. "He's going north with me."

Phil was led away by the irreverent porter, hugging tightly his unstrung violin to his bosom.

Thorpe lay awake for some time after retiring. Phil claimed a share of his thoughts.

Thorpe's winter in the woods had impressed upon him that a good cook and a fiddler will do more to keep men contented than high wages and easy work. So his protection of the cripple was not entirely disinterested. But his imagination persisted in occupying itself with the boy. What terrible life of want and vicious associates had he led in this terrible town? What treatment could have lit that wolf-gleam in his eyes? What hell had he inhabited that he was so eager to get away? In an hour or so he dozed. He dreamed that the cripple had grown to enormous proportions and was overshadowing his life. A slight noise outside his bedroom door brought him to his feet.

He opened the door and found that in the stillness of the night the poor deformed creature had taken the blankets from his bed and had spread them across the door-sill of the man who had befriended him.

CHAPTER TWENTY-NINE

THREE weeks later the steam barge *Pole Star* sailed down the reach of Saginaw Bay.

Thorpe had received letters from Carpenter advising him of a credit to him at a Marquette bank, and enclosing a draft sufficient for current expenses. Tim Shearer had helped make out the list of necessaries. In time everything was loaded, the gangplank hauled in, and the little band of Argonauts set their faces toward the point where the Big Dipper swings.

The weather was beautiful. Each morning the sun rose out of the frosty blue lake water, and set in a sea of deep purple. The moon, once again at the full, drew broad paths across the pathless waste. From the southeast blew daily the lake trades, to die at sunset, and then to return in the soft still nights from the west. A more propitious beginning for the adventure could not be imagined.

The ten horses in the hold munched their hay and oats as peaceably as though at home in their own stables. Jackson Hines had helped select them from the stocks of firms changing locality or going out of business. His judgment in such matters was infallible, but he had resolutely refused to take the position of barn-boss which Thorpe offered him.

"No," said he, "she's too far north. I'm gettin' old, and the rheumatics ain't what you might call abandonin' of me. Up there it's colder than hell on a stoker's holiday."

So Shearer had picked out a barn-boss of his own. This man was important, for the horses are the mainstay of logging operations. He had selected also a blacksmith, a cook, four teamsters, half a dozen cant-hook men, and as many handy with axe or saw.

"The blacksmith is also a good wood-butcher (carpenter)," explained Shearer. "Four teams is all we ought to keep going at a clip. If we need a few axe-men, we can pick 'em up at Marquette. I think this gang'll stick. I picked 'em."

There was not a young man in the lot. They were most of them in the prime of middle life, between thirty and forty, rugged in appearance, "cocky" in manner, with the swagger and the oath of so many buccaneers, hard as nails. Altogether Thorpe thought them about as rough a set of customers as he had ever seen. Throughout the day they played cards on deck, and spat tobacco juice abroad, and swore incessantly. Toward himself and Shearer their manner was an odd mixture of independent equality and a slight deference. It was as much as to say, "You're the boss, but I'm as good a man as you any day." They would be a rough, turbulent, unruly mob to handle, but under a strong man they might accomplish wonders.

Constituting the élite of the profession, as it were —whose swagger every lad new to the woods and river tried to emulate, to whom lesser lights looked up as heroes and models, and whose lofty, half-contemptuous scorn of everything and everybody outside their circle of " bully boys " was truly the aristocracy of class—Thorpe might have wondered at their consenting to work for an obscure little camp belonging to a greenhorn. Loyalty to and pride in the firm for which he works is a strong characteristic of the lumber-jack. He will fight at the drop of a hat on behalf of his " Old Fellows "; brag loud and long of the season's cut, the big loads, the smart methods of his camps; and even after he has been discharged for some flagrant debauch, he cherishes no rancor, but speaks with soft reminiscence to the end of his days concerning " that winter in '81 when the Old Fellows put in sixty million on Flat River."

For this reason he feels that he owes it to his reputation to ally himself only with firms of creditable size and efficiency. The small camps are for the youngsters. Occasionally you will see two or three of the veterans in such a camp, but it is generally a case of lacking something better.

The truth is, Shearer had managed to inspire in the minds of his cronies an idea that they were about to participate in a fight. He re-told Thorpe's story artistically, shading the yellows and the reds. He detailed the situation as it existed. The men agreed that the " young fellow had sand enough for a lake front." After that there needed but a little skillful maneuvring to inspire them with the idea that it would be a great thing to take a hand, to " make a camp " in spite of the big concern up-river.

Shearer knew that this attitude was tentative. Everything depended on how well Thorpe lived up to his reputation at the outset—how good a first impression of force and virility he would manage to convey—for the first impression possessed the power of transmuting the present rather ill-defined enthusiasm into loyalty or dissatisfaction. But Tim himself believed in Thorpe blindly. So he had no fears.

A little incident at the beginning of the voyage did much to reassure him. It was on the old question of whiskey.

Thorpe had given orders that no whiskey was to be brought aboard, as he intended to tolerate no high-sea orgies. Soon after leaving dock he saw one of the teamsters drinking from a pint flask. Without a word he stepped briskly forward, snatched the bottle from the man's lips, and threw it overboard. Then he turned sharp on his heel and walked away, without troubling himself as to how the fellow was going to take it.

The occurrence pleased the men, for it showed them they had made no mistake. But it meant little else. The chief danger really was lest they become too settled in the protective attitude. As they took it, they were about, good-naturedly, to help along a worthy greenhorn. This they considered exceedingly generous on their part, and in their own minds they were inclined to look on Thorpe much as a grown man would look on a child. There needed an occasion for him to prove himself bigger than they.

Fine weather followed them up the long blue reach of Lake Huron; into the noble breadth of the Detour Passage, past the opening through the Thousand Islands of the Georgian Bay; into the St. Mary's River. They were locked through after some delay on account of the grain barges from Duluth, and at last turned their prow westward in the Big Sea Water, beyond which lay Hiawatha's Po-ne-mah, the Land of the Hereafter.

Thorpe was about late that night, drinking in the mystic beauty of the scene. Northern lights, pale and dim, stretched their arc across beneath the Dipper. The air, soft as the dead leaves of spring, fanned his cheek. By and by the moon, like a red fire at sea, lifted itself from the waves. Thorpe made his way to the stern, beyond the square deckhouse, where he intended to lean on the rail in silent contemplation of the moon-path.

He found another before him. Phil, the little cripple, was peering into the wonderful east, its light in his eyes. He did not look at Thorpe when the latter approached, but seemed aware of his presence, for he moved swiftly to give room.

"It is very beautiful; isn't it, Phil?" said Thorpe after a moment.

"It is the Heart Song of the Sea," replied the cripple in a hushed voice.

Thorpe looked down surprised.

"Who told you that?" he asked.

But the cripple, repeating the words of a chance preacher, could explain himself no further. In a dim way the ready-made phrase had expressed the smothered poetic craving of his heart—the belief that the sea, the sky, the woods, the men and women, you, I, all have our Heart Songs, the Song which is most beautiful.

"The Heart Song of the Sea," he repeated gropingly. "I don't know . . . I play it," and he made the motion of drawing a bow across strings, "very still and low." And this was all Thorpe's question could elicit.

Thorpe fell silent in the spell of the night, and pondered over the chances of life which had cast on the shores of the deep as driftwood the soul of a poet.

"Your Song," said the cripple timidly, "some day I will hear it. Not yet. That night in Bay City, when you took me in, I heard it very dim. But I cannot play it yet on my violin."

"Has your violin a song of its own?" queried the man.

"I cannot hear it. It tries to sing, but there is something in the way. I cannot. Some day I will hear it and play it, but "—and he drew nearer Thorpe and touched his arm—" that day will be very bad for me. I lose something." His eyes of the wistful dog were big and wondering.

"Queer little Phil!" cried Thorpe laughing whimsically. "Who tells you these things?"

"Nobody," said the cripple dreamily, "they come when it is like to-night. In Bay City they do not come."

At this moment a third voice broke in on them.

"Oh, it's you, Mr. Thorpe," said the captain of the vessel. "Thought it was some of them lumber-jacks, and I was going to fire 'em below. Fine night."

"It is that," answered Thorpe, again the cold, unresponsive man of reticence. "When do you expect to get in, Captain?"

"About to-morrow noon," replied the captain, moving away. Thorpe followed him a short distance, discussing the landing. The cripple stood all night, his bright, luminous eyes gazing clear and unwinking at the moonlight, listening to his Heart Song of the Sea.

CHAPTER THIRTY

NEXT morning continued the traditions of its calm predecessors. Therefore by daybreak every man was at work. The hatches were opened, and soon between-decks was cumbered with boxes, packing cases, barrels, and crates. In their improvised stalls, the patient horses seemed to catch a hint of shore-going and whinnied. By ten o'clock there loomed against the strange coast line of the Pictured Rocks, a shallow bay and what looked to be a dock distorted by the northern mirage.

" That's her," said the captain.

Two hours later the steamboat swept a wide curve, slid between the yellow waters of two outlying reefs, and, with slackened speed, moved slowly toward the wharf of log cribs filled with stone.

The bay or the dock Thorpe had never seen. He took them on the captain's say-so. He knew very well that the structure had been erected by and belonged to Morrison & Daly, but the young man had had the foresight to purchase the land lying on the deep-water side of the bay. He therefore anticipated no trouble in unloading; for while Morrison & Daly owned the pier itself, the land on which it abutted belonged to him.

266

From the arms of the bay he could make out a dozen figures standing near the end of the wharf. When, with propeller reversed, the *Pole Star* bore slowly down toward her moorings, Thorpe recognized Dyer at the head of eight or ten woodsmen. The sight of Radway's old scaler somehow filled him with a quiet but dangerous anger, especially since that official, on whom rested a portion at least of the responsibility of the jobber's failure, was now found in the employ of the very company which had attempted that failure. It looked suspicious.

"Catch this line!" sung out the mate, hurling the coil of a handline on the wharf.

No one moved, and the little rope, after a moment, slid overboard with a splash.

The captain, with a curse, signalled full speed astern.

"Captain Morse!" cried Dyer, stepping forward. "My orders are that you are to land here nothing but M. & D. merchandise."

"I have a right to land," answered Thorpe. "The shore belongs to me."

"This dock doesn't," retorted the other sharply, "and you can't set foot on her."

"You have no legal status. You had no business building in the first place—" began Thorpe, and then stopped with a choke of anger at the futility of arguing legality in such a case.

The men had gathered interestedly in the waist of

the ship, cool, impartial, severely critical. The vessel, gathering speed astern, but not yet obeying her reversed helm, swung her bow in toward the dock. Thorpe ran swiftly forward, and during the instant of rubbing contact, leaped.

He alighted squarely upon his feet. Without an instant's hesitation, hot with angry energy at finding his enemy within reach of his hand, he rushed on Dyer, and with one full, clean in-blow stretched him stunned on the dock. For a moment there was a pause of astonishment. Then the woodsmen closed upon him.

During that instant Thorpe had become possessed of a weapon. It came hurling through the air from above to fall at his feet. Shearer, with the cool calculation of the pioneer whom no excitement can distract from the main issue, had seen that it would be impossible to follow his chief, and so had done the next best thing—thrown him a heavy iron belaying pin.

Thorpe was active, alert, and strong. The men could come at him only in front. As offset, he could not give ground, even for one step. Still, in the hands of a powerful man, the belaying pin is by no means a despicable weapon. Thorpe hit with all his strength and quickness. He was conscious once of being on the point of defeat. Then he had cleared a little space for himself. Then the men were on him again more savagely than ever. One fellow even succeeded in hitting him a glancing blow on the shoulder.

Then came a sudden crash. Thorpe was nearly thrown from his feet. The next instant a score of yelling men leaped behind and all around him. There ensued a moment's scuffle, the sound of dull blows; and the dock was clear of all but Dyer and three others who were, like himself, unconscious. The captain, yielding to the excitement, had run his prow plump against the wharf.

Some of the crew received the mooring lines. All was ready for disembarkation.

Bryan Moloney, a strapping Irish-American of the big-boned, red-cheeked type, threw some water over the four stunned combatants. Slowly they came to life. They were promptly yanked to their feet by the irate rivermen, who commenced at once to bestow sundry vigorous kicks and shakings by way of punishment. Thorpe interposed.

"Quit it!" he commanded. "Let them go!"

The men grumbled. One or two were inclined to be openly rebellious.

"If I hear another peep out of you," said Thorpe to these latter, "you can climb right aboard and take the return trip." He looked them in the eye until they muttered, and then went on: "Now, we've got to get unloaded and our goods ashore before those fellows report to camp. Get right moving, and hustle!"

If the men expected any comment, approval, or familiarity from their leader on account of their little fracas, they were disappointed. This was a good thing. The lumber-jack demands in his boss a certain fundamental unapproachability, whatever surface *bonhomie* he may evince.

So Dyer and his men picked themselves out of the trouble sullenly and departed. The ex-scaler had nothing to say as long as he was within reach, but when he had gained the shore, he turned.

" You won't think this is so funny when you get in the law-courts! " he shouted.

Thorpe made no reply. " I guess we'll keep even," he muttered.

" By the jumping Moses," snarled Scotty Parsons turning in threat.

" Scotty! " said Thorpe sharply.

Scotty turned back to his task, which was to help the blacksmith put together the wagon, the component parts of which the others had trundled out.

With thirty men at the job it does not take a great while to move a small cargo thirty or forty feet. By three o'clock the *Pole Star* was ready to continue her journey. Thorpe climbed aboard, leaving Shearer in charge.

" Keep the men at it, Tim," said he. " Put up the walls of the warehouse good and strong, and move the stuff in. If it rains, you can spread the tent over the roof, and camp in with the provisions

If you get through before I return, you might take a scout up the river and fix on a camp site. I'll bring back the lumber for roofs, floors, and trimmings with me, and will try to pick up a few axe-men for swamping. Above all things, have a good man or so always in charge. Those fellows won't bother us any more for the present, I think; but it pays to be on deck. So long."

In Marquette, Thorpe arranged for the cashing of his time checks and orders; bought lumber at the mills; talked contract with old Harvey, the mill-owner and prospective buyer of the young man's cut; and engaged four axe-men whom he found loafing about, waiting for the season to open.

When he returned to the bay he found the warehouse complete except for the roofs and gables. These, with their reinforcement of tar-paper, were nailed on in short order. Shearer and Andrews, the surveyor, were scouting up the river.

" No trouble from above, boys?" asked Thorpe.

" Nary trouble," they replied.

The warehouse was secured by padlocks, the wagon loaded with the tent and the necessaries of life and work. Early in the morning the little procession—laughing, joking, skylarking with the high spirits of men in the woods—took its way up the river-trail. Late that evening, tired, but still inclined to mischief, they came to the first dam, where Shearer and Andrews met them.

"How do you like it, Tim?" asked Thorpe that evening.

"She's all right," replied the riverman with emphasis; which, for him, was putting it strong.

At noon of the following day the party arrived at the second dam. Here Shearer had decided to build the permanent camp. Injin Charley was constructing one of his endless series of birch-bark canoes. Later he would paddle the whole string to Marquette, where he would sell them to a hardware dealer for two dollars and a half apiece.

To Thorpe, who had walked on ahead with his foreman, it seemed that he had never been away. There was the knoll; the rude camp with the deer hides; the venison hanging suspended from the pole; the endless broil and tumult of the clear north-country stream; the yellow glow over the hill opposite. Yet he had gone a nearly penniless adventurer; he returned at the head of an enterprise.

Injin Charley looked up and grunted as Thorpe approached.

"How are you, Charley?" greeted Thorpe reticently.

"You gettum pine? Good!" replied Charley in the same tone.

That was all; for strong men never talk freely of what is in their hearts. There is no need; they understand.

CHAPTER THIRTY-ONE

TWO months passed away. Winter set in. The camp was built and inhabited. Routine had established itself, and all was going well.

The first move of the M. & D. Company had been one of conciliation. Thorpe was approached by the walking-boss of the camps up-river. The man made no reference to or excuse for what had occurred, nor did he pretend to any hypocritical friendship for the younger firm. His proposition was entirely one of mutual advantage. The Company had gone to considerable expense in constructing the pier of stone cribs. It would be impossible for the steamer to land at any other point. Thorpe had undisputed possession of the shore, but the Company could as indisputably remove the dock. Let it stay where it was. Both companies could then use it for their mutual convenience.

To this Thorpe agreed. Baker, the walking-boss, tried to get him to sign a contract to that effect. Thorpe refused.

"Leave your dock where it is and use it when you want to," said he. "I'll agree not to interfere as long as you people behave yourselves."

The actual logging was opening up well. Both Shearer and Thorpe agreed that it would not do to be too ambitious the first year. They set about clearing their banking ground about a half mile below the first dam; and during the six weeks before snowfall cut three short roads of half a mile each. Approximately two million feet would be put in from these roads—which could be extended in years to come—while another million could be travoyed directly to the landing from its immediate vicinity.

"We won't skid them," said Tim. "We'll haul from the stump to the bank. And we'll tackle only a snow-road proposition: we ain't got time to monkey with buildin' sprinklers and plows this year. We'll make a little stake ahead, and then next year we'll do it right and get in twenty million. That railroad'll get along a ways by then, and men'll be more plenty."

Through the lengthening evenings they sat crouched on wooden boxes either side of the stove, conversing rarely, gazing at one spot with a steady persistency which was only an outward indication of the persistency with which their minds held to the work in hand. Tim, the older at the business, showed this trait more strongly than Thorpe. The old man thought of nothing but logging. From the stump to the bank, from the bank to the camp, from the camp to the stump again, his restless intelligence travelled tirelessly, picking up, turning over, examining the littlest details with an ever-fresh curiosity and interest. Nothing was too small to escape this deliberate scrutiny. Nothing was in so perfect a state that it did not bear one more inspection. He played the logging as a chess player his game. One by one he adopted the various possibilities, remote and otherwise, as hypotheses, and thought out to the uttermost copper rivet what would be the best method of procedure in case that possibility should confront him.

Occasionally Thorpe would introduce some other topic of conversation. The old man would listen to his remark with the attention of courtesy; would allow a decent period of silence to intervene; and then, reverting to the old subject without comment on the new, would emit one of his terse practical suggestions, result of a long spell of figuring. That is how success is made.

In the men's camp the crew lounged, smoked, danced, or played cards. In those days no one thought of forbidding gambling. One evening Thorpe, who had been too busy to remember Phil's violin—although he noticed, as he did every other detail of the camp, the cripple's industry, and the precision with which he performed his duties—strolled over and looked through the window. A dance was in progress. The men were waltzing, whirling solemnly round and round, gripping firmly each other's loose sleeves just above the elbow. At every third step of the waltz they stamped one foot.

Perched on a cracker box sat Phil. His head was thrust forward almost aggressively over his instrument, and his eyes glared at the dancing men with the old wolf-like gleam. As he played, he drew the bow across with a swift jerk, thrust it back with another, threw his shoulders from one side to the other in abrupt time to the music. And the music! Thorpe unconsciously shuddered; then sighed in pity. It was atrocious. It was not even in tune. Two out of three of the notes were either sharp or flat, not so flagrantly as to produce absolute disharmony, but just enough to set the teeth on edge. And the rendition was as colorless as that of a poor hand-organ.

The performer seemed to grind out his fearful stuff with a fierce delight, in which appeared little of the æsthetic pleasure of the artist. Thorpe was at a loss to define it.

" Poor Phil," he said to himself. " He has the musical soul without even the musical ear! "

Next day, while passing out of the cook camp he addressed one of the men:

" Well, Billy," he inquired, " how do you like your fiddler? "

" All *right*! " replied Billy with emphasis. " She's got some go to her."

In the woods the work proceeded finely. From

the travoy sledges and the short roads a constant stream of logs emptied itself on the bank. There long parallel skidways had been laid the whole width of the river valley. Each log as it came was dragged across those monster andirons and rolled to the bank of the river. The cant-hook men dug their implements into the rough bark, leaned, lifted, or clung to the projecting stocks until slowly the log moved, rolling with gradually increasing momentum. Then they attacked it with fury lest the momentum be lost. Whenever it began to deviate from the straight rolling necessary to keep it on the centre of the skids, one of the workers thrust the shoe of his cant-hook under one end of the log. That end promptly stopped; the other, still rolling, soon caught up; and the log moved on evenly, as was fitting.

At the end of the rollway the log collided with other logs and stopped with the impact of one bowling ball against another. The men knew that being caught between the two meant death or crippling for life. Nevertheless they escaped from the narrowing interval at the latest possible moment, for it is easier to keep a log rolling than to start it.

Then other men piled them by means of long steel chains and horses, just as they would have skidded them in the woods. Only now the logs mounted up and up until the skidways were thirty or forty feet high. Eventually the pile of logs would fill the banking ground utterly, burying the landing under a nearly continuous carpet of timber as thick as a two-story house is tall. The work is dangerous. A saw log containing six hundred board feet weighs about one ton. This is the weight of an ordinary iron safe. When one of them rolls or falls from even a moderate height, its force is irresistible. But when twenty or thirty cascade down the bold front of a skidway, carrying a man or so with them, the affair becomes a catastrophe.

Thorpe's men, however, were all old-timers, and nothing of the sort occurred. At first it made him catch his breath to see the apparent chances they took; but after a little he perceived that seeming luck was in reality a coolness of judgment and a long experience in the peculiar ways of that most erratic of inanimate cussedness—the pine log. The banks grew daily. Everybody was safe and sound.

The young lumberman had sense enough to know that, while a crew such as his is supremely effective, it requires careful handling to keep it good-humored and willing. He knew every man by his first name, and each day made it a point to talk with him for a moment or so. The subject was invariably some phase of the work. Thorpe never permitted himself the familiarity of introducing any other topic. By this course he preserved the nice balance between too great reserve, which chills the lumber-jack's rather independent enthusiasm, and the too great familiarity, which loses his respect. He never replied directly to an objection or a request, but listened to it non-committally; and later, without explanation or reasoning, acted as his judgment dictated. Even Shearer, with whom he was in most intimate contact, respected this trait in him. Gradually he came to feel that he was making a way with his men. It was a status, not assured as yet nor even very firm, but a status for all that.

Then one day one of the best men, a teamster, came in to make some objection to the cooking. As a matter of fact, the cooking was perfectly good. It generally is, in a well-conducted camp, but the lumber-jack is a great hand to growl, and he usually begins with his food.

Thorpe listened to his vague objections in silence. "All right," he remarked simply.

Next day he touched the man on the shoulder just as he was starting to work.

"Step into the office and get your time," said he.

"What's the matter?" asked the man.

"I don't need you any longer."

The two entered the little office. Thorpe looked through the ledger and van book, and finally handed the man his slip.

"Where do I get this?" asked the teamster, looking at it uncertainly.

"At the bank in Marquette," replied Thorpe without glancing around.

"Have I got to go 'way up to Marquette?"

"Certainly," replied Thorpe briefly.

"Who's going to pay my fare south?"

"You are. You can get work at Marquette."

"That ain't a fair shake," cried the man excitedly.

"I'll have no growlers in this camp," said Thorpe with decision.

"By God!" cried the man, "you damned——"

"You get out of here!" cried Thorpe with a concentrated blaze of energetic passion that made the fellow step back.

"I ain't goin' to get on the wrong side of the law by foolin' with this office," cried the other at the door, "but if I had you outside for a minute——"

"Leave this office!" shouted Thorpe.

"S'pose you make me!" challenged the man insolently.

In a moment the defiance had come, endangering the careful structure Thorpe had reared with such pains. The young man was suddenly angry in exactly the same blind, unreasoning manner as when he had leaped single-handed to tackle Dyer's crew.

Without a word he sprang across the shack, seized a two-bladed axe from the pile behind the door, swung it around his head and cast it full at the now frightened teamster. The latter dodged, and the swirling steel buried itself in the snowbank beyond.

Without an instant's hesitation Thorpe reached back for another. The man took to his heels.

"I don't want to see you around here again!" shouted Thorpe after him.

Then in a moment he returned to the office and sat down overcome with contrition.

"It might have been murder!" he told himself, awe-stricken.

But, as it happened, nothing could have turned out better.

Thorpe had instinctively seized the only method by which these strong men could be impressed. A rough-and-tumble attempt at ejectment would have been useless. Now the entire crew looked with vast admiration on their boss as a man who intended to have his own way no matter what difficulties or consequences might tend to deter him. And that is the kind of man they liked. This one deed was more effective in cementing their loyalty than any increase of wages would have been.

Thorpe knew that their restless spirits would soon tire of the monotony of work without ultimate interest. Ordinarily the hope of a big cut is sufficient to keep men of the right sort working for a record. But these men had no such hope—the camp was too small, and they were too few. Thorpe adopted the expedient, now quite common, of posting the results of each day's work in the men's shanty.

Three teams were engaged in travoying, and two

in skidding the logs, either on the banking ground, or along the road. Thorpe divided his camp into four sections, which he distinguished by the names of the teamsters. Roughly speaking, each of the three hauling teams had its own gang of sawyers and skidders to supply it with logs and to take them from it, for of the skidding teams, one was split;— the horses were big enough so that one of them to a skidway sufficed. Thus three gangs of men were performing each day practically the same work. Thorpe scaled the results, and placed them conspicuously for comparison.

Red Jacket, the teamster of the sorrels, one day was credited with 11,000 feet; while Long Pine Jim and Rollway Charley had put in but 10,500 and 10,250 respectively. That evening all the sawyers, swampers, and skidders belonging to Red Jacket's outfit were considerably elated; while the others said little and prepared for business on the morrow.

Once Long Pine Jim lurked at the bottom for three days. Thorpe happened by the skidway just as Long Pine arrived with a log. The young fellow glanced solicitously at the splendid buckskins, the best horses in camp.

" I'm afraid I didn't give you a very good team, Jimmy," said he, and passed on.

That was all; but men of the rival gangs had heard. In camp Long Pine Jim and his crew received chaffing with balefully red glares. Next day they stood at the top by a good margin, and always after were competitors to be feared.

Injin Charley, silent and enigmatical as ever, had constructed a log shack near a little creek over in the hardwood. There he attended diligently to the business of trapping. Thorpe had brought him a deer knife from Detroit; a beautiful instrument made of the best tool steel, in one long piece extending through the buck-horn handle. One could even break bones with it. He had also lent the Indian the assistance of two of his Marquette men in erecting the shanty; and had given him a barrel of flour for the winter. From time to time Injin Charley brought in fresh meat, for which he was paid. This with his trapping, and his manufacture of moccasins, snowshoes and birch canoes, made him a very prosperous Indian indeed. Thorpe rarely found time to visit him, but he often glided into the office, smoked a pipeful of the white man's tobacco in friendly fashion by the stove, and glided out again without having spoken a dozen words.

Wallace made one visit before the big snows came, and was charmed. He ate with gusto of the "salt-horse," baked beans, stewed prunes, mince pie, and cakes. He tramped around gaily in his moccasins or on the fancy snowshoes he promptly purchased of Injin Charley. There was nothing new to report in regard to financial matters. The loan had been negotiated easily on the basis of a mortgage guaranteed by Carpenter's personal signature. Nothing had been heard from Morrison & Daly.

When he departed, he left behind him four little long-eared, short-legged beagle hounds. They were solemn animals, who took life seriously. Never a smile appeared in their questioning eyes. Wherever one went, the others followed, pattering gravely along in serried ranks. Soon they discovered that the swamp over the knoll contained big white hares. Their mission in life was evident. Thereafter from the earliest peep of daylight until the men quit work at night they chased rabbits. The quest was hopeless, but they kept obstinately at it, wallowing with contained excitement over a hundred paces of snow before they would get near enough to scare their quarry to another jump. It used to amuse the hares. All day long the mellow bell-tones echoed over the knoll. It came in time to be part of the color of the camp, just as were the pines and birches, or the cold northern sky. At the fall of night, exhausted, trailing their long ears almost to the ground, they returned to the cook, who fed them and made much of them. Next morning they were at it as hard as ever. To them it was the quest for the Grail—hopeless, but glorious.

Little Phil, entrusted with the alarm clock, was the first up in the morning. In the fearful biting cold of an extinct camp, he lighted his lantern and with numb hands raked the ashes from the stove. A few sticks of dried pine topped by split wood of birch or maple, all well dashed with kerosene, took the flame eagerly. Then he awakened the cook, and stole silently into the office, where Thorpe and Shearer and Andrews, the surveyor, lay asleep. There quietly he built another fire, and filled the water-pail afresh. By the time this task was finished, the cook sounded many times a conch, and the sleeping camp awoke.

Later Phil drew water for the other shanties, swept out all three, split wood and carried it in to the cook and to the living-camps, filled and trimmed the lamps, perhaps helped the cook. About half the remainder of the day he wielded an axe, saw and wedge in the hardwood, collecting painfully—for his strength was not great—material for the constant fires it was his duty to maintain. Often he would stand motionless in the vast frozen, creaking forest, listening with awe to the voices which spoke to him alone. There was something uncanny in the misshapen dwarf with the fixed marble-white face and the expressive changing eyes—something uncanny, and something indefinably beautiful.

He seemed to possess an instinct which warned him of the approach of wild animals. Long before a white man, or even an Indian, would have suspected the presence of game, little Phil would lift his head with a peculiar listening toss. Soon, stepping daintily through the snow near the swamp edge, would come a deer; or pat-apat-patting on his broad hairy paws, a lynx would steal by. Except Injin Charley, Phil was the only man in that country who ever saw a beaver in the open daylight.

At camp sometimes when all the men were away and his own work was done, he would crouch like a raccoon in the far corner of his deep square bunk with the board ends that made of it a sort of little cabin, and play to himself softly on his violin. No one ever heard him. After supper he was docilely ready to fiddle to the men's dancing. Always then he gradually worked himself to a certain pitch of excitement. His eyes glared with the wolf-gleam, and the music was vulgarly atrocious and out of tune.

As Christmas drew near, the weather increased in severity. Blinding snow-squalls swept whirling from the northeast, accompanied by a high wind. The air was full of it—fine, dry, powdery, like the dust of glass. The men worked covered with it as a tree is covered after a sleet. Sometimes it was impossible to work at all for hours at a time; but Thorpe did not allow a bad morning to spoil a good afternoon. The instant a lull fell on the storm, he was out with his scaling rule, and he expected the men to give him something to scale. He grappled the fierce winter by the throat, and shook from it the price of success.

THE BLAZING OF THE TRAIL

Then came a succession of bright cold days and clear cold nights. The aurora gleamed so brilliantly that the forest was as bright as by moonlight. In the strange weird shadow cast by its waverings the wolves stole silently, or broke into wild ululations as they struck the trail of game. Except for these weird invaders, the silence of death fell on the wilderness. Deer left the country. Partridges crouched trailing under the snow. All the weak and timid creatures of the woods shrank into concealment and silence before these fierce woods-marauders with the glaring famine-struck eyes.

Injin Charley found his traps robbed. In return he constructed deadfalls, and dried several scalps. When spring came, he would send them out for the bounty. In the night, from time to time, the horses would awake trembling at an unknown terror. Then the long weird howl would shiver across the starlight near at hand, and the chattering man who rose hastily to quiet the horses' frantic kicking would catch a glimpse of gaunt forms skirting the edge of the forest.

And the little beagles were disconsolate, for their quarry had fled. In place of the fan-shaped triangular trail for which they sought, they came upon dog-like prints. These they sniffed at curiously, and then departed growling, the hair on their backbones erect and stiff.

CHAPTER THIRTY-TWO

BY the end of the winter some four million feet of logs were piled in the bed or upon the banks of the stream. To understand what that means, you must imagine a pile of solid timber a mile in length. This tremendous mass lay directly in the course of the stream. When the winter broke up, it had to be separated and floated piecemeal down the current. The process is an interesting and dangerous one, and one of great delicacy. It requires for its successful completion picked men of skill, and demands as toll its yearly quota of cripples and dead. While on the drive, men work fourteen hours a day, up to their waists in water filled with floating ice.

On the Ossawinamakee, as has been stated, three dams had been erected to simplify the process of driving. When the logs were in right distribution, the gates were raised, and the proper head of water floated them down.

Now the river being navigable, Thorpe was possessed of certain rights on it. Technically he was entitled to a normal head of water, whenever he needed it; or a special head, according to agreement 'vith the parties owning the dam. Early in the drive, he found that Morrison & Daly intended to cause him trouble. It began in a narrows of the river between high, rocky banks. Thorpe's drive was floating through close-packed. The situation was ticklish. Men with spiked boots ran here and there from one bobbing log to another, pushing with their peaveys, hurrying one log, retarding another, working like beavers to keep the whole mass straight. The entire surface of the water was practically covered with the floating timbers. A moment's reflection will show the importance of preserving a full head of water. The moment the stream should drop an inch or so, its surface would contract, the logs would then be drawn close together in the narrow space; and, unless an immediate rise should lift them up and apart from each other, a jam would form, behind which the water, rapidly damming, would press to entangle it the more.

This is exactly what happened. In a moment, as though by magic, the loose wooden carpet ground together. A log in the advance up-ended; another thrust under it. The whole mass ground together, stopped, and began rapidly to pile up. The men escaped to the shore in a marvellous manner of their own.

Tim Shearer found that the gate at the dam above had been closed. The man in charge had simply obeyed orders. He supposed M. & D. wished to back up the water for their own logs.

Tim indulged in some picturesque language.

"You ain't got no right to close off more'n enough to leave us th' nat'ral flow unless by agreement," he concluded, and opened the gates.

Then it was a question of breaking the jam. This had to be done by pulling out or chopping through certain "key" logs which locked the whole mass. Men stood under the face of imminent ruin—over them a frowning sheer wall of bristling logs, behind which pressed the weight of the rising waters—and hacked and tugged calmly until the mass began to stir. Then they escaped. A moment later, with a roar, the jam vomited down on the spot where they had stood. It was dangerous work. Just one half day later it had to be done again, and for the same reason.

This time Thorpe went back with Shearer. No one was at the dam, but the gates were closed. The two opened them again.

That very evening a man rode up on horseback inquiring for Mr. Thorpe.

"I'm he," said the young fellow.

The man thereupon dismounted and served a paper. It proved to be an injunction issued by Judge Sherman enjoining Thorpe against interfering with the property of Morrison & Daly—to wit, certain dams erected at designated points on the Ossawinamakee. There had not elapsed sufficient time since the commission of the offense for the other firm to secure the issuance of this interesting document, so it was at once evident that the whole affair had been prearranged by the up-river firm for the purpose of blocking off Thorpe's drive. After serving the injunction, the official rode away.

Thorpe called his foreman. The latter read the injunction attentively through a pair of steel-bowed spectacles.

"Well, what are you going to do?" he asked.

"Of all the consummate gall!" exploded Thorpe. "Trying to enjoin me from touching a dam when they're refusing me the natural flow! They must have bribed that fool judge. Why, his injunction isn't worth the powder to blow it up!"

"Then you're all right, ain't ye?" inquired Tim.

"It'll be the middle of summer before we get a hearing in court," said he. "Oh, they're a cute layout! They expect to hang me up until it's too late to do anything with the season's cut!"

He arose and began to pace back and forth.

"Tim," said he, "is there a man in the crew who's afraid of nothing and will obey orders?"

"A dozen," replied Tim promptly.

"Who's the best?"

"Scotty Parsons."

"Ask him to step here."

In a moment the man entered the office.

"Scotty," said Thorpe, "I want you to understand that I stand responsible for whatever I order you to do."

"All right, sir," replied the man.

"In the morning," said Thorpe, "you take two men and build some sort of a shack right over the sluice-gate of that second dam—nothing very fancy, but good enough to camp in. I want you to live there day and night. Never leave it, not even for a minute. The cookee will bring you grub. Take this Winchester. If any of the men from up-river try to go out on the dam, you warn them off. If they persist, you shoot near them. If they keep coming, you shoot *at* them. Understand?"

"You bet," answered Scotty with enthusiasm.

"All right," concluded Thorpe.

Next day Scotty established himself, as had been agreed. He did not need to shoot anybody. Daly himself came down to investigate the state of affairs, when his men reported to him the occupancy of the dam. He attempted to parley, but Scotty would have none of it.

"Get out!" was his first and last word.

Daly knew men. He was at the wrong end of the whip. Thorpe's game was desperate, but so was his need, and this was a backwoods country a long ways from the little technicalities of the law. It was one thing to serve an injunction; another to enforce it. Thorpe finished his drive with no more of the diffi-culties than ordinarily bother a riverman.

At the mouth of the river, booms of logs chained together at the ends had been prepared. Into the enclosure the drive was floated and stopped. Then a raft was formed by passing new manila ropes over the logs, to each one of which the line was fastened by a hardwood forked pin driven astride of it. A tug dragged the raft to Marquette.

Now Thorpe was summoned legally on two counts. First, Judge Sherman cited him for contempt of court. Second, Morrison & Daly sued him for alleged damages in obstructing their drive by holding open the dam-sluice beyond the legal head of water.

Such is a brief but true account of the *coup-de-force* actually carried out by Thorpe's lumbering firm in northern Michigan. It is better known to the craft than to the public at large, because eventually the affair was compromised. The manner of that compromise is to follow.

CHAPTER THIRTY-THREE

PENDING the call of trial, Thorpe took a three weeks' vacation to visit his sister. Time, filled with excitement and responsibility, had erased from his mind the bitterness of their parting. He had before been too busy, too grimly in earnest, to allow himself the luxury of anticipation. Now he found himself so impatient that he could hardly wait to get there. He pictured their meeting, the things they would say to each other.

As formerly, he learned on his arrival that she was not at home. It was the penalty of an attempted surprise. Mrs. Renwick proved not nearly so cordial as the year before; but Thorpe, absorbed in his eagerness, did not notice it. If he had, he might have guessed the truth: that the long propinquity of the fine and the commonplace, however safe at first from the insulation of breeding and natural kindliness, was at last beginning to generate sparks.

No, Mrs. Renwick did not know where Helen was: thought she had gone over to the Hughes's. The Hughes live two blocks down the street and three to the right, in a brown house back from the street. Very well, then; she would expect Mr. Thorpe to spend the night.

The latter wandered slowly down the charming driveways of the little western town. The broad dusty street was brown with sprinkling from numberless garden hose. A double row of big soft maples met over it, and shaded the sidewalk and part of the wide lawns. The grass was fresh and green. Houses with capacious verandas on which were glimpsed easy chairs and hammocks, sent forth a mild glow from a silk-shaded lamp or two. Across the evening air floated the sounds of light conversation and laughter from these verandas, the tinkle of a banjo, the thrum of a guitar. Automatic sprinklers whirled and hummed here and there. Their delicious artificial coolness struck refreshingly against the cheek.

Thorpe found the Hughes residence without difficulty, and turned up the straight walk to the veranda. On the steps of the latter a rug had been spread. A dozen youths and maidens lounged in well-bred ease on its soft surface. The gleam of white summer dresses, of variegated outing clothes, the rustle of frocks, the tinkle of low, well-bred laughter confused Thorpe, so that, as he approached the light from a tall lamp just inside the hall, he hesitated, vainly trying to make out the figures before him.

So it was that Helen Thorpe saw him first, and came fluttering to meet him.

"O Harry! What a surprise!" she cried, and flung her arms about his neck to kiss him.

"How do you do, Helen," he replied sedately.

This was the meeting he had anticipated so long. The presence of others brought out in him, irresistibly, the repression of public display which was so strong an element of his character.

A little chilled, Helen turned to introduce him to her friends. In the cold light of her commonplace reception she noticed what in a warmer effusion of feelings she would never have seen—that her brother's clothes were out of date and worn; and that, though his carriage was notably strong and graceful, the trifling constraint and dignity of his younger days had become almost an awkwardness after two years among uncultivated men. It occurred to Helen to be just a little ashamed of him.

He took a place on the steps and sat without saying a word all the evening. There was nothing for him to say. These young people talked thoughtlessly, as young people do, of the affairs belonging to their own little circle. Thorpe knew nothing of the cotillion, or the brake ride, or of the girl who visited Alice Southerland; all of which gave occasion for so much lively comment. Nor was the situation improved when some of them, in a noble effort at politeness turned the conversation into more general channels. The topics of the day's light talk were absolutely unknown to him. The plays, the new books, the latest popular songs, jokes depending for their point on an intimate knowledge of the prevailing vaudeville mode, were as unfamiliar to him as Miss Alice Southerland's guest. He had thought pine and forest and the trail so long, that he found these square-elbowed subjects refusing to be jostled aside by any trivialities.

So he sat there silent in the semi-darkness. This man, whose lightest experience would have aroused the eager attention of the entire party, held his peace because he thought he had nothing to say.

He took Helen back to Mrs. Renwick's about ten o'clock. They walked slowly beneath the broad-leaved maples, whose shadows danced under the tall electric lights—and talked.

Helen was an affectionate, warm-hearted girl. Ordinarily she would have been blind to everything except the delight of having her brother once more with her. But his apparently cold reception had first chilled, then thrown her violently into a critical mood. His subsequent social inadequacy had settled her into the common-sense level of everyday life.

"How have you done, Harry?" she inquired anxiously. "Your letters have been so vague."

"Pretty well," he replied. "If things go right, I hope some day to have a better place for you than this."

Her heart contracted suddenly. It was all she could do to keep from bursting into tears. One would have to realize perfectly her youth, the life to which she had been accustomed, the lack of encouragement she had labored under, the distastefulness of her surroundings, the pent-up dogged patience she had displayed during the last two years, the hopeless feeling of battering against a brick wall she always experienced when she received the replies to her attempts on Harry's confidence, to appreciate how the indefiniteness of his answer exasperated her and filled her with sullen despair. She said nothing for twenty steps. Then:

"Harry," she said quietly, "can't you take me away from Mrs. Renwick's this year?"

"I don't know, Helen. I can't tell yet. Not just now, at any rate."

"Harry," she cried, "you don't know what you're doing. I tell you I can't *stand* Mrs. Renwick any longer." She calmed herself with an effort, and went on more quietly. "Really, Harry, she's awfully disagreeable. If you can't afford to keep me anywhere else—" she glanced timidly at his face and for the first time saw the strong lines about the jaw and the tiny furrows between the eyebrows. "I know you've worked hard, Harry dear," she said with a sudden sympathy, "and that you'd give me more, if you could. But so have I worked hard. Now we ought to change this in some way. I can get a position as teacher, or some other work some-where. Won't you let me do that?"

Thorpe was thinking that it would be easy enough to obtain Wallace Carpenter's consent to his taking a thousand dollars from the profits of the year. But he knew also that the struggle in the courts might need every cent the new company could spare. It would look much better were he to wait until after the verdict. If favorable, there would be no diffi-culty about sparing the money. If adverse, there would be no money to spare. The latter contingency he did not seriously anticipate, but still it had to be considered. And so, until the thing was absolutely certain, he hesitated to explain the situation to Helen for fear of disappointing her!

"I think you'd better wait, Helen," said he. "There'll be time enough for all that later when it becomes necessary. You are very young yet, and it will not hurt you a bit to continue your education for a little while longer."

"And in the meantime stay with Mrs. Ren-wick?" flashed Helen.

"Yes. I hope it will not have to be for very long."

"How long do you think, Harry?" pleaded the girl.

"That depends on circumstances," replied Thorpe.

"Oh!" she cried indignantly.

"Harry," she ventured after a time, "why not write to Uncle Amos?"

Thorpe stopped and looked at her searchingly.

"You can't mean that, Helen," he said, drawing a long breath.

"But why not?" she persisted.

"You ought to know."

"Who would have done any different? If you had a brother and discovered that he had—appropriated—most all the money of a concern of which you were president, wouldn't you think it your duty to have him arrested?"

"No!" cried Thorpe suddenly excited. "Never! If he was my brother, I'd help him, even if he'd committed murder!"

"We differ there," replied the girl coldly. "I consider that Uncle Amos was a strong man who did his duty as he saw it, in spite of his feelings. That he had father arrested is nothing against him in my eyes. And his wanting us to come to him since seems to me very generous. I am going to write to him."

"You will do nothing of the kind," commanded Thorpe sternly. "Amos Thorpe is an unscrupulous man who became unscrupulously rich. He deliberately used our father as a tool, and then destroyed him. I consider that any one of our family who would have anything to do with him is a traitor!"

The girl did not reply.

Next morning Thorpe felt uneasily repentant for his strong language. After all, the girl did lead a monotonous life, and he could not blame her for rebelling against it from time to time. Her remarks had been born of the rebellion; they had meant nothing in themselves. He could not doubt for a moment her loyalty to the family.

But he did not tell her so. That is not the way of men of his stamp. Rather he cast about to see what he could do.

Injin Charley had, during the winter just past, occupied odd moments in embroidering with beads and porcupine quills a wonderful outfit of soft buckskin gauntlets, a shirt of the same material, and moccasins of moose-hide. They were beautifully worked, and Thorpe, on receiving them, had at once conceived the idea of giving them to his sister. To this end he had consulted another Indian near Marquette, to whom he had confided the task of reducing the gloves and moccasins. The shirt would do as it was, for it was intended to be worn as a sort of belted blouse. As has been said, all were thickly beaded, and represented a vast quantity of work. Probably fifty dollars could not have bought them, even in the north country.

Thorpe tendered this as a peace offering. Not understanding women in the least, he was surprised to see his gift received by a burst of tears and a sudden exit from the room. Helen thought he had bought the things; and she was still sore from the pinch of the poverty she had touched the evening before. Nothing will exasperate a woman more than to be presented with something expensive for which she does not particularly care, after being denied, on the ground of economy, something she wants very much.

Thorpe stared after her in hurt astonishment. Mrs. Renwick sniffed.

That afternoon the latter estimable lady attempted to reprove Miss Helen, and was snubbed; she persisted, and an open quarrel ensued.

"I will not be dictated to by you, Mrs. Renwick," said Helen, "and I don't intend to have you interfere in any way with my family affairs."

"They won't stand *much* investigation," replied Mrs. Renwick, goaded out of her placidity.

Thorpe entered to hear the last two speeches. He said nothing, but that night he wrote to Wallace Carpenter for a thousand dollars. Every stroke of the pen hurt him. But of course Helen could not stay here now.

"And to think, just to *think* that he let that woman insult me so, and didn't say a word!" cried Helen to herself.

Her method would have been to have acted irrevocably on the spot, and sought ways and means afterward. Thorpe's, however, was to perfect all his plans before making the first step.

Wallace Carpenter was not in town. Before the letter had followed him to his new address, and the answer had returned, a week had passed. Of course the money was gladly put at Thorpe's disposal. The latter at once interviewed his sister.

"Helen," he said, "I have made arrangements for some money. What would you like to do this year?"

She raised her head and looked at him with clear bright gaze. If he could so easily raise the money, why had he not done so before? He knew how much she wanted it. Her happiness did not count. Only when his quixotic ideas of family honor were attacked did he bestir himself.

"I am going to Uncle Amos's," she replied distinctly.

"What?" asked Thorpe incredulously.

For answer she pointed to a letter lying open on the table. Thorpe took it and read:

"My dear Niece:

"Both Mrs. Thorpe and myself more than rejoice that time and reflection have removed that, I must confess, natural prejudice which the unfortunate family affair, to which I will not allude, raised in your mind against us. As we said long ago, our home is yours when you may wish to make it so. You state your present readiness to come immediately. Unless you wire to the contrary, we shall expect you next Tuesday evening on the four:forty train. I shall be at the Central Station myself to meet you. If your brother is now with you, I should be pleased to see him also, and will be most happy to give him a position with the firm.

> "Aff. your uncle,
>
> "Amos Thorpe.

"New York, June 6, 1883."

On finishing the last paragraph the reader crumpled the letter and threw it into the grate.

"I am sorry you did that, Helen," said he, "but I don't blame you, and it can't be helped. We won't need to take advantage of his 'kind offer' now."

"I intend to do so, however," replied the girl coldly.

"What do you mean?"

"I mean," she cried, "that I am sick of waiting on your good pleasure. I waited, and slaved, and stood unbearable things for two years. I did it cheerfully. And in return I don't get a civil word, not a decent explanation, not even a—caress," she fairly sobbed out the last word. "I can't stand it any longer. I have tried and tried and tried, and then when I've come to you for the littlest word of encouragement, you have pecked at me with those stingy little kisses, and have told me I was young and ought to finish my education! You put me in uncongenial surroundings, and go off into the woods camping yourself. You refuse me money enough to live in a three-dollar boarding-house, and you buy expensive rifles and fishing tackle for yourself. You can't afford to send me away somewhere for the summer, but you bring me back gee-gaws you have happened to fancy, worth a month's board in the country. You haven't a cent when it is a question of what *I* want; but you raise money quick enough when your old family is insulted. Isn't it my family too? And then you blame me because, after waiting in vain two years for you to do something, I start out to do the best I can for myself. I'm not of age; but you're not my guardian!"

During this long speech Thorpe had stood motionless, growing paler and paler. Like most noble natures, when absolutely in the right, he was incapable of defending himself against misunderstandings. He was too wounded; he was hurt to the soul.

"You know that is not true, Helen," he replied, almost sternly.

"It *is* true!" she asseverated, "and I'm *through*!"

"It's a little hard," said Thorpe, passing his hand wearily before his eyes, "to work hard this way for years, and then——"

She laughed with a hard little note of scorn.

"Helen," said Thorpe with new energy, "I forbid you to have anything to do with Amos Thorpe. I think he is a scoundrel and a sneak."

"What grounds have you to think so?"

"None," he confessed, "that is, nothing definite. But I know men; and I know his type. Some day I shall be able to prove something. I do not wish you to have anything to do with him."

"I shall do as I please," she replied, crossing her hands behind her.

Thorpe's eyes darkened.

"We have talked this over a great many times," he warned, "and you've always agreed with me. Remember, you owe something to the family."

"Most of the family seem to owe something," she replied with a flippant laugh. "I'm sure I didn't choose the family. If I had, I'd have picked out a better one!"

The flippancy was only a weapon which she used unconsciously, blindly, in her struggle. The man could not know this. His face hardened, and his voice grew cold.

"You may take your choice, Helen," he said formally. "If you go into the household of Amos Thorpe, if you deliberately prefer your comfort to your honor, we will have nothing more in common."

They faced each other with the cool, deadly glance of the race, so similar in appearance but so unlike in nature.

"I, too, offer you a home, such as it is," repeated the man. "Choose!"

At the mention of the home for which means were

so quickly forthcoming when Thorpe, not she, considered it needful, the girl's eyes flashed. She stooped and dragged violently from beneath the bed a flat steamer trunk, the lid of which she threw open. A dress lay on the bed. With a fine dramatic gesture she folded the garment and laid it in the bottom of the trunk. Then she knelt, and without vouchsafing another glance at her brother standing rigid by the door, she began feverishly to arrange the folds.

The choice was made. He turned and went out.

CHAPTER THIRTY-FOUR

WITH Thorpe there could be no half-way measure. He saw that the rupture with his sister was final, and the thrust attained him in one of his unprotected points. It was not as though he felt either himself or his sister consciously in the wrong. He acquitted her of all fault, except as to the deadly one of misreading and misunderstanding. The fact argued not a perversion but a lack in her character. She was other than he had thought her.

As for himself, he had schemed, worked, lived only for her. He had come to her from the battle expecting rest and refreshment. To the world he had shown the hard, unyielding front of the unemotional; he had looked ever keenly outward; he had braced his muscles in the constant tension of endeavor. So much the more reason why, in the hearts of the few he loved, he, the man of action, should find repose; the man of sternness should discover that absolute peace of the spirit in which not the slightest motion of the will is necessary; the man of repression should be permitted affectionate, care-free expansion of the natural affection, of the full sympathy which will understand and not mistake for weakness. Instead of this, he was forced into refusing where he would rather have given; into denying where he would rather have assented; and finally into commanding where he longed most ardently to lay aside the cloak of authority. His motives were misread; his intentions misjudged; his love doubted.

But worst of all, Thorpe's mind could see no possibility of an explanation. If she could not see of her own accord how much he loved her, surely it was a hopeless task to attempt an explanation through mere words. If, after all, she was capable of misconceiving the entire set of his motives during the past two years, expostulation would be futile. In his thoughts of her he fell into a great spiritual dumbness. Never, even in his moments of most theoretical imaginings, did he see himself setting before her fully and calmly the hopes and ambitions of which she had been the mainspring. And before a reconciliation, many such rehearsals must take place in the secret recesses of a man's being.

Thorpe did not cry out, nor confide in a friend, nor do anything even so mild as pacing the floor. The only outward and visible sign a close observer might have noted was a certain dumb pain lurking in the depths of his eyes like those of a wounded spaniel. He was hurt, but did not understand. He suffered in silence, but without anger. This is at once the noblest and the most pathetic of human suffering.

At first the spring of his life seemed broken. He did not care for money; and at present disappointment had numbed his interest in the game. It seemed hardly worth the candle.

Then in a few days, after his thoughts had ceased to dwell constantly on the one subject, he began to look about him mentally. Beneath his other interests he still felt constantly a dull ache, something unpleasant, uncomfortable. Strangely enough it was almost identical in quality with the uneasiness that always underlay his surface-thoughts when he was worried about some detail of his business. Unconsciously—again as in his business—the combative instinct aroused. In lack of other object on which to expend itself, Thorpe's fighting spirit turned with energy to the subject of the lawsuit.

Under the unwonted stress of the psychological condition just described, he thought at white heat. His ideas were clear, and followed each other quickly, almost feverishly.

After his sister left the Renwicks, Thorpe himself went to Detroit, where he interviewed at once Northrop, the brilliant young lawyer whom the firm had engaged to defend its case.

"I'm afraid we have no show," he replied to Thorpe's question. "You see, you fellows were on the wrong side of the fence in trying to enforce the law yourselves. Of course you may well say that justice was all on your side. That does not count. The only recourse recognized for injustice lies in the law courts. I'm afraid you are due to lose your case."

"Well," said Thorpe, "they can't prove much damage."

"I don't expect that they will be able to procure a very heavy judgment," replied Northrop. "The facts I shall be able to adduce will cut down damages. But the costs will be very heavy."

"Yes," agreed Thorpe.

"And," then pursued Northrop with a dry smile, "they practically own Sherman. You may be in for contempt of court—at their instigation. As I understand it, they are trying rather to injure you than to get anything out of it themselves."

"That's it," nodded Thorpe.

"In other words, it's a case for compromise."

"Just what I wanted to get at," said Thorpe with satisfaction. "Now answer me a question. Suppose a man injures Government or State land by trespass. The land is afterward bought by another party. Has the latter any claim for damage against the trespasser? Understand me, the purchaser bought *after* the trespass was committed."

"Certainly," answered Northrop without hesitation. "Provided suit is brought within six years of the time the trespass was committed."

"Good! Now see here. These M. & D. people stole about a section of Government pine up on that river, and I don't believe they've ever bought in the land it stood on. In fact I don't believe they suspect that any one knows they've been stealing. How would it do, if I were to buy that section at the Land Office, and threaten to sue them for the value of the pine that originally stood on it?"

The lawyer's eyes glimmered behind the lenses of his pince-nez; but, with the caution of the professional man he made no other sign of satisfaction.

"It would do very well indeed," he replied, "but you'd have to prove they did the cutting, and you'll have to pay experts to estimate the probable amount of the timber. Have you the description of the section?"

"No," responded Thorpe, "but I can get it; and I can pick up witnesses from the woodsmen as to the cutting."

"The more the better. It is rather easy to discredit the testimony of one or two. How much, on a broad guess, would you estimate the timber to come to?"

"There ought to be about eight or ten million," guessed Thorpe after an instant's silence, "worth in the stump anywhere from sixteen to twenty thousand dollars. It would cost me only eight hundred to buy it."

"Do so, by all means. Get your documents and

evidence all in shape, and let me have them. I'll see that the suit is discontinued then. Will you sue them?"

"No, I think not," replied Thorpe. "I'll just hold it back as a sort of club to keep them in line."

The next day, he took the train north. He had something definite and urgent to do, and, as always with practical affairs demanding attention and resource, he threw himself whole-souled into the accomplishment of it. By the time he had bought the sixteen forties constituting the section, searched out a dozen witnesses to the theft, and spent a week with the Marquette expert in looking over the ground, he had fallen into the swing of work again. His experience still ached; but dully.

Only now he possessed no interests outside of those in the new country; no affections save the half-protecting, good-natured comradeship with Wallace, the mutual self-reliant respect that subsisted between Tim Shearer and himself, and the dumb, unreasoning dog-liking he shared with Injin Charley. His eye became clearer and steadier; his methods more simple and direct. The taciturnity of his mood redoubled in thickness. He was less charitable to failure on the part of subordinates. And the new firm on the Ossawinamakee prospered.

CHAPTER THIRTY-FIVE

FIVE years passed.

In that time Thorpe had succeeded in cutting a hundred million feet of pine. The money received for this had all been turned back into the Company's funds. From a single camp of twenty-five men, with ten horses and a short haul of half a mile, the concern had increased to six large, well-equipped communities of eighty to a hundred men apiece, using nearly two hundred horses, and hauling as far as eight or nine miles.

Near the port stood a mammoth sawmill capable of taking care of twenty-two million feet a year, about which a lumber town had sprung up. Lake schooners lay in a long row during the summer months, while busy loaders passed the planks from one to the other into the deep holds. Besides its original holding, the company had acquired about a hundred and fifty million more, back near the headwaters of tributaries to the Ossawinamakee. In the spring and early summer months, the drive was a wonderful affair.

During the four years in which the Morrison & Daly Company shared the stream with Thorpe, the two firms lived in complete amity and understanding. Northrop had played his cards skillfully. The older capitalists had withdrawn suit. Afterward they kept scrupulously within their rights, and saw to it that no more careless openings were left for Thorpe's shrewdness. They were keen enough business men, but had made the mistake, common enough to established power, of underrating the strength of an apparently insignificant opponent. Once they understood Thorpe's capacity, that young man had no more chance to catch them napping.

And as the younger man, on his side, never attempted to overstep his own rights, the interests of the rival firms rarely clashed. As to the few disputes that did arise, Thorpe found Mr. Daly singularly anxious to please. In the desire was no friendliness, however. Thorpe was watchful for treachery, and could hardly believe the affair finished when at the end of the fourth year the M. & D. sold out the remainder of its pine to a firm from Manistee, and transferred its operations to another stream a few miles east, where it had acquired more considerable holdings.

"They're altogether too confounded anxious to help us on that freight, Wallace," said Thorpe wrinkling his brow uneasily. "I don't like it. It isn't natural."

"No," laughed Wallace, "neither is it natural for a dog to draw a sledge. But he does it—when he has to. They're afraid of you, Harry: that's all."

Thorpe shook his head, but had to acknowledge that he could evidence no grounds for his mistrust.

The conversation took place at Camp One, which was celebrated in three states. Thorpe had set out to gather around him a band of good woodsmen. Except on a pinch he would employ no others.

" I don't care if I get in only two thousand feet this winter, and if a boy does that," he answered Shearer's expostulations, " it's got to be a good boy."

The result of his policy began to show even in the second year. Men were a little proud to say that they had put in a winter at " Thorpe's One." Those who had worked there during the first year were loyally enthusiastic over their boss's grit and resourcefulness, their camp's order, their cook's good " grub." As they were authorities, others perforce had to accept the dictum. There grew a desire among the better class to see what Thorpe's " One " might be like. In the autumn Harry had more applicants than he knew what to do with. Eighteen of the old men returned. He took them all, but when it came to distribution, three found themselves assigned to one or the other of the new camps. And quietly the rumor gained that these three had shown the least willing spirit during the previous winter. The other fifteen were sobered to the industry which their importance as veterans might have impaired.

Tim Shearer was foreman of Camp One; Scotty Parsons was drafted from the veterans to take charge of Two; Thorpe engaged two men known to Tim to boss Three and Four. But in selecting the "push" for Five he displayed most strikingly his keen appreciation of a man's relation to his environment. He sought out John Radway and induced him to accept the commission.

"You can do it, John," said he, "and I know it. I want you to try; and if you don't make her go, I'll call it nobody's fault but my own."

"I don't see how you dare risk it, after that Cass Branch deal, Mr. Thorpe," replied Radway, almost brokenly. "But I would like to tackle it, I'm dead sick of loafing. Sometimes it seems like I'd die, if I don't get out in the woods again."

"We'll call it a deal, then," answered Thorpe.

The result proved his sagacity. Radway was one of the best foremen in the outfit. He got more out of his men, he rose better to emergencies, and he accomplished more with the same resources than any of the others, excepting Tim Shearer. As long as the work was done for some one else, he was capable and efficient. Only when he was called upon to demand on his own account did the paralyzing shyness affect him.

But the one feature that did more to attract the very best element among woodsmen, and so make possible the practice of Thorpe's theory of success, was Camp One. The men's accommodations at the other five were no different and but little better than those in a thousand other typical lumber camps of both peninsulas. They slept in box-like bunks filled with hay or straw over which blankets were spread; they sat on a narrow hard bench or on the floor; they read by the dim light of a lamp fastened against the big cross beam; they warmed themselves at a huge iron stove in the centre of the room around which suspended wires and poles offered space for the drying of socks; they washed their clothes when the mood struck them. It was warm and comparatively clean. But it was dark, without ornament, cheerless.

The lumber-jack never expects anything different. In fact, if he were pampered to the extent of ordinary comforts, he would be apt at once to conclude himself indispensable; whereupon he would become worthless.

Thorpe, however, spent a little money—not much —and transformed Camp One. Every bunk was provided with a tick, which the men could fill with hay, balsam, or hemlock, as suited them. Cheap but attractive curtains on wires at once brightened the room and shut each man's "bedroom" from the main hall. The deacon seat remained, but was supplemented by a half-dozen simple and comfortable chairs. In the centre of the room stood a big round table over which glowed two hanging lamps. The table was littered with papers and magazines. Home life was still further suggested by a canary bird in a gilt cage, a sleepy cat, and two pots of red geraniums. Thorpe had further imported a washer-woman who dwelt in a separate little cabin under the hill. She washed the men's belongings at twenty-five cents a week, which amount Thorpe deducted from each man's wages, whether he had the washing done or not. This encouraged cleanliness. Phil scrubbed out every day, while the men were in the woods.

Such was Thorpe's famous Camp One in the days of its splendor. Old woodsmen will still tell you about it, with a longing reminiscent glimmer in the corners of their eyes as they recall its glories and the men who worked in it. To have " put in " a winter in Camp One was the mark of a master; and the ambition of every raw recruit to the forest. Probably Thorpe's name is remembered to-day more on account of the intrepid, skillful, loyal men his strange genius gathered about it, than for the her-culean feat of having carved a great fortune from the wilderness in but five years' time.

But Camp One was a privilege. A man entered it only after having proved himself; he remained in it only as long as his efficiency deserved the honor. Its members were invariably recruited from one of the other four camps; never from applicants who had not been in Thorpe's employ. A raw man was sent to Scotty, or Jack Hyland, or Radway, or Kerlie. There he was given a job, if he happened to suit, and men were needed. By and by, perhaps, when a member of Camp One fell sick or was given his time, Tim Shearer would send word to one of the other five that he needed an axe-man or a sawyer, or a loader, or teamster, as the case might be. The best man in the other camps was sent up.

So Shearer was foreman of a picked crew. Probably no finer body of men was ever gathered at one camp. In them one could study at his best the American pioneer. It was said at that time that you had never seen logging done as it should be until you had visited Thorpe's Camp One on the Ossawinamakee.

Of these men Thorpe demanded one thing—success. He tried never to ask of them anything he did not believe to be thoroughly possible; but he expected always that in some manner, by hook or crook, they would carry the affair through. No matter how good the excuse, it was never accepted. Accidents would happen, there as elsewhere; a way to arrive in spite of them always exists, if only a man is willing to use his wits, unflagging energy, and time. Bad luck is a reality; but much of what is called bad luck is nothing but a want of careful foresight, and Thorpe could better afford to be harsh occasionally to the genuine for the sake of eliminating the false. If a man failed, he left Camp One.

The procedure was very simple. Thorpe never explained his reasons even to Shearer.

" Ask Tom to step in a moment," he requested of the latter.

" Tom," he said to that individual, " I think I can use you better at Four. Report to Kerlie there."

And strangely enough, few even of these proud and independent men ever asked for their time, or preferred to quit rather than to work up again to the glories of their prize camp.

For while new recruits were never accepted at Camp One, neither was a man ever discharged there. He was merely transferred to one of the other fore-men.

It is necessary to be thus minute in order that the reader may understand exactly the class of men Thorpe had about his immediate person. Some of them had the reputation of being the hardest citizens in three States, others were mild as turtle doves. They were all pioneers. They had the independ-ence, the unabashed eye, the insubordination even, of the man who has drawn his intellectual and moral nourishment at the breast of a wild nature. They were afraid of nothing alive. From no one, were he chore-boy or president, would they take a single word—with the exception always of Tim Shearer and Thorpe. The former they respected because in their picturesque guild he was a master craftsman. The latter they adored and quoted and fought for in distant saloons, because he represented to them their own ideal, what they would be if freed from the heavy gyves of vice and executive incapacity that weighed them down.

And they were loyal. It was a point of honor with them to stay "until the last dog was hung." He who deserted in the hour of need was not only a renegade, but a fool. For he thus earned a magnificent licking if ever he ran up against a member of the "Fighting Forty." A band of soldiers they were, ready to attempt anything their commander ordered, devoted, enthusiastically admiring. And, it must be confessed, they were also somewhat on the order of a band of pirates. Marquette thought so each spring after the drive, when, hat-tilted, they surged swearing and shouting down to Denny Hogan's saloon. Denny had to buy new fixtures when they went away; but it was worth it.

Proud! it was no name for it. Boast! the fame of Camp One spread abroad over the land, and was believed in to about twenty per cent. of the anecdotes detailed of it—which was near enough the actual truth. Anecdotes disbelieved, the class of men from it would have given it a reputation. The latter was varied enough, in truth. Some people thought Camp One must be a sort of hell-hole of roaring, fighting devils. Others sighed and made rapid calculations of the number of logs they could put in, if only they could get hold of help like that.

Thorpe himself, of course, made his headquarters at Camp One. Thence he visited at least once a week all the other camps, inspecting the minutest details, not only of the work, but of the every-day life. For this purpose he maintained a light box sleigh and a pair of bays, though often, when the snow became deep, he was forced to snowshoes.

During the five years he had never crossed the Straits of Mackinaw. The rupture with his sister had made repugnant to him all the southern country. He preferred to remain in the woods. All winter long he was more than busy at his logging. Summers he spent at the mill. Occasionally he visited Marquette, but always on business. He became used to seeing only the rough faces of men. The vision of softer graces and beauties lost its distinctness before this strong, hardy northland, whose gentler moods were like velvet over iron, or like its own summer leaves veiling the eternal darkness of the pines.

He was happy because he was too busy to be anything else. The insistent need of success which he had created for himself absorbed all other sentiments. He demanded it of others rigorously. He could do no less than demand it of himself. It had practically become one of his tenets of belief. The chief end of any man, as he saw it, was to do well and successfully what his life found ready. Anything to further this fore-ordained activity was good; anything else was bad. These thoughts, aided by a disposition naturally fervent and single in purpose, hereditarily ascetic and conscientious—for his mother was of old New England stock—gave to him in the course of six years' striving a sort of daily and familiar religion to which he conformed his life.

Success, success, success. Nothing could be of more importance. Its attainment argued a man's efficiency in the Scheme of Things, his worthy fulfillment of the end for which a divine Providence had placed him on earth. Anything that interfered with it—personal comfort, inclination, affection, desire, love of ease, individual liking—was bad.

Luckily for Thorpe's peace of mind, his habit of looking on men as things helped him keep to this attitude of mind. His lumbermen were tools—good, sharp, efficient tools, to be sure, but only because he had made them so. Their loyalty aroused in his breast no pride nor gratitude. He expected loyalty. He would have discharged at once a man who did not show it. The same with zeal, intelligence, effort—they were the things he took for granted. As for the admiration and affection which the Fighting Forty displayed for him personally, he gave not a thought to it. And the men knew it, and loved him the more from the fact.

Thorpe cared for just three people, and none of

them happened to clash with his machine. They were Wallace Carpenter, little Phil, and Injin Charley.

Wallace, for reasons already explained at length, was always personally agreeable to Thorpe. Latterly, since the erection of the mill, he had developed unexpected acumen in the disposal of the season's cut to wholesale dealers in Chicago. Nothing could have been better for the firm. Thereafter he was often in the woods, both for pleasure and to get his partner's ideas on what the firm would have to offer. The entire responsibility of the city end of the business was in his hands.

Injin Charley continued to hunt and trap in the country round about. Between him and Thorpe had grown a friendship the more solid in that its increase had been mysteriously without outward cause. Once or twice a month the lumberman would snowshoe down to the little cabin at the forks. Entering, he would nod briefly and seat himself on a cracker-box.

" How do, Charley," said he.

" How do," replied Charley.

They filled pipes and smoked. At rare intervals one of them made a remark, tersely.

" Catch um three beaver las' week," remarked Charley.

" Good haul," commented Thorpe.

Or:

"I saw a mink track by the big boulder," offered Thorpe.

"H'm!" responded Charley in a long-drawn falsetto whine.

Yet somehow the men came to know each other better and better; and each felt that in an emergency he could depend on the other to the uttermost in spite of the difference in race.

As for Phil, he was like some strange, shy animal, retaining all its wild instincts, but led by affection to become domestic. He drew the water, cut the wood—none better. In the evening he played atrociously his violin—none worse—bending his great white brow forward with the wolf-glare in his eyes, swaying his shoulders with a fierce delight in the subtle dissonances, the swaggering exactitude of time, the vulgar rendition of the horrible tunes he played. And often he went into the forest and gazed wondering through his liquid poet's eyes at occult things. Above all, he worshipped Thorpe. And in turn the lumberman accorded him a good-natured affection. He was as indispensable to Camp One as the beagles.

And the beagles were most indispensable. No one could have got along without them. In the course of events and natural selection they had increased to eleven. At night they slept in the men's camp underneath or very near the stove. By daylight in the morning they were clamoring at the door. Never had they caught a hare. Never for a moment did their hopes sink. The men used sometimes to amuse themselves by refusing the requested exit. The little dogs agonized. They leaped and yelped, falling over each other like a tangle of angleworms. Then finally, when the door at last flung wide, they precipitated themselves eagerly and silently through the opening. A few moments later a single yelp rose in the direction of the swamp; the band took up the cry. From then until dark the glade was musical with baying. At supper time they returned straggling, their expression pleased, six inches of red tongue hanging from the corners of their mouths, ravenously ready for supper.

Strangely enough the big white hares never left the swamp. Perhaps the same one was never chased two days in succession. Or it is possible that the quarry enjoyed the harmless game as much as did the little dogs.

Once only while the snow lasted was the hunt abandoned for a few days. Wallace Carpenter announced his intention of joining forces with the diminutive hounds.

" It's a shame, so it is, doggies! " he laughed at the tried pack. " We'll get one to-morrow."

So he took his shotgun to the swamp, and after a half-hour's wait, succeeded in killing the hare. From that moment he was the hero of those ecstasized canines. They tangled about him everywhere. He hardly dared take a step for fear of crushing one of the open faces and expectant, pleading eyes looking up at him. It grew to be a nuisance. Wallace always claimed his trip was considerably shortened because he could not get away from his admirers.

CHAPTER THIRTY-SIX

FINANCIALLY the Company was rated high, and yet was heavily in debt. This condition of affairs by no means constitutes an anomaly in the lumbering business.

The profits of the first five years had been immediately reinvested in the business. Thorpe, with the foresight that had originally led him into this new country, saw farther than the instant's gain. He intended to establish in a few years more a big plant which would be returning benefices in proportion not only to the capital originally invested, but also in ratio to the energy, time, and genius he had himself expended. It was not the affair of a moment. It was not the affair of half-measures, of timidity.

Thorpe knew that he could play safely, cutting a few millions a year, expanding cautiously. By this method he would arrive, but only after a long period.

Or he could do as many other firms have done; start on borrowed money.

In the latter case he had only one thing to fear, and that was fire. Every cent, and many times over, of his obligations would be represented in the state of raw material. All he had to do was to cut it out by the very means which the yearly profits of his business would enable him to purchase. For the moment, he owed a great deal; without the shadow of a doubt mere industry would clear his debt, and leave him with substantial acquisitions created, practically, from nothing but his own abilities. The money obtained from his mortgages was a tool which he picked up an instant, used to fashion one of his own, and laid aside.

Every autumn the Company found itself suddenly in easy circumstances. At any moment that Thorpe had chosen to be content with the progress made, he could have, so to speak, declared dividends with his partner. Instead of undertaking more improvements, for part of which he borrowed some money, he could have divided the profits of the season's cut. But this he was not yet ready to do.

He had established five more camps, he had acquired over a hundred and fifty million more of timber lying contiguous to his own, he had built and equipped a modern high-efficiency mill, he had constructed a harbor breakwater and the necessary booms, he had bought a tug, built a boarding-house. All this costs money. He wished now to construct a logging railroad. Then he promised himself and Wallace that they would be ready to commence paying operations.

just right he must doctor it up; or get some more, even if he has to steal it. If he has hard luck, he must sit up nights to better it. It's none of my concern how hard or how easy a time a man has in doing what I tell him to. *I expect him to do it.* If I have to do all a man's thinking for him, I may as well hire Swedes and be done with it. I have too many details to attend to already without bothering about excuses."

The man stood puzzling over this logic.

" I ain't got any other job," he ventured.

" You can go to piling on the docks," replied Thorpe, " if you want to."

Thorpe was thus explicit because he rather liked Herrick. It was hard for him to discharge the man peremptorily, and he proved the need of justifying himself in his own eyes.

Now he sat back idly in the clean painted little room with the big square desk and the three chairs. Through the door he could see Collins, perched on a high stool before the shelf-like desk. From the open window came the clear, musical note of the circular saw, the fresh aromatic smell of new lumber, the bracing air from Superior sparkling in the offing. He felt tired. In rare moments such as these, when the muscles of his striving relaxed, his mind turned to the past. Old sorrows rose before him and looked at him with their sad eyes; the sorrows that had helped to make him what he was. He wondered where his sister was. She would be twenty-two years old now. A tenderness, haunting, tearful, invaded his heart. He suffered. At such moments the hard shell of his rough woods life seemed to rend apart. He longed with a great longing for sympathy, for love, for the softer influences that cradle even warriors between the clangors of the battles.

The outer door, beyond the cage behind which Collins and his shelf desk were placed, flew open. Thorpe heard a brief greeting, and Wallace Carpenter stood before him.

"Why, Wallace, I didn't know you were coming!" began Thorpe, and stopped. The boy, usually so fresh and happily buoyant, looked ten years older. Wrinkles had gathered between his eyes. "Why, what's the matter?" cried Thorpe.

He rose swiftly and shut the door into the outer office. Wallace seated himself mechanically.

"Everything! everything!" he said in despair. "I've been a fool! I've been blind!"

So bitter was his tone that Thorpe was startled. The lumberman sat down on the other side of the desk.

"That'll do, Wallace," he said sharply. "Tell me briefly what is the matter."

"I've been speculating!" burst out the boy.

"Ah!" said his partner.

"At first I bought only dividend-paying stocks

outright. Then I bought for a rise, but still outright. Then I got in with a fellow who claimed to know all about it. I bought on a margin. There came a slump. I met the margins because I am sure there will be a rally, but now all my fortune is in the thing. I'm going to be penniless. I'll lose it all."

"Ah!" said Thorpe.

"And the name of Carpenter is so old-established, so honorable!" cried the unhappy boy, "and my sister!"

"Easy!" warned Thorpe. "Being penniless isn't the worst thing that can happen to a man.

"No; but I am in debt," went on the boy more calmly. "I have given notes. When they come due, I'm a goner."

"How much?" asked Thorpe laconically.

"Thirty thousand dollars."

"Well, you have that amount in this firm."

"What do you mean?"

"If you want it, you can have it."

Wallace considered a moment.

"That would leave me without a cent," he replied.

"But it would save your commercial honor."

"Harry," cried Wallace suddenly, "couldn't this firm go on my note for thirty thousand more? Its credit is good, and that amount would save my margins."

"You are partner," replied Thorpe, "your signature is as good as mine in this firm."

"But you know I wouldn't do it without your consent," replied Wallace reproachfully. "O Harry!" cried the boy, "when you needed the amount, I let you have it!"

Thorpe smiled.

"You know you can have it, if it's to be had, Wallace. I wasn't hesitating on that account. I was merely trying to figure out where we can raise such a sum as sixty thousand dollars. We haven't got it."

"But you'll never have to pay it," assured Wallace eagerly. "If I can save my margins, I'll be all right."

"A man has to figure on paying whatever he puts his signature to," asserted Thorpe. "I can give you our note payable at the end of a year. Then I'll hustle in enough timber to make up the amount. It means we don't get our railroad, that's all."

"I knew you'd help me out. Now it's all right," said Wallace, with a relieved air.

Thorpe shook his head. He was already trying to figure how to increase his cut to thirty million feet.

"I'll do it," he muttered to himself, after Wallace had gone out to visit the mill. "I've been demanding success of others for a good many years; now I'll demand it of myself."

336

PART IV
THORPE'S DREAM GIRL

CHAPTER THIRTY-SEVEN

THE moment had struck for the woman. Thorpe did not know it, but it was true. A solitary, brooding life in the midst of grand surroundings, an active, strenuous life among great responsibilities, a starved, hungry life of the affections whence even the sister had withdrawn her love—all these had worked unobtrusively toward the formation of a single psychological condition. Such a moment comes to every man. In it he realizes the beauties, the powers, the vastnesses which unconsciously his being has absorbed. They rise to the surface as a need, which, being satisfied, is projected into the visible world as an ideal to be worshipped. Then is happiness and misery, beside which the mere struggle to dominate men becomes trivial, the petty striving with the forces of nature seems a little thing. And the woman he at that time meets takes on the qualities of the dream; she is more than woman, less than goddess; she is the best of that man made visible.

Thorpe found himself for the first time filled with the spirit of restlessness. His customary iron evenness of temper was gone, so that he wandered quickly from one detail of his work to another, without seeming to penetrate below the surface need of any one task. Out of the present his mind was always escaping to a mystic fourth dimension which he did not understand. But a week before, he had felt himself absorbed in the component parts of his enterprise, the totality of which arched far over his head, shutting out the sky. Now he was outside of it. He had, without his volition, abandoned the creator's standpoint of the god at the heart of his work. It seemed as important, as great to him, but somehow it had taken on a strange solidarity, as though he had left it a plastic beginning and returned to find it hardened into the shapes of finality. He acknowledged it admirable—and wondered how he had ever accomplished it! He confessed that it should be finished as it had begun—and could not discover in himself the Titan who had watched over its inception.

Thorpe took this state of mind much to heart, and in combating it expended more energy than would have sufficed to accomplish the work. Inexorably he held himself to the task. He filled his mind full of lumbering. The millions along the bank on section nine must be cut and travoyed directly on the rollways. It was a shame that the necessity should arise. From section nine Thorpe had hoped to lighten the expenses when finally he should begin operations on the distant and inaccessible headwaters of French Creek. Now there was no help for it. The instant necessity was to get thirty millions of pine logs down the river before Wallace Carpenter's notes came due. Every other consideration had to yield before that. Fifteen millions more could be cut on seventeen, nineteen, and eleven—regions hitherto practically untouched —by the men in the four camps inland. Camp One and Camp Three could attend to section nine.

These were details to which Thorpe applied his mind. As he pushed through the sun-flecked forest, laying out his roads, placing his travoy trails, spying the difficulties that might supervene to mar the fair face of honest labor, he had always this thought before him—that he must apply his mind. By an effort, a tremendous effort, he succeeded in doing so. The effort left him limp. He found himself often standing, or moving gently, his eyes staring sightless, his mind cradled on vague misty clouds of absolute inaction, his will chained so softly and yet so firmly that he felt no strength and hardly the desire to break from the dream that lulled him. Then he was conscious of the physical warmth of the sun, the faint sweet woods smells, the soothing caress of the breeze, the sleepy cicada-like note of the pine creeper. Through his half-closed lashes the tangled sunbeams made soft-tinted rainbows. He wanted nothing so much as to sit on the pine needles there in the golden flood of radiance, and dream—dream on—vaguely, comfortably, sweetly—dream of summer——

341

Thorpe, with a mighty and impatient effort, snapped the silken cords asunder.

"Lord, Lord!" he cried impatiently. "What's coming to me? I must be a little off my feed!"

And he hurried rapidly to his duties. After an hour of the hardest concentration he had ever been required to bestow on a trivial subject, he again unconsciously sank by degrees into the old apathy.

"Glad it isn't the busy season!" he commented to himself. "Here, I must quit this! Guess it's the warm weather. I'll get down to the mill for a day or two."

There he found himself incapable of even the most petty routine work. He sat to his desk at eight o'clock and began the perusal of a sheaf of letters, comprising a certain correspondence, which Collins brought him. The first three he read carefully; the following two rather hurriedly; of the next one he seized only the salient and essential points; the seventh and eighth he skimmed; the remainder of the bundle he thrust aside in uncontrollable impatience. Next day he returned to the woods.

The incident of the letters had aroused to the full his old fighting spirit, before which no mere instincts could stand. He clamped the iron to his actions and forced them to the way appointed. Once more his mental processes became clear and incisive, his commands direct and to the point. To all outward appearance Thorpe was as before.

He opened Camp One, and the Fighting Forty came back from distant drinking joints. This was in early September, when the raspberries were entirely done and the blackberries fairly in the way of vanishing. That able-bodied and devoted band of men was on hand when needed. Shearer, in some subtle manner of his own, had let them feel that this year meant thirty million or "bust." They tightened their leather belts and stood ready for commands. Thorpe set them to work near the river, cutting roads along the lines he had blazed to the inland timber on seventeen and nineteen. After much discussion with Shearer the young man decided to take out the logs from eleven by driving them down French Creek.

To this end a gang was put to clearing the creek-bed. It was a tremendous job. Centuries of forest life had choked the little stream nearly to the level of its banks. Old snags and stumps lay imbedded in the ooze; decayed trunks, moss-grown, blocked the current; leaning tamaracks, fallen timber, tangled vines, dense thickets gave to its course more the appearance of a tropical jungle than of a north-country brook-bed. All these things had to be removed, one by one, and either piled to one side or burnt. In the end, however, it would pay. French Creek was not a large stream, but it could be driven during the time of the spring freshets.

Each night the men returned in the beautiful

dream-like twilight to the camp. There they sat, after eating, smoking their pipes in the open air. Much of the time they sang, while Phil, crouching wolf-like over his violin, rasped out an accompaniment of dissonances. From a distance it softened and fitted pleasantly into the framework of the wilderness. The men's voices lent themselves well to the weird minor strains of the chanteys. These times—when the men sang, and the night-wind rose and died in the hemlock tops—were Thorpe's worst moments. His soul, tired with the day's iron struggle, fell to brooding. Strange thoughts came to him, strange visions. He wanted something—he knew not what; he longed, and thrilled, and aspired to a greater glory than that of brave deeds, a softer comfort than his old foster mother, the wilderness, could bestow.

The men were singing in a mighty chorus, swaying their heads in unison, and bringing out with a roar the emphatic words of the crude ditties written by some genius from their own ranks.

" *Come all ye sons of freedom throughout old Michigan,*
  Come all ye gallant lumbermen, list to a shanty man.
  On the banks of the Muskegon, where the rapid waters flow,
  OH!—we'll range the wild woods o'er while a-lumbering
    we go."

Here was the bold unabashed front of the pioneer, here was absolute certainty in the superiority of his calling—absolute scorn of all others. Thorpe passed his hand across his brow. The same spirit was once fully and freely his.

> " *The music of our burnished axe shall make the woods resound,*
> *And many a lofty ancient pine will tumble to the ground.*
> *At night around our shanty fire we'll sing while rude winds*
> *blow,*
> *OH!—we'll range the wild woods o'er while a-lumbering*
> *we go!* "

That was what he was here for. Things were going right. It would be pitiful to fail merely on account of this idiotic lassitude, this unmanly weakness, this boyish impatience and desire for play. He a woodsman! He a fellow with these big strong men!

A single voice, clear and high, struck into a quick measure:

> " *I am a jolly shanty boy,*
> *As you will soon discover;*
> *To all the dodges I am fly,*
> *A hustling pine-woods rover.*
> *A peavey-hook it is my pride,*
> *An axe I well can handle.*
> *To fell a tree or punch a bull*
> *Get rattling Danny Randall.* "

And then with a rattle and crash the whole Fighting Forty shrieked out the chorus:

> " *Bung yer eye! bung yer eye!* "

Active, alert, prepared for any emergency that might arise; hearty, ready for everything, from punching bulls to felling trees—that was something like! Thorpe despised himself. The song went on.

> " *I love a girl in Saginaw,*
> *She lives with her mother.*
> *I defy all Michigan*
> *To find such another.*
> *She's tall and slim, her hair is red,*
> *Her face is plump and pretty.*
> *She's my daisy Sunday best-day girl,*
> *And her front name stands for Kitty.*"

And again as before the Fighting Forty howled truculently:

> " *Bung yer eye! bung yer eye!* "

The words were vulgar, the air a mere minor chant. Yet Thorpe's mind was stilled. His aroused subconsciousness had been engaged in reconstructing these men entire as their songs voiced rudely the inner characteristics of their beings. Now his spirit halted, finger on lip. Their bravery, pride of caste, resource, bravado, boastfulness—all these he had checked off approvingly. Here now was the idea of the Mate. Somewhere for each of them was a " Kitty," a " daisy Sunday best-day girl "; the eternal feminine; the softer side; the tenderness, beauty, glory of even so harsh a world as they were compelled to inhabit. At the present or in the past these woods roisterers, this Fighting Forty, had known love. Thorpe arose abruptly and turned at random into the forest. The song pursued him as he went, but he heard only the clear sweet tones, not the words. And yet even the words would have spelled to his awakened sensibilities another idea— would have symbolized, however rudely, companionship and the human delight of acting a part before a woman.

> " *I took her to a dance one night,*
> *A mossback gave the bidding—*
> *Silver Jack bossed the shebang,*
> *And Big Dan played the fiddle.*
> *We danced and drank the livelong night*
> *With fights between the dancing,*
> *Till Silver Jack cleaned out the ranch*
> *And sent the mossbacks prancing.*"

And with the increasing war and turmoil of the quick water the last snout of the Fighting Forty mingled faintly and was lost.

> " *Bung yer eye! bung yer eye!* "

Thorpe found himself at the edge of the woods facing a little glade into which streamed the radiance of a full moon.

CHAPTER THIRTY-EIGHT

THERE he stood and looked silently, not understanding, not caring to inquire. Across the way a white-throat was singing, clear, beautiful, like the shadow of a dream. The girl stood listening.

Her small fair head was inclined ever so little sideways and her finger was on her lips as though she wished to still the very hush of night, to which impression the inclination of her supple body lent its grace. The moonlight shone full upon her countenance. A little white face it was, with wide clear eyes and a sensitive, proud mouth that now half parted like a child's. Her eyebrows arched from her straight nose in the peculiarly graceful curve that falls just short of pride on the one side and of power on the other, to fill the eyes with a pathos of trust and innocence. The man watching could catch the poise of her long white neck and the molten moon-fire from her tumbled hair—the color of corn-silk, but finer.

And yet these words mean nothing. A painter might have caught her charm, but he must needs be a poet as well—and a great poet, one capable of grandeurs and subtleties.

348

THORPE'S DREAM GIRL

To the young man standing there rapt in the spell of vague desire, of awakened vision, she seemed most like a flower or a mist. He tried to find words to formulate her to himself, but did not succeed. Always it came back to the same idea—the flower and the mist. Like the petals of a flower most delicate was her questioning, upturned face; like the bend of a flower most rare the stalk of her graceful throat; like the poise of a flower most dainty the attitude of her beautiful, perfect body sheathed in a garment that outlined each movement, for the instant in suspense. Like a mist the glimmering of her skin, the shining of her hair, the elusive moon-like quality of her whole personality as she stood there in the ghost-like clearing listening, her fingers on her lips.

Behind her lurked the low, even shadow of the forest where the moon was not, a band of velvet against which the girl and the light-touched twigs and bushes and grass blades were etched like frost against a black window pane. There was something, too, of the frost-work's evanescent spiritual quality in the scene—as though at any moment, with a puff of the balmy summer wind, the radiant glade, the hovering figure, the filagreed silver of the entire setting would melt into the accustomed stern and menacing forest of the northland, with its wolves, and its wild deer, and the voices of its sterner calling.

Thorpe held his breath and waited. Again the white-throat lifted his clear, spiritual note across the brightness, slow, trembling with ecstasy. The girl never moved. She stood in the moonlight like a beautiful emblem of silence, half real, half fancy, part woman, wholly divine, listening to the little bird's message.

For the third time the song shivered across the night; then Thorpe with a soft sob, dropped his face in his hands and looked no more.

He did not feel the earth beneath his knees, nor the whip of the sumach across his face; he did not see the moon shadows creep slowly along the fallen birch; nor did he notice that the white-throat had hushed its song. His inmost spirit was shaken. Something had entered his soul and filled it to the brim, so that he dared no longer stand in the face of radiance until he had accounted with himself. Another drop would overflow the cup.

Ah, sweet God, the beauty of it, the beauty of it! That questing, child-like starry gaze, seeking so purely to the stars themselves! That flower face, those drooping, half-parted lips! That inexpressible, unseizable something they had meant! Thorpe searched humbly — eagerly — then with agony through his troubled spirit, and in its furthermost depths saw the mystery as beautifully remote as ever. It approached and swept over him and left him gasping passion-racked. Ah, sweet God, the beauty of it! the beauty of it! the vision! the dream!

He trembled and sobbed with his desire to seize it, with his impotence to express it, with his failure even to appreciate it as his heart told him it should be appreciated.

He dared not look. At length he turned and stumbled back through the moonlit forest crying on his old gods in vain.

At the banks of the river he came to a halt. There in the velvet pines the moonlight slept calmly, and the shadows rested quietly under the breezeless sky. Near at hand the river shouted as ever its cry of joy over the vitality of life, like a spirited boy before the face of inscrutable nature. All else was silence. Then from the waste boomed a strange, hollow note, rising, dying, rising again, instinct with the spirit of the wilds. It fell, and far away sounded a heavy but distant crash. The cry lifted again. It was the first bull moose calling across the wilderness to his mate.

And then, faint but clear, down the current of a chance breeze drifted the chorus of the Fighting Forty.

> " *The forests so brown at our stroke go down,*
> *And cities spring up where they fell;*
> *While logs well run and work well done*
> *Is the story the shanty boys tell.*"

Thorpe turned from the river with a thrust forward of his head. He was not a religious man, and in his six years' woods experience had never been to church. Now he looked up over the tops of the pines to where the Pleiades glittered faintly among the brighter stars.

"Thanks, God," said he briefly.

CHAPTER THIRTY-NINE

FOR several days this impression satisfied him completely. He discovered, strangely enough, that his restlessness had left him, that once more he was able to give to his work his former energy and interest. It was as though some power had raised its finger and a storm had stilled, leaving calm, unruffled skies.

He did not attempt to analyze this; he did not even make an effort to contemplate it. His critical faculty was stricken dumb and it asked no questions of him. At a touch his entire life had changed. Reality or vision, he had caught a glimpse of something so entirely different from anything his imagination or experience had ever suggested to him, that at first he could do no more than permit passively its influences to adjust themselves to his being.

Curiosity, speculation, longing — all the more active emotions remained in abeyance while outwardly, for three days, Harry Thorpe occupied himself only with the needs of the Fighting Forty at Camp One.

In the early morning he went out with the gang. While they chopped or heaved, he stood by serene

353

Little questions of expediency he solved. Dilemmas he discussed leisurely with Tim Shearer. Occasionally he lent a shoulder when the peaveys lacked of prying a stubborn log from its bed. Not once did he glance at the nooning sun. His patience was quiet and sure. When evening came he smoked placidly outside the office, listening to the conversation and laughter of the men, caressing one of the beagles, while the rest slumbered about his feet, watching dreamily the night shadows and the bats. At about nine o'clock he went to bed, and slept soundly. He was vaguely conscious of a great peace within him, a great stillness of the spirit, against which the metallic events of his craft clicked sharply in vivid relief. It was the peace and stillness of a river before it leaps.

Little by little the condition changed. The man felt vague stirrings of curiosity. He speculated aimlessly as to whether or not the glade, the moonlight, the girl, had been real or merely the figments of imagination. Almost immediately the answer leaped at him from his heart. Since she was so certainly flesh and blood, whence did she come? what was she doing there in the wilderness? His mind pushed the query aside as unimportant, rushing eagerly to the essential point: When could he see her again? How find for the second time the vision before which his heart felt the instant need of prostrating itself. His placidity had gone. That morning he made some vague excuse to Shearer and set out blindly down the river.

He did not know where he was going, any more than did the bull moose plunging through the trackless wilderness to his mate. Instinct, the instinct of all wild natural creatures, led him. And so, without thought, without clear intention even—most would say by accident—he saw her again. It was near the "pole trail"; which was less like a trail than a rail-fence.

For when the snows are deep and snowshoes not the property of every man who cares to journey, the old-fashioned "pole trail" comes into use. It is merely a series of horses built of timber across which thick Norway logs are laid, about four feet from the ground to form a continuous pathway. A man must be a tight-rope walker to stick to the pole trail when ice and snow have sheathed its logs. If he makes a misstep, he is precipitated ludicrously into feathery depths through which he must flounder to the nearest timber horse before he can remount. In summer, gas has been said, it resembles nothing so much as a thick one-rail fence of considerable height, around which a fringe of light brush has grown.

Thorpe reached the fringe of bushes, and was about to dodge under the fence, when he saw her. So he stopped short, concealed by the leaves and the timber horse.

She stood on a knoll in the middle of a grove of

monster pines. There was something of the cathedral in the spot. A hush dwelt in the dusk, the long columns lifted grandly to the Roman arches of the frond, faint murmurings stole here and there like whispering acolytes. The girl stood tall and straight among the tall, straight pines like a figure on an ancient tapestry. She was doing nothing—just standing there—but the awe of the forest was in her wide, clear eyes.

The great sweet feeling clutched the young man's throat again. But while the other—the vision of the frost-work glade and the spirit-like figure of silence—had been unreal and phantasmagoric, this was of the earth. He looked, and looked, and looked again. He saw the full pure curve of her cheek's contour, neither oval nor round, but like the outline of a certain kind of plum. He appreciated the half-pathetic downward droop of the corners of her mouth—her red mouth in dazzling, bewitching contrast to the milk-whiteness of her skin. He caught the fineness of her nose, straight as a Grecian's, but with some faint suggestion about the nostrils that hinted at piquance. And the waving corn-silk of her altogether charming and unruly hair, the superb column of her long neck on which her little head poised proudly like a flower, her supple body, whose curves had the long undulating grace of the current in a swift river, her slender white hand with the pointed fingers—all these he saw one after the other, and his soul shouted within him at the sight. He wrestled with the emotions that choked him. "Ah, God! Ah, God!" he cried softly to himself like one in pain. He, the man of iron frame, of iron nerve, hardened by a hundred emergencies, trembled in every muscle before a straight, slender girl, clad all in brown, standing alone in the middle of the ancient forest.

In a moment she stirred slightly, and turned. Drawing herself to her full height, she extended her hands over her head palm outward, and, with an indescribably graceful gesture, half mockingly bowed a ceremonious adieu to the solemn trees. Then with a little laugh she moved away in the direction of the river.

At once Thorpe proved a great need of seeing her again. In his present mood there was nothing of the awe-stricken peace he had experienced after the moonlight adventure. He wanted the sight of her as he had never wanted anything before. He must have it, and he looked about him fiercely as though to challenge any force in Heaven or Hell that would deprive him of it. His eyes desired to follow the soft white curve of her cheek, to dance with the light of her corn-silk hair, to delight in the poetic movements of her tall, slim body, to trace the full outline of her chin, to wonder at the carmine of her lips, red as a blood-spot on the snow. These things must be at once. The strong man desired it.

And finding it impossible, he raged inwardly and tore the tranquillities of his heart, as on the shores of the distant Lake of Stars, the bull-moose trampled down the bushes in his passion.

So it happened that he ate hardly at all that day, and slept ill, and discovered the greatest difficulty in preserving the outward semblance of ease which the presence of Tim Shearer and the Fighting Forty demanded.

And next day he saw her again, and the next, because the need of his heart demanded it, and because, simply enough, she came every afternoon to the clump of pines by the old pole trail.

Now had Thorpe taken the trouble to inquire, he could have learned easily enough all there was to be known of the affair. But he did not take the trouble. His consciousness was receiving too many new impressions, so that in a manner it became bewildered. At first, as has been seen, the mere effect of the vision was enough; then the sight of the girl sufficed him. But now curiosity awoke and a desire for something more. He must speak to her, touch her hand, look into her eyes. He resolved to approach her, and the mere thought choked him and sent him weak.

When he saw her again from the shelter of the pole trail, he dared not, and so stood there prey to a novel sensation—that of being baffled in an intention. It awoke within him a vast passion compounded part of rage at himself, part of longing for that which he could not take, but most of love for the girl. As he hesitated in one mind but in two decisions, he saw that she was walking slowly in his direction.

Perhaps a hundred paces separated the two. She took them deliberately, pausing now and again to listen, to pluck a leaf, to smell the fragrant balsam and fir tops as she passed them. Her progression was a series of poses, the one of which melted imperceptibly into the other without appreciable pause of transition. So subtly did her grace appeal to the sense of sight, that out of mere sympathy the other senses responded with fictions of their own. Almost could the young man behind the trail savor a faint fragrance, a faint music that surrounded and preceded her like the shadows of phantoms. He knew it as an illusion, born of his desire, and yet it was a noble illusion, for it had its origin in her.

In a moment she had reached the fringe of brush about the pole trail. They stood face to face.

She gave a little start of surprise, and her hand leaped to her breast, where it caught and stayed. Her child-like down-drooping mouth parted a little more, and the breath quickened through it. But her eyes, her wide, trusting, innocent eyes, sought his and rested.

He did not move. The eagerness, the desire, the long years of ceaseless struggle, the thirst for affection, the sob of awe at the moonlit glade, the love —all these flamed in his eyes and fixed his gaze in an unconscious ardor that had nothing to do with convention or timidity. One on either side of the spike-marked old Norway log of the trail they stood, and for an appreciable interval the duel of their glances lasted—he masterful, passionate, exigent; she proud, cool, defensive in the aloofness of her beauty. Then at last his prevailed. A faint color rose from her neck, deepened, and spread over her face and forehead. In a moment she dropped her eyes.

"Don't you think you stare a little rudely—Mr. Thorpe?" she asked.

CHAPTER FORTY

THE vision was over, but the beauty remained. The spoken words of protest made her a woman. Never again would she, nor any other creature of the earth, appear to Thorpe as she had in the silver glade or the cloistered pines. He had had his moment of insight. The deeps had twice opened to permit him to look within. Now they had closed again. But out of them had fluttered a great love and the priestess of it. Always, so long as life should be with him, Thorpe was destined to see in this tall graceful girl with the red lips and the white skin and the corn-silk hair, more beauty, more of the great mysterious spiritual beauty which is eternal, than her father or her mother or her dearest and best. For to them the vision had not been vouchsafed, while he had seen her as the highest symbol of God's splendor.

Now she stood before him, her head turned half away, a faint flush still tingeing the chalk-white of her skin, watching him with a dim, half-pleading smile in expectation of his reply.

"Ah, moon of my soul! light of my life!" he cried, but he cried it within him, though it

361

almost escaped his vigilance to his lips. What he really said sounded almost harsh in consequence.

"How did you know my name?" he asked.

She planted both elbows on the Norway and framed her little face deliciously with her long pointed hands.

"If Mr. Harry Thorpe can ask that question," she replied, "he is not quite so impolite as I had thought him."

"If you don't stop pouting your lips, I shall kiss them!" cried Harry—to himself.

"How is that?" he inquired breathlessly.

"Don't you know who I am?" she asked in return.

"A goddess, a beautiful woman!" he answered ridiculously enough.

She looked straight at him. This time his gaze dropped.

"I am a friend of Elizabeth Carpenter, who is Wallace Carpenter's sister, who I believe is Mr. Harry Thorpe's partner."

She paused as though for comment. The young man opposite was occupied in many other more important directions. Some moments later the words trickled into his brain, and some moments after that he realized their meaning.

"We wrote Mr. Harry Thorpe that we were about to descend on his district with wagons and tents and Indians and things, and asked him to come and see us."

"Ah, heart o' mine, what clear, pure eyes she has! How they look at a man to drown his soul!"

Which, even had it been spoken, was hardly the comment one would have expected.

The girl looked at him for a moment steadily, then smiled. The change of countenance brought Thorpe to himself, and at the same moment the words she had spoken reached his comprehension.

"But I never received the letter. I'm so sorry," said he. "It must be at the mill. You see, I've been up in the woods for nearly a month."

"Then we'll have to forgive you."

"But I should think they would have done something for you at the mill——"

"Oh, we didn't come by way of your mill. We drove from Marquette."

"I see," cried Thorpe, enlightened. "But I'm sorry I didn't know. I'm sorry you didn't let me know. I suppose you thought I was still at the mill. How did you get along? Is Wallace with you?"

"No," she replied, dropping her hands and straightening her erect figure. "It's horrid. He was coming, and then some business came up and he couldn't get away. We are having the loveliest time though. I do adore the woods. Come," she cried impatiently, sweeping aside to leave a way clear, "you shall meet my friends."

Thorpe imagined she referred to the rest of the tenting party. He hesitated.

"I am hardly in fit condition," he objected.

She laughed, parting her red lips. "You are extremely picturesque just as you are," she said with rather embarrassing directness. "I wouldn't have you any different for the world. But my friends don't mind. They are used to it." She laughed again.

Thorpe crossed the pole trail, and for the first time found himself by her side. The warm summer odors were in the air, a dozen lively little birds sang in the brush along the rail, the sunlight danced and flickered through the openings.

Then suddenly they were among the pines, and the air was cool, the vista dim, and the bird-songs inconceivably far away.

The girl walked directly to the foot of a pine three feet through and soaring up an inconceivable distance through the still twilight.

"This is Jimmy," said she gravely. "He is a dear good old rough bear when you don't know him, but he likes me. If you put your ear close against him," she confided, suiting the action to the word, "you can hear him talking to himself. This little fellow is Tommy. I don't care so much for Tommy because he's sticky. Still, I like him pretty well, and here's Dick, and that's Bob, and the one just beyond is Jack."

"Where is Harry?" asked Thorpe.

"I thought one in a woods was quite sufficient," she replied with the least little air of impertinence.

"Why do you name them such common, every-day names?" he inquired.

"I'll tell you. It's because they are so big and grand themselves, that it did not seem to me they needed high-sounding names. What do you think?" she begged with an appearance of the utmost anxiety.

Thorpe expressed himself as in agreement. As the half-quizzical conversation progressed, he found their relations adjusting themselves with increasing rapidity. He had been successively the mystic devotee before his vision, the worshipper before his goddess; now he was unconsciously assuming the attitude of the lover before his mistress. It needs always this humanizing touch to render the greatest of all passions livable.

And as the human element developed, he proved at the same time greater and greater difficulty in repressing himself, and greater and greater fear of the results in case he should not do so. He trembled with the desire to touch her long slender hand, and as soon as his imagination had permitted him that much, he had already crushed her to him and had kissed passionately her starry face. Words hovered on his lips longing for flight. He withheld them by an effort that left him almost incoherent, for he feared with a deadly fear lest he lose forever what the vision had seemed to offer to his hand.

So he said little, and that lamely, for he dreaded to say too much. To her playful sallies he had no *riposte*. And in consequence he fell more silent with another boding—that he was losing his cause outright for lack of a ready word.

He need not have been alarmed. A woman in such a case hits as surely as a man misses. Her very daintiness and preciosity of speech indicated it. For where a man becomes stupid and silent, a woman covers her emotions with words and a clever speech. Not in vain is a proud-spirited girl stared down in such a contest of looks; brave deeds simply told by a friend are potent to win interest in advance; a straight, muscular figure, a brown skin, a clear, direct eye, a carriage of power and acknowledged authority, strike hard at a young imagination; a mighty passion sweeps aside the barriers of the heart. Such a victory, such a friend, such a passion had Thorpe.

And so the last-spoken exchange between them meant nothing; but if each could have read the unsaid words that quivered on the other's heart, Thorpe would have returned to the Fighting Forty more tranquilly, while she would probably not have returned to the camping party at all for a number of hours.

" I do not think you had better come with me,"

she said. "Make your call and be forgiven on your own account. I don't want to drag you in at my chariot wheels."

"All right. I'll come this afternoon," Thorpe had replied.

"I love her, I must have her. I must go—at once," his soul had cried, "quick—now—before I kiss her!"

"How strong he is," she said to herself, "how brave-looking; how honest! He is different from the other men. He is magnificent."

CHAPTER FORTY-ONE

THAT afternoon Thorpe met the other members of the party, offered his apologies and explanations, and was graciously forgiven. He found the personnel to consist of, first of all, Mrs. Cary, the chaperone, a very young married woman of twenty-two or thereabouts; her husband, a youth of three years older, clean-shaven, light-haired, quiet-mannered; Miss Elizabeth Carpenter, who resembled her brother in the characteristics of good-looks, vivacious disposition, and curly hair; an attendant satellite of the masculine persuasion called Morton; and last of all the girl whom Thorpe had already so variously encountered and whom he now met as Miss Hilda Farrand. Besides these were Ginger, a squab negro built to fit the galley of a yacht; and three Indian guides. They inhabited tents, which made quite a little encampment.

Thorpe was received with enthusiasm. Wallace Carpenter's stories of his woods partner, while never doing more than justice to the truth, had been of a warm color tone. One and all owned a lively curiosity to see what a real woodsman might be like. When he proved to be handsome and well-mannered, as well as picturesque, his reception was no longer in doubt.

Nothing could exceed his solicitude as to their comfort and amusement. He inspected personally the arrangement of the tents, and suggested one or two changes conducive to the littler comforts. This was not much like ordinary woods-camping. The largest wall-tent contained three folding cots for the women, over which, in the daytime, were flung bright - colored Navajo blankets. Another was spread on the ground. Thorpe later, however, sent over two bear-skins, which were acknowledgedly an improvement. To the tent pole a mirror of size was nailed, and below it stood a portable wash-stand. The second tent, devoted to the two men, was not quite so luxurious; but still boasted of little conveniences the true woodsman would never con-sider worth the bother of transporting. The third, equally large, was the dining tent. The other three, smaller, and on the A-tent order, served re-spectively as sleeping-rooms for Ginger and the Indi-ans, and as a general storehouse for provisions and impedimenta.

Thorpe sent an Indian to Camp One for the bear-skins, put the rest to digging a trench around the sleeping tents in order that a rain-storm might not cause a flood, and ordered Ginger to excavate a square hole some feet deep, which he intended to utilize as a larder.

Then he gave Morton and Cary hints as to the deer they wished to capture, pointed out the best trout-pools, and issued advice as to the compassing of certain blackberries, not far distant.

Simple things enough they were to do—it was as though a city man were to direct a newcomer to Central Park, or impart to him a test for the destinations of trolley lines—yet Thorpe's new friends were profoundly impressed with his knowledge of occult things. The forest was to them, as to most, more or less of a mystery, unfathomable except to the favored of genius. A man who could interpret it, even a little, into the speech of everyday comfort and expediency possessed a strong claim to their imaginations. When he had finished these practical affairs, they wanted him to sit down and tell them more things—to dine with them, to smoke about their camp-fire in the evening. But here they encountered a decided check. Thorpe became silent, almost morose. He talked in monosyllables, and soon went away. They did not know what to make of him, and so were, of course, the more profoundly interested. The truth was, his habitual reticence would not have permitted a great degree of expansion in any case, but now the presence of Hilda made any but an attitude of hushed waiting for her words utterly impossible to him. He wished well to them all. If there was anything he could do for them, he would gladly undertake it. But he would not act the lion nor tell of his, to them, interesting adventures.

However, when he discovered that Hilda had ceased visiting the clump of pines near the pole trail, his desire forced him back among these people. He used to walk in swiftly at almost any time of day, casting quick glances here and there in search of his divinity.

"How do, Mrs. Cary," he would say. "Nice weather. Enjoying yourself?"

On receiving the reply he would answer heartily, "That's good!" and lapse into silence. When Hilda was about he followed every movement of hers with his eyes, so that his strange conduct lacked no explanation or interpretation, in the minds of the women at least. Thrice he redeemed his reputation for being an interesting character by conducting the party on little expeditions here and there about the country. Then his woodcraft and resourcefulness spoke for him. They asked him about the lumbering operations, but he seemed indifferent.

"Nothing to interest you," he affirmed. "We're just cutting roads now. You ought to be here for the drive."

To him there was really nothing interesting in the cutting of roads nor the clearing of streams. It was all in a day's work.

Once he took them over to see Camp One. They were immensely pleased, and were correspondingly loud in exclamations. Thorpe's comments were brief and dry. After the noon dinner he had the unfortunate idea of commending the singing of one of the men.

"Oh, I'd like to hear him," cried Elizabeth Carpenter. "Can't you get him to sing for us, Mr. Thorpe?"

Thorpe went to the men's camp, where he singled out the unfortunate lumber-jack in question.

"Come on, Archie," he said. "The ladies want to hear you sing."

The man objected, refused, pleaded, and finally obeyed what amounted to a command. Thorpe re-entered the office with triumph, his victim in tow.

"This is Archie Harris," he announced heartily. "He's our best singer just now. Take a chair, Archie."

The man perched on the edge of the chair and looked straight out before him.

"Do sing for us, won't you, Mr. Harris?" requested Mrs. Cary in her sweetest tones.

The man said nothing, nor moved a muscle, but turned a brick-red. An embarrassed silence of expectation ensued.

"Hit her up, Archie," encouraged Thorpe.

"I ain't much in practice no how," objected the man in a little voice, without moving.

"I'm sure you'll find us very appreciative," said Elizabeth Carpenter.

"Give us a song, Archie, let her go," urged Thorpe impatiently.

"All right," replied the man very meekly.

Another silence fell. It got to be a little awful. The poor woodsman, pilloried before the regards of this polite circle, out of his element, suffering cruelly, nevertheless made no sign nor movement one way or the other. At last when the situation had almost reached the breaking point of hysteria, he began.

His voice ordinarily was rather a good tenor. Now he pitched it too high; and went on straining at the high notes to the very end. Instead of offering one of the typical woods chanteys, he conceived that before so grand an audience he should give something fancy. He therefore struck into a sentimental song of the cheap music-hall type. There were nine verses, and he drawled through them all, hanging whiningly on the nasal notes in the fashion of the untrained singer. Instead of being a performance typical of the strange woods genius, it was merely an atrocious bit of cheap sentimentalism, badly rendered.

The audience listened politely. When the song was finished it murmured faint thanks.

"Oh, give us 'Jack Haggerty,' Archie," urged Thorpe.

But the woodsman rose, nodded his head awkwardly, and made his escape. He entered the men's camp swearing, and for the remainder of the day made none but blasphemous remarks.

The beagles, however, were a complete success. They tumbled about, and lolled their tongues, and laughed up out of a tangle of themselves in a fascinating manner. Altogether the visit to Camp One was a success, the more so in that on the way back, for the first time, Thorpe found that chance—and Mrs. Cary—had allotted Hilda to his care.

A hundred yards down the trail they encountered Phil. The dwarf stopped short, looked attentively at the girl, and then softly approached. When quite near to her he again stopped, gazing at her with his soul in his liquid eyes.

"You are more beautiful than the sea at night," he said directly.

The others laughed. "There's sincerity for you, Miss Hilda," said young Mr. Morton.

"Who is he?" asked the girl after they had moved on.

"Our chore-boy," answered Thorpe with great brevity, for he was thinking of something much more important.

After the rest of the party had gone ahead, leaving them sauntering more slowly down the trail, he gave it voice.

"Why don't you come to the pine grove any more?" he asked bluntly.

"Why?" countered Hilda in the manner of women.

"I want to see you there. I want to talk with you. I can't talk with all that crowd around."

"I'll come to-morrow," she said—then with a little mischievous laugh, "if that'll make you talk."

"You must think I'm awfully stupid," agreed Thorpe bitterly.

"Ah, no! Ah, no!" she protested softly. "You must not say that."

She was looking at him very tenderly, if he had only known it, but he did not, for his face was set in discontented lines straight before him.

"It is true," he replied.

They walked on in silence, while gradually the dangerous fascination of the woods crept down on them. Just before sunset a hush falls on nature. The wind has died, the birds have not yet begun their evening songs, the light itself seems to have left off sparkling and to lie still across the land-scape. Such a hush now lay on their spirits. Over the way a creeper was droning sleepily a little chant —the only voice in the wilderness. In the heart of the man, too, a little voice raised itself alone.

"Sweetheart, sweetheart, sweetheart!" it breathed over and over again. After a while he said it gently in a half voice.

"No, no, hush!" said the girl, and she laid the soft, warm fingers of one hand across his lips, and looked at him from a height of superior soft-eyed tenderness as a woman might look at a child. "You must not. It is not right."

Then he kissed the fingers very gently before they were withdrawn, and she said nothing at all in rebuke, but looked straight before her with troubled eyes.

The voices of evening began to raise their jubilant notes. From a tree near by the olive thrush sang like clockwork; over beyond carolled eagerly a black-throat, a myrtle warbler, a dozen song sparrows, and a hundred vireos and creepers. Down deep in the blackness of the ancient woods a hermit thrush uttered his solemn bell-note, like the tolling of the spirit of peace. And in Thorpe's heart a thousand tumultuous voices that had suddenly roused to clamor, died into nothingness at the music of her softly protesting voice.

CHAPTER FORTY-TWO

THORPE returned to Camp One shortly after dark. He found there Scotty Parsons, who had come up to take charge of the crew engaged in clearing French Creek. The man brought him a number of letters sent on by Collins, among which was one from Wallace Carpenter.

After commending the camping party to his companion's care, and giving minute directions as to how and where to meet it, the young fellow went on to say that affairs were going badly on the Board.

"Some interest that I haven't been able to make out yet has been hammering our stocks down day after day," he wrote. "I don't understand it, for the stocks are good—they rest on a solid foundation of value—and intrinsically are worth more than is bid for them right now. Some powerful concern is beating them down for a purpose of its own. Sooner or later they will let up, and then we'll get things back in good shape. I am amply protected now, thanks to you, and am not at all afraid of losing my holdings. The only difficulty is that I am unable to predict exactly when the other fellows will decide that they have accomplished whatever they are about, and let up. It may not be before next year. In that case I couldn't help you out on those notes when they come due. So put in your best licks, old man. You may have to pony up for a little while, though, of course, sooner or later I can put it all back. Then, you bet your life, I keep out of it. Lumbering's good enough for yours truly.

" By the way, you might shine up to Hilda Farrand and join the rest of the fortune-hunters. She's got it to throw to the birds, and in her own right. Seriously, old fellow, don't put yourself into a false position through ignorance. Not that there is any danger to a hardened old woodsman like you."

Thorpe went to the group of pines by the pole trail the following afternoon because he had said he would, but with a new attitude of mind. He had come into contact with the artificiality of conventional relations, and it stiffened him. No wonder she had made him keep silence the afternoon before! She had done it gently and nicely, to be sure, but that was part of her good-breeding. Hilda found him formal, reserved, polite; and marvelled at it. In her was no coquetry. She was as straightforward and sincere as the look of her eyes.

They sat down on a log. Hilda turned to him with her graceful air of confidence.

" Now talk to me," said she.

" Certainly," replied Thorpe in a practical tone of voice, " what do you want me to talk about? "

She shot a swift, troubled glance at him, concluded herself mistaken, and said:

"Tell me about what you do up here—your life—all about it."

"Well—" replied Thorpe formally, "we haven't much to interest a girl like you. It is a question of saw logs with us"—and he went on in his dryest, most technical manner to detail the process of manufacture. It might as well have been bricks.

The girl did not understand. She was hurt. As surely as the sun tangled in the distant pine frond, she had seen in his eyes a great passion. Now it was coldly withdrawn.

"What has happened to you?" she asked finally, out of her great sincerity.

"Me? Nothing," replied Thorpe.

A forced silence fell upon him. Hilda seemed gradually to lose herself in reverie. After a time she said softly:

"Don't you love this woods?"

"It's an excellent bunch of pine," replied Thorpe bluntly. "It'll cut three million at least."

"Oh!" she cried drawing back, her hands pressed against the log either side of her, her eyes wide.

After a moment she caught her breath convulsively, and Thorpe became conscious that she was studying him furtively with a quickening doubt.

After that, by the mercy of God, there was no more talk between them. She was too hurt and shocked and disillusioned to make the necessary effort to go away. He was too proud to put an end to the position. They sat there apparently absorbed in thought, while all about them the accustomed life of the woods drew nearer and nearer to them, as the splash of their entrance into it died away.

A red squirrel poised thirty feet above them, leaped, and clung swaying to a sapling-top a dozen yards from the tree he had quitted. Two chickadees, upside down, uttering liquid undertones, searched busily for insects next their heads. Wilson's warblers, pine creepers, black-throats, myrtle and magnolia warblers, oven birds, peewits, blue-jays, purple finches, passed silently or noisily, each according to his kind. Once a lone spruce hen dusted herself in a stray patch of sunlight until it shimmered on a tree trunk, raised upward, and disappeared, to give place to long level dusty shafts that shot here and there through the pines laying the spell of sunset on the noisy woods brawlers.

Unconsciously the first strain of opposition and of hurt surprise had relaxed. Each thought vaguely his thoughts. Then in the depths of the forest, perhaps near at hand, perhaps far away, a single hermit thrush began to sing. His song was of three solemn deep liquid notes; followed by a slight rhetorical pause as of contemplation; and then, deliberately, three notes more on a different key—and so on without haste and without pause. It is the most digni-

fied, the most spiritual, the holiest of woods utter-
ances. Combined with the evening shadows and the
warm soft air, it offered to the heart an almost irresistible appeal. The man's artificial antagonism
modified; the woman's disenchantment began to
seem unreal.

Then subtly over and through the bird-song another sound became audible. At first it merely repeated the three notes faintly, like an echo, but with
a rich, sad undertone that brought tears. Then,
timidly and still softly, it elaborated the theme,
weaving in and out through the original three the
glitter and shimmer of a splendid web of sound,
spreading before the awakened imagination a broad
river of woods-imagery that reflected on its surface
all the subtler moods of the forest. The pine shadows, the calls of the wild creatures, the flow of the
brook, the splashes of sunlight through the trees, the
sigh of the wind, the shout of the rapid—all these
were there, distinctly to be felt in their most ethereal
and beautiful forms. And yet it was all slight and
tenuous as though the crack of a twig would break
it through—so that over it continually like a grand
full organ-tone repeated the notes of the bird itself.

With the first sigh of the wonder-music the girl
had started and caught her breath in the exquisite
pleasure of it. As it went on they both forgot
everything but the harmony and each other.

" Ah, beautiful! " she murmured.

" What is it? " he whispered marvelling.

" A violin—played by a master."

The bird suddenly hushed, and at once the strain abandoned the woods-note and took another motif. At first it played softly in the higher notes, a tinkling lightsome little melody that stirred a kindly surface-smile over a full heart. Then suddenly, without transition, it dropped to the lower register, and began to sob and wail in the full vibrating power of a great passion.

And the theme it treated was love. It spoke solemnly, fearfully of the greatness of it, the glory. These as abstractions it amplified in fine full-breathed chords that swept the spirit up and up as on the waves of a mighty organ. Then one by one the voices of other things were heard—the tinkling of laughter, the roar of a city, the sob of a grief, a cry of pain suddenly shooting across the sound, the clank of a machine, the tumult of a river, the puff of a steamboat, the murmuring of a vast crowd— and one by one, without seeming in the least to change their character, they merged imperceptibly into, and were part of the grand-breathed chords, so that at last all the fames and ambitions and passions of the world came, in their apotheosis, to be only parts of the master-passion of them all.

And while the echoes of the greater glory still swept beneath their uplifted souls like ebbing waves, so that they still sat rigid and staring with the majesty of it, the violin softly began to whisper. Beautiful it was as a spirit, beautiful beyond words, beautiful beyond thought. Its beauty struck sharp at the heart. And they two sat there hand in hand dreaming—dreaming—dreaming——

At last the poignant ecstasy seemed slowly, slowly to die. Fainter and fainter ebbed the music. Through it as through a mist the solemn aloof forest began to show to the consciousness of the two. They sought each other's eyes gently smiling. The music was very soft and dim and sad. They leaned to each other with a sob. Their lips met. The music ceased.

Alone in the forest side by side they looked out together for a moment into that eternal vision which lovers only are permitted to see. The shadows fell. About them brooded the inscrutable pines stretching a canopy over them enthroned. A single last shaft of the sun struck full upon them, a single light-spot in the gathering gloom. They were beautiful.

And over behind the trees, out of the light and the love and the beauty, little Phil huddled, his great shaggy head bowed in his arms. Beside him lay his violin, and beside that his bow, broken. He had snapped it across his knee. That day he had heard at last the Heart Song of the Violin, and uttering it, had bestowed love. But in accordance with his prophecy he had that day lost what he cared for most in all the world, his friend.

CHAPTER FORTY-THREE

THAT was the moon of delight. The days passed through the hazy forest like stately figures from an old masque. In the pine grove on the knoll the man and the woman had erected a temple to love, and love showed them one to the other.

In Hilda Farrand was no guile, no coquetry, no deceit. So perfect was her naturalism that often by those who knew her least she was considered affected. Her trust in whomever she found herself with attained so directly its reward; her unconsciousness of pose was so rhythmically graceful; her ignorance and innocence so triumphantly effective, that the mind with difficulty rid itself of the belief that it was all carefully studied. This was not true. She honestly did not know that she was beautiful; was unaware of her grace; did not realize the potency of her wealth.

This absolute lack of self-consciousness was most potent in overcoming Thorpe's natural reticence. He expanded to her. She came to idolize him in a manner at once inspiring and touching in so beautiful a creature. In him she saw reflected all the lofty attractions of character which she herself possessed,

384

but of which she was entirely unaware. Through his words she saw to an ideal. His most trivial actions were ascribed to motives of a dignity which would have been ridiculous, if it had not been a little pathetic. The woods-life, the striving of the pioneer kindled her imagination. She seized upon the great facts of them and fitted those facts with reasons of her own. Her insight perceived the adventurous spirit, the battle-courage, the indomitable steadfastness which always in reality lie back of these men of the frontier to urge them into the life; and of them constructed conscious motives of conduct. To her fancy the lumbermen, of whom Thorpe was one, were self-conscious agents of advance. They chose hardship, loneliness, the strenuous life because they wished to clear the way for a higher civilization. To her it seemed a great and noble sacrifice. She did not perceive that while all this is true, it is under the surface, the real spur is a desire to get on, and a hope of making money. For, strangely enough, she differentiated sharply the life and the reasons for it. An existence in subduing the forest was to her ideal; the making of a fortune through a lumbering firm she did not consider in the least important. That this distinction was most potent, the sequel will show.

In all of it she was absolutely sincere, and not at all stupid. She had always had all she could spend, without question. Money meant nothing to her, one way or the other. If need was, she might have experienced some difficulty in learning how to economize, but none at all in adjusting herself to the necessity of it. The material had become, in all sincerity, a basis for the spiritual. She recognized but two sorts of motives; of which the ideal, comprising the poetic, the daring, the beautiful, were good; and the material, meaning the sordid and selfish, were bad. With her the mere money-getting would have to be allied with some great and poetic excuse.

That is the only sort of aristocracy, in the popular sense of the word, which is real; the only scorn of money which can be respected.

There are some faces which symbolize to the beholder many subtleties of soul-beauty which by no other method could gain expression. Those subtleties may not, probably do not, exist in the possessor of the face. The power of such a countenance lies not so much in what it actually represents, as in the suggestion it holds out to another. So often it is with a beautiful character. Analyze it carefully, and you will reduce it generally to absolute simplicity and absolute purity—two elements common enough in adulteration; but place it face to face with a more complex personality, and mirror-like it will take on a hundred delicate shades of ethical beauty, while at the same time preserving its own lofty spirituality.

Thus Hilda Farrand reflected Thorpe. In the clear mirror of her heart his image rested transfigured. It was as though the glass were magic, so that the gross and material was absorbed and lost, while the more spiritual qualities reflected back. So the image was retained in its entirety, but etherealized, refined. It is necessary to attempt, even thus faintly and inadequately, a sketch of Hilda's love, for a partial understanding of it is necessary to the comprehension of what followed the moon of delight.

That moon saw a variety of changes.

The bed of French Creek was cleared. Three of the roads were finished, and the last begun. So much for the work of it.

Morton and Cary shot four deer between them, which was unpardonably against the law, caught fish in plenty, smoked two and a half pounds of tobacco, and read half of one novel. Mrs. Cary and Miss Carpenter walked a total of over a hundred miles, bought twelve pounds of Indian work of all sorts, embroidered the circle of two embroidery frames, learned to paddle a birch-bark canoe, picked fifteen quarts of berries, and gained six pounds in weight. All the party together accomplished five picnics, four explorations, and thirty excellent camp-fires in the evening. So much for the fun of it.

Little Phil disappeared utterly, taking with him his violin, but leaving his broken bow. Thorpe has it even to this day. The lumberman caused search and inquiry on all sides. The cripple was never heard of again. He had lived his brief hour, taken his subtle artist's vengeance of misplayed notes on the crude appreciation of men too coarse-fibred to recognize it, brought together by the might of sacrifice and consummate genius two hearts on the brink of misunderstanding;—now there was no further need for him, he had gone. So much for the tragedy of it.

" I saw you long ago," said Hilda to Thorpe. " Long, long ago, when I was quite a young girl. I had been visiting in Detroit, and was on my way all alone to catch an early train. You stood on the corner thinking, tall and straight and brown, with a weather-beaten old hat and a weather-beaten old coat and weather-beaten old moccasins, and such a proud, clear, undaunted look on your face. I have remembered you ever since."

And then he told her of the race to the Land Office, while her eyes grew brighter and brighter with the epic splendor of the story. She told him that she had loved him from that moment—and believed her telling; while he, the unsentimental leader of men, persuaded himself and her that he had always in some mysterious manner carried her image prophetically in his heart. So much for the love of it.

In the last days of the month of delight Thorpe

received a second letter from his partner, which to some extent awakened him to the realities.

"My dear Harry," it ran. "I have made a startling discovery. The other fellow is Morrison. I have been a blind, stupid dolt, and am caught nicely. You can't call me any more names than I have already called myself. Morrison has been in it from the start. By an accident I learned he was behind the fellow who induced me to invest, and it is he who has been hammering the stock down ever since. They couldn't lick you at your game, so they tackled me at mine. I'm not the man you are, Harry, and I've made a mess of it. Of course their scheme is plain enough on the face of it. They're going to involve me so deeply that I will drag the firm down with me.

"If you can fix it to meet those notes, they can't do it. I have ample margin to cover any more declines they may be able to bring about. Don't fret about that. Just as sure as you can pay that sixty thousand, just so sure we'll be ahead of the game at this time next year. For God's sake get a move on you, old man. If you don't—good Lord! The firm'll bust because she can't pay; I'll bust because I'll have to let my stock go on margins—it'll be an awful smash. But you'll get there, so we needn't worry. I've been an awful fool, and I've no right to do the getting into trouble and leave you to the hard work of getting out again. But as part-

ner I'm going to insist on your having a salary—
etc."

The news aroused all Thorpe's martial spirit.
Now at last the mystery surrounding Morrison &
Daly's unnatural complaisance was riven. It had
come to grapples again. He was glad of it. Meet
those notes? Well I guess so! He'd show them
what sort of a proposition they had tackled. Sneak-
ing, underhanded scoundrels! taking advantage of a
mere boy. Meet those notes? You bet he would;
and then he'd go down there and boost those stocks
until M. & D. looked like a last year's bird's nest.
He thrust the letter in his pocket and walked buoy-
antly to the pines.

The two lovers sat there all the afternoon drinking in half sadly the joy of the forest and of being
near each other, for the moon of delight was almost
done. In a week the camping party would be breaking up, and Hilda must return to the city. It was
uncertain when they would be able to see each other
again, though there was talk of getting up a winter
party to visit Camp One in January. The affair
would be unique.

Suddenly the girl broke off and put her fingers to
her lips. For some time, dimly, an intermittent and
faint sound had been felt, rather than actually
heard, like the irregular muffled beating of a heart.
Gradually it had insisted on the attention. Now at
last it broke through the film of consciousness.

" What is it? " she asked.

Thorpe listened. Then his face lit mightily with the joy of battle.

" My axe-men," he cried. " They are cutting the road."

A faint call echoed. Then without warning, nearer at hand the sharp ring of an axe sounded through the forest.

PART V
THE FOLLOWING OF THE TRAIL

CHAPTER FORTY-FOUR

FOR a moment they sat listening to the clear staccato knocking of the distant blows, and the more forceful thuds of the man nearer at hand. A bird or so darted from the direction of the sound and shot silently into the thicket behind them.

"What are they doing? Are they cutting lumber?" asked Hilda.

"No," answered Thorpe, "we do not cut saw logs at this time of year. They are clearing out a road."

"Where does it go to?"

"Well, nowhere in particular. That is, it is a logging road that starts at the river and wanders up through the woods where the pine is."

"How clear the axes sound. Can't we go down and watch them a little while?"

"The main gang is a long distance away; sound carries very clearly in this still air. As for that fellow you hear so plainly, he is only clearing out small stuff to get ready for the others. You wouldn't see anything different from your Indian chopping the cordwood for your camp fire. He won't chop out any big trees."

" Let's not go, then," said Hilda submissively.

" When you come up in the winter," he pursued, " you will see any amount of big timber felled."

" I would like to know more about it," she sighed, a quaint little air of childish petulance graving two lines between her eyebrows. " Do you know, Harry, you are a singularly uncommunicative sort of being. I have to guess that your life is interesting and picturesque—that is," she amended, " I should have to do so if Wallace Carpenter had not told me a little something about it. Sometimes I think you are not nearly poet enough for the life you are living. Why, you are wonderful, you men of the north, and you let us ordinary mortals who have not the gift of divination imagine you entirely occupied with how many pounds of iron chain you are going to need during the winter." She said these things lightly as one who speaks things not for serious belief.

" It is something that way," he agreed with a laugh.

" Do you know, sir," she persisted, " that I really don't know anything at all about the life you lead here? From what I have seen, you might be perpetually occupied in eating things in a log cabin, and in disappearing to perform some mysterious rites in the forest." She looked at him with a smiling mouth but tender eyes, her head tilted back slightly.

" It's a good deal that way, too," he agreed again.

" We use a barrel of flour in Camp One every two
and a half days! "

She shook her head in a faint negation that only
half understood what he was saying, her whole heart
in her tender gaze.

" Sit there," she breathed very softly, pointing to
the dried needles on which her feet rested, but without altering the position of her head or the steadfastness of her look.

He obeyed.

" Now tell me," she breathed, still in the fascinated monotone.

" What? " he inquired.

" Your life; what you do; all about it. You
must tell me a story."

Thorpe settled himself more lazily, and laughed
with quiet enjoyment. Never had he felt the expansion of a similar mood. The barrier between
himself and self-expression had faded, leaving not
the smallest *débris* of the old stubborn feeling.

" The story of the woods," he began, " the story
of the saw log. It would take a bigger man than I
to tell it. I doubt if any one man ever would be big
enough. It is a drama, a struggle, a battle. Those
men you hear there are only the skirmishers extending the firing line. We are fighting always with
Time. I'll have to hurry now to get those roads
done and a certain creek cleared before the snow.
Then we'll have to keep on the keen move to finish

our cutting before the deep snow; to haul our logs before the spring thaws; to float them down the river while the freshet water lasts. When we gain a day we have scored a victory; when the wilderness puts us back an hour, we have suffered a defeat. Our ammunition is Time; our small shot the minutes, our heavy ordnance the hours!"

The girl placed her hand on his shoulder. He covered it with his own.

"But we win!" he cried. "We win!"

"That is what I like," she said softly, "— the strong spirit that wins!" She hesitated, then went on gently, "But the battlefields, Harry; to me they are dreadful. I went walking yesterday morning, before you came over, and after a while I found myself in the most awful place. The stumps of trees, the dead branches, the trunks lying all about, and the glaring hot sun over everything! Harry, there was not a single bird in all that waste, a single green thing. You don't know how it affected me so early in the morning. I saw just one lonesome pine tree that had been left for some reason or another, standing there like a sentinel. I could shut my eyes and see all the others standing, and almost hear the birds singing and the wind in the branches, just as it is here." She seized his fingers in her other hand. "Harry," she said earnestly, "I don't believe I can ever forget that experience, any more than I could have forgotten a battlefield, were I to see one. I can shut my eyes now, and can see this place, our dear little wooded knoll wasted and blackened as that was."

The man twisted his shoulder uneasily and withdrew his hand.

"Harry," she said again, after a pause, "you must promise to leave this woods until the very last. I suppose it must all be cut down some day, but I do not want to be here to see after it is all over."

Thorpe remained silent.

"Men do not care much for keepsakes, do they, Harry?—they don't save letters and flowers as we girls do—but even a man can feel the value of a great beautiful keepsake such as this, can't he, dear? Our meeting-place—do you remember how I found you down there by the old pole trail, staring as though you had seen a ghost?—and that beautiful, beautiful music! It must always be our most sacred memory. Promise me you will save it until the very, very last."

Thorpe said nothing because he could not rally his faculties. The sentimental association connected with the grove had actually never occurred to him. His keepsakes were impressions which he carefully guarded in his memory. To the natural masculine indifference toward material bits of sentiment he had added the instinct of the strictly portable early developed in the rover. He had never even possessed a photograph of his sister. Now this sudden discovery that such things might be part of the woof of another person's spiritual garment came to him ready-grown to the proportions of a problem.

In selecting the districts for the season's cut, he had included in his estimates this very grove. Since then he had seen no reason for changing his decision. The operations would not commence until winter. By that time the lovers would no longer care to use it as at present. Now rapidly he passed in review a dozen expedients by which his plan might be modified to permit of the grove's exclusion. His practical mind discovered flaws in every one. Other bodies of timber promising a return of ten thousand dollars were not to be found near the river, and time now lacked for the cutting of roads to more distant forties.

"Hilda," he broke in abruptly at last, "the men you hear are clearing a road to this very timber."

"What do you mean?" she asked.

"This timber is marked for cutting this very winter."

She had not a suspicion of the true state of affairs. "Isn't it lucky I spoke of it!" she exclaimed. "How could you have forgotten to countermand the order! You must see to it to-day; now!"

She sprang up impulsively and stood waiting for him. He arose more slowly. Even before he spoke her eyes dilated with the shock from her quick intuitions.

" Hilda, I cannot," he said.

She stood very still for some seconds.

" Why not? " she asked quietly.

" Because I have not time to cut a road through to another bunch of pine. It is this or nothing."

" Why not nothing, then? "

" I want the money this will bring."

His choice of a verb was unfortunate. The employment of that one little word opened the girl's mind to a flood of old suspicions which the frank charm of the northland had thrust outside. Hilda Farrand was an heiress and a beautiful girl. She had been constantly reminded of the one fact by the attempts of men to use flattery of the other as a key to her heart and her fortune. From early girlhood she had been sought by the brilliant impecunious of two continents. The continued experience had varnished her self-esteem with a glaze of cynicism sufficiently consistent to protect it against any but the strongest attack. She believed in no man's protestations. She distrusted every man's motives as far as herself was concerned. This attitude of mind was not unbecoming in her for the simple reason that it destroyed none of her graciousness as regards other human relations besides that of love. That men should seek her in matrimony from a selfish motive was as much to be expected as that flies should seek the sugar bowl. She accepted the fact as one of nature's laws, annoying enough but inevitable; a thing to guard against, but not one of sufficient moment to grieve over.

With Thorpe, however, her suspicions had been lulled. There is something virile and genuine about the woods and the men who inhabit them that strongly predisposes the mind to accept as proved in their entirety all the other virtues. Hilda had fallen into this state of mind. She endowed each of the men whom she encountered with all the robust qualities she had no difficulty in recognizing as part of nature's charm in the wilderness. Now at a word her eyes were opened to what she had done. She saw that she had assumed unquestioningly that her lover possessed the qualities of his environment.

Not for a moment did she doubt the reality of her love. She had conceived one of those deep, uplifting passions possible only to a young girl. But her cynical experience warned her that the reality of that passion's object was not proven by any test besides the fallible one of her own poetizing imagination. The reality of the ideal she had constructed might be a vanishable quantity even though the love of it was not. So to the interview that ensued she brought, not the partiality of a loving heart, nor even the impartiality of one sitting in judgment, but rather the perverted prejudice of one who actually fears the truth.

"Will you tell me for what you want the money?" she asked.

THE FOLLOWING OF THE TRAIL

The young man caught the note of distrust. At once, instinctively, his own confidence vanished. He drew within himself, again beyond the power of justifying himself with the needed word.

"The firm needs it in the business," said he.

Her next question countered instantaneously.

"Does the firm need the money more than you do me?"

They stared at each other in the silence of the situations that had so suddenly developed. It had come into being without their volition, as a dust cloud springs up on a plain.

"You do not mean that, Hilda," said Thorpe quietly. "It hardly comes to that."

"Indeed it does," she replied, every nerve of her fine organization strung to excitement. "I should be more to you than any firm."

"Sometimes it is necessary to look after the bread and butter," Thorpe reminded her gently, although he knew that was not the real reason at all.

"If your firm can't supply it, I can," she answered. "It seems strange that you won't grant my first request of you, merely because of a little money."

"It isn't a little money," he objected, catching man-like at the practical question. "You don't realize what an amount a clump of pine like this stands for. Just in saw logs, before it is made into lumber, it will be worth about thirty thousand dollars—of course there's the expense of logging to pay out of that," he added, out of his accurate business conservatism, "but there's ten thousand dollars' profit in it."

The girl, exasperated by cold details at such a time, blazed out. "I never heard anything so ridiculous in my life!" she cried. "Either you are not at all the man I thought you, or you have some better reason than you have given. Tell me, Harry; tell me at once. You don't know what you are doing."

"The firm needs it, Hilda," said Thorpe, "in order to succeed. If we do not cut this pine, we may fail."

In that he stated his religion. The duty of success was to him one of the loftiest of abstractions, for it measured the degree of a man's efficiency in the station to which God had called him. The money, as such, was nothing to him.

Unfortunately the girl had learned a different language. She knew nothing of the hardships, the struggles, the delight of winning for the sake of victory rather than the sake of spoils. To her, success meant getting a lot of money. The name by which Thorpe labelled his most sacred principle, to her represented something base and sordid. She had more money herself than she knew. It hurt her to the soul that the condition of a small money-making machine, as she considered the lumber firm, should be weighed even for an instant against her love. It was a great deal Thorpe's fault that she so saw the firm. He might easily have shown her the great forces and principles for which it stood.

"If I were a man," she said, and her voice was tense, "if I were a man and loved a woman, I would be ready to give up everything for her. My riches, my pride, my life, my honor, my soul even—they would be as nothing, as less than nothing to me—if I loved. Harry, don't let me think I am mistaken. Let this miserable firm of yours fail, if fail it must for lack of my poor little temple of dreams," she held out her hands with a tender gesture of appeal. The affair had gone beyond the preservation of a few trees. It had become the question of an ideal. Gradually, in spite of herself, the conviction was forcing itself upon her that the man she had loved was no different from the rest; that the greed of the dollar had corrupted him too. By the mere yielding to her wishes, she wanted to prove the suspicion wrong.

Now the strange part of the whole situation was, that in two words Thorpe could have cleared it. If he had explained that he needed the ten thousand dollars to help pay a note given to save from ruin a foolish friend, he would have supplied to the affair just the higher motive the girl's clear spirituality demanded. Then she would have shared enthusiastically in the sacrifice, and been the more loving and repentant from her momentary doubt. All she needed was that the man should prove himself actuated by a noble, instead of a sordid, motive. The young man did not say the two words, because in all honesty he thought them unimportant. It seemed to him quite natural that he should go on Wallace Carpenter's note. That fact altered not a bit the main necessity of success. It was a man's duty to make the best of himself—it was Thorpe's duty to prove himself supremely efficient in his chosen calling; the mere coincidence that his partner's troubles worked along the same lines meant nothing to the logic of the situation. In stating baldly that he needed the money to assure the firm's existence, he imagined he had adduced the strongest possible reason for his attitude. If the girl was not influenced by that, the case was hopeless.

It was the difference of training rather than the difference of ideas. Both clung to unselfishness as the highest reason for human action; but each expressed the thought in a manner incomprehensible to the other.

" I cannot, Hilda," he answered steadily.

" You sell me for ten thousand dollars! I cannot believe it! Harry! Harry! Must I put it to you as a choice? Don't you love me enough to spare me that?"

He did not reply. As long as it remained a dilemma, he would not reply. He was in the right.

"Do you need the money more than you do me? more than you do love?" she begged, her soul in her eyes; for she was begging also for herself. "Think, Harry; it is the last chance!"

Once more he was face to face with a vital decision. To his surprise he discovered in his mind no doubt as to what the answer should be. He experienced no conflict of mind; no hesitation; for the moment, no regret. During all his woods life he had been following diligently the trail he had blazed for his conduct. Now his feet carried him unconsciously to the same end. There was no other way out. In the winter of his trouble the clipped trees alone guided him, and at the end of them he found his decision. It is in crises of this sort, when a little reflection or consideration would do wonders to prevent a catastrophe, that all the forgotten deeds, decisions, principles, and thoughts of a man's past life combine solidly into the walls of fatality, so that in spite of himself he finds he must act in accordance with them. In answer to Hilda's question he merely inclined his head.

"I have seen a vision," said she simply, and lowered her head to conceal her eyes. Then she looked at him again. "There can be nothing better than love," she said.

"Yes, one thing," said Thorpe, "—the duty of success."

The man had stated his creed; the woman hers.

The one is born perfect enough for love; the other must work, must attain the completeness of a fulfilled function, must succeed, to deserve it.

She left him then, and did not see him again. Four days later the camping party left. Thorpe sent Tim Shearer over, as his most efficient man, to see that they got off without difficulty, but himself retired on some excuse to Camp Four. Three weeks gone in October he received a marked newspaper announcing the engagement of Miss Hilda Farrand to Mr. Hildreth Morton of Chicago.

He had burned his ships, and stood now on an unfriendly shore. The first sacrifice to his jealous god had been consummated, and now, live or die, he stood pledged to win his fight.

CHAPTER FORTY-FIVE

WINTER set in early and continued late; which in the end was a good thing for the year's cut. The season was capricious, hanging for days at a time at the brink of a thaw, only to stiffen again into severe weather. This was trying on the nerves. For at each of these false alarms the six camps fell into a feverish haste to get the job finished before the break-up. It was really quite extraordinary how much was accomplished under the nagging spur of weather conditions and the cruel rowelling of Thorpe.

The latter had now no thought beyond his work, and that was the thought of a madman. He had been stern and unyielding enough before, goodness knows, but now he was terrible. His restless energy permeated every molecule in the economic structure over which he presided, roused it to intense vibration. Not for an instant was there a resting spell. The veriest chore-boy talked, thought, dreamed of nothing but saw logs. Men whispered vaguely of a record cut. Teamsters looked upon their success or failure to keep near the top on the day's haul as a signal victory or a disgraceful defeat. The difficulties of snow, accident, topography which an ever-watchful nature threw down before the rolling car of this industry, were swept aside like straws. Little time was wasted and no opportunities. It did not matter how smoothly affairs happened to be running for the moment, every advantage, even the smallest, was eagerly seized to advance the work. A drop of five degrees during the frequent warm spells brought out the sprinklers, even in dead of night; an accident was white-hot in the forge almost before the crack of the iron had ceased to echo. At night the men fell into their bunks like sandbags, and their last conscious thought, if indeed they had any at all, was of eagerness for the morrow in order that they might push the grand total up another notch. It was madness; but it was the madness these men loved.

For now to his old religion Thorpe had added a fanaticism, and over the fanaticism was gradually creeping a film of doubt. To the conscientious energy which a sense of duty supplied, was added the tremendous kinetic force of a love turned into other channels. And in the wild nights while the other men slept, Thorpe's half-crazed brain was revolving over and over again the words of the sentence he had heard from Hilda's lips: "There can be nothing better than love."

His actions, his mind, his very soul vehemently denied the proposition. He clung as ever to his high Puritanic idea of man's purpose. But down deep in

a very tiny, sacred corner of his heart a very small
voice sometimes made itself heard when other, more
militant voices were still: " It may be; it may be! "

The influence of this voice was practically nothing. It made itself heard occasionally. Perhaps
even, for the time being, its weight counted on the
other side of the scale; for Thorpe took pains to
deny it fiercely, both directly and indirectly by increased exertions. But it persisted; and once in a
moon or so, when the conditions were quite favorable, it attained for an instant a shred of belief.

Probably never since the Puritan days of New
England has a community lived as sternly as did
that winter of 1888 the six camps under Thorpe's
management. There was something a little inspiring about it. The men fronted their daily work with
the same grim-faced, clear-eyed steadiness of veterans going into battle; with the same confidence,
the same sure patience that disposes effectively of
one thing before going on to the next. There was
little merely excitable bustle; there was no rest.
Nothing could stand against such a spirit. Nothing
did. The skirmishers which the wilderness threw
out were brushed away. Even the inevitable delays
seemed not so much stoppages as the instant's pause
of a heavy vehicle in a snowdrift, succeeded by the
momentary acceleration as the plunge carried it
through. In the main, and by large, the machine
moved steadily and inexorably.

And yet one possessed of the finer spiritual intuitions could not have shaken off the belief in an impending struggle. The feel of it was in the air. Nature's forces were too mighty to be so slightly overcome; the splendid energy developed in these camps too vast to be wasted on facile success. Over against each other were two great powers, alike in their calm confidence, animated with the loftiest and most dignified spirit of enmity. Slowly they were moving toward each other. The air was surcharged with the electricity of their opposition. Just how the struggle would begin was uncertain; but its inevitability was as assured as its magnitude. Thorpe knew it, and shut his teeth, looking keenly about him. The Fighting Forty knew it, and longed for the grapple to come. The other camps knew it, and followed their leader with perfect trust. The affair was an epitome of the historic combats begun with David and Goliath. It was an affair of Titans. The little courageous men watched their enemy with cat's eyes.

The last month of hauling was also one of snow. In this condition were few severe storms, but each day a little fell. By and by the accumulation amounted to much. In the woods where the wind could not get at it, it lay deep and soft above the tops of bushes. The grouse ate browse from the slender hardwood tips like a lot of goldfinches, or precipitated themselves headlong down through five

feet of snow to reach the ground. Often Thorpe
would come across the irregular holes of their entrance. Then if he took the trouble to stamp about
a little in the vicinity with his snowshoes, the bird
would spring unexpectedly from the clear snow,
scattering a cloud with its strong wings. The deer,
herded together, tramped "yards" where the feed
was good. Between the yards ran narrow trails.
When the animals went from one yard to another
in these trails, their ears and antlers alone were
visible. On either side of the logging roads the snow
piled so high as to form a kind of rampart. When
all this water in suspense should begin to flow, and
to seek its level in the water-courses of the district,
the logs would have plenty to float them, at least.

So late did the cold weather last that, even with
the added plowing to do, the six camps beat all
records. On the banks at Camp One were nine
million feet; the totals of all five amounted to
thirty-three million. About ten million of this was
on French Creek; the remainder on the main banks
of the Ossawinamakee. Besides this the firm up-
river, Sadler & Smith, had put up some twelve
million more. The drive promised to be quite an
affair.

About the fifteenth of April attention became
strained. Every day the mounting sun made heavy
attacks on the snow: every night the temperature
dropped below the freezing point. The river began

to show more air holes, occasional open places. About the centre the ice looked worn and soggy. Some one saw a flock of geese high in the air. Then came rain.

One morning early, Long Pine Jim came into the men's camp bearing a huge chunk of tallow. This he held against the hot stove until its surface had softened, when he began to swab liberal quantities of grease on his spiked river shoes, which he fished out from under his bunk.

" She's comin', boys," said he.

He donned a pair of woolen trousers that had been chopped off at the knee, thick woolen stockings, and the river shoes. Then he tightened his broad leather belt about his heavy shirt, cocked his little hat over his ear, and walked over in the corner to select a peavey from the lot the blacksmith had just put in shape. A peavey is like a cant-hook except that it is pointed at the end. Thus it can be used either as a hook or a pike. At the same moment Shearer, similarly attired and equipped, appeared in the doorway. The opening of the portal admitted a roar of sound. The river was rising.

" Come on, boys, she's on! " said he sharply.

Outside, the cook and cookee were stowing articles in the already loaded wanigan. The scow contained tents, blankets, provisions, and a portable stove. It followed the drive, and made a camp wherever expediency demanded.

" Lively, boys, lively! " shouted Thorpe. " She'll be down on us before we know it! "

Above the soft creaking of dead branches in the wind sounded a steady roar, like the bellowing of a wild beast lashing itself to fury. The freshet was abroad, forceful with the strength of a whole winter's accumulated energy.

The men heard it and their eyes brightened with the lust of battle. They cheered.

CHAPTER FORTY-SIX

A T the banks of the river, Thorpe rapidly issued
his directions. The affair had been all prearranged. During the week previous he and his
foremen had reviewed the situation, examining the
state of the ice, the heads of water in the three dams.
Immediately above the first rollways was Dam
Three with its two wide sluices through which a
veritable flood could be loosened at will; then four
miles farther lay the rollways of Sadler & Smith,
the up-river firm; and above them tumbled over a
forty-five foot ledge the beautiful Siscoe Falls; these
first rollways of Thorpe's — spread in the broad
marsh flat below the dam—contained about eight
millions; the rest of the season's cut was scattered
for thirty miles along the bed of the river.

Already the ice cementing the logs together had
begun to weaken. The ice had wrenched and tugged
savagely at the locked timbers until they had, with a
mighty effort, snapped asunder the bonds of their
hibernation. Now a narrow lane of black rushing
water pierced the rollways, to boil and eddy in the
consequent jam three miles below.

To the foremen Thorpe assigned their tasks, call-

416

ing them to him one by one, as a general calls his aids.

"Moloney," said he to the big Irishman, "take your crew and break that jam. Then scatter your men down to within a mile of the pond at Dam Two, and see that the river runs clear. You can tent for a day or so at West Bend or some other point about half-way down; and after that you had better camp at the dam. Just as soon as you get logs enough in the pond, start to sluicing them through the dam. You won't need more than four men there, if you keep a good head. You can keep your gates open five or six hours. And Moloney!"

"Yes, sir."

"I want you to be careful not to sluice too long. There is a bar just below the dam, and if you try to sluice with the water too low, you'll centre and jam there, as sure as shooting."

Bryan Moloney turned on his heel and began to pick his way down-stream over the solidly banked logs. Without waiting the command, a dozen men followed him. The little group bobbed away irregularly into the distance, springing lightly from one timber to the other, holding their quaintly fashioned peaveys in the manner of a rope-dancer's balancing pole. At the lowermost limit of the rollways each man pried a log into the water, and, standing gracefully erect on this unstable craft, floated out down the current to the scene of his dangerous labor.

"Kerlie," went on Thorpe, "your crew can break rollways with the rest until we get the river fairly filled, and then you can move on down-stream as fast as you are needed. Scotty, you will have the rear. Tim and I will boss the river."

At once the signal was given to Ellis, the dam watcher. Ellis and his assistants thereupon began to pry with long iron bars at the ratchets of the heavy gates. The chore-boy bent attentively over the ratchet-pin, lifting it delicately to permit another inch of raise, dropping it accurately to enable the men at the bars to seize a fresh purchase. The river's roar deepened. Through the wide sluiceways a torrent foamed and tumbled. Immediately it spread through the brush on either side to the limits of the freshet banks, and then gathered for its leap against the uneasy rollways. Along the edge of the dark channel the face of the logs seemed to crumble away. Farther in toward the banks where the weight of timber still outbalanced the weight of the flood, the tiers grumbled and stirred, restless with the stream's calling. Far down the river, where Bryan Moloney and his crew were picking at the jam, the water in eager streamlets sought the interstices between the logs, gurgling excitedly like a mountain brook.

The jam creaked and groaned in response to the

pressure. From its face a hundred jets of water spurted into the lower stream. Logs up-ended here and there, rising from the bristling surface slowly, like so many arms from lower depths. Above, the water eddied back foaming; logs shot down from the rollways, paused at the slackwater, and finally hit with a hollow and resounding *boom!* against the tail of the jam. A moment later they too up-ended, so becoming an integral part of the *chevaux de frise*.

The crew were working desperately. Down in the heap somewhere, two logs were crossed in such a manner as to lock the whole. They sought those logs.

Thirty feet above the bed of the river six men clamped their peaveys into the soft pine; jerking, pulling, lifting, sliding the great logs from their places. Thirty feet below, under the threatening face, six other men coolly picked out and set adrift, one by one, the timbers not inextricably imbedded. From time to time the mass creaked, settled, perhaps even moved a foot or two; but always the practised rivermen, after a glance, bent more eagerly to their work.

Outlined against the sky, big Bryan Moloney stood directing the work. He had gone at the job on the bias of indirection, picking out a passage at either side that the centre might the more easily " pull." He knew by the tenseness of the log he stood on that, behind the jam, power had gathered sufficient to push the whole tangle down-stream. Now he was offering it the chance.

Suddenly the six men below the jam scattered. Four of them, holding their peaveys across their bodies, jumped lightly from one floating log to another in the zigzag to shore. When they stepped on a small log they re-leaped immediately, leaving a swirl of foam where the little timber had sunk under them; when they encountered one larger, they hesitated for a barely perceptible instant. Thus their progression was of fascinating and graceful irregularity. The other two ran the length of their footing, and, overleaping an open of water, landed heavily and firmly on the very ends of two small floating logs. In this manner the force of the jump rushed the little timbers end-on through the water. The two men, maintaining marvellously their balance, were thus ferried to within leaping distance of the other shore.

In the meantime a barely perceptible motion was communicating itself from one particle to another through the centre of the jam. A cool and observant spectator might have imagined that the broad timber carpet was changing a little its pattern, just as the earth near the windows of an arrested railroad train seems for a moment to retrogress. The crew redoubled its exertions, clamping its peaveys here and there, apparently at random, but in reality with the most definite of purposes. A sharp *crack* exploded immediately underneath. There could no longer exist any doubt as to the motion, although it was as yet sluggish, glacial. Then in silence a log shifted—in silence and slowly —but with irresistible force. Jimmy Powers quietly stepped over it, just as it menaced his leg. Other logs in all directions up-ended. The jam crew were forced continually to alter their positions, riding the changing timbers bent-kneed, as a circus rider treads his four galloping horses.

Then all at once down by the face something crashed. The entire stream became alive. It hissed and roared, it shrieked, groaned and grumbled. At first slowly, then more rapidly, the very forefront of the centre melted inward and forward and down-ward until it caught the fierce rush of the freshet and shot out from under the jam. Far up-stream, bristling and formidable, the tons of logs, grinding savagely together, swept forward.

The six men and Bryan Moloney—who, it will be remembered, were on top—worked until the last moment. When the logs began to cave under them so rapidly that even the expert rivermen found dif-ficulty in " staying on top," the foreman set the example of hunting safety.

" She ' pulls,' boys," he yelled.

Then in a manner wonderful to behold, through the smother of foam and spray, through the crash and yell of timbers protesting the flood's hurrying, through the leap of destruction, the drivers zig-zagged calmly and surely to the shore.

All but Jimmy Powers. He poised tense and eager on the crumbling face of the jam. Almost immediately he saw what he wanted, and without pause sprang boldly and confidently ten feet straight downward, to alight with accuracy on a single log floating free in the current. And then in the very glory and chaos of the jam itself he was swept down-stream.

After a moment the constant acceleration in speed checked, then commenced perceptibly to slacken. At once the rest of the crew began to ride down-stream. Each struck the caulks of his river boots strongly into a log, and on such unstable vehicles floated miles with the current. From time to time, as Bryan Moloney indicated, one of them went ashore. There, usually at a bend of the stream where the likelihood of jamming was great, they took their stands. When necessary, they ran out over the face of the river to separate a congestion likely to cause trouble. The rest of the time they smoked their pipes.

At noon they ate from little canvas bags which had been filled that morning by the cookee. At sunset they rode other logs down the river to where their camp had been made for them. There they ate hugely, hung their ice-wet garments over a tall framework constructed around a monster fire, and turned in on hemlock branches.

THE FOLLOWING OF THE TRAIL

All night long the logs slipped down the moonlit current, silently, swiftly, yet without haste. The porcupines invaded the sleeping camp. From the whole length of the river rang the hollow *boom*, *boom*, *boom*, of timbers striking one against the other.

The drive was on.

CHAPTER FORTY-SEVEN

IN the meantime the main body of the crew under Thorpe and his foremen were briskly tumbling the logs into the current. Sometimes under the urging of the peaveys, but a single stick would slide down; or again a double tier would cascade with the roar of a little Niagara. The men had continually to keep on the tension of an alert, for at any moment they were called upon to exercise their best judgment and quickness to keep from being carried downward with the rush of the logs. Not infrequently a frowning sheer wall of forty feet would hesitate on the brink of plunge. Then Shearer himself proved his right to the title of riverman.

Shearer wore caulks nearly an inch in length. He had been known to ride ten miles, without shifting his feet, on a log so small that he could carry it without difficulty. For cool nerve he was unexcelled.

" I don't need you boys here any longer," he said quietly.

When the men had all withdrawn, he walked confidently under the front of the rollway, glancing with practised eye at the perpendicular wall of logs over him. Then, as a man pries jack-straws, he clamped his peavey and tugged sharply. At once the rollway flattened and toppled. A mighty splash, a hurl of flying foam and crushing timbers, and the spot on which the riverman had stood was buried beneath twenty feet of solid green wood. To Thorpe it seemed that Shearer must have been overwhelmed, but the riverman always mysteriously appeared at one side or the other, nonchalant, urging the men to work before the logs should have ceased to move. Tradition claimed that only once in a long woods life had Shearer been forced to " take water " before a breaking rollway: and then he saved his peavey. History stated that he had never lost a man on the river, simply and solely because he invariably took the dangerous tasks upon himself.

As soon as the logs had caught the current, a dozen men urged them on. With their short peaveys, the drivers were enabled to prevent the timbers from swirling in the eddies—one of the first causes of a jam. At last, near the foot of the flats, they abandoned them to the stream, confident that Moloney and his crew would see to their passage down the river.

In three days the rollways were broken. Now it became necessary to start the rear.

For this purpose Billy Camp, the cook, had loaded his cook-stove, a quantity of provisions, and a supply of bedding, aboard a scow. The scow was built of tremendous hewn timbers, four or five inches thick, to withstand the shock of the logs. At either end were long sweeps to direct its course. The craft was perhaps forty feet long, but rather narrow, in order that it might pass easily through the chute of a dam. It was called the " wanigan."

Billy Camp, his cookee, and his crew of two were now doomed to tribulation. The huge, unwieldy craft from that moment was to become possessed of the devil. Down the white water of rapids it would bump, smashing obstinately against boulders, impervious to the frantic urging of the long sweeps; against the roots and branches of the stream side it would scrape with the perverseness of a vicious horse; in the broad reaches it would sulk, refusing to proceed; and when expediency demanded its pause, it would drag Billy Camp and his entire crew at the rope's end, while they tried vainly to snub it against successively uprooted trees and stumps. When at last the wanigan was moored fast for the night—usually a mile or so below the spot planned —Billy Camp pushed back his battered old brown derby hat, the badge of his office, with a sigh of relief. To be sure he and his men had still to cut wood, construct cooking and camp fires, pitch tents, snip browse, and prepare supper for seventy men; but the hard work of the day was over. Billy Camp did not mind rain or cold—he would cheerfully cook away with the water dripping from his battered derby to his chubby and cold-purpled nose—but he did mind the wanigan. And the worst of it was, he got no sympathy nor aid from the crew. From either bank he and his anxious struggling assistants were greeted with ironic cheers and facetious remarks. The tribulations of the wanigan were as the salt of life to the spectators.

Billy Camp tried to keep back of the rear in clear water, but when the wanigan so disposed, he found himself jammed close in the logs. There he had a chance in his turn to become spectator, and so to repay in kind some of the irony and facetiousness.

Along either bank, among the bushes, on sand-bars, and in trees, hundreds and hundreds of logs had been stranded when the main drive passed. These logs the rear crew were engaged in restoring to the current.

And as a man had to be able to ride any kind of a log in any water; to propel that log by jumping on it, by rolling it squirrel fashion with the feet, by punting it as one would a canoe; to be skillful in pushing, prying, and poling other logs from the quarter deck of the same cranky craft; as he must be prepared at any and all times to jump waist deep into the river, to work in ice-water hours at a stretch; as he was called upon to break the most dangerous jams on the river, representing, as they did, the accumulation which the jam crew had left behind them, it was naturally considered the height of glory to belong to the rear crew. Here were the best of the Fighting Forty—men with a reputation as " white-water birlers "—men afraid of nothing.

Every morning the crews were divided into two sections under Kerlie and Jack Hyland. Each crew had charge of one side of the river, with the task of cleaning it thoroughly of all stranded and entangled logs. Scotty Parsons exercised a general supervisory eye over both crews. Shearer and Thorpe travelled back and forth the length of the drive, riding the logs down-stream, but taking to a partly submerged pole trail when ascending the current. On the surface of the river in the clear water floated two long graceful boats called bateaux. These were in charge of expert boatmen—men able to propel their craft swiftly forward, backward and sideways, through all kinds of water. They carried in racks a great supply of pike-poles, peaveys, axes, rope and dynamite, for use in various emergencies. Intense rivalry existed as to which crew " sacked " the farthest down-stream in the course of the day. There was no need to urge the men. Some stood upon the logs, pushing mightily with the long pike-poles. Others, waist deep in the water, clamped the jaws of their peaveys into the stubborn timbers, and, shoulder bent, slid them slowly but surely into the swifter waters. Still others, lining up on either side of one of the great brown tree trunks, carried it bodily to its appointed place. From one end of the rear to the other shouts, calls, warnings, and jokes flew back and forth. Once or twice a vast roar of Homeric laughter went up as some unfortunate slipped and soused into the water. When the current slacked, and the logs hesitated in their run, the entire crew hastened, bobbing from log to log, down-river to see about it. Then they broke the jam, standing surely on the edge of the great darkness, while the ice water sucked in and out of their shoes.

Behind the rear Big Junko poled his bateau backward and forward exploding dynamite. Many of the bottom tiers of logs in the rollways had been frozen down, and Big Junko had to loosen them from the bed of the stream. He was a big man, this, as his nickname indicated, built of many awkwardnesses. His cheekbones were high, his nose flat, his lips thick and slobbery. He sported a wide, ferocious straggling mustache and long eyebrows, under which gleamed little fierce eyes. His forehead sloped back like a beast's, but was always hidden by a disreputable felt hat. Big Junko did not know much, and had the passions of a wild animal, but he was a reckless riverman and devoted to Thorpe. Just now he exploded dynamite.

The sticks of powder were piled amidships. Big Junko crouched over them, inserting the fuses and caps, closing the openings with soap, finally lighting them, and dropping them into the water alongside, where they immediately sank. Then a few strokes of a short paddle took him barely out of danger. He huddled down in his craft, waiting. One, two, three seconds passed. Then a hollow boom shook the stream. A cloud of water sprang up, strangely beautiful. After a moment the great brown logs rose suddenly to the surface from below, one after the other, like leviathans of the deep. And Junko watched, dimly fascinated, in his rudimentary animal's brain, by the sight of the power he had evoked to his aid.

When night came the men rode down-stream to where the wanigan had made camp. There they slept, often in blankets wetted by the wanigan's eccentricities, to leap to their feet at the first cry in early morning. Some days it rained, in which case they were wet all the time. Almost invariably there was a jam to break, though strangely enough almost every one of the old-timers believed implicitly that "in the full of the moon logs will run free at night."

Thorpe and Tim Shearer nearly always slept in a dog tent at the rear; though occasionally they passed the night at Dam Two, where Bryan Moloney and his crew were already engaged in sluicing the logs through the chute.

The affair was simple enough. Long booms arranged in the form of an open V guided the drive to the sluice gate, through which a smooth apron of water rushed to turmoil in an eddying pool below.

THE FOLLOWING OF THE TRAIL

Two men tramped steadily backward and forward on the booms, urging the logs forward by means of long pike poles to where the suction could seize them. Below the dam, the push of the sluice water forced them several miles down-stream, where the rest of Bryan Moloney's crew took them in charge.

Thus through the wide gate nearly three-quarters of a million feet an hour could be run—a quantity more than sufficient to keep pace with the exertions of the rear. The matter was, of course, more or less delayed by the necessity of breaking out such roll-ways as they encountered from time to time on the banks. At length, however, the last of the logs drifted into the wide dam pool. The rear had arrived at Dam Two, and Thorpe congratulated himself that one stage of his journey had been completed. Billy Camp began to worry about shooting the wanigan through the sluiceway.

CHAPTER FORTY-EIGHT

THE rear had been tenting at the dam for two days, and was about ready to break camp, when Jimmy Powers swung across the trail to tell them of the big jam.

Ten miles along the river bed the stream dropped over a little half-falls into a narrow, rocky gorge. It was always an anxious spot for the river drivers. In fact, the plunging of the logs head-on over the fall had so gouged out the soft rock below that an eddy of great power had formed in the basin. Shearer and Thorpe had often discussed the advisability of constructing an artificial apron of logs to receive the impact. Here, in spite of all efforts, the jam had formed—first a little centre of a few logs in the middle of the stream, dividing the current, and shunting the logs to right and left; then "wings" growing out from either bank, built up from logs shunted too violently; finally a complete stoppage of the channel, and the consequent rapid piling up as the pressure of the drive increased. Now the bed was completely filled, far above the level of the falls, by a tangle that defied the jam crew's best efforts.

The rear at once took the trail down the river.

Thorpe and Shearer and Scotty Parsons looked over the ground.

"She may 'pull,' if she gets a good start," decided Tim.

Without delay the entire crew was set to work. Nearly a hundred men can pick a great many logs in the course of a day. Several times the jam started, but always "plugged" before the motion had become irresistible. This was mainly because the rocky walls narrowed at a slight bend to the west, so that the drive was throttled, as it were. It was hoped that perhaps the middle of the jam might burst through here, leaving the wings stranded. The hope was groundless.

"We'll have to shoot," Shearer reluctantly decided.

The men were withdrawn. Scotty Parsons cut a sapling twelve feet long, and trimmed it. Big Junko thawed his dynamite at a little fire, opening the ends of the packages in order that the steam generated might escape. Otherwise the pressure inside the oiled paper of the package was capable of exploding the whole affair. When the powder was warm, Scotty bound twenty of the cartridges around the end of the sapling, adjusted a fuse in one of them, and soaped the opening to exclude water. Then Big Junko thrust the long javelin down into the depths of the jam, leaving a thin stream of smoke behind him as he turned away. With sinister, evil eye he watched the smoke for an instant, then zigzagged awkwardly over the jam, the long, ridiculous tails of his brown cutaway coat flopping behind him as he leaped. A scant moment later the hoarse dynamite shouted.

Great chunks of timber shot to an inconceivable height; entire logs lifted bodily into the air with the motion of a fish jumping; a fountain of water gleamed against the sun and showered down in fine rain. The jam shrugged and settled. That was all; the " shot " had failed.

The men ran forward, examining curiously the great hole in the log formation.

" We'll have to flood her," said Thorpe.

So all the gates of the dam were raised, and the torrent tried its hand. It had no effect. Evidently the affair was not one of violence, but of patience. The crew went doggedly to work.

Day after day the *clank*, *clank*, *clink* of the peaveys sounded with the regularity of machinery. The only practicable method was to pick away the flank logs, leaving a long tongue pointing down-stream from the centre to start when it would. This happened time and again, but always failed to take with it the main jam. It was cruel hard work; a man who has lifted his utmost strength into a peavey knows that. Any but the Fighting Forty would have grumbled.

Collins, the bookkeeper, came up to view the

tangle. Later a photographer from Marquette took some views, which, being exhibited, attracted a great deal of attention, so that by the end of the week a number of curiosity seekers were driving over every day to see the Big Jam. A certain Chicago journalist in search of balsam health of lungs even sent to his paper a little item. This, unexpectedly, brought Wallace Carpenter to the spot. Although reassured as to the gravity of the situation, he remained to see.

The place was an amphitheatre for such as chose to be spectators. They could stand or sit on the summit of the gorge cliffs, overlooking the river, the fall, and the jam. As the cliff was barely sixty feet high, the view lacked nothing in clearness.

At last Shearer became angry.

"We've been monkeying long enough," said he. "Next time we'll leave a centre that *will* go out. We'll shut the dams down tight and dry-pick out two wings that'll start her."

The dams were first run at full speed, and then shut down. Hardly a drop of water flowed in the bed of the stream. The crews set laboriously to work to pull and roll the logs out in such flat fashion that a head of water should send them out.

This was even harder work than the other, for they had not the floating power of water to help them in the lifting. As usual, part of the men worked below, part above.

Jimmy Powers, curly-haired, laughing-faced, was irrepressible. He badgered the others until they threw bark at him and menaced him with their peaveys. Always he had at his tongue's end the proper quip for the occasion, so that in the long run the work was lightened by him. When the men stopped to think at all, they thought of Jimmy Powers with very kindly hearts, for it was known that he had had more trouble than most, and that the coin was not made too small for him to divide with a needy comrade. To those who had seen his mask of whole-souled good-nature fade into serious sympathy, Jimmy Powers's poor little jokes were very funny indeed.

"Did 'je see th' Swede at the circus las' summer?" he would howl to Red Jacket on the top tier.

"No," Red Jacket would answer, "was he there?"

"Yes," Jimmy Powers would reply; then, after a pause—"in a cage!"

It was a poor enough jest, yet if you had been there, you would have found that somehow the log had in the meantime leaped of its own accord from that difficult position.

Thorpe approved thoroughly of Jimmy Powers; he thought him a good influence. He told Wallace so, standing among the spectators on the cliff-top.

"He is all right," said Thorpe. "I wish I had more like him. The others are good boys, too."

Five men were at the moment tugging futilely at a reluctant timber. They were attempting to roll one end of it over the side of another projecting log, but were continually foiled, because the other end was jammed fast. Each bent his knees, inserting his shoulder under the projecting peavey stock, to straighten in a mighty effort.

"Hire a boy!" "Get some powder of Junko!" "Have Jimmy *talk* it out!" "Try that little one over by the corner," called the men on top of the jam.

Everybody laughed, of course. It was a fine spring day, clear-eyed and crisp, with a hint of new foliage in the thick buds of the trees. The air was so pellucid that one distinguished without difficulty the straight entrance to the gorge a mile away, and even the West Bend, fully five miles distant.

Jimmy Powers took off his cap and wiped his forehead.

"You boys," he remarked politely, "think you are boring with a mighty big auger."

"My God!" screamed one of the spectators on top of the cliff.

At the same instant Wallace Carpenter seized his friend's arm and pointed.

Down the bed of the stream from the upper bend rushed a solid wall of water several feet high. It flung itself forward with the headlong impetus of a cascade. Even in the short interval between the

437

visitor's exclamation and Carpenter's rapid gesture, it had loomed into sight, twisted a dozen trees from the river bank, and foamed into the entrance of the gorge. An instant later it collided with the tail of the jam.

Even in the railroad rush of those few moments several things happened. Thorpe leaped for a rope. The crew working on top of the jam ducked instinctively to right and left and began to scramble toward safety. The men below, at first bewildered and not comprehending, finally understood, and ran toward the face of the jam with the intention of clambering up it. There could be no escape in the narrow cañon below, the walls of which rose sheer.

Then the flood hit square. It was the impact of irresistible power. A great sheet of water rose like surf from the tail of the jam; a mighty cataract poured down over its surface, lifting the free logs; from either wing timbers crunched, split, rose suddenly into wracked prominence, twisted beyond the semblance of themselves. Here and there single logs were even projected bodily upward, as an apple seed is shot from between the thumb and forefinger. Then the jam moved.

Scotty Parsons, Jack Hyland, Red Jacket, and the forty or fifty topmen had reached the shore. By the wriggling activity which is a riverman's alone, they succeeded in pulling themselves beyond the snap of death's jaws. It was a narrow thing for most of them, and a miracle for some.

Jimmy Powers, Archie Harris, Long Pine Jim, Big Nolan, and Mike Moloney, the brother of Bryan, were in worse case. They were, as has been said, engaged in " flattening " part of the jam about eight or ten rods below the face of it. When they finally understood that the affair was one of escape, they ran toward the jam, hoping to climb out. Then the crash came. They heard the roar of the waters, the wrecking of the timbers, they saw the logs bulge outward in anticipation of the break. Immediately they turned and fled, they knew not where.

All but Jimmy Powers. He stopped short in his tracks, and threw his battered old felt hat defiantly full into the face of the destruction hanging over him. Then, his bright hair blowing in the wind of death, he turned to the spectators standing helpless and paralyzed, forty feet above him.

It was an instant's impression—the arrested motion seen in the flash of lightning—and yet to the onlookers it had somehow the quality of time. For perceptible duration it seemed to them they stared at the contrast between the raging hell above and the yet peaceable river bed below. They were destined to remember that picture the rest of their natural lives, in such detail that each one of them could almost have reproduced it photographically by simply closing his eyes. Yet afterward, when they attempted to recall definitely the impression, they knew it could have lasted but a fraction of a second, for the reason that, clear and distinct in each man's mind, the images of the fleeing men retained definite attitudes. It was the instantaneous photography of events.

"So long, boys," they heard Jimmy Powers's voice. Then the rope Thorpe had thrown fell across a caldron of tortured waters and of tossing logs.

CHAPTER FORTY-NINE

DURING perhaps ten seconds the survivors watched the end of Thorpe's rope trailing in the flood. Then the young man with a deep sigh began to pull it toward him.

At once a hundred surmises, questions, ejaculations broke out.

"What happened?" cried Wallace Carpenter.

"What was that man's name?" asked the Chicago journalist with the eager instinct of his profession.

"This is terrible, terrible, terrible!" a white-haired physician from Marquette kept repeating over and over.

A half dozen ran toward the point of the cliff to peer down-stream, as though they could hope to distinguish anything in that waste of flood water.

"The dam's gone out," replied Thorpe. "I don't understand it. Everything was in good shape, as far as I could see. It didn't act like an ordinary break. The water came too fast. Why, it was as dry as a bone until just as that wave came along. An ordinary break would have eaten through little by little before it burst, and Davis should have been able to stop it. This came all at once, as if the dam had disappeared. I don't see."

His mind of the professional had already begun to query causes.

"How about the men?" asked Wallace. "Isn't there something I can do?"

"You can head a hunt down the river," answered Thorpe. "I think it is useless until the water goes down. Poor Jimmy! He was one of the best men I had. I wouldn't have had this happen——"

The horror of the scene was at last beginning to filter through numbness into Wallace Carpenter's impressionable imagination.

"No, no!" he cried vehemently. "There is something criminal about it to me! I'd rather lose every log in the river!"

Thorpe looked at him curiously. "It is one of the chances of war," said he, unable to refrain from the utterance of his creed. "We all know it."

"I'd better divide the crew and take in both banks of the river," suggested Wallace in his constitutional necessity of doing something.

"See if you can't get volunteers from this crowd," suggested Thorpe. "I can let you have two men to show you trails. If you can make it that way, it will help me out. I need as many of the crew as possible to use this flood water."

"O Harry!" cried Carpenter, shocked. "You

can't be going to work again to-day after that horrible sight, before we have made the slightest effort to recover the bodies!"

"If the bodies can be recovered, they shall be," replied Thorpe quietly. "But the drive will not wait. We have no dams to depend on now, you must remember, and we shall have to get out on freshet water."

"Your men won't work. I'd refuse just as they will!" cried Carpenter, his sensibilities still suffering.

Thorpe smiled proudly. "You do not know them. They are mine. I hold them in the hollow of my hand!"

"By Jove!" cried the journalist in sudden enthusiasm. "By Jove! that is magnificent!"

The men of the river crew had crouched on their narrow footholds while the jam went out. Each had clung to his peavey, as is the habit of rivermen. Down the current past their feet swept the *débris* of flood. Soon logs began to swirl by—at first few, then many—from the remaining rollways which the river had automatically broken. In a little time the eddy caught up some of these logs, and immediately the inception of another jam threatened. The rivermen, without hesitation, as calmly as though catastrophe had not thrown the weight of its moral terror against their stoicism, sprang, peavey in hand, to the insistent work.

" By Jove! " said the journalist again. " That is magnificent! They are working over the spot where their comrades died! "

Thorpe's face lit with gratification. He turned to the young man.

" You see," he said in proud simplicity.

With the added danger of freshet water, the work went on.

At this moment Tim Shearer approached from inland, his clothes dripping wet, but his face retaining its habitual expression of iron calmness. " Anybody caught? " was his first question as he drew near.

" Five men under the face," replied Thorpe briefly.

Shearer cast a glance at the river. He needed to be told no more.

" I was afraid of it," said he. " The rollways must be all broken out. It's saved us that much, but the freshet water won't last long. It's going to be a close squeak to get 'em out now. Don't exactly figure on what struck the dam. Thought first I'd go right up that way, but then I came down to see about the boys."

Carpenter could not understand this apparent callousness on the part of men in whom he had always thought to recognize a fund of rough but genuine feeling. To him the sacredness of death was incompatible with the insistence of work. To these others the two, of grim necessity, went hand in hand.

"Where were you?" asked Thorpe of Shearer.

"On the pole trail. I got in a little, as you see."

In reality the foreman had had a close call for his life. A toughly-rooted basswood alone had saved him.

"We'd better go up and take a look," he suggested. "Th' boys has things going here all right."

The two men turned toward the brush.

"Hi, Tim," called a voice behind him.

Red Jacket appeared clambering up the cliff.

"Jack told me to give this to you," he panted, holding out a chunk of strangely twisted wood.

"Where'd he get this?" inquired Thorpe, quickly. "It's a piece of the dam," he explained to Wallace, who had drawn near.

"Picked it out of the current," replied the man.

The foreman and his boss bent eagerly over the morsel. Then they stared with solemnity into each other's eyes.

"Dynamite, by God!" exclaimed Shearer.

CHAPTER FIFTY

FOR a moment the three men stared at each other without speaking.

"What does it mean?" almost whispered Carpenter.

"Mean? Foul play!" snarled Thorpe. "Come on, Tim."

The two struck into the brush, threading the paths with the ease of woodsmen. It was necessary to keep to the high inland ridges for the simple reason that the pole trail had by now become impassable. Wallace Carpenter, attempting to follow them, ran, stumbled, and fell through brush that continually whipped his face and garments, continually tripped his feet. All he could obtain was a vanishing glimpse of his companions' backs. Thorpe and his foreman talked briefly.

"It's Morrison and Daly," surmised Shearer. "I left them 'count of a trick like that. They wanted me to take charge of Perkinson's drive and hang her a purpose. I been suspecting something—they've been layin' too low."

Thorpe answered nothing. Through the site of the old dam they found a torrent pouring from the

446

narrowed pond, at the end of which the dilapidated wings flapping in the current attested the former structure. Davis stood staring at the current.

Thorpe strode forward and shook him violently by the shoulder.

"How did this happen?" he demanded hoarsely. "Speak!"

The man turned to him in a daze. "I don't know," he answered.

"You ought to know. How was that 'shot' exploded? How did they get in here without you seeing them? Answer me!"

"I don't know," repeated the man. "I jest went over in th' bresh to kill a few pa'tridges, and when I come back I found her this way. I wasn't goin' to close down for three hours yet, and I thought they was no use a hangin' around here."

"Were you hired to watch this dam, or weren't you?" demanded the tense voice of Thorpe. "Answer me, you fool."

"Yes, I was," returned the man, a shade of aggression creeping into his voice.

"Well, you've done it well. You've cost me my dam, and you've killed five men. If the crew finds out about you, you'll go over the falls, sure. You get out of here! Pike! Don't you ever let me see your face again!"

The man blanched as he thus learned of his comrades' deaths. Thorpe thrust his face at him, lashed by circumstances beyond his habitual self-control.

"It's men like you who make the trouble," he stormed. "Damn fools who say they didn't mean to. It isn't enough not to mean to. They should *mean not to*! I don't ask you to think. I just want you to do what I tell you, and you can't even do that."

He threw his shoulder into a heavy blow that reached the dam-watcher's face, and followed it immediately by another. Then Shearer caught his arm, motioning the dazed and bloody victim of the attack to get out of sight. Thorpe shook his foreman off with one impatient motion, and strode away up the river, his head erect, his eyes flashing, his nostrils distended.

"I reckon you'd better mosey," Shearer dryly advised the dam watcher; and followed.

Late in the afternoon the two men reached Dam Three, or rather the spot on which Dam Three had stood. The same spectacle repeated itself here, except that Ellis, the dam watcher, was nowhere to be seen.

"The dirty whelps," cried Thorpe, "they did a good job!"

He thrashed about here and there, and so came across Ellis blindfolded and tied. When released, the dam watcher was unable to give any account of his assailants.

" They came up behind me while I was cooking," he said. " One of 'em grabbed me and the other one kivered my eyes. Then I hears the ' shot ' and knows there's trouble."

Thorpe listened in silence. Shearer asked a few questions. After the low-voiced conversation Thorpe arose abruptly.

" Where you going? " asked Shearer.

But the young man did not reply. He swung, with the same long, nervous stride, into the down-river trail.

Until late that night the three men—for Ellis insisted on accompanying them—hurried through the forest. Thorpe walked tirelessly, upheld by his violent but repressed excitement. When his hat fell from his head, he either did not notice the fact, or did not care to trouble himself for its recovery, so he glanced through the trees bareheaded, his broad white brow gleaming in the moonlight. Shearer noted the fire in his eyes, and from the coolness of his greater age, counselled moderation.

" I wouldn't stir the boys up," he panted, for the pace was very swift. " They'll kill some one over there, it'll be murder on both sides."

He received no answer. About midnight they came to the camp.

Two great fires leaped among the trees, and the men, past the idea of sleep, grouped between them, talking. The lesson of twisted timbers was not lost to their experience, and the evening had brought its accumulation of slow anger against the perpetrators of the outrage. These men were not given to oratorical mouthings, but their low-voiced exchanges between the puffings of a pipe led to a steadier purpose than that of hysteria. Even as the woodsmen joined their group, they had reached the intensity of execution. Across their purpose Thorpe threw violently his personality.

"You must not go," he commanded.

Through their anger they looked at him askance.

"I forbid it," Thorpe cried.

They shrugged their indifference and arose. This was an affair of caste brotherhood; and the blood of their mates cried out to them.

"The work," Thorpe shouted hoarsely. "The work! We must get those logs out! We haven't time!"

But the Fighting Forty had not Thorpe's ideal. Success meant a day's work well done; while vengeance stood for a righting of the realities which had been unrighteously overturned. Thorpe's dry-eyed, burning, almost mad insistence on the importance of the day's task had not its ordinary force. They looked upon him from a standpoint apart, calmly, dispassionately, as one looks on a petulant child. The grim call of tragedy had lifted them above little mundane things.

Then swiftly between the white, strained face of

the madman trying to convince his heart that his mind had been right, and the fanatically exalted rivermen, interposed the sanity of Radway. The old jobber faced the men calmly, almost humorously, and somehow the very bigness of the man commanded attention. When he spoke, his coarse, good-natured, every-day voice fell through the tense situation, clarifying it, restoring it to the normal.

"You fellows make me sick," said he. "You haven't got the sense God gave a rooster. Don't you see you're playing right in those fellows' hands? What do you suppose they dynamited them dams for? To kiil our boys? Don't you believe it for a minute. They never dreamed we was dry-pickin' that jam. They sent some low-lived whelp down there to hang our drive, and by smoke it looks like they was going to succeed, thanks to you muttonheads.

"'Spose you go over and take 'em apart; what then? You have a scrap; probably you lick 'em." The men growled ominously, but did not stir. "You whale daylights out of a lot of men who probably don't know any more about this here shooting of our dams than a hog does about a ruffled shirt. Meanwhile your drive hangs. Well? Well? Do you suppose the men who were back of that shooting, do you suppose Morrison and Daly give a tinker's dam how many men of theirs you lick? What they want is to hang our drive. If they

451

hang our drive, it's cheap at the price of a few black eyes."

The speaker paused and grinned good-humoredly at the men's attentive faces. Then suddenly his own became grave, and he swung into his argument all the impressiveness of his great bulk.

"Do you want to know how to get even?" he asked, shading each word. "Do you want to know how to make those fellows sing so small you can't hear them? Well, I'll tell you. *Take out this drive!* Do it in spite of them! Show them they're no good when they buck up against Thorpe's One! Our boys died doing their duty—the way a riverman ought to. *Now hump yourselves!* Don't let 'em die in vain!"

The crew stirred uneasily, looking at each other for approval of the conversion each had experienced. Radway, seizing the psychological moment, turned easily toward the blaze.

"Better turn in, boys, and get some sleep," he said. "We've got a hard day to-morrow." He stooped to light his pipe at the fire. When he had again straightened his back after rather a prolonged interval, the group had already disintegrated. A few minutes later the cookee scattered the brands of the fire from before a sleeping camp.

Thorpe had listened non-committally to the colloquy. He had maintained the suspended attitude of a man who is willing to allow the trial of other methods, but who does not therefore relinquish his own. At the favorable termination of the discussion he turned away without comment. He expected to gain this result. Had he been in a more judicial state of mind he might have perceived at last the reason, in the complicated scheme of Providence, for his long connection with John Radway.

CHAPTER FIFTY-ONE

BEFORE daylight Injin Charley drifted into the camp to find Thorpe already out. With a curt nod the Indian seated himself by the fire, and, producing a square plug of tobacco and a knife, began leisurely to fill his pipe. Thorpe watched him in silence. Finally Injin Charley spoke in the red man's clear-cut, imitative English, a pause between each sentence.

" I find trail three men," said he. " Both dam, three men. One man go down river. Those men have cork-boot. One man no have cork-boot. He boss."

The Indian suddenly threw his chin out, his head back, half closed his eyes in a cynical squint. As by a flash Dyer, the scaler, leered insolently from behind the Indian's stolid mask.

" How do you know? " said Thorpe.

For answer the Indian threw his shoulders forward in Dyer's nervous fashion.

" He make trail big by the toe, light by the heel. He make trail big on inside."

Charley arose and walked, after Dyer's springy fashion, illustrating his point in the soft wood ashes of the immediate fireside.

454

Thorpe looked doubtful. "I believe you are right, Charley," said he. "But it is mighty little to go on. You can't be sure."

"I sure," replied Charley.

He puffed strongly at the heel of his smoke, then arose, and without farewell disappeared in the forest.

Thorpe ranged the camp impatiently, glancing often at the sky. At length he laid fresh logs on the fire and aroused the cook. It was bitter cold in the early morning. After a time the men turned out of their own accord, at first yawning with insufficient rest, and then becoming grimly tense as their returned wits reminded them of the situation.

From that moment began the wonderful struggle against circumstances which has become a by-word among rivermen everywhere. A forty-day drive had to go out in ten. A freshet had to float out thirty million feet of logs. It was tremendous; as even the men most deeply buried in the heavy hours of that time dimly realized. It was epic; as the journalist, by now thoroughly aroused, soon succeeded in convincing his editors and his public. Fourteen, sixteen, sometimes eighteen hours a day, the men of the driving crew worked like demons. Jams had no chance to form. The phenomenal activity of the rear crew reduced by half the inevitable sacking. Of course, under the pressure, the lower dam had gone out. Nothing was to be depended on but sheer dogged grit. Far up-river Sadler & Smith had hung their drive for the season. They had stretched heavy booms across the current, and so had resigned themselves to a definite but not extraordinary loss. Thorpe had at least a clear river.

Wallace Carpenter could not understand how human flesh and blood endured. The men themselves had long since reached the point of practical exhaustion, but were carried through by the fire of their leader. Work was dogged until he stormed into sight; then it became frenzied. He seemed to impart to those about him a nervous force and excitability as real as that induced by brandy. When he looked at a man from his cavernous, burning eyes, that man jumped.

It was all willing enough work. Several definite causes, each adequate alone to something extraordinary, focussed to the necessity. His men worshipped Thorpe; the idea of thwarting the purposes of their comrades' murderers retained its strength; the innate pride of caste and craft—the sturdiest virtue of the riverman—was in these picked men increased to the dignity of a passion. The great psychological forces of a successful career gathered and made head against the circumstances which such careers always arouse in polarity.

Impossibilities were puffed aside like thistles. The men went at them headlong. They gave way before the rush. Thorpe always led. Not for a single instant of the day nor for many at night was he at rest. He was like a man who has taken a deep breath to reach a definite goal, and who cannot exhale until the burst of speed be over. Instinctively he seemed to realize that a let-down would mean collapse.

After the camp had fallen asleep, he would often lie awake half of the few hours of their night, every muscle tense, staring at the sky. His mind saw definitely every detail of the situation as he had last viewed it. In advance his imagination stooped and sweated to the work which his body was to accomplish the next morning. Thus he did everything twice. Then at last the tension would relax. He would fall into uneasy sleep. But twice that did not follow. Through the dissolving iron mist of his striving, a sharp thought cleaved like an arrow. It was that after all he did not care. The religion of Success no longer held him as its devoutest worshipper. He was throwing the fibres of his life into the engine of toil, not because of moral duty, but because of moral pride. He meant to succeed in order to prove to himself that he had not been wrong.

The pain of the arrow-wound always aroused him from his doze with a start. He grimly laughed the thought out of court. To his waking moments his religion was sincere, was real. But deep down in his subconsciousness, below his recognition, the other influence was growing like a weed. Perhaps the vision, not the waking, had been right. Perhaps that far-off beautiful dream of a girl which Thorpe's idealism had constructed from the reactionary necessities of Thorpe's harsh life had been more real than his forest temples of his ruthless god! Perhaps there were greater things than to succeed, greater things than success. Perhaps, after all, the Power that put us here demands more that we cleave one to the other in loving-kindness than that we learn to blow the penny whistles it has tossed us. And then the keen, poignant memory of the dream girl stole into the young man's mind, and in agony was immediately thrust forth. He would not think of her. He had given her up. He had cast the die. For success he had bartered her, in the noblest, the loftiest spirit of devotion. He refused to believe that devotion fanatical; he refused to believe that he had been wrong. In the still darkness of the night he would rise and steal to the edge of the dully roaring stream. There, his eyes blinded and his throat choked with a longing more manly than tears, he would reach out and smooth the round rough coats of the great logs.

"We'll do it!" he whispered to them—and to himself. "We'll do it! We can't be wrong. God would not have let us!"

CHAPTER FIFTY-TWO

WALLACE CARPENTER'S search expedition had proved a failure, as Thorpe had foreseen, but at the end of the week, when the water began to recede, the little beagles ran upon a mass of flesh and bones. The man was unrecognizable, either as an individual or as a human being. The remains were wrapped in canvas and sent for interment in the cemetery at Marquette. Three of the others were never found. The last did not come to light until after the drive had quite finished.

Down at the booms the jam crew received the drive as fast as it came down. From one crib to another across the broad extent of the river's mouth, heavy booms were chained end to end effectually to close the exit to Lake Superior. Against these the logs caromed softly in the slackened current, and stopped. The cribs were very heavy with slanting, instead of square, tops, in order that the pressure might be downward instead of sidewise. This guaranteed their permanency. In a short time the surface of the lagoon was covered by a brown carpet of logs running in strange patterns like windrows of fallen grain. Finally, across the straight middle distance of the river, appeared little agitated specks leaping back and forth. Thus the rear came in sight and the drive was all but over.

Up till now the weather had been clear but oppressively hot for this time of year. The heat had come suddenly and maintained itself well. It had searched out with fierce directness all the patches of snow lying under the thick firs and balsams of the swamp edge, it had shaken loose the anchor ice of the marsh bottoms, and so had materially aided the success of the drive by increase of water. The men had worked for the most part in undershirts. They were as much in the water as out of it, for the icy bath had become almost grateful. Hamilton, the journalist, who had attached himself definitely to the drive, distributed bunches of papers, in which the men read that the unseasonable condition prevailed all over the country.

At length, however, it gave signs of breaking. The sky, which had been of a steel blue, harbored great piled thunder-heads. Occasionally athwart the heat shot a streak of cold air. Toward evening the thunder-heads shifted and finally dissipated, to be sure, but the portent was there.

Hamilton's papers began to tell of disturbances in the South and West. A washout in Arkansas derailed a train; a cloudburst in Texas wiped out a camp; the cities along the Ohio River were enjoying their annual flood with the usual concomitants of floating houses and boats in the streets. The men wished they had some of that water here.

So finally the drive approached its end and all concerned began in anticipation to taste the weariness that awaited them. They had hurried their powers. The few remaining tasks still confronting them all at once seemed more formidable than what they had accomplished. They could not contemplate further exertion. The work for the first time became dogged, distasteful. Even Thorpe was infected. He, too, wanted more than anything else to drop on the bed in Mrs. Hathaway's boarding-house, there to sponge from his mind all colors but the dead gray of rest. There remained but a few things to do. A mile of sacking would carry the drive beyond the influence of freshet water. After that there would be no hurry.

He looked around at the hard, fatigue-worn faces of the men about him, and in the obsession of his wearied mood he suddenly felt a great rush of affection for these comrades who had so unreservedly spent themselves for his affair. Their features showed exhaustion, it is true, but their eyes gleamed still with the steady half-humorous purpose of the pioneer. When they caught his glance they grinned good-humoredly.

All at once Thorpe turned and started for the bank.

" That'll do, boys," he said quietly to the nearest group. " She's down ! "

It was noon. The sackers looked up in surprise. Behind them, to their very feet, rushed the soft smooth slope of Hemlock Rapids. Below them flowed a broad, peaceful river. The drive had passed its last obstruction. To all intents and purposes it was over.

Calmly, with matter-of-fact directness, as though they had not achieved the impossible; as though they, a handful, had not cheated nature and powerful enemies, they shouldered their peaveys and struck into the broad wagon road. In the middle distance loomed the tall stacks of the mill with the little board town about it. Across the eye spun the thread of the railroad. Far away gleamed the broad expanses of Lake Superior.

The cook had, early that morning, moored the wanigan to the bank. One of the teamsters from town had loaded the men's " turkeys " on his heavy wagon. The wanigan's crew had thereupon trudged into town.

The men paired off naturally and fell into a dragging, dogged walk. Thorpe found himself unexpectedly with Big Junko. For a time they plodded on without conversation. Then the big man ventured a remark.

" I'm glad she's over," said he. " I got a good stake comin'."

"Yes," replied Thorpe indifferently.

"I got most six hundred dollars comin'," persisted Junko.

"Might as well be six hundred cents," commented Thorpe, "it'd make you just as drunk."

Big Junko laughed self-consciously but without the slightest resentment.

"That's all right," said he, "but you betcher life I don't blow this stake."

"I've heard that talk before," shrugged Thorpe.

"Yes, but this is different. I'm goin' to git married on this. How's *that*?"

Thorpe, his attention struck at last, stared at his companion. He noted the man's little twinkling animal eyes, his high cheek-bones, his flat nose, his thick and slobbery lips, his straggling, fierce mustache and eyebrows, his grotesque long-tailed cutaway coat. So to him, too, this primitive man reaching dully from primordial chaos, the great moment had yielded its vision.

"Who is she?" he asked abruptly.

"She used to wash at Camp Four."

Thorpe dimly remembered the woman now—an overweighted creature with a certain attraction of elfishly blowing hair, with a certain pleasing full-cheeked, full-bosomed health.

The two walked on in re-established silence. Finally the giant, unable to contain himself longer, broke out again.

"I do like that woman," said he with a quaintly deliberate seriousness. "That's the finest woman in this district."

Thorpe felt the quick moisture rush to his eyes. There was something inexpressibly touching in those simple words as Big Junko uttered them.

"And when you are married," he asked, "what are you going to do? Are you going to stay on the river?"

"No, I'm goin' to clear a farm. The woman she says that's the thing to do. I like the river, too. But you bet when Carrie says a thing, that's plenty good enough for Big Junko."

"Suppose," suggested Thorpe, irresistibly impelled toward the attempt, "suppose I should offer you two hundred dollars a month to stay on the river. Would you stay?"

"Carrie don't like it," replied Junko.

"Two hundred dollars is big wages," persisted Thorpe. "It's twice what I give Radway."

"I'd like to ask Carrie."

"No, take it or leave it now."

"Well, Carrie says she don't like it," answered the riverman with a sigh.

Thorpe looked at his companion fixedly. Somehow the bestial countenance had taken on an attraction of its own. He remembered Big Junko as a wild beast when his passions were aroused, as a man whose honesty had been doubted.

" You've changed, Junko," said he.

" I know," said the big man. " I been a scalawag all right. I quit it. I don't know much, but Carrie she's smart, and I'm goin' to do what she says. When you get stuck on a good woman like Carrie, Mr. Thorpe, you don't give much of a damn for anything else. Sure! That's right! It's the biggest thing top o' earth! "

Here it was again, the opposing creed. And from such a source. Thorpe's iron will contracted again.

" A woman is no excuse for a man's neglecting his work," he snapped.

" Shorely not," agreed Junko serenely. " I aim to finish out my time all right, Mr. Thorpe. Don't you worry none about that. I done my best for you. And," went on the riverman in the expansion of this unwonted confidence with his employer, " I'd like to rise to remark that you're the best boss I ever had, and we boys wants to stay with her till there's skating in hell! "

" All right," murmured Thorpe indifferently.

His momentary interest had left him. Again the reactionary weariness dragged at his feet. Suddenly the remaining half mile to town seemed very long indeed.

CHAPTER FIFTY-THREE

WALLACE CARPENTER and Hamilton, the journalist, seated against the sun-warmed bench of Mrs. Hathaway's boarding-house, commented on the band as it stumbled into the wash-room.

"Those men don't know how big they are," remarked the journalist. "That's the way with most big men. And that man Thorpe belongs to another age. I'd like to get him to telling his experiences; he'd be a gold mine to me."

"And would require about as much trouble to ' work,' " laughed Wallace. "He won't talk."

"That's generally the trouble, confound 'em," sighed Hamilton. "The fellows who *can* talk haven't anything to say; and those who have something to tell are dumb as oysters. I've got him in though." He spread one of a roll of papers on his knees. "I got a set of duplicates for you. Thought you might like to keep them. The office tells me," he concluded modestly, "that they are attracting lots of attention, but are looked upon as being a rather clever sort of fiction."

Wallace picked up the sheet. His eye was at once met by the heading, " ' So long, boys,' " in let-

ters a half inch in height, and immediately underneath in smaller type, " said Jimmy Powers, and
threw his hat in the face of death."

" It's all there," explained the journalist, " —the
jam and the break, and all this magnificent struggle
afterward. It makes a great yarn. I feel tempted
sometimes to help it out a little—artistically, you
know—but of course that wouldn't do. She'd make
a ripping yarn, though, if I could get up some
motive outside mere trade rivalry for the blowing
up of those dams. That would just round it off."

Wallace Carpenter was about to reply that such a
motive actually existed, when the conversation was
interrupted by the approach of Thorpe and Big
Junko. The former looked twenty years older after
his winter. His eye was dull, his shoulders drooped,
his gait was inelastic. The whole bearing of the
man was that of one weary to the bone.

" I've got something here to show you, Harry,"
cried Wallace Carpenter, waving one of the papers.
" It was a great drive and here's something to remember it by."

" All right, Wallace, by and by," replied Thorpe
dully. " I'm dead. I'm going to turn in for a
while. I need sleep more than anything else. I
can't think now."

He passed through the little passage into the
" parlor bedroom," which Mrs. Hathaway always
kept in readiness for members of the firm. There

he fell heavily asleep almost before his body had met the bed.

In the long dining-room the rivermen consumed a belated dinner. They had no comments to make. It was over.

The two on the veranda smoked. To the right, at the end of the sawdust street, the mill sang its varying and lulling keys. The odor of fresh-sawed pine perfumed the air. Not a hundred yards away the river slipped silently to the distant blue Superior, escaping between the slanting stone-filled cribs which held back the logs. Down the south and west the huge thunder-heads gathered and flashed and grumbled, as they had done every afternoon for days previous.

"Queer thing," commented Hamilton finally, "these cold streaks in the air. They are just as distinct as though they had partitions around them."

"Queer climate anyway," agreed Carpenter.

Excepting always for the mill, the little settlement appeared asleep. The main booms were quite deserted. Not a single figure, armed with its picturesque pike-pole, loomed athwart the distance. After a while Hamilton noticed something.

"Look here, Carpenter," said he, "what's happening out there? Have some of your confounded logs *sunk*, or what? There don't seem to be near so many of them somehow."

"No, it isn't that," proffered Carpenter after a

moment's scrutiny, " there are just as many logs, but they are getting separated a little so you can see the open water between them."

" Guess you're right. Say, look here, I believe that the river is rising! "

" Nonsense, we haven't had any rain."

" She's rising just the same. I'll tell you how I know; you see that spile over there near the left-hand crib? Well, I sat on the boom this morning watching the crew, and I whittled the spile with my knife—you can see the marks from here. I cut the thing about two feet above the water. Look at it now."

" She's pretty near the water line, that's right," admitted Carpenter.

" I should think that might make the boys *hot*," commented Hamilton. " If they'd known this was coming, they needn't have hustled so to get the drive down."

" That's so," Wallace agreed.

About an hour later the younger man in his turn made a discovery.

" She's been rising right along," he submitted. " Your marks are nearer the water, and, do you know, I believe the logs are beginning to feel it. See, they've closed up the little openings between them, and they are beginning to crowd down to the lower end of the pond."

" I don't know anything about this business,"

hazarded the journalist, " but by the mere look of the thing I should think there was a good deal of pressure on that same lower end. By Jove, look there! See those logs up-end? I believe you're going to have a jam right here in your own booms! "

" I don't know," hesitated Wallace, " I never heard of its happening."

" You'd better let some one know."

" I hate to bother Harry or any of the rivermen. I'll just step down to the mill. Mason—he's our mill foreman—he'll know."

Mason came to the edge of the high trestle and took one look.

" Jumpin' fish-hooks! " he cried. " Why, the river's up six inches and still a comin'! Here you, Tom! " he called to one of the yard hands, " you tell Solly to get steam on that tug double quick, and have Dave hustle together his driver crew."

" What you going to do? " asked Wallace.

" I got to strengthen the booms," explained the mill foreman. " We'll drive some piles across between the cribs."

" Is there any danger? "

" Oh, no, the river would have to rise a good deal higher than she is now to make current enough to hurt. They've had a hard rain up above. This will go down in a few hours."

After a time the tug puffed up to the booms, escorting the pile driver. The latter towed a little raft of long sharpened piles, which it at once began to drive in such positions as would most effectually strengthen the booms. In the meantime the thunder-heads had slyly climbed the heavens, so that a sudden deluge of rain surprised the workmen. For an hour it poured down in torrents; then settled to a steady gray beat. Immediately the aspect had changed. The distant rise of land was veiled; the brown expanse of logs became slippery and glistening; the river below the booms was picked into staccato points by the drops; distant Superior turned lead color and seemed to tumble strangely athwart the horizon.

Solly, the tug captain, looked at his mooring hawsers and then at the nearest crib.

"She's riz two inches in th' las' two hours," he announced, "and she's runnin' like a mill race." Solly was a typical north-country tug captain, short and broad, with a brown, clear face, and the steadiest and calmest of steel-blue eyes. "When she begins to feel th' pressure behind," he went on, "there's goin' to be trouble."

Toward dusk she began to feel that pressure. Through the rainy twilight the logs could be seen raising their ghostly arms of protest. Slowly, without tumult, the jam formed. In the van the logs crossed silently; in the rear they pressed in, were sucked under in the swift water, and came to rest at the bottom of the river. The current of the river began to protest, pressing its hydraulics through the narrowing crevices. The situation demanded attention.

A breeze began to pull off shore in the body of rain. Little by little it increased, sending the water by in gusts, ruffling the already hurrying river into greater haste, raising far from the shore dimly perceived white-caps. Between the roaring of the wind, the dash of rain, and the rush of the stream, men had to shout to make themselves heard.

" Guess you'd better rout out the boss," screamed Solly to Wallace Carpenter; " this damn water's comin' up an inch an hour right along. When she backs up once, she'll push this jam out sure."

Wallace ran to the boarding-house and roused his partner from a heavy sleep. The latter understood the situation at a word. While dressing, he explained to the younger man wherein lay the danger.

" If the jam breaks once," said he, " nothing top of earth can prevent it from going out into the Lake, and there it'll scatter, Heaven knows where. Once scattered, it is practically a total loss. The salvage wouldn't pay the price of the lumber."

They felt blindly through the rain in the direction of the lights on the tug and pile-driver. Shearer, the water dripping from his flaxen mustache, joined them like a shadow.

" I heard you come in," he explained to Carpenter. At the river he announced his opinion. " We can hold her all right," he assured them. " It'll take a few more piles, but by morning the storm'll be over, and she'll begin to go down again."

The three picked their way over the creaking, swaying timber. But when they reached the pile-driver, they found trouble afoot. The crew had mutinied, and refused longer to drive piles under the face of the jam.

" If she breaks loose, she's going to bury us," said they.

" She won't break," snapped Shearer, " get to work."

" It's dangerous," they objected sullenly.

" By God, you get off this driver," shouted Solly. " Go over and lie down in a ten-acre lot, and see if you feel safe there!"

He drove them ashore with a storm of profanity and a multitude of kicks, his steel-blue eyes blazing.

" There's nothing for it but to get the boys out again," said Tim; " I kinder hate to do it."

But when the Fighting Forty, half asleep but dauntless, took charge of the driver, a catastrophe made itself known. One of the ejected men had tripped the lifting chain of the hammer after another had knocked away the heavy preventing block, and so the hammer had fallen into the river and was lost. None other was to be had. The pile-driver was useless.

A dozen men were at once despatched for cables,

chains, and wire ropes from the supply at the ware-house.

"I'd like to have those whelps here," cried Shearer, "I'd throw them under the jam."

"It's part of the same trick," said Thorpe grimly; "those fellows have their men everywhere among us. I don't know whom to trust."

"You think it's Morrison & Daly?" queried Carpenter astonished.

"Think? I know it. They know as well as you or I that if we save these logs, we'll win out in the stock exchange; and they're not such fools as to let us save them if it can be helped. I have a score to settle with those fellows; and when I get through with this thing I'll settle it all right."

"What are you going to do now?"

"The only thing there is to be done. We'll string heavy booms, chained together, between the cribs, and then trust to heaven they'll hold. I think we can hold the jam. The water will begin to flow over the bank before long, so there won't be much increase of pressure over what we have now; and as there won't be any shock to withstand, I think our heavy booms will do the business."

He turned to direct the boring of some long boom logs in preparation for the chains. Suddenly he whirled again to Wallace with so strange an expression in his face that the young man almost cried out. The uncertain light of the lanterns showed dimly the streaks of rain across his countenance. and his eye flared with a look almost of panic.

"I never thought of it!" he said in a low voice. "Fool that I am! I don't see how I missed it. Wallace, don't you see what those devils will do next?"

"No, what do you mean?" gasped the younger man.

"There are twelve million feet of logs up river in Sadler & Smith's drive. Don't you see what they'll do?"

"No, I don't believe——"

"Just as soon as they find out that the river is booming, and that we are going to have a hard time to hold our jam, they'll let loose those twelve million on us. They'll break the jam, or dynamite it, or something. And let me tell you that a very few logs hitting the tail of our jam will start the whole shooting match so that no power on earth can stop it."

"I don't imagine they'd think of doing that——" began Wallace by way of assurance.

"Think of it! You don't know them. They've thought of everything. You don't know that man Daly. Ask Tim, he'll tell you."

"Well, the ——"

"I've got to send a man up there right away. Perhaps we can get there in time to head them off. They have to send their man over—— By the way," he queried, struck with a new idea, " how long have you been driving piles? "

" Since about three o'clock."

" Six hours," computed Thorpe. " I wish you'd come for me sooner."

He cast his eye rapidly over the men.

" I don't know just who to send. There isn't a good enough woodsman in the lot to make Siscoe Falls through the woods a night like this. The river trail is too long; and a cut through the woods is blind. Andrews is the only man I know of who could do it, but I think Billy Mason said Andrews had gone up on the Gunther track to run lines. Come on; we'll see."

With infinite difficulty and caution, they reached the shore. Across the gleaming logs shone dimly the lanterns at the scene of work, ghostly through the rain. Beyond, on either side, lay impenetrable drenched darkness, racked by the wind.

" *I* wouldn't want to tackle it," panted Thorpe. " If it wasn't for that cursed tote road between Sadler's and Daly's, I wouldn't worry. It's just too easy for *them*."

Behind them the jam cracked and shrieked and groaned. Occasionally was heard, beneath the sharper noises, a dull *boom*, as one of the heavy timbers, forced by the pressure from its resting-place, shot into the air, and fell back on the bristling surface.

Andrews had left that morning.

"Tim Shearer might do it," suggested Thorpe, "but I hate to spare him."

He picked his rifle from its rack and thrust the magazine full of cartridges.

"Come on, Wallace," said he, "we'll hunt him up."

They stepped again into the shriek and roar of the storm, bending their heads to its power, but indifferent, in the already drenched condition of their clothing, to the rain. The sawdust street was saturated like a sponge. They could feel the quick water rise about the pressure at their feet. From the invisible houses they heard a steady monotone of flowing from the roofs. Far ahead, dim in the mist, sprayed the light of lanterns.

Suddenly Thorpe felt a touch on his arm. Faintly he perceived at his elbow the high lights of a face from which the water streamed.

"Injin Charley!" he cried, "the very man!"

CHAPTER FIFTY-FOUR

RAPIDLY Thorpe explained what was to be done, and thrust his rifle into the Indian's hands. The latter listened in silence and stolidity, then turned, and without a word departed swiftly in the darkness. The two white men stood a minute attentive. Nothing was to be heard but the steady beat of rain and the roaring of the wind.

Near the bank of the river they encountered a man, visible only as an uncertain black outline against the glow of the lanterns beyond. Thorpe, stopping him, found Big Junko.

"This is no time to quit," said Thorpe, sharply.

"I 'aint quittin'," replied Big Junko.

"Where are you going, then?"

Junko was partially and stammeringly unresponsive.

"Looks bad," commented Thorpe. "You'd better get back to your job."

"Yes," agreed Junko helplessly. In the momentary slack tide of work, the giant had conceived the idea of searching out the driver crew for purposes of pugilistic vengeance. Thorpe's suspicions stung him, but his simple mind could see no direct way to explanation.

478

THE FOLLOWING OF THE TRAIL

All night long in the chill of a spring rain and wind-storm the Fighting Forty and certain of the mill crew gave themselves to the labor of connecting the slanting stone cribs so strongly, by means of heavy timbers chained end to end, that the pressure of a break in the jam might not sweep aside the defences. Wallace Carpenter, Shorty, the chore-boy, and Anderson, the barn-boss, picked a danger-ous passage back and forth carrying pails of red-hot coffee which Mrs. Hathaway constantly prepared. The cold water numbed the men's hands. With difficulty could they manipulate the heavy chains through the auger holes; with pain they twisted knots, bored holes. They did not complain. Behind them the jam quivered, perilously near the bursting point. From it shrieked aloud the demons of pres-sure. Steadily the river rose, an inch an hour. The key might snap at any given moment—they could not tell—and with the rush they knew very well that themselves, the tug, and the disabled pile-driver would be swept from existence. The worst of it was that the blackness shrouded their experience into uselessness; they were utterly unable to tell by the ordinary visual symptoms how near the jam might be to collapse.

However, they persisted, as the old-time riverman always does, so that when dawn appeared the bar-rier was continuous and assured. Although the pressure of the river had already forced the logs against the defences, the latter held the strain well.

The storm had settled into its gait. Overhead the sky was filled with gray, beneath which darker scuds flew across the zenith before a howling southwest wind. Out in the clear river one could hardly stand upright against the gusts. In the fan of many directions furious squalls swept over the open water below the booms, and an eager boiling current rushed to the lake.

Thorpe now gave orders that the tug and driver should take shelter. A few moments later he expressed himself as satisfied. The dripping crew, their harsh faces gray in the half-light, picked their way to the shore.

In the darkness of that long night's work no man knew his neighbor. Men from the river, men from the mill, men from the yard all worked side by side. Thus no one noticed especially a tall, slender, but well-knit individual dressed in a faded mackinaw and a limp slouch hat which he wore pulled over his eyes. This young fellow occupied himself with the chains. Against the racing current the crew held the ends of the heavy booms, while he fastened them together. He worked well, but seemed slow. Three times Shearer hustled him on after the others had finished, examining closely the work that had been done. On the third occasion he shrugged his shoulder somewhat impatiently.

The men straggled to shore, the young fellow just described bringing up the rear. He walked as though tired out, hanging his head and dragging his feet. When, however, the boarding-house door had closed on the last of those who preceded him, and the town lay deserted in the dawn, he suddenly became transformed. Casting a keen glance right and left to be sure of his opportunity, he turned and hurried recklessly back over the logs to the centre booms. There he knelt and busied himself with the chains.

In his zigzag progression over the jam he so blended with the morning shadows as to seem one of them, and he would have escaped quite unnoticed had not a sudden shifting of the logs under his feet compelled him to rise for a moment to his full height. So Wallace Carpenter, passing from his bedroom, along the porch, to the dining-room, became aware of the man on the logs.

His first thought was that something demanding instant attention had happened to the boom. He therefore ran at once to the man's assistance, ready to help him personally or to call other aid as the exigency demanded. Owing to the precarious nature of the passage, he could not see beyond his feet until very close to the workman. Then he looked up to find the man, squatted on the boom, contemplating him sardonically.

" Dyer! " he exclaimed.

" Right, my son," said the other coolly.

"What are you doing?"

"If you want to know, I am filing this chain."

Wallace made one step forward and so became aware that at last firearms were taking a part in this desperate game.

"You stand still," commanded Dyer from behind the revolver. "It's unfortunate for you that you happened along, because now you'll have to come with me till this little row is over. You won't have to stay long; your logs'll go out in an hour. I'll just trouble you to go into the brush with me for a while."

The scaler picked his file from beside the weakened link.

"What have you against us, anyway, Dyer?" asked Wallace. His quick mind had conceived a plan. At the moment, he was standing near the outermost edge of the jam, but now as he spoke he stepped quietly to the boom log.

Dyer's black eyes gleamed at him suspiciously, but the movement appeared wholly natural in view of the return to shore.

"Nothing," he replied. "I didn't like your gang particularly, but that's nothing."

"Why do you take such nervy chances to injure us?" queried Carpenter.

"Because there's something in it," snapped the scaler. "Now about face; mosey!"

Like a flash Wallace wheeled and dropped into

the river, swimming as fast as possible below water before his breath should give out. The swift current hurried him away. When at last he rose for air, the spit of Dyer's pistol caused him no uneasiness. A moment later he struck out boldly for shore.

What Dyer's ultimate plan might be, he could not guess. He had stated confidently that the jam would break " in an hour." He might intend to start it with dynamite. Wallace dragged himself from the water and commenced breathlessly to run toward the boarding-house.

Dyer had already reached the shore. Wallace raised what was left of his voice in a despairing shout. The scaler mockingly waved his hat, then turned and ran swiftly and easily toward the shelter of the woods. At their border he paused again to bow in derision. Carpenter's cry brought men to the boarding-house door. From the shadows of the forest two vivid flashes cut the dusk. Dyer staggered, turned completely about, seemed partially to recover, and disappeared. An instant later, across the open space where the scaler had stood, with rifle a-trail, the Indian leaped in pursuit.

CHAPTER FIFTY-FIVE

"WHAT is it?" "What's the matter?" "What the hell's up?" "What's happened?" burst on Wallace in a volley.

"It's Dyer," gasped the young man. "I found him on the boom! He held me up with a gun while he filed the boom chains between the centre piers. They're just ready to go. I got away by diving. Hurry and put in a new chain; you haven't much time!"

"He's a gone-er now," interjected Solly grimly.— "Charley is on his trail—and he is hit."

Thorpe's intelligence leaped promptly to the practical question.

"Injin Charley, where'd he come from? I sent him up Sadler's & Smith's. It's twenty miles, even through the woods."

As though by way of colossal answer the whole surface of the jam moved inward and upward, thrusting the logs bristling against the horizon.

"She's going to break!" shouted Thorpe, starting on a run toward the river. "A chain, quick!"

The men followed, strung high with excitement. Hamilton, the journalist, paused long enough to

484

glance up-stream. Then he, too, ran after them, screaming that the river above was full of logs. By that they all knew that Injin Charley's mission had failed, and that something under ten million feet of logs were racing down the river like so many battering rams.

At the boom the great jam was already a-tremble with eagerness to spring. Indeed a miracle alone seemed to hold the timbers in their place.

"It's death, certain death, to go out on that boom," muttered Billy Mason.

Tim Shearer stepped forward coolly, ready as always to assume the perilous duty. He was thrust back by Thorpe, who seized the chain, cold-shut and hammer which Scotty Parsons brought, and ran lightly out over the booms, shouting:

"Back! back! Don't follow me, on your lives! Keep 'em back, Tim!"

The swift water boiled from under the booms. *Bang! smash! bang!* crashed the logs, a mile upstream, but plainly audible above the waters and the wind. Thorpe knelt, dropped the cold-shut through on either side of the weakened link, and prepared to close it with his hammer. He intended further to strengthen the connection with the other chain.

"Lem' me hold her for you. You can't close her alone," said an unexpected voice next his elbow.

Thorpe looked up in surprise and anger. Over

him leaned Big Junko. The men had been unable to prevent his following. Animated by the blind devotion of the animal for its master, and further stung to action by that master's doubt of his fidelity, the giant had followed to assist as he might.

"You damned fool," cried Thorpe exasperated, then held the hammer to him, "strike while I keep the chain underneath," he commanded.

Big Junko leaned forward to obey, kicking strongly his caulks into the barked surface of the boom log. The spikes, worn blunt by the river work already accomplished, failed to grip. Big Junko slipped, caught himself by an effort, overbalanced in the other direction, and fell into the stream. The current at once swept him away, but fortunately in such a direction that he was enabled to catch the slanting end of a "dead head" log whose lower end was jammed in the crib. The dead head was slippery, the current strong; Big Junko had no crevice by which to assure his hold. In another moment he would be torn away.

"Let go and swim!" shouted Thorpe.

"I can't swim," replied Junko in so low a voice as to be scarcely audible.

For a moment Thorpe stared at him.

"Tell Carrie," said Big Junko.

Then there beneath the swirling gray sky, under the frowning jam, in the midst of flood waters, Thorpe had his second great Moment of Decision.

He did not pause to weigh reasons or chances, to discuss with himself expediency, or the moralities of failure. His actions were foreordained, mechanical. All at once the great forces which the winter had been bringing to power crystallized into something bigger than himself or his ideas. The trail lay before him; there was no choice.

Now clearly, with no shadow of doubt, he took the other view: There could be nothing better than Love. Men, their works, their deeds were little things. Success was a little thing; the opinion of men a little thing. Instantly he felt the truth of it.

And here was Love in danger. That it held its moment's habitation in clay of the coarser mould had nothing to do with the great elemental truth of it. For the first time in his life Thorpe felt the full crushing power of an abstraction. Without thought, instinctively, he drew before the necessity of the moment all that was lesser. It was the triumph of what was real in the man over that which environment, alienation, difficulties had raised up within him.

At Big Junko's words, Thorpe raised his hammer and with one mighty blow severed the chains which bound the ends of the booms across the opening. The free end of one of the poles immediately swung down with the current in the direction of Big Junko. Thorpe like a cat ran to the end of the boom, seized the giant by the collar, and dragged him through the water to safety.

" Run! " he shouted. " Run for your life! "

The two started desperately back, skirting the edge of the logs which now the very seconds alone seemed to hold back. They were drenched and blinded with spray, deafened with the crash of timbers settling to the leap. The men on shore could no longer see them for the smother. The great crush of logs had actually begun its first majestic sliding motion when at last they emerged to safety.

At first a few of the loose timbers found the opening, slipping quietly through with the current; then more; finally the front of the jam dove forward; and an instant later the smooth, swift motion had gained its impetus and was sweeping the entire drive down through the gap.

Rank after rank, like soldiers charging, they ran. The great fierce wind caught them up ahead of the current. In a moment the open river was full of logs jostling eagerly onward. Then suddenly, far out above the uneven tossing skyline of Superior, the strange northern " loom," or mirage, threw the spectres of thousands of restless timbers rising and falling on the bosom of the lake.

CHAPTER FIFTY-SIX

THEY stood and watched them go.

"Oh, the great man! Oh, the great man!" murmured the writer, fascinated.

The grandeur of the sacrifice had struck them dumb. They did not understand the motives beneath it all, but the fact was patent. Big Junko broke down and sobbed.

After a time the stream of logs through the gap slackened. In a moment more, save for the inevitably stranded few, the booms were empty. A deep sigh went up from the attentive multitude.

"She's *gone*!" said one man, with the emphasis of a novel discovery; and groaned.

Then the awe broke from about their minds, and they spoke many opinions and speculations. Thorpe had disappeared. They respected his emotion and did not follow him.

"It was just plain damn foolishness;—but it was great!" said Shearer. "That no-account jackass of a Big Junko ain't worth as much per thousand feet as good white pine."

Then they noticed a group of men gathering about the office steps, and on it some one talking. Collins, the bookkeeper, was making a speech.

Collins was a little hatchet-faced man, with straight, lank hair, near-sighted eyes, a timid, order-loving disposition, and a great suitability for his profession. He was accurate, unemotional, and valuable. All his actions were as dry as the saw-dust in the burner. No one had ever seen him ex-cited. But he was human; and now his knowledge of the Company's affairs showed him the dramatic contrast. *He knew!* He knew that the property of the firm had been mortgaged to the last dollar in order to assist expansion, so that not another cent could be borrowed to tide over present difficulty. He knew that the notes for sixty thousand dollars covering the loan to Wallace Carpenter came due in three months; he knew from the long table of statis-tics which he was eternally preparing and comparing that the season's cut should have netted a profit of two hundred thousand dollars—enough to pay the interest on the mortgages, to take up the notes, and to furnish a working capital for the ensuing year. These things he knew in the strange concrete arith-metical manner of the routine bookkeeper. Other men saw a desperate phase of firm rivalry; he saw a struggle to the uttermost. Other men cheered a rescue: he thrilled over the magnificent gesture of the Gambler scattering his stake in largesse to Death.

It was the simple turning of the hand from full-breathed prosperity to lifeless failure.

His view was the inverse of his master's. To Thorpe it had suddenly become a very little thing in contrast to the great, sweet elemental truth that the dream girl had enunciated. To Collins the affair was miles vaster than the widest scope of his own narrow life.

The firm could not take up its notes when they came due; it could not pay the interest on the mortgages, which would now be foreclosed; it could not even pay in full the men who had worked for it —that would come under a court's adjudication.

He had therefore watched Thorpe's desperate sally to mend the weakened chain, in all the suspense of a man whose entire universe is in the keeping of the chance moment. It must be remembered that at bottom, below the outer consciousness, Thorpe's final decision had already grown to maturity. On the other hand, no other thought than that of accomplishment had even entered the little bookkeeper's head. The rescue and all that it had meant had hit him like a stroke of apoplexy, and his thin emotions had curdled to hysteria. Full of the idea he appeared before the men.

With rapid, almost incoherent speech he poured it out to them. Professional caution and secrecy were forgotten. Wallace Carpenter attempted to push through the ring for the purpose of stopping him. A gigantic riverman kindly but firmly held him back.

" I guess it's just as well we hears this," said the latter.

It all came out—the loan to Carpenter, with a hint at the motive: the machinations of the rival firm on the Board of Trade; the notes, the mortgages, the necessity of a big season's cut; the reasons the rival firm had for wishing to prevent that cut from arriving at the market; the desperate and varied means they had employed. The men listened silent. Hamilton, his eyes glowing like coals, drank in every word. Here was the master motive he had sought; here was the story great to his hand!

" That's what we ought to get," cried Collins, almost weeping, " and now we've gone and bust, just because that infernal river-hog had to fall off a boom. By God, it's a shame! Those scalawags have done us after all! "

Out from the shadows of the woods stole Injin Charley. The whole bearing and aspect of the man had changed. His eye gleamed with a distant far-seeing fire of its own, which took no account of anything but some remote vision. He stole along a most furtively, but with a proud upright carriage of his neck, a backward tilt of his fine head, a distention of his nostrils that lent to his appearance a panther-like pride and stealthiness. No one saw him. Suddenly he broke through the group and mounted the steps beside Collins.

" The enemy of my brother is gone," said he

simply in his native tongue, and with a sudden gesture held out before them—a scalp.

The medieval barbarity of the thing appalled them for a moment. The days of scalping were long since past, had been closed away between the pages of forgotten histories, and yet here again before them was the thing in all its living horror. Then a growl arose. The human animal had tasted blood.

All at once like wine their wrongs mounted to their heads. They remembered their dead comrades. They remembered the heart-breaking days and nights of toil they had endured on account of this man and his associates. They remembered the words of Collins, the little bookkeeper. They hated. They shook their fists across the skies. They turned and with one accord struck back for the railroad right-of-way which led to Shingleville, the town controlled by Morrison & Daly.

The railroad lay for a mile straight through a thick tamarack swamp, then over a nearly treeless cranberry plain. The tamarack was a screen between the two towns. When half-way through the swamp, Red - Jacket stopped, removed his coat, ripped the lining from it, and began to fashion a rude mask.

"Just as well they don't recognize us," said he.

"Somebody in town will give us away," suggested Shorty the chore-boy.

"No, they won't; they're all here," assured Kerlie.

It was true. Except for the women and children, who were not yet about, the entire village had assembled. Even old Vanderhoof, the fire-watcher of the yard, hobbled along breathlessly on his rheumatic legs. In a moment the masks were fitted. In a moment more the little band had emerged from the shelter of the swamp, and so came into full view of its objective point.

Shingleville consisted of a big mill; the yards, now nearly empty of lumber; the large frame boarding-house; the office; the stable; a store; two saloons; and a dozen dwellings. The party at once fixed its eyes on this collection of buildings, and trudged on down the right-of-way with unhastening grimness.

Their approach was not unobserved. Daly saw them; and Baker, his foreman, saw them. The two at once went forth to organize opposition. When the attacking party reached the mill-yard, it found the boss and the foreman standing alone on the sawdust, revolvers drawn.

Daly traced a line with his toe.

"The first man that crosses that line gets it," said he.

They knew he meant what he said. An instant's pause ensued, while the big man and the little faced a mob. Daly's rivermen were still on drive. He knew the mill men too well to depend on them. Truth to tell, the possibility of such a raid as this had not occurred to him; for the simple reason that he did not anticipate the discovery of his complicity with the forces of nature. Skillfully carried out, the plan was a good one. No one need know of the weakened link, and it was the most natural thing in the world that Sadler & Smith's drive should go out with the increase of water.

The men grouped swiftly and silently on the other side of the sawdust line. The pause did not mean that Daly's defence was good. I have known of a crew of striking mill men being so bluffed down, but not such men as these.

"Do you know what's going to happen to you?" said a voice from the group. The speaker was Radway, but the contractor kept himself well in the background. "We're going to burn your mill; we're going to burn your yards; we're going to burn your whole shooting match, you low-lived whelp!"

"Yes, and we're going to string you to your own trestle!" growled another voice harshly.

"Dyer!" said Injin Charley, simply, shaking the wet scalp arm's length toward the lumbermen.

At this grim interruption a silence fell. The owner paled slightly; his foreman chewed a nonchalant straw. Down the still and deserted street crossed and recrossed the subtle occult influences of a half-hundred concealed watchers. Daly and his subordinate were very much alone, and very much in danger. Their last hour had come; and they knew it.

With the recognition of the fact, they immediately raised their weapons in the resolve to do as much damage as possible before being overpowered.

Then suddenly, full in the back, a heavy stream of water knocked them completely off their feet, rolled them over and over on the wet sawdust, and finally jammed them both against the trestle, where it held them, kicking and gasping for breath, in a choking cataract of water. The pistols flew harmlessly into the air. For an instant the Fighting Forty stared in paralyzed astonishment. Then a tremendous roar of laughter saluted this easy vanquishment of a formidable enemy.

Daly and Baker were pounced upon and captured. There was no resistance. They were too nearly strangled for that. Little Solly and old Vanderhoof turned off the water in the fire hydrant and disconnected the hose they had so effectively employed.

"There, damn you!" said Rollway Charley, jerking the mill man to his feet. "How do *you* like too much water, hey?"

The unexpected comedy changed the party's mood. It was no longer a question of killing. A number broke into the store, and shortly emerged, bearing pails of kerosene with which they deluged the slabs on the windward side of the mill. The flames caught the structure instantly. A thousand sparks, borne by the off-shore breeze, fastened like so many stinging insects on the lumber in the yard.

It burned as dried balsam thrown on a camp fire. The heat of it drove the onlookers far back in the village, where in silence they watched the destruction. From behind locked doors the inhabitants watched with them.

The billow of white smoke filled the northern sky. A whirl of gray wood ashes, light as air, floated on and ever on over Superior. The site of the mill, the squares where the piles of lumber had stood, glowed incandescence over which already a white film was forming.

Daly and his man were slapped and cuffed hither and thither at the men's will. Their faces bled, their bodies ached as one bruise.

"That squares us," said the men. "If we can't cut this year, neither kin you. It's up to *you* now!"

Then, like a destroying horde of locusts, they gutted the office and the store, smashing what they could not carry to the fire. The dwellings and saloons they did not disturb. Finally, about noon, they kicked their two prisoners into the river, and took their way stragglingly back along the right-of-way.

"I surmise we took that town apart *some*!" remarked Shorty with satisfaction.

"I should rise to remark," replied Kerlie. Big

Junko said nothing, but his cavernous little animal eyes glowed with satisfaction. He had been the first to lay hands on Daly; he had helped to carry the petroleum; he had struck the first match; he had even administered the final kick.

At the boarding-house they found Wallace Carpenter and Hamilton seated on the veranda. It was now afternoon. The wind had abated somewhat, and the sun was struggling with the still flying scuds.

"Hello, boys," said Wallace, "been for a little walk in the woods?"

"Yes, sir," replied Jack Hyland, "we——"

"I'd rather not hear," interrupted Wallace. "There's quite a fire over east. I suppose you haven't noticed it."

Hyland looked gravely eastward.

"Sure 'nough!" said he.

"Better get some grub," suggested Wallace.

After the men had gone in, he turned to the journalist.

"Hamilton," he began, "write all you know about the drive, and the break, and the rescue, but as to the burning of the mill——"

The other held out his hand.

"Good," said Wallace offering his own.

And that was as far as the famous Shingleville raid ever got. Daly did his best to collect even circumstantial evidence against the participants, but in vain. He could not even get any one to say that a single member of the village of Carpenter had absented himself from town that morning. This might have been from loyalty, or it might have been from fear of the vengeance the Fighting Forty would surely visit on a traitor. Probably it was a combination of both. The fact remains, however, that Daly never knew surely of but one man implicated in the destruction of his plant. That man was Injin Charley, but Injin Charley promptly disappeared.

After an interval, Tim Shearer, Radway and Kerlie came out again.

"Where's the boss?" asked Shearer.

"I don't know, Tim," replied Wallace seriously. "I've looked everywhere. He's gone. He must have been all cut up. I think he went out in the woods to get over it. I am not worrying. Harry has lots of sense. He'll come in about dark."

"Sure!" said Tim.

"How about the boy's stakes?" queried Radway. "I hear this is a bad smash for the firm."

"We'll see that the men get their wages all right," replied Carpenter, a little disappointed that such a question should be asked at such a time.

"All right," rejoined the contractor. "We're all going to need our money this summer."

CHAPTER FIFTY-SEVEN

THORPE walked through the silent group of men without seeing them. He had no thought for what he had done, but for the triumphant discovery he had made in spite of himself. This he saw at once as something to glory in and as a duty to be fulfilled.

It was then about six o'clock in the morning. Thorpe passed the boarding-house, the store, and the office, to take himself as far as the little open shed that served the primitive town as a railway station. There he set the semaphore to flag the east-bound train from Duluth. At six thirty-two, the train happening on time, he climbed aboard. He dropped heavily into a seat and stared straight in front of him until the conductor had spoken to him twice.

"Where to, Mr. Thorpe?" he asked.

The latter gazed at him uncomprehendingly.

"Oh! Mackinaw City," he replied at last.

"How're things going up your way?" inquired the conductor by way of conversation while he made out the pay-slip.

"Good!" responded Thorpe mechanically.

The act of paying for his fare brought to his consciousness that he had but a little over ten dollars

500

with him. He thrust the change back into his
pocket, and took up his contemplation of nothing.
The river water dripped slowly from his "cork"
boots to form a pool on the car floor. The heavy
wool of his short driving trousers steamed in the
car's warmth. His shoulders dried in a little cloud
of vapor. He noticed none of these things, but
stared ahead, his gaze vacant, the bronze of his face
set in the lines of a brown study, his strong capable
hands hanging purposeless between his knees. The
ride to Mackinaw City was six hours long, and the
train in addition lost some ninety minutes; but in
all this distance Thorpe never altered his pose nor
his fixed attitude of attention to some inner voice.

The car-ferry finally landed them on the southern
peninsula. Thorpe descended at Mackinaw City to
find that the noon train had gone. He ate a lunch
at the hotel—borrowed a hundred dollars from the
agent of Louis Sands, a lumberman of his acquaintance; and seated himself rigidly in the little waiting-
room, there to remain until the nine-twenty that
night. When the cars were backed down from the
siding, he boarded the sleeper. In the doorway
stood a disapproving colored porter.

"Yo'll fin' the smokin' cah up fo'wu'd, suh," said
the latter, firmly barring the way.

"It's generally forward," answered Thorpe.

"This yeah's th' sleepah," protested the function-
ary. "You pays extry."

" I am aware of it," replied Thorpe curtly. " Give me a lower."

" Yessah! " acquiesced the darkey, giving way, but still in doubt. He followed Thorpe curiously, peering into the smoking-room on him from time to time. A little after twelve his patience gave out. The stolid gloomy man of lower six seemed to in tend sitting up all night.

" Yo' berth is ready, sah," he delicately suggested.

Thorpe arose obediently, walked to lower six, and, without undressing, threw himself on the bed. Afterward the porter, in conscientious discharge of his duty, looked diligently beneath the seat for boots to polish. Happening to glance up, after fruitless search, he discovered the boots still adorning the feet of their owner.

" Well, for th' *lands* sake! " ejaculated the scandalized negro, beating a hasty retreat.

He was still more scandalized when, the following noon, his strange fare brushed by him without bestowing the expected tip.

Thorpe descended at Twelfth Street in Chicago without any very clear notion of where he was going. For a moment he faced the long park-like expanse of the lake front, then turned sharp to his left and picked his way south up the interminable reaches of Michigan Avenue. He did this without any conscious motive—mainly because the reaches seemed interminable, and he proved the need of walking. Block after block he clicked along, the caulks of his boots striking fire from the pavement. Some people stared at him a little curiously. Others merely glanced in his direction, attracted more by the expression of his face than the peculiarity of his dress. At that time rivermen were not an uncommon sight along the water front.

After an interval he seemed to have left the smoke and dirt behind. The street became quieter. Boarding-houses and tailors' shops ceased. Here and there appeared a bit of lawn, shrubbery, flowers. The residences established an uptown crescendo of magnificence. Policemen seemed trimmer, better-gloved. Occasionally he might have noticed in front of one of the sandstone piles a besilvered pair champing before a stylish vehicle. By and by he came to himself to find that he was staring at the deep-carved lettering in a stone horse-block before a large dwelling.

His mind took the letters in one after the other, perceiving them plainly before it accorded them recognition. Finally he had completed the word *Farrand*. He whirled sharp on his heel, mounted the broad white stone steps, and rang the bell.

It was answered almost immediately by a clean-shaven, portly and dignified man with the most impassive countenance in the world. This man looked upon Thorpe with lofty disapproval.

"Is Miss Hilda Farrand at home?" he asked.

"I cannot say," replied the man. "If you will step to the back door, I will ascertain."

"The flowers will do. Now see that the south room is ready, Annie," floated a voice from within.

Without a word, but with a deadly earnestness, Thorpe reached forward, seized the astonished servant by the collar, yanked him bodily outside the door, stepped inside, and strode across the hall toward a closed portière whence had come the voice. The riverman's long spikes cut little triangular pieces from the hardwood floor. Thorpe did not notice that. He thrust aside the portière.

Before him he saw a young and beautiful girl. She was seated, and her lap was filled with flowers. At his sudden apparition, her hands flew to her heart, and her lips slightly parted. For a second the two stood looking at each other, just as nearly a year before their eyes had crossed over the old pole trail.

To Thorpe the girl seemed more beautiful than ever. She exceeded even his retrospective dreams of her, for the dream had persistently retained something of the quality of idealism which made the vision unreal, while the woman before him had become human flesh and blood, adorable, to be desired. The red of this violent unexpected encounter rushed to her face, her bosom rose and fell in a fluttering catch for breath; but her eyes were steady and inquiring.

Then the butler pounced on Thorpe from behind with the intent to do great bodily harm.

"Morris!" commanded Hilda sharply, "what are you doing?"

The man cut short his heroism in confusion.

"You may go," concluded Hilda.

Thorpe stood straight and unwinking by the straight portière. After a moment he spoke.

"I have come to tell you that you were right and I was wrong," said he steadily. "You told me there could be nothing better than love. In the pride of my strength I told you this was not so. I was wrong."

He stood for another instant, looking directly at her, then turned sharply, and head erect walked from the room.

Before he had reached the outer door the girl was at his side.

"Why are you going?" she asked.

"I have nothing more to say."

"*Nothing?*"

"Nothing at all."

She laughed happily to herself.

"But I have—much. Come back."

They returned to the little morning room, Thorpe's caulked boots gouging out the little triangular furrows in the hardwood floor. Neither noticed that. Morris, the butler, emerged from his hiding and held up the hands of horror.

"What are you going to do now?" she catechised, facing him in the middle of the room. A long tendril of her beautiful corn-silk hair fell across her eyes; her red lips parted in a faint wistful smile; beneath the draperies of her loose gown the pure slender lines of her figure leaned toward him.

"I am going back," he replied patiently.

"I knew you would come," said she. "I have been expecting you."

She raised one hand to brush back the tendril of hair, but it was a mechanical gesture, one that did not stir even the surface consciousness of the strange half-smiling, half-wistful, starry gaze with which she watched his face.

"O Harry," she breathed, with a sudden flash of insight, "you are a man born to be much misunderstood."

He held himself rigid, but in his veins was creeping a molten fire, and the fire was beginning to glow dully in his eye. Her whole being called him. His heart leaped, his breath came fast, his eyes swam. With almost hypnotic fascination the idea obsessed him—to kiss her lips, to press the soft body of the young girl, to tumble her hair down about her flower face. He had not come for this. He tried to steady himself, and by an effort that left him weak he succeeded. Then a new flood of passion overcame him.

In the later desire was nothing of the old humble adoration. It was elemental, real, almost a little savage. He wanted to seize her so fiercely as to hurt her. Something caught his throat, filled his lungs, weakened his knees. For a moment it seemed to him that he was going to faint.

And still she stood there before him, saying nothing, leaning slightly toward him, her red lips half parted, her eyes fixed almost wistfully on his face.

" Go away ! " he whispered hoarsely at last. The voice was not his own. " Go away ! Go away ! "

Suddenly she swayed to him.

" O Harry, Harry," she whispered, " must I *tell* you? Don't you *see*? "

The flood broke through him. He seized her hungrily. He crushed her to him until she gasped; he pressed his lips against hers until she all but cried out with the pain of it; he ran his great brown hands blindly through her hair until it came down about them both in a cloud of spun light.

" Tell me ! " he whispered. " Tell me ! "

" Oh ! oh ! " she cried. " Please ! What is it? "

" I do not believe it," he murmured savagely.

She drew herself from him with gentle dignity.

" I am not worthy to say it," she said soberly, " but I love you with all my heart and soul ! "

Then for the first and only time in his life Thorpe fell to weeping, while she, understanding, stood by and comforted him.

CHAPTER FIFTY-EIGHT

THE few moments of Thorpe's tears eased the emotional strain under which, perhaps unconsciously, he had been laboring for nearly a year past. The tenseness of his nerves relaxed. He was able to look on the things about him from a broader standpoint than that of the specialist, to front life with saving humor. The deep breath after striving could at last be taken.

In this new attitude there was nothing strenuous, nothing demanding haste; only a deep glow of content and happiness. He savored deliberately the joy of a luxurious couch, rich hangings, polished floor, subdued light, warmed atmosphere. He watched with soul-deep gratitude the soft girlish curves of Hilda's body, the poise of her flower head, the piquant, half-wistful, half-childish set of her red lips, the clear star-like glimmer of her dusky eyes. It was all near to him; his.

"Kiss me, dear," he said.

She swayed to him again, deliciously graceful, deliciously unself-conscious, trusting, adorable. Already in the little nothingnesses of manner, the trifles of mental and bodily attitude, she had as sumed that faint trace of the maternal which to the observant tells so plainly that a woman has given herself to a man.

She leaned her cheek against her hand, and her hand against his shoulder.

"I have been reading a story lately," said she, "that has interested me very much. It was about a man who renounced all he held most dear to shield a friend."

"Yes," said Thorpe.

"Then he renounced all his most valuable possessions because a poor common man needed the sacrifice."

"Sounds like a medieval story," said he with unconscious humor.

"It happened recently," rejoined Hilda. "I read it in the papers."

"Well, he blazed a good trail," was Thorpe's sighing comment. "Probably he had his chance. We don't all of us get that. Things go crooked and get tangled up, so we have to do the best we can. I don't believe *I'd* have done it."

"Oh, you are delicious!" she cried.

After a time she said very humbly: "I want to beg your pardon for misunderstanding you and causing you so much suffering. I was very stupid, and didn't see why you could not do as I wanted you to."

"That is nothing to forgive. I acted like a fool."

"I have known about you," she went on. "It

has all come out in the *Telegram*. It has been very exciting. Poor boy, you look tired."

He straightened himself suddenly. "I have forgotten—actually forgotten," he cried a little bitterly. "Why, I am a pauper, a bankrupt, I——"

"Harry," she interrupted gently, but very firmly, "you must not say what you were going to say. I cannot allow it. Money came between us before. It must not do so again. Am I not right, dear?"

She smiled at him with the lips of a child and the eyes of a woman.

"Yes," he agreed after a struggle, "you are right. But now I must begin all over again. It will be a long time before I shall be able to claim you. I have my way to make."

"Yes," said she diplomatically.

"But you!" he cried suddenly. "The papers remind me. How about that Morton?"

"What about him?" asked the girl, astonished. "He is very happily engaged."

Thorpe's face slowly filled with blood.

"You'll break the engagement at once," he commanded a little harshly.

"Why should I break the engagement?" demanded Hilda, eying him with some alarm.

"I should think it was obvious enough."

"But it isn't," she insisted. "Why?"

Thorpe was silent—as he always had been in emergencies, and as he was destined always to be.

His was not a nature of expression, but of action. A crisis always brought him, like a bulldog, silently to the grip.

Hilda watched him puzzled, with bright eyes, like a squirrel. Her quick brain glanced here and there among the possibilities, seeking the explanation. Already she knew better than to demand it of him.

"You actually don't think he's engaged to *me*!" she burst out finally.

"Isn't he?" asked Thorpe.

"Why no, stupid! He's engaged to Elizabeth Carpenter, Wallace's sister. Now *where* did you get that silly idea?"

"I saw it in the paper."

"And you believe all you see! Why didn't you ask Wallace—but of course you wouldn't! Harry, you are the most incoherent dumb old brute I ever saw! I could shake you! Why don't you say something occasionally when it's needed, instead of sitting dumb as a sphinx and getting into all sorts of trouble? But you never will. I know you. You dear old bear! You *need* a wife to interpret things for you. You speak a different language from most people." She said this between laughing and crying; between a sense of the ridiculous uselessness of withholding a single timely word, and a tender pathetic intuition of the suffering such a nature must endure. In the prospect of the future she saw her use. It gladdened her and filled her with a serene happiness possible only to those who feel themselves a necessary and integral part in the lives of the ones they love. Dimly she perceived this truth. Dimly beyond it she glimpsed that other great truth of nature, that the human being is rarely completely efficient alone, that in obedience to his greater use he must take to himself a mate before he can succeed.

Suddenly she jumped to her feet with an exclamation.

" O Harry! I'd forgotten utterly! " she cried in laughing consternation. " I have a luncheon here at half-past one! It's almost that now. I must run and dress. Just look at me; just *look*! *You* did that! "

" I'll wait here until the confounded thing is over," said Thorpe.

" Oh, no, you won't," replied Hilda decidedly. " You are going down town right now and get something to put on. Then you are coming back here to stay."

Thorpe glanced in surprise at his driver's clothes, and his spiked boots.

" Heavens and earth! " he exclaimed, " I should think so! How am I to get out without ruining the floor? "

Hilda laughed and drew aside the portière.

" Don't you think you have done that pretty well already? " she asked. " There, don't look so solemn.

512

THE FOLLOWING OF THE TRAIL

We're not going to be sorry for a single thing we've done to-day, are we? " She stood close to him holding the lapels of his jacket in either hand, searching his face wistfully with her fathomless dusky eyes.

" No, sweetheart, we are not," replied Thorpe soberly.

CHAPTER FIFTY-NINE

SURELY it is useless to follow the sequel in detail, to tell how Hilda persuaded Thorpe to take her money. She aroused skillfully his fighting blood, induced him to use one fortune to rescue another. To a woman such as she this was not a very difficult task in the long run. A few scruples of pride; that was all.

"Do not consider its being mine," she answered to his objections. "Remember the lesson we learned so bitterly. Nothing can be greater than love, not even our poor ideals. You have my love; do not disappoint me by refusing so little a thing as my money."

"I hate to do it," he replied; "it doesn't look right."

"You must," she insisted. "I will not take the position of rich wife to a poor man; it is humiliating to both. I will not marry you until you have made your success."

"That is right," said Thorpe heartily.

"Well, then, are you going to be so selfish as to keep me waiting while you make an entirely new start, when a little help on my part will bring your plans to completion?"

514

She saw the shadow of assent in his eyes.

"How much do you need?" she asked swiftly.

"I must take up the notes," he explained. "I must pay the men. I may need something on the stock market. If I go in on this thing, I'm going in for keeps. I'll get after those fellows who have been swindling Wallace. Say a hundred thousand dollars."

"Why, it's nothing," she cried.

"I'm glad you think so," he replied grimly.

She ran to her dainty escritoire, where she scribbled eagerly for a few moments.

"There," she cried, her eyes shining, "there is my check book all signed in blank. I'll see that the money is there."

Thorpe took the book, staring at it with sightless eyes. Hilda, perched on the arm of his chair, watched his face closely, as later became her habit of interpretation.

"What is it?" she asked.

Thorpe looked up with a pitiful little smile that seemed to beg indulgence for what he was about to say.

"I was just thinking, dear. I used to imagine I was a strong man, yet see how little my best efforts amount to. I have put myself into seven years of the hardest labor, working like ten men in order to succeed. I have foreseen all that mortal could foresee. I have always thought, and think now, that a man is no man unless he works out the sort of success for which he is fitted. I have done fairly well until the crises came. Then I have been absolutely powerless, and if left to myself, I would have failed. At the times when a really strong man would have used effectively the strength he had been training, I have fallen back miserably on outer aid. Three times my affairs have become critical. In the crises I have been saved, first by a mere boy; then by an old illiterate man; now by a weak woman!"

She heard him through in silence.

"Harry," she said soberly when he had quite finished, "I agree with you that God meant the strong man to succeed; that without success the man has not fulfilled his reason for being. But, Harry, *are you quite sure that God meant him to succeed alone?*"

The dusk fell through the little room. Out in the hallway a tall clock ticked solemnly. A noiseless servant appeared in the doorway to light the lamps, but was silently motioned away.

"I had not thought of that," said Thorpe at last.

"You men are so selfish," went on Hilda. "You would take everything from us. Why can't you leave us the poor little privilege of the occasional deciding touch, the privilege of succor. It is all that weakness can do for strength."

"And why," she went on after a moment, "why is not that, too, a part of a man's success—the gathering about him of people who can and will supplement his efforts? Who was it inspired Wallace Carpenter with confidence in an unknown man? You. What did it? Those very qualities by which you were building your success. Why did John Radway join forces with you? How does it happen that your men are of so high a standard of efficiency? Why am I willing to give you everything, *everything*, to my heart and soul? Because it is you who ask it. Because you, Harry Thorpe, have woven us into your fortune, so that we have no choice. Depend upon us in the crises of your work! Why, so are you dependent on your ten fingers, your eyes, the fibre of your brain! Do you think the less of your fulfillment for that?"

So it was that Hilda Farrand gave her lover confidence, brought him out from his fanaticism, launched him afresh into the current of events. He remained in Chicago all that summer, giving orders that all work at the village of Carpenter should cease. With his affairs that summer we have little to do. His common-sense treatment of the stock market, by which a policy of quiescence following an outright buying of the stock which he had previously held on margins, retrieved the losses already sustained, and finally put both partners on a firm financial footing. That is another story. So too is his reconciliation with and understanding of his sister. It came about through Hilda, of course.

Perhaps in the inscrutable way of Providence the estrangement was of benefit—even necessary—for it had thrown him entirely within himself during his militant years.

Let us rather look to the end of the summer. It now became a question of re-opening the camps. Thorpe wrote to Shearer and Radway, whom he had retained, that he would arrive on Saturday noon, and suggested that the two begin to look about for men. Friday, himself, Wallace Carpenter, Elizabeth Carpenter, Morton, Helen Thorpe, and Hilda Farrand boarded the north-bound train.

CHAPTER SIXTY

THE train of the South Shore Railroad shot its
way across the broad reaches of the northern
peninsula. On either side of the right-of-way lay
mystery in the shape of thickets so dense and over-
grown that the eye could penetrate them but a few
feet at most. Beyond them stood the forests. Thus
Nature screened her intimacies from the impertinent
eye of a new order of things.

Thorpe welcomed the smell of the northland. He
became almost eager, explaining, indicating to the
girl at his side.

"There is the Canada balsam," he cried. "Do
you remember how I showed it to you first? And
yonder the spruce. How stuck up your teeth were
when you tried to chew the gum before it had been
heated. Do you remember? Look! Look there!
It's a white pine! Isn't it a grand tree? It's the
finest tree in the forest, by my way of thinking,
so tall, so straight, so feathery, and so dignified.
See, Hilda, look quick! There's an old logging
road all filled with raspberry vines. We'd
find lots of partridges there, and perhaps a bear.

Wouldn't you just like to walk down it about sunset?"

"Yes, Harry."

"I wonder what we're stopping for. Seems to me they are stopping at every squirrel's trail. Oh, this must be Seney. Yes, it is. Queer little place, isn't it? but sort of attractive. Good deal like our town. You have never seen Carpenter, have you? Location's fine, anyway; and to me it's sort of picturesque. You'll like Mrs. Hathaway. She's a buxom, motherly woman who runs the boarding-house for eighty men, and still finds time to mend my clothes for me. And you'll like Solly. Solly's the tug captain, a mighty good fellow, true as a gun barrel. We'll have him take us out, some still day. We'll be there in a few minutes now. See the cranberry marshes. Sometimes there's a good deal of pine on little islands scattered over it, but it's very hard to log, unless you get a good winter. We had just such a proposition when I worked for Radway. Oh, you'll like Radway, he's as good as gold. Helen!"

"Yes," replied his sister.

"I want you to know Radway. He's the man who gave me my start."

"All right, Harry," laughed Helen. "I'll meet anybody or anything from bears to Indians."

"I know an Indian too—Geezigut, an Ojibwa— we called him Injin Charley. He was my first friend in the north woods. He helped me get my timber. This spring he killed a man—a good job, too—and is hiding now. I wish I knew where he is. But we'll see him some day. He'll come back when the thing blows over. See! See!"

"What?" they all asked, breathless.

"It's gone. Over beyond the hills there I caught a glimpse of Superior."

"You are ridiculous, Harry," protested Helen Thorpe laughingly. "I never saw you so. You are a regular boy!"

"Do you like boys?" he asked gravely of Hilda.

"Adore them!" she cried.

"All right, I don't care," he answered his sister in triumph.

The air brakes began to make themselves felt, and shortly the train came to a grinding stop.

"What station is this?" Thorpe asked the colored porter.

"Shingleville, sah," the latter replied.

"I thought so. Wallace, when did their mill burn, anyway? I haven't heard about it."

"Last spring, about the time you went down."

"Is *that* so? How did it happen?"

"They claim incendiarism," parried Wallace cautiously.

Thorpe pondered a moment, then laughed. "I am in the mixed attitude of the small boy," he observed, "who isn't mean enough to wish anybody's property destroyed, but who wishes that if there is a fire, to be where he can see it. I am sorry those fellows had to lose their mill, but it was a good thing for us. The man who set that fire did us a good turn. If it hadn't been for the burning of their mill, they would have made a stronger fight against us in the stock market."

Wallace and Hilda exchanged glances. The girl was long since aware of the inside history of those days.

"You'll have to tell them that," she whispered over the back of her seat. "It will please them."

"Our station is next!" cried Thorpe, "and it's only a little ways. Come, get ready!"

They all crowded into the narrow passageway near the door, for the train barely paused.

"All right, sah," said the porter, swinging down his little step.

Thorpe ran down to help the ladies. He was nearly taken from his feet by a wild-cat yell, and a moment later that result was actually accomplished by a rush of men that tossed him bodily onto its shoulders. At the same moment, the mill and tug whistles began to screech, miscellaneous firearms exploded. Even the locomotive engineer, in the spirit of the occasion, leaned down heartily on his whistle rope. The sawdust street was filled with screaming, jostling men. The homes of the town were brilliantly draped with cheesecloth, flags and bunting.

For a moment Thorpe could not make out what had happened. This turmoil was so different from the dead quiet of desertion he had expected, that he was unable to gather his faculties. All about him were familiar faces upturned to his own. He distinguished the broad, square shoulders of Scotty Parsons, Jack Hyland, Kerlie, Bryan Moloney; Ellis grinned at him from the press; Billy Camp, the fat and shiny drive cook; Mason, the foreman of the mill; over beyond howled Solly, the tug captain, Rollway Charley, Shorty, the chore-boy; everywhere were features that he knew. As his dimming eyes travelled here and there, one by one the Fighting Forty, the best crew of men ever gathered in the northland, impressed themselves on his consciousness. Saginaw birlers, Flat River drivers, woodsmen from the forests of lower Canada, bully boys out of the Muskegon waters, peavey men from Au Sable, white-water daredevils from the rapids of the Menominee—all were there to do him honor, him in whom they had learned to see the supreme qualities of their calling. On the outskirts sauntered the tall form of Tim Shearer, a straw peeping from beneath his flax-white mustache, his eyes glimmering under his flax-white eyebrows. He did not evidence as much excitement as the others, but the very bearing of the man expressed the deepest satisfaction.

Perhaps he remembered that zero morning so many years before when he had watched the thinly clad, shivering chore-boy set his face for the first time toward the dark forest.

Big Junko and Anderson deposited their burden on the raised platform of the office steps. Thorpe turned and fronted the crowd.

At once pandemonium broke loose, as though the previous performance had been nothing but a low-voiced rehearsal.

The men looked upon their leader and gave voice to the enthusiasm that was in them. He stood alone there, straight and tall, the muscles of his brown face set to hide his emotion, his head thrust back proudly, the lines of his strong figure tense with power—the glorification in finer matter of the hardy, reliant men who did him honor.

" Oh, aren't you *proud* of him? " gasped Hilda, squeezing Helen's arm with a little sob.

In a moment Wallace Carpenter, his countenance glowing with pride and pleasure, mounted the platform and stood beside his friend, while Morton and the two young ladies stopped half-way up the steps.

At once the racket ceased. Every one stood at attention.

" Mr. Thorpe," Wallace began, " at the request of your friends here, I have a most pleasant duty to fulfill. They have asked me to tell you how glad

they are to see you; that is surely unnecessary. They
have also asked me to congratulate you on having
won the fight with our rivals."

"You done 'em good." "Can't down the Old
Fellow," muttered joyous voices.

"But," said Wallace, "I think that I first have
a story to tell on my own account.

"At the time the jam broke this spring, we owed
the men here for a year's work. At that time I considered their demand for wages ill-timed and grasp-
ing. I wish to apologize. After the money was
paid them, instead of scattering, they set to work
under Jack Radway and Tim Shearer to salvage
your logs. They have worked long hours all summer. They have invested every cent of their year's
earnings in supplies and tools, and now they are
prepared to show you the Company's booms, three
million feet of logs, rescued by their grit and hard
labor from total loss."

At this point the speaker was interrupted. "Saw
off," "Shut up," "Give us a rest," growled the
audience. "Three million feet ain't worth talkin'
about," "You make me tired," "Say your little say
the way you oughter," "Found purty nigh two
millions pocketed on Mare's Island, or we wouldn't
a had that much," "Damn-fool undertaking, any-
how."

"Men," cried Thorpe, "I have been very fortunate. From failure success has come. But never

look on 527

have I been more fortunate than in my friends. The firm is now on its feet. It could afford to lose three times the logs it lost this year——"

He paused and scanned their faces.

"But," he continued suddenly, "it cannot now, nor ever can afford to lose what those three million feet represent—the friends it has made. I can pay you back the money you have spent and the time you have put in——" Again he looked them over, and then for the first time since they have known him his face lighted up with a rare and tender smile of affection. "But, comrades, I shall not offer to do it: the gift is accepted in the spirit with which it was offered——"

He got no further. The air was rent with sound. Even the members of his own party cheered. From every direction the crowd surged inward. The women and Morton were forced up the platform to Thorpe. The latter motioned for silence.

"Now, boys, we have done it," said he, "and so will go back to work. From now on you are my comrades in the fight."

His eyes were dim; his breast heaved; his voice shook. Hilda was weeping from excitement. Through the tears she saw them all looking at their leader, and in the worn, hard faces glowed the affection and admiration of a dog for its master. Something there was especially touching in this, for strong men rarely show it. She felt a great wave of excitement sweep over her. Instantly she was standing by Thorpe, her eyes streaming, her breast throbbing with emotion.

"Oh!" she cried, stretching her arms out to them passionately, "Oh! I love you; I love you all!"

THE END